WHITE PEAK

WHITE PEAK

RONAN FROST

ST. MARTIN'S PRESS ✠ NEW YORK

WHITE PEAK. Copyright © 2019 by Steven Savile. All rights reserved. Printed in the United States of America. For information, address St. Martin's Press, 175 Fifth Avenue, New York, N.Y. 10010.

www.stmartins.com

The Library of Congress Cataloging-in-Publication Data is available upon request.

ISBN 978-1-250-13008-2 (hardcover)
ISBN 978-1-250-13009-9 (ebook)

Our books may be purchased in bulk for promotional, educational, or business use. Please contact your local bookseller or the Macmillan Corporate and Premium Sales Department at 1-800-221-7945, extension 5442, or by email at MacmillanSpecialMarkets@macmillan.com.

First Edition: May 2019

10 9 8 7 6 5 4 3 2 1

FOR CHAZ BRENCHLEY,

WHO HAS BEEN MY FRIEND EVERY DAY SINCE THOSE IMMORTAL WORDS "THIS COULD BE THE BEGINNING OF A BEAUTIFUL FRIENDSHIP" WERE FIRST UTTERED.

OURS IS A FRIENDSHIP KEPT SAFE IN A LITTLE BOX UNDER THE BED THAT CAN NEVER BE LOST.

WHITE PEAK

ONE

Ryerson McKenna listened to his wife's death on the telephone.

He fed another quarter into the slot. The radio was playing his favorite song. No one in the roadside diner said a word. They all stared at him.

He pressed the phone against his ear.

"Rye? Rye? Can you hear me?"

"I'm still here," he said, then cupped his hand over the mouthpiece to yell at the waitress behind the counter, "I need coins. Quickly. Please."

On the screen above her head the words ACTIVE SHOOTER scrolled across the aerial shot of the black smoke and Sheridan Meadows shopping mall where less than five minutes ago the shooter had rammed a truck through the plate glass windows of the anchor store and kept on driving right into the heart of the perfume department. The smoke was more than just the settling of debris; the truck, with a beer company logo on the side, had been carrying a crude fertilizer bomb that had detonated less than sixty seconds after the engine died, barely giving the driver time to get free of the vehicle and start shooting his way clear.

Ryerson was down to three bucks in change, enough to keep the line alive for less than two minutes at the rate the pay phone was eating through the coins.

He pushed it all into the slot.

He couldn't afford to let the connection die. The cell phone networks were overloaded. No other calls were getting through. If the line dropped, he lost contact with Hannah. It was as simple as that.

Three gunshots in rapid succession punctuated his next words. "I'm going to get you out of there, Hannah, I promise." It was a stupid thing to promise, but he needed her to believe him. This was what he did for other people; he could do it for her. "Just stay with me, okay?"

"Okay," she said, unaware that the clock on their call was running out fast.

The world narrowed to vivid snapshots, brittle too-bright images of a life that had, in a couple of seconds, become incredibly fragile: the foam crescent of his lips slowly sliding down the side of the glass as his coffee went cold in the booth; the yolk of his sunny-side up eggs congealing on the greasy plate; the short-order cook with grease on the front of his apron and bacon sizzling on the hot plate; the candy-stripe straws in the glass jar on the countertop; the yellow sunflowers on the tables, petals wilting in the too-warm interior; the trucker leaning against the bar with a piece of green from his burger stuck between his teeth as he hit on the waitress; the coffeepot burning dry with nothing but dregs in the bottom.

The trucker emptied out his pockets, pushing another three bucks in quarters toward Rye, who fumbled them up and fed them into the phone, buying another two minutes on the open line.

The cash drawer chimed as the waitress opened it, scooping out another handful of silver. It still wasn't enough. No one paid by cash anymore. Not even tips. She pushed the tip jar across the counter. There was maybe another seven or eight minutes in there at best.

"More. I need more," he said, his gaze sweeping across the diners. Not including the two waitstaff, there were seven people in there with him, and two of those were kids. One of the diners, an art student type with plastic flowers in her hair, pushed back her chair and went around the table with her hat, collecting every last quarter the diners had between them, and brought it over to him.

He could only pray it was going to be enough to stay with Hannah until she was out of there.

The problem was he didn't have a religious bone in his body.

He stared at the screen, trying to think.

He needed to do this like it was a complete stranger in there, not the woman who was his world: keep her moving, keep her away from the crowds, find a place to either hide out or get out.

"Han, I need you to look for the mirrors," he said, thinking on his feet. "You should be able to see rows of them between the storefronts?"

"I see some," she said.

"Good. That's great. Okay. You need to find the one that opens into the service corridors. It's probably in the middle. Don't panic if it doesn't immediately open, some are false fronts. You need to find the one that opens, and go through it, before that main aisle becomes a shooting gallery."

He regretted the choice of words as soon as they were out of his mouth.

She breathed heavily in his ear. Running. It was hard to hear anything over the screams and panic on the open line. It was mid-afternoon. Not peak hours, but there must have been a thousand-plus people in the mall. More, probably, counting employees.

He was forty miles away, helpless, and his money was running out. It was one of the modern pay phones, with a little LCD display counting down the cents.

He fed the coins from the tip jar into the phone. "I need more," he shouted at the girl with the hat. She nodded, but they both knew she couldn't just magic up money from nowhere. Thinking on her feet, she ran outside to the parking lot.

"I can see them," Hannah repeated, but this time she wasn't talking about the mirrored doors. Another burst of gunfire under-lined exactly what she could see.

"Get out of there, Han. Don't look at anyone. Just focus on the mirrors. Get through the mirrors."

"Oh god, oh god . . . oh god . . . Rye . . . Oh god . . . They just . . . oh god."

"Hannah, listen to me. Hannah, you can't help anyone. I need you to concentrate on my voice. You're coming home to me. Okay?" She didn't answer him. "Go through the mirrored doors. Hannah, can you hear me? You need to get out of there."

The girl with the hat came back into the diner and offered up more coins. Her hands were shaking as she held out the hat. There was a felt flower pinned to the front, and maybe six bucks in coins and a pearl button inside it. It wasn't going to buy him enough time.

He needed more.

Rye grabbed a handful of silver and fumbled the coins into the slot, each one adding precious seconds to the call.

The message on the television screen changed, the ticker adding more detail to underscore the horror: EXPLOSION AT SHOPPING MALL. EYEWITNESS REPORTS OF MULTIPLE SHOOTERS. CASUALTIES.

Multiple shooters.

He'd been concentrating on getting her away from a single point of danger, but before he could think about how that changed things she was back with him. "I'm through. I'm in some sort of passageway. It's all concrete and pipes." As the mirrored doors closed behind her they muted the sounds of dying. "I can see signs for Bay One and Bay Two."

"Follow the one that's heading away from the shooting," he said. "Every time you get a choice, head away from the shooting. Eventually you'll see signs for the fire exits."

"I can see an arrow," she said breathlessly.

"Follow it."

He heard her hustling down the service corridor. The count-down on the phone said he had less than ninety seconds with her. She was on her way out now, away from the worst of it. He looked up at the television screen, thinking: *god help those other people. . . .* There was a distance to it now.

He'd made good on his promise.

She was on her way out.

"I can see light up ahead," Hannah told him.

"Great," he said, "head toward it. You're coming home, love. Just get out of there. Don't stop. Don't look back. Just run and keep on running until you're behind the wheel."

For the next dollar, the only sounds he heard were Hannah's heavy breathing and the slap of her footsteps echoing in the in-dustrial passage.

And then they stopped.

Again, he cupped his hand over the mouthpiece. "I need more money." He saw the poker machine beside the door and pointed. The waitress understood. She grabbed the key for the coin box and emptied it out, spreading the coins out across the counter. She sorted through them quickly.

He looked up at the television screen.

The message hadn't changed.

"Rye," Hannah said in his ear, only that, but it was the way that she'd suddenly stopped, like there was nothing else to say, the way that last footstep had dragged as she faltered, the way her breathing had changed in that last second, that told him she was in trouble.

Multiple shooters.

He'd led her away from one straight into the path of another.

There were no last I love yous.

With eleven seconds left on the display, the gunshots rang out. Seven of them in less than a second. There was no more brutal sound in the world. With nine seconds left on the display he heard the phone fall from her hand. Eight, silence. Seven, silence. Six and the only sound was the slow measured approach of heavy booted feet. Five, and it was the scratch of the cell phone's case on the concrete floor as the gunman picked it up. Three, a man's voice told him, "She can't come to the phone right now."

The one thing he didn't hear in any one of those last eleven seconds was Hannah breathing.

One final shot killed any remaining hope.

The waitress had more money for him.

He didn't take it.

TWO

Rye didn't make a good widower.

He didn't look after himself. Didn't eat properly. Didn't go to bed, sleeping on the couch instead because he couldn't face going into the bedroom where she should have been. He didn't clear her clothes out of the closet or any of her lotions and soaps and perfumes from the medicine cabinet in the bathroom. He didn't take her last note down from the refrigerator door, even though it was a reminder that she would be home late because she was going to the mall. He didn't get rid of any of the happy stuff they'd spent too little time together amassing: the shared record collection, the book she'd never finish reading, the teacup she kept beside the kettle and the stupidly expensive rooibos and honeybush tea bags she liked so much, the photograph albums she'd insisted on instead of backing everything up to the cloud. In other words, all of the stuff that made Hannah Hannah.

He didn't take his ring off, either.

He wasn't ready to let go of who he had been.

He stared at the bottle, knowing that was one way out.

But every time he reached for the bottle, the one thing he kept coming back to was how much shit she would have given him for living this badly, and that stopped him. It didn't heal the Hannah-shaped hole in his world, though.

He couldn't remember the last time he'd cooked a meal.

When he did eat, like today, it was at the diner.

He pushed open the door and went inside.

Aggie, the waitress, offered him a smile and started with his coffee, not asking what he wanted. Why would she? He was a creature of habit. He'd been having the same stuff for five months. She never let on if she realized it was what he'd ordered the day Hannah had died.

Aggie steamed the milk while he took a seat at the counter. She was thirty-seven, in an on-again off-again, mostly off-again, relationship with Declan, the short-order cook, whose real name was something East European with a jumble of consonants that just made Declan so much easier to say, so it stuck. She was short, just nudging five foot, with delicate elfin features and a complexion that didn't appreciate the grease in the air. She smiled a lot. He quite liked Aggie because she knew better than to ask how he was doing. She just let him be.

He looked up at the television screen. It was still tuned to the local twenty-four-hour news cycle, waiting for the next tragedy to revel in. Aggie was in the middle of spooning froth onto the top of his drink. Some piss-poor Springsteen clone was on the radio. Little slices of Americana.

He'd started coming here after the shooting. At first it felt like a way of connecting with Hannah, as though the pay phone on the wall might ring, and he'd hear her voice on the other end of the line. Then it became a way of punishing himself with the constant reminder that he'd paid to listen to his wife die one quarter at a time.

They hadn't known how to talk to him the second time he turned up at their counter, or the third or the fourth. Instead, Aggie and Dec had put a plate of scrambled eggs and a coil of sausage in front of him and simply said, "Eat." It was the first hot food he'd eaten in three days, but he didn't tell them that.

He didn't tell them he'd just been to identify Hannah's body, either.

The aftermath of the Sheridan Mall Massacre—that was what they called it on the news, savoring the alliteration of the Mall Massacre—had been chaos. It had taken the police five hours to secure the scene, fifteen more to recover the bodies. The next twenty-four hours was about identifying them, even if social media was filled with lists of the dead, official channels just took *longer,* not able to make any mistakes.

They'd warned him that they'd done their best to make her look peaceful, but there was some damage to her body.

They'd promised that it would be like looking at her sleeping, but that was a lie. Asleep, the body is so full of life: little twitches and muscular tics, the rapid-eye flutter of dreaming, the barely perceptible flare of nostrils; the body was a landscape of tiny movement. Dead, it was absolutely still. That's what they meant when they said she looked peaceful. All of those little tics of life were gone.

Identifying her body took its toll on his psyche.

He couldn't understand how people could forgive or move on. He was going to carry this grief, this anger, until the day he joined her in the ground.

Rye heard the bell chime above the door as new customers entered the diner.

He didn't turn around.

He took a sip of coffee as Aggie put a plate down in front of him.

His favorite song came on the radio.

"Turn it off," he said.

Aggie didn't need telling twice. She knew the significance of the song. It was a ghost that haunted the roadside diner. None of them could stand to listen to it these days. It was burned into their collective memories; the soundtrack of that day.

He felt the presence of someone standing behind him, before the man asked, "Ryerson McKenna?"

"Who wants to know?" he grunted, not looking around.

The man put an envelope on the counter beside him.

"Someone suing me?"

"No idea. I'm only paid to see these get into the right hands. You have yourself a good day," the courier said, and a couple of seconds later Ryerson heard the bell again as the guy left.

"Bastards, the lot of them," Aggie said, but Rye was looking at the envelope. It was too small to be a subpoena.

He opened it.

Inside there was a single black business card, with gold lettering. The words: *Do You Deserve a Second Chance?* were printed on one side, the other was blank. He assumed the whole mysterious "we're not telling you what this is all about" thing was meant to intrigue him. It didn't. It bored him. He didn't play games.

He pushed the card aside and concentrated on his food. It was good, or at least good enough, and that was all he ever asked. He had a second cup of coffee before he pushed back the barstool.

He left without the card.

As he stepped out into the warm night, he saw a giant of a man—easily twice as broad as he was, muscular, hairless, black skin slick with sweat, his white shirt stretched painfully across huge ham hock biceps—leaning against a quarter of a million dollars' worth of yellow sports car. The man watched him for a moment. How he could ever fit inside the cramped confines of the automobile was a puzzle for physicists everywhere. Seeing Rye step out into the light, the man pushed himself away from the wing and wandered over.

"Mr. McKenna?" he asked, his voice a deep basso profundo.

"No," Rye said, walking away.

The big man smiled. "Do you mind if I ask whether you intend to respond to the invitation?"

"You can ask," he said. "I don't have to answer."

"True, so?"

"I'm not interested in whatever you are selling."

"That's a pity, I suspect you're everything the boss hoped you would be."

"I'm sure he's used to disappointment."

"Actually, no, he tends to get his way when it comes to things he cares passionately about."

"Well, then perhaps it's time he experiences what the rest of us go through every day. He can send me a thank-you card. He obviously knows where to find me."

"It's a fair question," the big man said. "Do you deserve a second chance?"

"No," Rye McKenna said, and walked away.

THREE

The knock at the door dragged him out of the recurring nightmare.

He lay on his back looking at the ceiling, disoriented. The ceiling fan wobbled in its arc. It did nothing for the ventilation. Half a dozen red pinpricks of light dotted around the dark room could easily have been a metaphor for his life on standby.

The knock came again, more insistent this time.

"All right, all right, keep your hair on. I'm coming," he called. His jeans were across the back of the couch, as was his shirt. He dressed quickly, still buttoning when he opened the door.

It was the black guy from the diner.

"We're going to have to stop meeting like this," Rye said.

"My employer is going to need an answer."

"Like I told you, I'm not interested."

"I think you might be. Can I come in?"

"Knock yourself out," Rye said.

The man took residence in one of the room's two armchairs. He looked like he was settling in for a child's tea party, twice as big as the chair beneath him. He put an envelope on the table. He didn't say anything until Rye had closed the door and sunk back down into the memory foam seat. "Okay, let's get this over with shall we? Who's your employer and why the fuck won't he leave me alone?"

"My employer has asked that I repeat his offer, now that you've had some time to think about it: Do you deserve a second chance?"

"Look, not being funny, but why does he care? I assume it's a he? Only a man would pull this kind of bullshit."

"He cares because he himself was the recipient of a second chance and it is safe to say that it changed his life. Now he finds himself in a position of being able to help others. He is aware of your situation and would like to do the same for you, if you are ready to help yourself?"

"Take a look around you, what do you think?"

"What I think doesn't come into it, Mr. McKenna."

"So, who is this mysterious benefactor of mine?"

"I am not at liberty to say. Yet. There are certain things we need to discuss first."

"What about you? Am I allowed to know who you are?"

"Of course. My name is Guuleed."

"That trips off the tongue," Rye said.

"It means *victor*."

"Okay, so, for the next few minutes I'm going to call you Vic. That work for you?"

"I've been called worse," the big man said.

"Okay, Vic, don't take this the wrong way, but this whole thing stinks. First a courier shows up with an enigmatic note, then you're waiting for me outside the diner, and now you're here. I feel like I'm being stalked. And why? Because your boss wants to change my life?"

"Perhaps it would help if I told you something about myself? I have been in this country for three years now. I am a refugee of the Somali Civil War, the *Dagaal Sokeeye Soomal* in my own language. I was born into war, I will almost certainly die in war when my time comes. I am resigned to this. But for now, I am here, and life is good. Before America, life was not so good. Both of my parents were murdered by the Barre regime. My three brothers died in the fighting at Mogadishu. I am the last of my line. There is no denying nature, I am a lion, my friend. There is blood on my soul that no amount of praying will cleanse. And yet, thanks to my employer, I have been given a second chance."

"I'm happy for you," Rye said.

"That is to say, I think you should listen to his offer." Vic leaned forward and with two fingers pushed the envelope across the table toward Rye. "Open it."

He did as he was told. Inside was a photograph taken from a crude low-resolution security camera. It was from the service corridors in the Sheridan Meadows mall. In the middle of the shot was a man, his features blurred with movement. He carried an assault rifle. Rye was intimately familiar with both the weapon and the man who had killed his wife.

"Is this supposed to mean something?"

"His name is Matthew Langley."

"I know what his name *was*," he corrected the tense. Tactical Response had taken the shooter out in the process of securing the scene. He was six feet under. Rotting.

"Is," the black man repeated. "It was decided that it was in the public interest to report that all three gunmen lost their lives in the assault on the mall. That was a lie for the media."

"It doesn't work like that," Rye said. "The cops won't just hide a mass murderer. That's not how the law works. This is America not Mogadishu. Secret prisons? American citizens spirited away in the middle of the night? It doesn't matter what their crimes are, it just doesn't work like that. There are laws."

"Yes, there are laws, and yet that is exactly what they did. And it is not the first time, nor will it be the last. This country hides the truth within lies, just as my homeland did. Tomorrow Langley is going to be moved to a black site where he will essentially disappear forever."

Rye shook his head. "How do you know this?"

"My employer is well connected, Mr. McKenna. It is his business to know."

"You'll excuse me if I don't swallow this shit, right?"

"I will, but that doesn't change the fact that in forty-five minutes a prisoner transport is leaving and my employer has gone to great lengths to clear the way for you to ride on that bus. It is up to you whether you are on it or not, of course, but arrangements have been made for you to spend an hour in a cell with your wife's killer. The guards will be under the impression that you are Martin Blake. You will be provided with a driver's license and other paperwork in Blake's name. Blake is serving seven to ten and is registered to be on a transport out before dawn, so the window is finite."

"This is what your boss means by a second chance?"

"No, he views this as offering you closure. Your second chance would begin the moment you board the transport out of the prison facility."

"Right, so what is this? Some sort of test of my moral compass? If I get on that bus, do I pass or fail? I mean, what kind of man turns down an offer of alone time with his wife's murderer?" Despite himself, Rye felt his heart rate quicken at the thought of it. "Isn't that what you're supposed to dream of, the chance to extract vengeance. Who do you think I am?"

The black man said nothing for a moment, seeming to mull the conundrum over. "A man in considerable pain, I think." He put the photograph back in the envelope. "I have seen security footage from inside the mall. I know what he did to your wife. I have listened to your call. I have heard your last words together. I know what I would do in your place."

"And what is that?"

"I would tear him apart with my bare hands and eat his heart while it was still hot in my fist. But then I am not a forgiving man." Rye barked out a laugh at that. "But that is my truth. It does not have to be yours."

"Right, you say that while at the same time offering me the chance to kill someone. . . ."

"Yes. My employer believes that this arrangement will allow you to move on with your life. All you have to do is say the word and you will be sharing a cell with Matthew Langley before sunrise. What you do in those four walls is between you and your conscience. There will be no comebacks. You have my word on that."

"Have we reached the point where you tell me who this mysterious employer of yours is yet?"

"No. That time, if it comes, is later. After you have made your peace with Matthew Langley."

"Not being funny, but that's awfully convenient. How do I know you aren't setting me up? For all I know you could be wearing a wire."

Vic unbuttoned his shirt, opening it on a ruin of scar tissue that made a patchwork out of his torso. It was a mess. There was no wire. He saw Rye looking and explained, "As I said, he saved me."

"What I don't get is, why me?"

"My employer is assembling a team of people with unique skill sets. He will explain more when you meet."

"You mean if?"

"No, if you had no intention of taking his offer you would have asked me to leave by now. I suggest you clean your teeth, your breath is rancid. That won't go down well with the warders. But be quick, it's a thirty-minute drive to our rendezvous with the transport and we only have thirty-six minutes before it leaves."

FOUR

They drove in silence.

Vic wasn't a man of many words.

The car traveled low, making it feel even faster than it was. Vic worked the stick, roaring the engine toward the red line. There were no streetlights on this stretch of road. It was far enough out of the town limits for the various municipal departments to wash their hands if anything went wrong. He took the cloverleaf,

powering around the exit ramp and peeled away. The clock was
ticking. It had taken Rye a few minutes to get his stuff together,
freshen up, gargle with mouthwash, and lock up. Those few minutes had eaten into their time.

Vic drove like a man possessed, making up time on the road.
The canary yellow Lavoisier hybrid sports car handled like a dream,
but at over a quarter of a million dollars it ought to. The Lavoisier
was Rask Labs first venture into the luxury car market. There were
only twenty-six in the world and one of them had turned up in
the farthest reaches of Butt-fuck, Wyoming, promising revenge.

They pulled into the rest stop with four minutes to spare.

"Give me your wallet, your keys, anything you have that might
be used to identify you. From here on you are Martin Blake. You
answer to Martin Blake and only Martin Blake. Understood?"

He nodded.

"You have never heard the name Ryerson McKenna before,"
Vic continued. "You talk to no one. You keep your head down.
They are very dangerous people, Mr. McKenna—"

"Blake," he said.

"—and no one on the inside knows of my employer's arrangement. Once you get on that bus you are on your own."

"Meaning they're going to treat me like scum?"

Vic nodded. "It has to be that way. Anything else would raise
red flags later. This way Blake takes the fall for whatever you chose
to do in his name."

"I can live with it," he said.

He took his watch off—a gift from Hannah—and dropped it
into the envelope Vic held out for his personal effects. He took the
coins and keys out of his pocket, and his cell phone, and dropped
them into the envelope with the watch.

"I hope so."

"So, tell me, what is Martin Blake in there for? The real one."

"Blake is a member of the Brethren, a white supremacist movement in South Carolina. Last week he drove a flatbed loaded with
a fertilizer bomb into a trailer park outside of Charleston. He killed
seven people, wiping out three generations of the same family:
grandmother, both parents, and four kids aged between two and

twelve. Hate is a powerful thing in some people. Earlier that night there had been an altercation between Blake and the father at a restaurant in the city. Tempers flared when he was told he would have to wait because the family had taken the last table. Eyewitness reports claim Blake told the waitress that, 'It didn't used to be like this, niggers used to know their place.' Blake left the restaurant but followed the family home, then returned in the middle of the night with the bomb. He waited until he knew everyone was asleep before, using a brick to weigh down the gas, he steered the flatbed into the trailer."

"Jesus Christ."

"Has very little to do with what Blake believes."

"And this is the man I am tonight."

"It could be worse, you could be him tomorrow as well." Vic handed him a wallet filled with the usual ID, loyalty cards, and a billfold with half a dozen dead presidents in it. The last thing he handed Rye was a power bar. "Eat up."

He didn't need telling twice.

A bright yellow school bus turned into the rest stop as he took the last bite. Its engine idled as it pulled up alongside the piss-yellow lights of the toilet block. The driver disembarked, unzipping before he was through the door. A guard came around the side of the bus, saw them and nodded.

"I'll be waiting for you whatever you decide to do when you come face-to-face with Langley. I hope, whatever happens between now and sunrise, you slay your demons. A man cannot live beneath the burden you carry, my friend."

Rye said nothing.

He opened the door and got out of the car.

"Blake?" the guard called.

He nodded.

"Inside. Quick."

He did as he was told, taking up one of the vacant seats half-way back. The interior was dark save for the splash-back of the piss-yellow light from outside, but it was enough for him to see the silver of handcuffs chained to the floor. He sank back into the leather seat and put his hands out, allowing the guard to cuff him before the driver returned. There were seven other passengers on the bus, each one a candidate for their own Lifetime movie. The closest to him, a Latino with gang tats crawling up the side of his face, hawked and spat in his direction. He looked around him. Seven faces. All of them black or Latino.

Rye did what Martin Blake would have done: lunged forward and lashed out with a booted foot, missing and earning mocking laughter from his fellow prisoners.

"I'm gonna fuck you up real good when we get to where we're going," the spitter promised.

Rye met his unflinching stare.

The man continued. "Oh yeah, we know all about you and what you did to that family. Gonna be a reckoning. Let's see just how superior you really are, eh?"

What the hell had he got himself into?

FIVE

The bus pulled up outside the chain-link fence.

There were four armed guards waiting to usher them inside.

It was night, but you'd never know it. The place was lit up with powerful searchlights cutting across the killing ground between the prison's windowless walls and the fence.

The guard who'd smuggled him onto the transport walked down the line, to the front, where he pulled a lever that released the security bar and sprung their cuffs. The mechanism was a more advanced version of the roll bar in a roller-coaster carriage. Rye sat up straight, spreading his legs to brace himself. His ankles were chained. He wasn't sure when trouble would hit, only that it would, somewhere between here and the cell. But given what waited for him in that cell, he could handle a metric fuckton of trouble happily.

"On your feet," the guard said, banging his baton against the side of the bus to hustle them along. "File out."

Rye did as he was told.

The roof of the bus was low, forcing him to stoop as he shuffled toward the rear doors.

He was fourth in line.

The spitter was three short dragging footsteps behind him. Rye concentrated on the scuff of the spitter's soft-soled shoes, making sure there was no change in the pattern—any sort of change in his footsteps would be the first indication of a lunge.

He jumped down, misjudging the length of the chain shackling his ankles, and stumbled.

The spitter jumped down behind him, moving quickly enough to send him sprawling in the dirt.

"Watch yourself," the spitter mocked.

"Shut up," one of the guards snapped. "We don't put up with any shit in here. You better learn that fast. Once you're through those doors you cease to be. You are nothing. You shit when we say. You piss when we want you to. We want you to suck on dick, you suck on dick. Your ass is our ass. *Comprende?*"

He said nothing.

"I asked if you understood?"

He nodded.

"I'm not hearing you, what did you say?"

"Understood," Rye said, not meeting the man's eye.

The nearest guard hauled him back to his feet. The name on his uniform read: LAW, which he seemed to take literally.

"That's better. Wasn't so hard, was it? Now hustle that lazy ass inside before I die of fucking pneumonia standing around in the freezing fucking cold waiting for you to get your shit together."

The chain-links formed a crude tunnel. On the far side, the exercise yard was bathed in floodlights leaving nowhere for a would-be escapee to hide.

An alarm sounded, just once, and the huge steel doors at the end of the tunnel opened with a hydraulic hiss.

Inside, they were processed and sent through to the shower block to be hosed down and deloused.

"Strip," Law ordered. "My colleague will come along with a garbage bag. Put your stuff in there. The next time you see your things you'll be free men," Law said. He was lying. With the exception of Rye McKenna, none of the people who'd come in on the transport were getting out. Not waiting for Rye to start undressing, the guard drove his baton into the back of his legs. Rye's knees buckled, but he didn't fall. He slapped his hand up against the tiles to keep his balance, which earned a second punishing blow, this one to the base of the spine. He straightened up, pulling his shirt up over his head and unbuckling his belt. He peeled his jeans down, then stepped out of his boxers and took off his socks. He stood naked before the guards, eyes fixed squarely on the tiles in front of him. The guard leaned in close, his lips up against his ear as he breathed, *"You'll have an hour when the cameras outside your cell aren't working."* A third blow, this one a punch driven into his kidneys, left him gasping, one hand flat on the tiles to stop himself from falling forward. Law stepped in behind him, so close he could make an educated guess at his religious persuasion. "I'll take that," Law said, taking his belt.

The guard rolled the belt and pocketed it.

Law walked along the line of naked men, running his baton across the small of their backs one after the other, then walked back the other way. His booted feet echoed loudly on the tiled floor. The tiles were good for washing the blood and piss away.

It seemed to take forever for the pressure hose to hit him. When it finally did, the spray was fierce enough to bully him two steps closer to the wall before he found his balance against it.

It was *freezing.*

He gritted his teeth, feeling his skin shrivel.

He was a full minute under the spray.

When the hose finally shut off he looked up to see another guard waiting with an orange coverall in her hands. It had his borrowed name on it.

"Welcome to your new home, Mr. Blake. I hope you'll be very uncomfortable with us."

"Won't be here long," the spitter said, drawing a finger slowly across the curve of his throat.

"Shut your mouth, Gonzalo, unless you want me to shut it for you," Law said, putting the baton to work again.

Rye took the orange coverall and a pair of plastic-soled prison-issue sneakers and dressed without saying a word.

The guard disappeared through the door.

He waited until he was told to follow.

The eight of them shuffled along the corridor.

The place reeked of the twin odors of cabbage and urine, fused forever together. Night-lights lit the way.

Law curled a finger, "Follow me, Blake. The rest of you, it can be a long lonely first night. We've got a pool on who will be the first to break." He grinned at Rye. "Don't let me down. We'll all be listening."

The walk to the cell was as daunting and depressing as any he'd ever taken, right up there with the short walk to the observation room in the mortuary, though at the end of that journey there had been a dead body waiting for him on the slab. The smell didn't get any better the deeper he got into the complex. He noted several security cameras, a small red light beside each lens. Law was good for his word; the cameras outside his cell weren't working.

The door was open. It was a mag-lock. There was no key.

"In you go," the guard said, following him inside. The room was basic, two wire-frame beds with thin mattresses and a single sheet folded on top with a pillow at the head, and between the beds a toilet without a lid. He took the belt from his pocket and put it on the pillow of one of the cell's two beds. "Don't make a mess. It's got to look like he's sleeping, otherwise when it comes time to move you out the alarm's going to be raised and Marty Blake will be going nowhere, you understand?"

"Why are you doing this?"

"Why do you care?" The other man said.

"Just curious."

"You want the truth? I don't care what you do to Langley when that door behind me closes. You can slice his balls off or put his eyes out with your thumbs. Doesn't matter to me. He deserves everything you do to him. What he did to those people . . . in your place I'd hope there was someone like me to give me the chance to make sure he paid for what he did. Justice. Retribution.

Whatever you want to call it. It's yours. That good enough for you?"

Rye nodded. "And the guy who sorted it out?"

"Not my secret to tell, pal. Okay, make yourself comfortable. Langley will be joining you in about forty minutes."

Law left him, drawing the door into place behind him. The magnetic locks engaged with a deep resonating chime like the tolling of a bell. In those harmonics hid a voice that quietly promised a reckoning.

He made both beds.

Law had said he needed it to look like Langley was sleeping; you didn't do that on an unmade bed. Then he sat down on one, with his back against the wall, and held the leather belt in his hands. He hadn't considered how he would do it, but alone with his thoughts he had plenty of time to imagine the way the meeting would play out.

The reality was nothing like he envisioned.

SIX

He didn't know what he'd been expecting, even after seeing the still from the surveillance camera, but it wasn't this.

Matthew Langley wasn't some demonic colossus of a man. He was the weedy runt of his particular litter. He stumbled as Law pushed him into the cell. He looked surprised to see that he wasn't alone. He had lank greasy black hair that was too long for his face and hollow cheeks with half a dozen angry red pimple-heads cratering them.

Rye couldn't picture him ever looking frightening, but put an assault rifle in his hands and a balaclava over his face and Rye had the portrait of a mass murderer standing in front of him.

The kid couldn't have been much more than eighteen or nineteen.

Rye tried to imagine being so full of hate you couldn't contain it all within your flesh.

He was a kid.

His mind kept coming back to that.

Matthew Langley was a kid.

Rye looked at him standing there in his dark red jumpsuit looking like he was playing dress up.

The color designated the risk; Martin Blake's orange put him as medium risk, red was high risk, dark red marked the kid as the worst of the worst, a candidate for supermax.

"You all right?" Langley asked, taking up a seat on the empty bed.

"Been better," Rye said. They weren't the words he'd imagined greeting his wife's killer with.

"What you in for?"

"Murder," he said, which wasn't, technically, a lie.

"Me too."

"Well, would you look at us, two bad hombres," Rye said.

The kid laughed. It was a wheezy nasal sound.

"Who'd you do?"

Rye looked down at his hands. For a moment he thought about telling Martin Blake's story, but he wanted the kid to know who he was in here with, and for however long he had left to understand the true meaning of fear. "You first."

"Why not," the kid said, like he was trading war stories. "Sheridan Mall. That was me."

"I thought they killed the guys who did that?"

"That's what you're supposed to think."

"Why'd you do it? Some sort of political thing?"

The kid's face twisted into a passable sneer. "Nah. That's all bullshit. Those niggers who pledge themselves to ISIS then go shoot up a mall, they're just cunts, same as the closet fags who shoot up a nightclub because they secretly wanna suck some cock and don't like what that says about them."

"So, what, you depressed? Looking to martyr yourself?"

"Just like Jesus," the kid said and laughed that laugh again.

Rye was going to take that sound to the grave.

"Just angry then?"

"Sure, if you want a reason, that's as good as any. Some people just wanna watch the world burn. Why'd you do yours?"

"Justice," he said, pushing himself away from the wall. He felt the belt beneath him. He reached down for it.

"There you go, that's what I call a reason. Good for you, man. That's some pure motivation there. What they do to you?"

Rye stood.

"They killed the woman I loved. And you have no idea how much I hate using that word, *loved*, instead of *love*. That one extra letter changes a man. It took a good man and made him into a murderer."

"Fuck man, that's heavy. Why'd *they* do it?"

"You tell me," Rye said, grabbing the kid by the ankles and hauling him off the bed in one sudden, violent, motion. The base of Langley's spine jarred against the metal frame. As he hit the floor Rye drove a soft-soled foot into the *V* between the kid's legs, kicking him hard enough to ram his testicles back up into his throat.

He stood over Langley as he gagged and gasped, choking and clutching his cock.

Rye tangled his fist in the kid's greasy hair and jerked his head back, forcing Matthew Langley to look into his eyes. "Let me give you one more clue, make it easy for you: *she can't come to the phone right now.* Ring any bells?"

Langley started to answer.

Rye punched him in the throat with his free hand. "I don't want to hear it."

He stood over him. All the anger, all the rage, all the desperation he'd felt over the last six months flooded through Rye McKenna in that moment. He was a black angel dispensing justice. He was vengeance. He was wrath.

But most of all he was human.

He looped the belt through the buckle and dropped it over the kid's head like he was playing lasso, then pulled it tight, and kept on pulling on it as the buckle bit deep into Langley's Adam's apple. The kid clawed at the leather, desperately trying to get his fingers under the belt as though that could somehow save him. His eyes bulged in his face as his brain was starved of oxygen. The leather took the heads off two of the pimples, leaving blood on Langley's hollow check. Rye kept on pulling on the belt until the kid's legs kicked out desperately, and then stopped. He let go of the end of the belt. This wasn't him. He wanted it to be. He wanted to be Death.

But he couldn't.

He learned something about himself in that moment: whatever else he was, Rye McKenna wasn't a murderer.

But that didn't mean the kid got to live.

He stood over him.

"I'm going to leave that belt with you. You're going to hang yourself. You understand?"

Matthew Langley stared up at him. "You can't make me."

"I think we both know that I can," Rye said. "I'm giving you a way out. The alternative will be worse."

He handed the kid the belt.

SEVEN

He felt nothing.

Not satisfied, not avenged, not empty or changed.

He was the only prisoner on the transport.

Getting out had been easy. Law had turned up maybe forty minutes after Langley had hung himself from the pipe. The guard took one look at the body in the bed and grunted, "Good enough," before he led him away. The lights beside the camera, Rye noted, were still red. He didn't know who this mysterious benefactor of his was, but the man had some juice.

The transport, another battered yellow school bus with the words PRISONER TRANSPORT stenciled on the side, waited in the lot. It was a different driver. He wasn't chained into his seat this time. The driver put on the radio as they peeled out onto the highway. The station offered some sort of bebop. The tune was familiar, but he couldn't have picked the players out of a lineup.

"Your clothes are in the sack on the back seat," the driver called back. "Figure you might want to get changed."

Everything was there.

With the dark country rolling by outside, Martin Blake ceased to be as Rye reclaimed his life.

"Mind me asking, what did it feel like?" And that was the question that had prompted the realization that he felt nothing. "I like to think I'd be able to do it," the driver continued. "You hear people say it, don't you, how they'd give anything for a few minutes alone with the killer. . . ."

"It's not how you would imagine," Rye said, still trying to process it himself. "I can tell you this much, you build the guy up in your head until he's a monster. He's this black hole responsible for sucking all of the living out of your life. But when you come face-to-face with him you don't see some devil, no matter how desperately you need him to be that, he's just some snotty-nosed kid who happened to be the one who pulled the trigger."

"Shit."

"I don't feel like Dirty Harry, put it that way."

The driver didn't say anything else for a while. It obviously wasn't the answer he'd expected.

Rye bundled the orange jumpsuit into a ball and stuffed it into the garbage sack and dumped it on the back seat. He went to sit up front.

"I heard what happened to you," the driver said as he took his seat. "Just wanted to say I'm sorry, man. I can't imagine."

He'd heard the same thing countless times over the last six months: *I can't imagine.* He didn't have to. He'd lived through it. But it was over now, wasn't it? That's what this night had been about. The gift of closure from his mysterious benefactor.

Matthew Langley was dead, and in dying knew exactly why.

Hannah was avenged.

So why did he feel so hollow?

"It doesn't give you your life back," he said, answering his own question.

The driver nodded thoughtfully.

"You think it will. You think seeing the killer die will solve everything, but it doesn't change a thing. Hannah's still dead, I'm still living alone the life we were meant to share. It isn't some magic wand solution that makes everything all right."

"Would you do it again if you had a do-over?"

He didn't hesitate.

"Yes."

EIGHT

Vic waited for him at the same rest stop.

The big man had his eyes closed, hands crossed behind his head, and seemed to be asleep.

For all he knew, Vic had been there all night cramped in his ludicrously expensive sports car waiting for him to return from the lockup.

Rye walked slowly across the gravel to the car, savoring the chill bite of the predawn air on his skin.

He might have only been inside for a few hours, but he felt dirty. No, not dirty. Unclean. There was a difference.

He opened the passenger's-side door and clambered in.

"I trust you had a fruitful trip?" Vic said.

"He's dead, if that's what you mean."

"I know. Andy Law radioed ahead. His body hasn't been discovered yet, though it's only a matter of time. But don't worry, no one knows you were there, only that Martin Blake was a temporary inmate. Any fallout will burn him without ever touching you."

It wasn't just morally ambiguous, it was disturbing how callously these people were prepared to play with someone's life, even a racist murdering prick like Blake deserved some sort of protection by the law—you had to believe that if you believed in the rule of law—but the rules were different for these people. They were the church in a society that worshiped money.

"I'm good," Rye said. "I didn't kill him. I just gave him the belt, he chose to take the easy way out."

"Good. Here." He offered Rye the envelope with the rest of his life in it. Rye took it, and in return gave the black man everything that marked him as Martin Blake.

"Only one question remains, Mr. McKenna: Am I to drive you back to your home, or should I take you to meet my employer?"

"So, I'll finally get to know who my mysterious benefactor is?"

"You will, but only if you choose to meet him. If you want me to take you home, we will part ways with a handshake and I will wish you the very best with the rest of your life."

Rye nodded. "Assuming I say yes and finally get to see the wizard hiding behind his curtain pulling the levers, I can still walk away, right? You're not about to produce a film of me watching Matthew Langley hang himself and say you own my soul?"

"Where would be the fun in my answering that one?" His smile was genuine. "You can walk away at any time, Mr. McKenna, but I would suggest you ask yourself this: What have you got to lose by listening? Perhaps you will learn something you didn't know you needed to hear? When I was in your place, I did. I wouldn't be the man I am today if I'd chosen to walk away from my invitation."

Rye nodded. "And that's a good thing?"

"I believe so."

"Fine, let's do it. Take me to your leader."

"A wise decision."

"We'll see soon enough."

They drove all through the day, heading into the sunset, and on into the night. Vic stopped twice at charging stations. That was one drawback with the whole hybrid eco-warrior sports car, they were limited in where they could refuel, making some legs of the journey a kind of treasure hunt. Vic was a good conversationalist, though in all the hours on the road he gave nothing away about his employer. Eventually they left the interstate, the lanes narrowing down to a single lane, the asphalt giving way to a dusty track that ended at a huge iron gate. The gate appeared to have been wrought in the shape of a winged man or an angel, it was hard to tell as it glided effortlessly open as they approached.

"Icarus," Vic said. "It's all about reaching for the sun."

"Is there a clue in that," he asked with a wry smile.

"You'll find out soon enough."

Beyond the gate was a richly cultivated landscape with woodland on the left and a lake off to the right. It was like entering a walled city, the grandeur of it was inescapable. The gravel driveway twisted and turned up a series of switchbacks that climbed a steep hill, before leveling out to reveal the house at the heart of it all. The manor house was immense, with dozens of gables and climbing plants clinging to the white-painted cedar façade. There were rose beds and granite stairs bordered by plant pots as big as him overflowing with colorful blossoms. More climbers, these ones on thin, reedy stalks, entwined the banisters on either side of the stairs leading up to a terrace where an older man, in his early fifties, sat drinking his mint julep and enjoying the cool of the night. Japonicas grew along the wall beneath the terrace.

Five cars were lined up outside the house; one Rye noticed was an Aston Martin Vanquish Zagato Volante. There were only ninety-nine in the world. It was a stunning piece of engineering worth more than Rye's house.

"She's beautiful, isn't she?"

"Well, not that I'm complaining about your wheels, but if the boss had given me a choice between the two, I'd have come to impress the new boy in that."

The other cars were variants of the same, super cars; nothing that would have looked at home in the lot outside Walmart.

Vic pulled in and killed the engine.

"Any last-minute advice?"

"Just be yourself," Vic said, clambering out. "He's really not that intimidating when you get to know him."

The man on the terrace raised his glass in greeting as they approached. He had more salt than pepper in his goatee, and more crags and crevices on his face than any amount of laughter could cause. He looked deeply tired. "Join me, Ryerson. You don't mind if I call you that, do you?"

"It's my name."

"Indeed it is. I think it's about time we had a chat, don't you?"

NINE

"You took the words right out of my mouth," Rye said, taking one of the three empty seats around the table. He had his back to the wall, looking out across the grounds. It was an old habit, don't leave your back open for someone to sneak up behind you.

"Guuleed, would you fetch our guest a drink?" The big man looked at him, his gaze implacable. It left Rye feeling judged without having opened his mouth. "Ryerson, what's your poison? No, don't tell me, let me guess." The man made a show of looking him up and down. "You strike me as a single malt soul?"

"Normally you'd be right, but tonight I think a decent cup of coffee will do just fine. I've got a feeling I'm going to need to keep a clear head for this."

The old man smiled. "As you wish. You have a preferred bean? Something rich and fruity or more mellow?"

"Surprise me. As long as it's hand roasted by naked virgins on some mountainside I'm sure it'll be just great."

"Guuleed, see to it, would you?"

"Of course, Mr. Rask."

Rask.

Like the car. It made sense. Who else had that kind of pull, but someone like Greg Rask? The next question was: What could a man like Greg Rask want with him?

"Now, how would you like to do this? Trade some small talk first, or get straight down to business? You must be tired, after everything. Perhaps you'd like to freshen up first?"

"I'm good. Why don't you just give me your sales pitch and we'll see where we go from there?"

"Very well," Rask said, taking a sip of his drink. "I'm not sure what you know about me—"

"I didn't even know your name until a few seconds ago," Rye said.

"Very true. I am sure you can appreciate the need for discretion, given our little arrangement. Greg Rask. It truly is a pleasure to meet you," he held out his hand to be shaken. Rye took it, surprised to find it was like holding a leathery bag of brittle bird bones. There was very little strength behind the handshake.

"I'll tell you if I agree later," Rye said. "We may end up hating each other."

That brought another wry smile from the older man. "I am a lucky man. You might not think it to look at the facts, especially considering the beginning of my story. I was orphaned before I was seven years old, but the other way of looking at it is that I walked away from the plane crash that killed my mother and everyone else on it. Luck, I tend to think, depends a lot on perspective. Imagine a really lucky man who's running late, rushing to an airport to catch a flight, everything goes his way, every light turns green for him, every junction is clear for him to race through, customs is a breeze, the TSA wave him through, everything just goes his way. Then there's the unlucky guy booked on the same flight, he's coming the other way, hitting every light, and getting more and more frustrated because he's not going to make the flight. Everything's against him. Traffic on his cross streets is an absolute bitch, and he's losing time at every intersection. He just knows he's going to get stuck in customs and the TSA are going to strip-search him and stick three fingers up his ass while his bags are put on the wrong flight, all of it. So, because nothing goes his way he misses the flight where the lucky guy makes it. When that plane stalls and falls out of the sky, who's the lucky one, really?"

Rask had a point. Rye had thought about Hannah and what might have happened if she hadn't chosen that day to run her errands, meaning she never would have come face-to-face with Matthew Langley or his bitter little tribe of trench-coat mafia.

"Do you want to know what saved my life?" Rask asked, without waiting for Rye to answer. "A stranger wanted to hit on my mother. She was a beautiful woman, so I can hardly blame him, but life pivots on such inconsequential things. Fate is a fickle bastard, not that I need to tell you that. We swapped seats, so he could talk to her and I could look out of the window. A piece of metal twisted off the hull and went right through the back of his chair, and I walked away with barely a scratch. A couple of bruises. I don't remember much of the crash beyond that, just that we changed seats. Which brings me to you."

"How so?"

"You don't know whether to feel lucky you're alive, or unlucky that you lost everything. It took me a while to decide which way I wanted to look at it, but eventually I decided it was all about second chances. I got a second bite at life that day. I was lucky again in that I showed a certain aptitude for the new world, grasping the concept of coding and computers in those early days of the dotcom boom and being able to imagine the future in terms of possibilities where others couldn't. First, working out of my bedroom, still financed by the payout from the airline, I set up Raskurity, offering people online security while everyone was obsessed with viruses and identity theft, and then the true stroke of luck, used that code to create a secure platform for people to buy and sell anything anywhere in the world, and all for the cost of a half percent or a single dollar fee, whichever is lower. Last year we averaged one point five million transactions a day through the site. Over seven billion dollars were traded, and in terms of pure profit we banked over five hundred million dollars. It's obscene, of course. And worse when you realize there's the double dip, because the second best thing I ever did was develop the app that allows people to actually spend their money. Seven billion dollars went through that app last year alone, and we took five percent in transaction fees, meaning we banked another three hundred and fifty million essentially for doing nothing."

"Must be nice."

"It is, but the important thing isn't the money, it's what we can do with it. Just through these two enterprises Rask Labs banks one and a quarter billion dollars. That money goes into the development of the car Guuleed drove you here in, for instance; into the development of our smart phones, which are being prepped for sale at under forty bucks a phone for the developing world market; the RASKos software we've been developing for a few years

now, a free-to-the-end-user operating system that addresses security and anonymity concerns in this new era of Big Brother,
available on a free license to the end user; and our most recent
venture, of course, the Messier 44 space program. And so much
more."

It was an impressive sales pitch. There weren't many men like
Greg Rask in the world.

"It's all about what you can imagine for the future. Shouldn't
everyone have access to pure drinking water? I think so, conse-
quently we are looking into portable purifiers that can be used in
artesian wells, each costing no more than a buck and lasting for a
year or more before they need to be replaced. How can we tackle
pollution and the problem posed by non-biodegradable plastics?
It's not about straws and plastic bags. That's barely even the tip of
the iceberg. Two thirds of the plastic we consume is through pack-
aging and we only recycle about ten percent of that. We need to
think big. Not just more recycling plants. But how do you sell it
to people who most of the time couldn't give a crap? Call it national security. Tell people that by supporting homegrown recy-
clate plastic industries they are guaranteeing themselves access to
vital materials for their economic growth. It worked for gold in
the nineteenth century. Tax reductions for industry that source re-
cyclate material rather than virgin plastics. Put emergency taxes on
virgin resin. Things like that are bigger than one man. In the long
run what I want to do is transform that waste plastic into energy.
In the next three years we're opening the first four Rask Technical
Labs, pharmaceutical research facilities, and we're also developing a
new kind of prosthesis for vets that is intuitive and responds as
close to naturally as anything I've ever seen. Every cent we bring
in is being channeled into trying to imagine a better future.
Over the next eighteen months we're also opening half a dozen
educational facilities offering free tuition to students from poor
backgrounds who show an aptitude for the sciences. And all of it
paid for by people's insatiable hunger to buy stuff."

"I'm sure there's some sort of metaphor for modern living in
there," Rye said.

"Absolutely. I'm lucky. I've always been lucky. The motivation behind everything we do at Rask these days is to make the world a better place for those who can't afford to live in it. Not just aid programs, either. Drop-ship food in the desert, you might feed hungry people for a week. Drop-ship farming tools, seeds and such, and they can feed themselves for years. We do a goat donation program where for every five-dollar donation we provide a family with a goat so that they can produce their own milk, their own cheese; but it's not about giving, it's about educating, too. So, there's sex ed programs, there's health awareness, vaccines, you name it."

"And you want me to be a part of this?" Rye said. "I'm not sure I'm much use unless you're planning on flying me to somewhere I can dig a well or work as security for your doctors out there?"

"Neither of which are what I have in mind for you."

"Enlighten me."

"Before we get into the specifics, there's one other thing you need to know about me; I am dying."

"I guessed," Rye said, "but I'm still not seeing where I come in, unless you're looking for an heir or a kidney donor?"

"One of the many things we are working on at the moment is a series of bionic organs."

"Like the Six Million Dollar Man?"

"But considerably more expensive," Rask said. "We're developing a computerized chipset that is a combination of silicon nanotechnology and living human cells that work to replicate the organ functions, so the bio-kidney would filter blood, removing waste product, the bio-liver would replicate the metabolic processes, break down fats, and produce energy. The whole idea is really quite brilliant. The bionic organs are driven by a series of microchips that essentially form a scaffold for the living cells to grow on, so that the chipset becomes a biological hybrid, much like the technology behind the Lavoisier you were driving."

"Sounds like something out of the future."

"Like I said, if you can imagine it, it's just a case of developing the knowledge to make it possible. We're still about a year or so away from human trials, but we know the science works. The chipset is capable of balancing the levels of sodium and potassium in the body, filtering waste and toxins from the bloodstream."

"But?"

"What felt like a vague concept a decade ago is now an inevitability. Our miraculous device won't be approved in time to save me. And I'm not ready to go yet."

"I sympathize, but short of giving you one of my own organs, which isn't happening, I don't see how I come into this?"

Rask took another drink as Vic appeared over his shoulder balancing a silver tray with a French press, creamer, and single bone china cup on it and proceeded to ease down the press before he poured out a fragrant drink for Rye. "In the last year I have spent a not inconsiderable sum chasing every supposed miracle cure and wonder drug out there. You name it, I've tried it. Ancient Chinese dietary remedies, exercise regimen designed for body and mind, acupuncture, herbal teas, even faith healers. Experimental drugs, banned pharmaceuticals. Anything and everything. Nothing has worked."

"I really am sorry."

"I'm not looking for sympathy," Rask said.

"What are you looking for?"

"A man of your unique talents," he said. "I know you. I know your background, right down to your field of academic study. I've read your doctoral thesis and found it fascinating. There is so much we still don't truly understand about our recent history, but it strikes me you are a man who knows the value of the past. Equally, I am familiar with your passion for dangerous sports and your reputation as a real-life Spider-Man. You are exactly what I am looking for, that balance of brawn and brain."

"You're flattering me," Rye said. "But I'll take it."

Rask nodded. "I have located an antiquities dealer in Stockholm who, I believe, is in the process of restoring a painting which contains a hidden map. I am willing to pay a considerable sum of money for that piece of art."

"I'm guessing the guy doesn't want to sell," Rye said. "So, what? You expect me to convince this guy to sell up? Bribery? Blackmail? Or am I supposed to steal it?"

"Rather than theft, perhaps just find out what, if not money, he truly wants for it, and broker the deal? I would leave the particulars up to you. As I said, I've done my due diligence, I know you are nothing if not resourceful, but I would prefer it if you didn't break any laws. I have clearance for the Gulfstream to leave in the morning. You and Guuleed are both listed on the passenger manifest, but of course, you can still say no and walk away tonight as agreed."

"You could send anyone to pick up that painting."

"But I don't want to send anyone. I want to send *you*."

"And we circle right back around to the same question that's been bugging me from the moment that courier dropped off the invitation: Why me?"

"Because you experienced something no one should ever have to. You had your own equivalent of that plane crash and walked away while the one person you loved didn't. The invitation asked if you deserve a second chance. The wording was very specific, because until you feel that you do you will become more and more self-destructive and truly come to believe that death should be the end of your story. I'll be honest, I've got no use for you if that's the way you want to go. Perhaps it's time to meet the rest of the team so you can make your decision?"

Rye shook his head. "I'd rather not. Let's just say I am willing to travel, just to test the waters—what do I get out of the deal apart from this magical second chance?"

"You will be generously compensated," Rask said, not actually offering a number.

"I'm sure, but are we talking health care, dental, 401(k), paid vacation? It would help to be able to visualize it."

"I can help you with that." Rask fished in his pocket for something, then tossed it across the table. The unfurled wings dug into his palm as Rye closed his hand around the Aston Martin's key ring. "For one, the job comes with a company car."

TEN

Rask didn't actually give him a choice in the matter. It was a lesson in how he operated. If he thought it was time for Rye to meet the team, then it was time for Rye to meet the team, end of discussion.

He led Rye down the hallway to a drawing room where the rest of his team were unwinding.

There were four of them in there, two men, two women.

Rye nodded to them as he entered the room, feeling very much like this was the real interview.

The drawing room was anything but the classic Southern-charm plantation retreat he'd expected. Rye's first impression was more military in nature: this was a debriefing room. It was bigger than he'd expected, too, with modern technology juxtaposed against conservative charm. One entire wall comprised twelve huge high-definition displays capable of showing either a single image as a visual mosaic or spliced into a dozen individual ones. On the second wall there were heavy antique bookcases filled with priceless first editions and folio editions. Recessed spotlights were set into the ceiling. They were dimmed low.

The room was dominated by antique leather armchairs and a Chesterfield couch that was being used as a bed by a very tall black man.

The rest of Rask's team sat in three of the four armchairs.

Rask did the introductions.

The man lying on the couch was Carter Vickers, a thief. Carter didn't look much like a thief, but then what was a thief supposed to look like? He was a good four inches taller than Rye, reed thin, and radiated confidence. The half smile he offered Rye made him look like someone used to trying and failing to charm himself out of trouble.

Next to him was Olivia Meyer. She was pure Celtic fire with an almost albino-white complexion, her shoulder-length flame-red hair framing fine bones and heart-shaped lips. She was born in Cork, her father from a small town just outside Waterford, her mother from the ice of northern Sweden, and Olivia herself was a curious blend of both gene pools, fire and ice. Her Celtic heritage was obvious in her features, while her Swedish side manifested itself in other ways, most of them skin-deep, including a ruthless calm. Olivia Meyer was a linguistics expert, fluent in a dozen tongues, and specializing in dead languages.

On the other side of the room, Iskra Zima inclined her head in greeting when Rask reached her. Iskra was a Russian defector raised to be a Cold War weapon long after the Cold War had supposedly ended. Before she defected, she was GRU, part of the Sixth Directorate in Syria, ex–Soviet intelligence. She had trained in martial arts and tradecraft, and was by far the most dangerous person in the room. She had lived the kind of life that carved itself out on every inch of her skin. Rye had the distinct impression that the Russian only smiled when she wanted to emphasize just how eager she was to hurt you.

"What is it with you people and your unpronounceable names? First Vic, now you. I'm going to get your name wrong every time I try and say it, so I'm just going to call you Ice, if that works for you?"

"It is appropriate," she said, a trace of the Russian still in her accent. She sounded cultured.

They, each of them, had their own stories, of course, their own flaws. They were all broken, like him. Vic had made a point of telling him how Rask collected people that he believed deserved a second chance—meaning at one time or another each of these people had received the same black card and a visit from Vic asking if they deserved a second shot at life.

And then there was Jeremiah Byrne, the cuckoo in this nest of soldiers. He was a space archaeologist, though what that entailed was beyond Rye.

"I use satellite telemetry to search for remnants of lost civilizations."

"Okay, that sounds pretty cool, actually," Rye said, nodding.

"Most recently, I discovered proof of an entire lost city within the Amazon rain forest, which is what brought me here."

"Nice. Lost cities. Very *Indiana Jones*."

"He is also something of a tech guru," Rask said. "*Newsweek* once called him the man who broke the internet." Which had Byrne rolling his eyes, but he didn't deny it, Rye noticed.

"Perhaps you should tell us who the fuck you are?" Carter said, grinning. "Fair's fair, after all."

"Not much to tell," Rye said.

"Oh, don't be so modest," Rask told him. "One of the youngest competitors in the Vendée Globe yacht race—"

"Which I didn't finish."

"—lasting over one hundred days out there alone, that's something. You've been a regular competitor in the X Games—"

"I broke my leg and needed metal pins. I tore my rotator cuff. I ruptured my ACL and countless other minor injuries. It's three years since I last took part."

"—but remain an active base jumper, an accomplished ice climber, builderer—"

"Arrested three times for night-climbing the façades of several famous buildings isn't exactly a claim to fame."

"Scaling the Petronas Tower, CN Tower, Sears Tower, and the Millennium Tower, however, is. Five years ago, you were featured in an article in *Time* magazine, even though you weren't featured by name, where they called you the real Spider-Man. That article also discussed your obsession with the urban exploration scene, especially roof-topping, though I believe you prefer to call it roof-and-tunnel hacking?"

"That was another life." He fiddled idly with the watch hanging from his wrist. It had been a wedding gift from Hannah. Right now, it felt like all he had left of her. "I got old. I settled down."

"Maybe so, but it doesn't change the fact that you are the real Spider-Man, and that person will always be in you. And that is who we've identified as the missing link in terms of our team here."

ELEVEN

The first thing he noticed about Stockholm was the air.

It tasted different in his lungs. It was hard to explain the difference, only that it felt more *vital*. He stood on the asphalt looking up at the stars. It was the same sky he'd grown up with, but everything was in the wrong place, as though god had scooped up all the stars and decided to play dice with the universe, letting them fall where they may. He smiled at that. Beside him, Vic stuffed his hands in his pockets. "Strange to think the sun will be coming up again in a couple of hours." Which of course was true. This time of year, the city had maybe four hours of darkness at best. It was every bit as disconcerting as the stars being in the wrong place.

The airport walls were adorned with photographs of famous Swedes welcoming them. He had no idea who half of them were, which was as much down to his shortcomings as theirs.

Rather than wait in the snaking queue of travelers for a cab that could easily be an hour in arriving, they turned and went back into the terminal, riding the elevator down to the subterranean station, and took the express into the central station.

The second thing he noticed, stepping off the train, was the women.

It was a hoary old cliché to say that Scandinavian women were gorgeous, tall, endlessly blond, with equally endless legs, but confronted by the city in summer it was hard to deny the cliché had its foundation in reality. Though these days it was a considerably more multicultural place, the Viking heritage ran strong in the nightlife. Most bizarrely, stepping onto the platform expecting the reek of grease and engine smoke, he was surrounded by the heady fragrances of designer perfumes. Even the station smelled good. He couldn't help but smile as he followed Vic through to the main hall, looking for signs to the taxi ranks.

The demographics settled into a more interracial balance around them. A dozen languages rose and fell, some snatches of conversation sounding like mynah birds singing; others much more guttural, like hammers chipping off rocks. People hugged hello and good-bye. There were tears and smiles. All of life was here on some miniature scale.

He checked the boards. They promised half a dozen more arrivals before they closed for the night. There were half as many departures lined up, with the station already closing up. Half of the concessions were already closed, steel shutters rolled down across their doors. There was a café with no food left in the glass display cabinets and a florist in the process of retrieving the brightly colored waterfall of blossoms that had spilled out onto the concourse.

She smiled at him and Vic as they walked past.

Up ahead he saw a man holding a sign with his name on it.

"Looks like our ride's here," Vic said.

"Give me a second, I'm just going to grab a coffee," he said, which proved more of a challenge than he'd expected as he put a handful of dollars on the counter, then realized he couldn't pay with them. He felt about two inches tall. The barista just smiled. "We take cards." But he didn't have any plastic on him. Vic had wanted minimal ties that linked back to their real lives in case things went sideways. The barista ended up offering him a cup on the house, black and strong enough to descale his arteries. "Welcome to Sweden," she said. Rye walked toward the huge granite portico where Vic waited for him.

Their driver was a young refugee who had come over from Syria twelve months earlier and already spoke better English than a lot of the Americans Rye'd encountered. He showed them to a waiting car that looked like something he had brought with him from the war zone. Rye couldn't help but smile at the beaded cushion on the driver's seat. The driver held the door open for them, eager to please.

"So, what are you? Like the Swedish version of Uber?" Rye asked, as they settled in for the short ride to the waterfront.

"Ammar," the driver said.

It took him a moment to realize it was the kid's name.

"Pleased to meet you, Ammar. You know where we need to go?"

"Oh yes, the most expensive street in the whole country, everyone knows it," he said, not worrying about the blinkers as he pulled out into traffic. It was still bright daylight despite the fact it was less than an hour short of midnight. Ammar drove quickly, weaving in and out of back streets and off-ramps to cut across the city with the confidence only a taxi driver could possess. They didn't get to see much of it through the windows, until he brought them around a particularly seedy corner and up a street so tight Rye and Vic could have reached out of either side window and dragged their fingers down the walls closing in on them. It was a shortcut around the back of the Grand Hotel and Berzelii Park. They emerged on the waterfront beside the golden statues of the national theater on Strandvägen. "Not far now," Ammar assured them. Up ahead, on the right, row upon row of luxury yachts were moored, bobbing in the surf. To the left, imposing buildings older than the country they called home housed embassies and the rich, if not the famous, of the old town.

"Did you know Hitler loved this city?" Rye said, not sure why he did.

Vic raised an eyebrow. "All the blond hair and blue eyes?"

"It's true. Not only was Sweden neutral during the war, high-ranking members of the Third Reich loved the place so much they bought residences here. Himmler and Goering had apartments in the city. So, on the one hand, you had places like the Swedish Match Factory running intel for the Polish resistance, and on the other, you had them playing the Germans for profit."

"That's different."

"That it is," Rye agreed.

"Here we are," Ammar said, slowing the car to a crawl alongside an avenue of ancient trees. They were coming into bloom, the season here a few weeks behind back home. The branches were weighed down with buds and sap. Ammar killed the engine as they pulled up across the street from an antiquarian bookstore. A light burned in a window upstairs, despite the relatively bright night.

Vic opened the passenger door, still holding the handle as he told the driver, "Just wait here. We won't be long."

"I live to serve," Ammar said.

Rye couldn't be entirely sure the man was joking. He opened his own door while Vic got out the other side, into the road.

The four lanes were empty of traffic. The nearest car was still several hundred yards away. They crossed the white line divider. Before they reached the sidewalk, a huge explosion tore out the façade of the store, the shards of glass chased out into the street by fire. The shriek of masonry ripped from its foundations and metal twisted beyond salvage was deafening. The savagery of the explosion punched Rye off his feet. Beside him, Vic went down sprawling across the blacktop, face and hands torn up from the lethal spray of glass fragments. Rye lay on his back for a moment. He couldn't hear anything from the world outside of his head. The only noise that existed was the pounding of blood through his skull. He looked across the street to see the flames licking at the timber frames of the windows. Everything beyond where the glass should have been was fire.

The sheer heat coming off the blaze was intense.

He rose unsteadily, mind racing.

The books burned.

Had they arrived at that shop ten seconds earlier, they'd have been knocking on that glass door as the explosion shredded the storefront. Thirty seconds earlier and they'd have been inside. And it wouldn't have been a few cuts and bruises he'd be nursing.

He looked at Vic.

The big man was getting to his feet. Ammar was out of the car, shaking his head, and on his own cell phone, jabbering away in a singsong language that could have been any of a dozen variants of Arabic.

Rye couldn't look at the fire; the ferocious heat stung tears from his eyes.

He took a step toward the building, and then stopped dead in his tracks as a burning man launched himself through the upstairs window, screaming as he tried to fly.

TWELVE

The man hung in the air, wings of fire unfurling behind him.

And then, like Lucifer, he fell.

Rye stood rooted to the spot.

He couldn't move.

It was as though he'd been given a front row seat with a view straight down into Hell. He froze, as the man hit the ground, the flames still burning, his arms and legs bent at unnatural angles. He wasn't screaming anymore. He didn't writhe against the flames. He lay there as the fire consumed his clothes and got at his flesh.

Vic moved fast. He threw his coat over the unmoving man, beating the flames out with his bare hands while Rye and Ammar just stood there, locked in the horror of it all.

It was useless. There was no saving him.

But that didn't stop Vic from smothering the flames.

Rye saw the man's burns and knew enough to know it was a mercy he hadn't made it.

He looked from the dead man back to the burning building.

He wasn't a big fan of coincidence.

In his experience, coincidence just meant you couldn't see who was pulling the strings.

In the distance he heard the first sirens. That was one thing about these socialist countries, the response time of the emergency services was *fast*. They had maybe two to three minutes before the first responders were on the scene, and already Swedes had begun to gather, drawn out onto the yacht decks by the explosion. Of course, it wasn't that long ago the city had been the victim of its first real terror attack—a disaffected man denied asylum had stolen a delivery truck and driven it headlong down the main shopping street and into the plate glass windows of the city's premier department store, claiming the lives of too many people in the process.

Rye started toward the building, but Vic stopped him. "It's pointless," the big man called. "We are here for a painting. There's no way anything made of canvas could survive in there. The heat, the flames. It's gone."

But Rye didn't listen. He pulled off his borrowed sweater and started to wrap it around his face to fashion a makeshift mask. Before Vic could stop him, he plunged into the burning building.

The heat came at him in waves.

It was unlike anything he'd ever experienced. It made the heat of a Wyoming summer feel like Siberia. He couldn't hear much beyond the sheer ferocity of the flames consuming row upon row of precious manuscripts, but every few seconds one of the glass cabinets succumbed to the conflagration. The glass shattered, each time ringing out clear and crisp like a gunshot. The heat stung his eyes, drawing out tears. He blinked against them, trying to see through the thickening black smoke. It was impossible. He pushed his way deeper into the store. The tables with rare leather-bound volumes danced with flames, the books on them barely recognizable as the fire consumed them. The flames chased up the walls, rippling out across the ceiling above him.

The heat was unbearable.

The timber frames in the old building sagged as the fire scored into them, biting deeper and deeper into the ancient heart as the wealth of inflammable material fed the flames. All around him the timber frame snapped with its own tiny detonations as the fire dried every last ounce of moisture out of the wood.

Rye shielded his eyes, biting back on the need to cough.

He called out, his voice muffled by the sleeve tied over his mouth.

There was no answer.

But that didn't mean there was no one else in here.

He forced himself to walk deeper into the rising inferno, feeling the bite of the fire against his skin. He wouldn't be able to withstand the heat much longer. He could feel his clothes beginning to sear to his skin. And still the heat rose as everything in the old store fed it.

He couldn't see anything obviously in the process of restoration, but why would the dealer have it down here on display? He had to have a workshop somewhere. The man had come crashing through the window of the floor above, which made upstairs a good place to start looking, if he could find a way up without getting himself killed.

Breathing hard, he forced himself to go deeper into the store.

He picked his way through the detritus of the explosion. It quickly became obvious that it wasn't rooted in some tragic gas leak or other accident. He saw fragments of the incendiary device, military issue, amid the rubble where the back half of the store had been utterly destroyed. There was a gaping hole in the ceiling that was filled with smoke and flame.

All around, the old building answered his progress with a chorus of failures as the integrity of the structure was undermined by the blaze. He found a staircase leading up but knew the likelihood of ever being able to come back down this way again was virtually zero. He didn't let that deter him. All he could think was that whatever that hidden map led to someone thought it was worth killing for, which right now made it worth risking his life to salvage. That was what having nothing left to lose meant.

Rye climbed the stairs two and three at a time, rising above the smoke.

He emerged on a landing. There was less air here than down below.

Three doors faced him on the landing.

The stairway rose to a third level, disappearing into thick choking black smoke halfway.

He didn't go up. He hadn't been in the building a full minute and already he was struggling. He looked left and right, trying to orient himself in the smoke. The stuff got through his makeshift mask into his throat. It was getting harder and harder to breathe and was only going to get worse. Every instinct in his body screamed at him to turn around and get out of the building on Strandvägen, but he went against them all and followed the worst of the fire toward the front of the house, each step harder than the last as the heat scoured his skin.

Somewhere out beyond the smoke he heard the frantic rising cries of sirens.

He pushed on, feeling the heat rising up through the floorboards as the flames consuming the story below worked their way through them. With each step they groaned desperately.

Rye ventured deeper, moving into the first doorway. He felt the rush of fresh air through the shattered window in direct contrast to the oxygen thief stealing every last ounce of air from the building.

He stepped into the room.

The open fireplace was the only thing not alight. The bookshelves lining one of the three other walls shimmered like a gateway to Hell, especially with half of the floorboards ending in a jagged hole where the explosion had torn up through them. Flames rushed in a funnel up from the first floor. Smoke billowed out through the shattered bay windows while the drapes around them burned.

In the middle of the room a draftsman's table was angled up. He saw a canvas weighted down on it. Part of the paint had begun to blister and wouldn't survive the fire much longer. There was a second table being used as a desk, that was rigged up with a curious arm and camera attachment that was hooked up to a huge iMac. There was a palm-sized portable drive on the table beside it. There was no way he could get the computer out of there. He snatched up the portable hard drive and stuffed it into his back pocket, leaving the cables still dangling from the back of the machine.

Behind him, a sudden backdraft of heat was chased by a groan so deep in the fabric of the building it sounded as though the whole place was coming apart.

Several of the lower stairs caved in on themselves, cutting him off.

He was into his second minute, with no way out.

Rye crossed the room to the draftsman's table and rescued the painting, rolling it up without looking at it, and crossed the room to the window.

The gaping hole in the floorboards was a problem.

He couldn't exactly drag the table across the room to bridge the gap, which meant he was going to have to do something stupid if he wanted to get out of there alive.

THIRTEEN

That was what he did.

With the floor crumbling beneath his feet, Rye stuffed the rolled-up canvas inside his shirt. He ran across the short distance, getting up as much speed as he could as he launched himself over the gaping hole where the floorboards had collapsed, kicking up through the blinding smoke and the rising flames, knowing that he only had one shot at this. Get it wrong and he was following the dead man all the way down and, short of learning how to fly in a couple of seconds, joining him in the morgue.

And part of him thought that wasn't such a bad place to be, just for a moment, a fleeting thought.

The bay windows dominated the outer wall, the center of the frame a crucifix of thicker timber supporting smaller windows set into the arch above. The cross brace was two inches deep, meaning there was two inches of handhold for him to catch and hold before he fell to the street below. This catch-and-release was basic stuff for a skilled climber, but that was a different life. It was a long time since he'd tried anything quite as reckless as this.

He couldn't think about it; letting doubt in was potentially lethal. It meant second-guessing everything. It meant micro-fractions of delay between mind and body as risks were calculated and put down. Those tiny slivers of time were the difference between making a landing and not.

Everything came down to instinct.

Rye had to trust who he was.

Or at least had been.

He reached out with his right hand still in the upward arc of his leap. The flames closed around him as he kicked through them.

His palm hit the cross brace dead center, arresting his flight. He used his momentum to pivot his body, twisting hard so instead of facing out toward the street his body came around one-eighty, which gave him the chance to reach out with his left hand even as he let go with his right. He faced the window he'd just jumped through, painfully aware that there was nothing between him and the twenty-five-foot drop to the sidewalk.

His focus was on the release, eyes taking in every inch of the façade at once.

He grabbed for the window ledge with his left hand as his body slammed into the stone wall. The impact jarred through his ribs and knees.

His fingers started to slip.

Flames rushed over his head, the fire tearing through the apartment block. The smoke rose, billowing up in thick black clouds to shroud the front of the building. The fire's appetite for destruction was voracious. It scorched deep into the red bricks, coating them black.

Rye heard people screaming down below, but there was no way he was about to look.

Three fingers carried his entire weight.

It was impossible to hold on for more than a few seconds.

The blistering paint betrayed him.

As he lost his grip, Rye adjusted his weight, kicking out with his feet and scrabbling around for any sort of purchase he could find.

He didn't dare breathe.

Which was a mistake.

It was unnatural.

He needed to trust that his skills, rusty or not, wouldn't abandon him when he needed them the most.

His toe caught on one of the letters of the bookstore's signage, giving him hope. He used it to give him leverage for a precious second to change his grip, the fingers of his right hand fastening on one of the decorative bricks proclaiming the age of the building. It was enough. He clung to the side of the building, breathing hard, the cries of people down below urging him to safety. Nine times out of ten, ascending was easier than descending, but climbing to the roof wasn't an option with the fire taking hold inside. It wouldn't be too long before the entire place went up in smoke. There was no obvious fire escape set into the façade, unlike back home where fire regs demanded it. The only real option he had lay in a decorative trellis and the climbing plants pitting the surface of the red brick—but that still meant negotiating five or six handholds sideways across the sheer wall without falling.

The drop was far enough to do serious damage, even if he tried to control his fall.

He couldn't hold on to the wall forever; his fingers were weakening fast.

Taking his weight on the toes of one foot, he felt out for a new handhold, reading the rough surface with his fingers.

He made it across. There was a small surveillance camera hidden within the climbing plants.

The trellis offered little reassurance; he felt the screws anchoring it to the wall pull away beneath him as he started down, and, still more than ten feet from the ground, was forced to jump.

Conscious of the portable drive in his back pocket, he landed badly, trying to protect it, and twisted his knee as he tried to roll with his body's natural momentum.

He lay on his back, looking up at the flames billowing out through the shattered window.

Vic's disapproving face loomed over him. The big man reached down. Rye thought he was offering to help him back to his feet, but as he reached up Vic ignored his hand.

"I think it's obvious what Mr. Rask sees in you," he said, retrieving the rolled-up canvas from inside Rye's shirt. "We need to get out of here."

A small crowd had gathered. Several people were on their cell phones, recording it for posterity or Twitter.

"Let's go find our ride."

FOURTEEN

Which was easier said than done. Ammar was nowhere to be found, and the sirens were on top of them.

Rye saw the flashing blue lights turn the same corner they had only a few moments ago. He pushed through the crowd, heading in the opposite direction. Voices yelled at his back. He didn't understand the words but didn't need to. "Come on," he urged. Vic didn't need telling twice.

They started to run.

The objection of the voices grew louder, but they were soon lost beneath the swell of sirens as more cop cars powered into the street, slewing sideways across the blacktop to form a temporary roadblock.

To the right, the yachts bobbed on the slight tidal roll of the water. To the left, a labyrinth of streets waited to swallow them whole. He turned and turned again, still moving away from the burning bookstore, trying to see Ammar's taxi within the descending chaos, but neither it nor the man was anywhere to be seen.

"What's the plan?" he called back to Vic.

"Distance first. We've got what we came for."

"What about—?" He cast a lingering look back toward the barrier of cops and saw a couple of the onlookers pointing at their backs, and knew they were being sold out. They had no more than three hundred yards on the cops, which in a strange city was nothing. Without thinking about it, Rye darted down one of the narrow side alleyways that in turn led to an even narrower alleyway that ended in a series of steps seemingly carved straight into the side of the hill. There was a tunnel beneath the staircase. The nondescript façade marked it as either a nuclear bunker or a parking garage.

Rye took the steps two and three at a time, not slowing, not looking back. He pushed himself hard, arms and legs pumping furiously as he climbed. There were over one hundred steps rising to the next street. Only once he reached the top did he turn in time to see two uniformed officers starting up the bottom steps after them.

The climb was hardest on Vic. He was built for sudden explosive strength, not this kind of muscle-burning endurance. He imagined the stairs a couple of months later, with the snow in place. It didn't bear thinking about. At the top of the stairs, the big man looked left and right, and made a decision: with an explosive burst of pace he charged toward one of the many glorious pre-twenties-decadence structures with their heavy oak doors and endless rows of buzzers keeping friend and foe alike out.

Sweden was a country struggling to reinvent itself—or at least, from what he'd seen of it, Stockholm was a city undergoing an identity crisis. Everywhere there seemed to be construction canvases hiding the work going on beneath as the city looked for a modern replacement to the brutalist architecture that had crushed the personality out of what had once been a beautiful place. The street they were on was one of the stubborn remnants of Germanic influence that predated those modernist monstrosities. Vic hit every single buzzer on the panel, top to bottom, knowing that someone would hit the door lock without actually asking who was there. He was right. Even as he was trying to convince a stranger to open the door, someone else triggered the lock. He pushed the door open and the pair of them hid inside.

The foyer was brown marbled stone, oak trim, and scuffed white paint. The problem was that the light came on as soon as the motion sensor was tripped, meaning the door was lit up like a big arrow pointing "This Way!" to the cops on their heels.

Vic didn't hesitate: he half bent to pull his shoe off, then jumped to shatter the lightbulb with its heel, plunging them into the same darkness that claimed the rest of the street.

"Get away from the doors," he said, leading them toward the back of the building. There was a second door that led out to a courtyard overlooked on all sides by apartments. He ran his fingers around the door frame. It took Rye a second to realize he was reassuring himself there was no magnetic seal that once broken would trip an alarm. The door, he saw, was an ancient thing. And heavy. Still holding his shoe, Vic tried the door. It was locked. Without anything to finesse it, he had no choice but to put his shoe back on and kick out the lock plate. It took four blows, each surely loud enough to bring the full weight of the law raining down on them, but the wood splintered around the metal, and he was able to force the door open.

They faced the same problem in reverse on the other side of the courtyard, but before Vic could shatter one of the small panel windows above the lock, Rye had found an alternate way out: a stable-style set of double doors that weren't locked. With a couple of streets between them and the scene of the crime, they were hardly out of the woods, especially given the lack of foot traffic at this time of night. They needed to find somewhere to disappear, even if only for half an hour or so, just until the immediate danger passed.

The streets around them were alive with sounds. Cars coming and going. Music, muted but definitely there. And voices. Drinkers. Exactly what they needed: a crowd of drunks to get lost in.

"This way," Rye said, pointing in the direction of the noise. Vic understood what he was thinking. Sometimes it was just smarter to hide in plain sight. He nodded. They set off toward the night's drinkers hoping there were enough of them to lose themselves among.

They turned a corner to see not one but two pubs with terraces filled with drinkers, dozens of people standing with glasses in hand, leaning against the yellow wall, while others sat around garden tables that spilled out into the street. The rise and fall of buzzed conversation welcomed them. Rye saw an empty table and steered Vic toward it. Vic sat with his back to the street, giving him a better view of who came and went around them.

A waitress came out to take their order, repeating herself when Rye said, "I'm sorry, I don't speak Swedish?"

"No problem. What can I get you?"

"Two beers," Vic said, keeping it easy. After all, they weren't here to drink.

She left them to themselves.

Rye tried to scan the street behind him through the reflections in the window, but it was a futile exercise. Vic seemed relaxed enough, so he had to assume there was no immediate danger.

Two cops, both built like rejects from some Scandinavian Terminator movie, walked down the street. They walked in step, hands easy but never far from the guns on their hips as they approached the drinkers.

The empty glasses on their table were the perfect camouflage. Rye reached for one and cradled it in his hands, nursing it.

The cops fell into conversation with a couple of the guys leaning against the wall. Words were exchanged. It was impossible to tell what was being said, but the tone sounded almost angry.

Rye raised the empty glass to his lips, doing his best to listen—and realized that they were the only people not talking. "So, I really want to go to Abba, The Museum," he said, suddenly, doing a little Keyser Söze, from the movie *The Usual Suspects,* thanks to the small sticker in the window that advertised the place.

"What are you talking about?" Vic asked, lost by the sudden non sequitur.

"It's supposed to be great," Rye said. "If you're into kaftans and flairs."

"I have no idea what you are talking about." The big man smiled as the waitress returned balancing a tray with their drinks.

She put the glasses down on the table between them. Vic reached for his wallet, even though he hadn't had time to change any money.

Rye looked from him to the cops and back to him as Vic took out his credit card. The waitress, he realized, had a handheld card reader in the front pocket of her apron.

She ran the card and handed the reader to Vic to put in his numbers.

One of the drinkers, a blonde propped up against the wall, raised her hand and pointed off in the opposite direction, nodding, and when questioned by the cops, nodding again more forcefully.

The cops worked their way back through the drinkers to the street and set off running in the opposite direction. Fast.

The helpful soul who'd sent them off on a wild-goose chase raised her glass when she saw Rye watching and offered him a flirtatious smile.

FIFTEEN

They were booked into a boutique hotel in the city, but Vic had no intention of staying there.

He wasn't sold on staying in the city, period.

Instead, after their taxi driver had dropped them off at their hotel, they made a show of walking in but carried on straight through the foyer and walked out of a second set of doors on the far side, out of the view of the street just in case anyone was watching.

They walked two blocks on back streets before crossing the main street to check into another hotel under false names. When the receptionist asked for their passports, Vic slipped her five hundred bucks and said, "If you could find us an empty room that isn't in the system, that would be excellent." She didn't seem convinced but pocketed the money.

"The room is meant to be empty, so don't make a mess. You'll need to be out before housekeeping arrives."

"Of course," Vic agreed.

"I don't want to know what you're planning on doing in there."

"Sleeping," Rye said, but the woman didn't look like she was buying it. But then, this was a country where prostitution was a tax-paying career, and what went on between two consenting adults, same sex or not, was none of her business.

The first thing Vic did when they were in the room was call Rask.

He unrolled the canvas and laid it out on one of the twin beds. Rye studied it, not sure what, exactly, he was looking for. There was no obvious map. It was a curious artifact. There was a considerable amount of damage to the oils on the left-hand side, with the paint blistered and charred in places. Nothing about the image, which appeared to be heavily symbolic in nature, suggested it was any sort of treasure map. Part of the canvas was given over to a tree of sorts, though it was no natural tree, but rather more akin to a glass sculpture wrapped in pastel-shaded angel wings and lit by a gloriously golden sun. No, not one sun, he realized there were three of them, in a triangle, though two were faded and less obvious than the main one, and appeared to be wreathed in flames that encompassed all three suns. There were rocks, and shadow shapes within the landscape that were disproportionately built, arms too long, legs unnaturally jointed, that wore crowns like kings. The figures, with their crowns and spears, towered over smaller ones, easily half again as tall as them. The rocks were dusted with snow, meaning they must be part of some mountain range? A lot of the painting was too damaged to make out any real detail.

"We've got a problem," Vic told Rask. The big man stared out through the window at the hotel farther down the main street.

Rye looked closer at one of the towering kings and changed his mind; the figure looked more like a knight. The entire image put him in mind of Arthurian knights questing after the Holy Grail, but he couldn't have said why, exactly. Perhaps it was the way the angel's wings seemed to form a chalice around the figures on the mountainside? The piece conveyed spiritual promise, but in truth it wasn't particularly good. There was a partial signature: *avatsky*. The rest of Helena Blavatsky's signature was lost beneath a ruptured bubble of oil.

"Okay, I'm putting you on speaker. I'm with Rye. We're both fine, but someone beat us to the punch. As we pulled up outside the dealer's an IED took the place out."

"What about Christoffer?"

"Dead," Vic said.

There was momentary silence, but Rask wasn't mourning the dealer, he was thinking two steps ahead.

"Thirty seconds earlier and we'd have been in there," Rye said, wanting Rask to understand the fine margins life and, in this case, death, turned on.

"But you weren't, which is something we should all be grateful for. I assume the painting was destroyed in the blaze?"

"You'd be wrong," Rye said.

"Our friend here took it upon himself to run into the burning building," Vic explained.

"I can see that," a new voice came onto the line. "And so can half of the world, so I'd say you've got two problems, not one. Someone's put footage of the new boy clinging to the front of the burning building up on Twitter. The thing's going viral. They've got a nice close-up of your face, too, and don't kill the camera until after Guuleed helps you back to your feet."

"Meaning you can see him take the rolled-up canvas from me first," Rye said, realizing what that meant.

"That you can. So, assuming the explosion wasn't just bad luck and a gas main blowing," that earned a snort from Vic. "It was set by someone who knew you were coming—"

"And if they see the video they know we've got the painting," Rye finished for Rask, not liking the implications of where he ended up.

"Precisely," Rask agreed.

"What do you want to do?" Vic asked.

"We need to get the pair of you out of there," Rask said. "I'll have Jeremiah see what he can find out about the bomber from here. You should relocate as soon as possible."

"Already done," Vic reassured him. "And even though our ride ditched us, we made sure our eventual taxi driver thinks we checked into the first hotel, just in case he sees the footage and realizes who his passengers were."

"You can never be too careful. It's a pity we can't get eyes on the actual painting until you get back here."

"It wasn't the only thing I rescued from the fire," Rye said. "There's this." He put the portable drive on the bed.

"I'm sure it's fantastic," the other voice said. "But given I can't actually *see* what you're talking about I'll just have to take your word for it."

"It's a portable hard drive," Rye said. "I've got no idea what's on it, but it was attached to the rig that had been used to photograph the painting. So, I'm thinking it includes the scans the dealer was using for authentication."

"Excellent," Rask said.

Vic was already taking a laptop out of his only piece of luggage. It wasn't a regular Best Buy kind of laptop, either. It was a rugged, shielded, military machine with satellite linkup. He held out a hand for the drive. Rye passed it to him as he powered up the machine. The thing was fast. The satellite linkup was active in less than twenty seconds. "It's all yours, Jerm."

"Cover me, I'm going in," the speaker—Jeremiah Byrne, Rask's space archaeologist—said gleefully.

"Can I say something?" Rye asked, not sure he felt entirely comfortable speaking up.

"Of course, you are among friends now, Mr. McKenna. Speak your mind," Rask told him.

"Okay, it might be different in your world, but in mine you don't kill someone lightly. So, whatever we've got here, it's important enough for someone to kill for. Which means the minute they know we've got it they're going to come after it. Meaning they're going to come after us."

"Indeed they are," Rask agreed. "Things are about to get interesting."

"I'm not sure I like your definition of interesting," Rye said.

"Don't be silly, Mr. McKenna. Of course you do. We're not so different, you and me. We like it when things get messy. It makes life fun."

"You're a very strange man."

"New man, whatever your name is, I need you to do something for me. Have you got a knife? Something sharp?"

"Not on me, no."

"Find one."

"I have a razor, will that work?" Vic offered.

"Perfect. I need you to pick a spot on the canvas and scrape away the oil paint."

The big man reached into his bag again, and after a couple of seconds had stripped the blade from his cheap disposable razor. He carefully worked the blade across the rough surface, scratching away the top layer.

"What do you see?"

"What am I looking for?"

"I see something, I think," Rye said, leaning closer. "Can you scratch away a little more?"

"Carefully," Rask said, down the open line. "You don't want to destroy the painting."

"I've got a feeling it won't matter," Rye said.

"What do you mean?" Rask asked as Vic peeled away another small patch of paint, no more than a thumbnail in size, but it was enough. Beneath it, Rye could see a faint grayscale shadow, as though the image above had somehow burned into the canvas. He'd need to see more of it to be sure, but it looked as though a photographic-quality copy of the hallucinatory painting had been transferred onto the canvas for someone to paint over. It was crude, like kids who used grease-proof paper for tracing, but effective in terms of creating a passable replica.

"It's a forgery," Rye said.

SIXTEEN

"What made you suspect it was a fake?" Rye asked Jeremiah Byrne.

"Bookkeeping," Rask's tech guru explained. "There's a directory that's mainly invoices. Seems Christoffer has been a very naughty boy."

"How so?"

"He liked to sell the same thing to several buyers at once."

"Naughty, naughty."

"Very naughty. Excluding us, he had three buyers lined up for our piece."

"Which rather suggests none of us were buying the original," Rask concluded. "I don't suppose his appointment calendar is there?"

"No, but it shouldn't be too hard to get into. Everything's backed up to the cloud. Just need to know where to look."

"It would be helpful to know if one of those buyers had a meeting set up with him today," Rask said.

"Find the bomber, find the painting," Rye agreed, following his train of thought.

"It's somewhere to start," Byrne said.

And then Rye remembered the camera. "There was a surveillance camera hidden in the climbing plants on the front of the building."

"Was there indeed? Well then, let's see how our luck holds shall we?" Byrne set to work on the other end of the line; the ghost echo of key taps the only sound for a moment as everyone in both rooms held their breath. "You, my new friend, are a legend." He could hear the grin in Byrne's voice. "There was indeed a camera, an IP camera, that's essentially a webcam that streams the signal wirelessly over the network to any backup drive you want, and you only went and stole the right drive. It's all here. I'm going to need to scrub through it, but there's a good chance our bomber's face is on here somewhere. You did good. We've got our break."

"Assuming he looks up at the camera."

"Why did you have to go and ruin my good mood?"

"Okay," Rask said, more to himself than anyone else. "I'm going to send the others over there to meet you. Rye, it seems like an opportune time to ask if you're in or out?"

He thought about it for a moment and realized the last few hours was the longest single span of time he'd gone without thinking about Hannah or trying—not particularly well—to hide his grief. He wasn't sure how he felt about that. "Technically I haven't finished collecting the painting," he said, which was no kind of answer at all.

"Is that your way of saying you're in?"

"No. Just stating a fact."

"Hate to interrupt the negotiations," Byrne cut across them. "But check your phones. I'm sending you the face of our bomber."

SEVENTEEN

True to his word, Jeremiah Byrne sent the image through moments later.

It wasn't a great shot, with half of the man's face obscured, but it was better than nothing.

A lot better than nothing.

A second image followed it. "One good thing about the location is that it's basically on Embassy Row. There are dozens and dozens of security and traffic cams up and down the street and looking over the marina along the opposite side of the road. While you boys were flirting I scrubbed the traffic cams and came back with a hit. A black sedan bearing French diplomatic plates entered the street thirteen minutes before you. It didn't leave until thirty seconds *after* you pulled up."

"He was watching us?"

"Looks that way."

"So why not wait the extra few seconds for us to get across the road and make sure we were taken out in the blast?" Rye wondered.

"Ever think you're not that important?" Byrne said helpfully. "Sometimes the world doesn't revolve around us, no matter how special mommy says we are. The good news is that thanks to the wonders of technology I managed to track the car through the traffic cams across the city. The bad news is that Stockholm isn't exactly wired with all those paranoid Big Brother cams like London and Paris, so I lost it again. But I can tell you it wasn't headed back to the French embassy. It's difficult to project a destination, but I took a gamble and ran a root search that isolated camera feeds at major and minor transport hubs in a fifty-mile radius of the city. The car turned up in a hospital parking lot fifteen minutes from the dealer's."

"How does that work?"

"Heliport. One of only six in the city. I checked with LFV,

Swedish air traffic control. Less than an hour ago an unscheduled takeoff from that hospital registered a flight path all the way through to Paris. Now, it may be a case of two and two making me Patsy Paranoid, but French diplomatic plates combined with a long-range private-charter helicopter capable of making the nearly thousand-mile flight to Paris, I'd say our bomber has serious resources and is long gone."

"Guuleed?" Rask said.

"Sir?"

"Your first course of action is to find that car, understood?"

"Sir."

"If there's anything that links it back to the bomber in any meaningful way, I want to know. There are sixty people working at the diplomatic mission in the city, and any number of visitors claiming diplomatic immunity. The embassy also runs a military service. There's no telling how many people use that car regularly, but anything we can do to winnow the numbers down enough to put a name to the half face we've got here, I want done."

"Understood," the big man said.

"I'm running the image through facial recognition," Byrne told them. "But there's no guarantee we'll get any sort of match. It's a low-quality image, bad angle, and only a partial, but if we can get enough hits on the few points of similarity we might get lucky. I'm taking a run at the law enforcement data center. The gendarmerie run a monolithic Linux kernel called GendBuntu; it's all open source, running from a centralized location in Issy-les-Moulineaux, just south of Paris. If he's known to any of the sub directorates, organized crime, counterterrorism, border police, or diplomatic protection, we'll find him."

"And if he isn't?" Rye asked.

"You really are determined to piss on my cornflakes today, aren't you, Sunshine? If he's not in there, you better hope you turn up something at your end. That's why they call it teamwork. I'll hold up my end, you worry about yours."

"Good man," Rask said approvingly. "Guuleed, when you are

done at the hospital I want you and Ryerson to rendezvous with the others in Paris, assuming Jeremiah is correct and that is where the trail leads. I want that painting."

"Sir."

It felt like a lot of effort for a so-so piece of art, but then it wasn't about the art, was it? It was all about the hidden map and whatever it led to. And that was wrapped up in Rask's desperate search for a cure for whatever was killing him.

But what Rye couldn't fathom was what sort of map could lead to a miracle?

EIGHTEEN

They took a taxi from the hotel to the hospital.

There were more than a hundred cars still in the visitor's lot, most bathed in early morning sun as the night had already given up being dark, bringing tomorrow with it much quicker than it would back home. Rye walked the line of cars, looking for one displaying diplomatic plates. It didn't take him long to find it. He reached out to try the door handle.

"Don't touch," Vic said. "When people wipe down surfaces for prints they often forget the most obvious areas—inside the handles." He proceeded to use tape on the inside of the handle to lift any prints it held.

"Nice," Rye said appreciatively, as Vic adhered it to a contrast paper.

"One partial," he said, as he pocketed it. "Not going to help much." He tried the handle. It didn't open. "Keep watch."

Vic didn't mess around; he took off his jacket, wrapped it around his fist, and punched out the tinted glass. He reached inside to open the door and clambered into the driver's seat. He slung the pack from his shoulder and dumped it on the passenger seat, then rooted around inside the glove box for anything that might have been left behind. There was a medallion for the embassy's parking garage, and the usual manuals and the service log book, but nothing particularly useful in terms of identifying the last driver. He reached under the seats, fumbling blindly, but came up empty-handed.

The car was clean.

He reached into the pack for a black light, and ran the beam across the dash, wheel, and other obvious places the driver might have touched. Even without the luminol it was obvious they'd all been wiped down.

He repeated the tape trick on the inside of the silver handle, this time coming out with a better print, which on a quick visual comparison seemed to be a match for the partial he'd taken from the door. It would need Jeremiah Byrne's computers to piece it together and see if it turned up a hit on Europol or elsewhere.

Across the parking lot the hospital's automatic doors slid open as a woman wearing black combat fatigues walked out into the night.

"We've got company," Rye told him.

Vic stuffed his equipment back into the pack, shouldered the bag, and got out of the car.

Wishing it was darker, the two of them hurried off to disappear within the anonymity of the parking lot, moving from car to car as the security guard headed across the blacktop to check out the diplomatic vehicle dumped by the bomber. Give it an hour or so and that car would be the center of some serious attention, assuming Swedish law enforcement were on the ball, but for now they were still ahead of the game.

"We need to get back to the airport."

"An Uber, an Uber, my kingdom for an Uber," Rye said, as they moved their way back toward the highway, looking to flag down a ride.

NINETEEN

It was midafternoon by the time they touched down in Paris.

Byrne had a name for them: Sébastien Guérin.

That in itself wasn't particularly helpful, given the fact the man was as good as a ghost.

"He's rich," Byrne explained. They were still on the hardstand, waiting for clearance to disembark. "I mean seriously, properly, chateaux-in-the-mountains rich. But beyond that, well, you need to see for yourselves."

"What do you mean?" Rye asked.

"I'm sending you through some stuff I found, tell me what you think."

A couple of seconds later his phone pinged. He opened the message to see a series of newspaper cuttings featuring photographs of Sébastien Guérin. The first couple were the usual sort of rich and famous hobnobbing with the man lurking in the background, caught by the camera in the company of an actress or an heiress, usually accompanied by the same question: Who is the mystery beau? Most of the bold and the beautiful were in their prime, and that would date the photograph around the fifties.

The third was interesting for who else was in it, as it appeared to be considerably older than the first paparazzi shots.

The four other men in the photograph wore the unmistakable uniforms of the Third Reich.

He didn't immediately recognize any of their faces, so it could conceivably have been some costume party in poor taste rather than a meeting of the Führer's inner circle.

"The man in the middle is Bruno Beger, he was a German racial anthropologist who was part of the Nazi expedition into Tibet, beside him is Ernst Schäfer, who headed that expedition. The man on the right is more immediately recognizable, Rudolf Hess, who at the time of the photo was deputy führer, the second most powerful man in Nazi Germany. The fourth man is Edmund Kiss, an archaeologist who wrote a substantial body of work relating to the occult and ancient mysticism. All four men were guests of the Thule Society, and members of the SS Ahnenerbe, the occult division of the SS. Indeed, the trip to Tibet, if you believe the more fanciful stories around it, was a front for Himmler's search for the Holy Grail."

The fourth photograph was different again, and all the more chilling for it. It was a grainy image of a prison chamber containing a guillotine, and a prisoner on his knees waiting for the blade to fall. Sébastien Guérin appeared to be his executioner. It could have been taken anywhere between the fifties and seventies, it was impossible to tell, but it was unmistakably Guérin, and he didn't appear to have aged a day since the previous photo and this one. He wasn't named in either of them.

"Who the hell is this guy?"

A rich man playing executioner?

Unsurprisingly, the article was in French. Rye could only pick out a few words here and there, but it seemed to be about the man escaping execution, and in the process claiming the life of a warder and the nurse who was due to deliver a mercy injection to calm his nerves before the guillotine took off his head.

"He was only the third man to escape La Santé Prison in over one hundred and fifty years. La Santé has housed some impressive inmates: Carlos the Jackal; Gorguloff, who assassinated their president; Bastien-Thiry, the assassin who came within inches of killing de Gaulle; Manuel Noriega. It's one of those places where you go in and you don't get out again."

The final photograph was every bit as shocking as the last.

It was considerably more modern than the others and appeared to be a newspaper cutting. It was a crowd scene, panic written on the face of those fleeing the scene of the Paris terror attack at the Bataclan a couple of years ago, and there, in the background, with blood on his face, was Sébastien Guérin, not a day older than the first photograph despite the years in between. "Facial recognition

picked the image up. There's nothing to say it's really him, but if
it is . . ."

"He's aging really well."

"To say the least. The guy in that photograph should be over a
hundred years old."

TWENTY

Early evening, and they were still several hours ahead of the rest
of Rask's team.

They had an address for Guérin, a chateau an hour or so to the
south of the city.

"What do you want to do?" Rye asked Vic.

The big man looked toward the rental car desk. "You up for a
bit of sightseeing?"

They hired a big Volvo SUV. There was a saying he'd heard
somewhere: back home a hundred years was a long time, over here
a hundred miles was a long way. That couldn't have been more
evident in a single journey if the route planner had deliberately
attempted to bury them in an avalanche of history. Buildings on
either side were older than his country, some five hundred, even
six hundred years old, their white stone façades polished and shining in the early evening sun as it slowly lowered toward the horizon. Across six lanes of traffic he saw the huge rising spires of the
ancient cathedral on the banks of the Seine and the iconic iron
tower that rose protectively over its city.

So many other landmarks were lost behind row upon row of
cramped and crowded streets overflowing with life.

The Autoroute du Soliel avoided congestion with the promise
of the sun. They drove without music, the GPS's voice occasionally prompting them to change lane or take an exit as they negotiated the journey from the airport to Sébastien Guérin's estate.

They left the crowded roads behind for an avenue of yew trees
whose branches grew together over the road to create a leafy tun-

nel that stretched on for more than a mile. The deeper into the tunnel they drove the more the atmosphere around them seemed to change and the temperature drop until it felt decidedly chilly inside the car. The grass along the roadside was high and unkempt. Branches, weighed down heavily by their leaves, dragged almost low enough to scrape the roof of the SUV in places.

The wrought-iron gates were the first indication they had that they were in the right place. The intricate latticework of iron formed three spheres that seemed to be surrounded by an aura of flame. The metal rendering was delicate and precise. He'd seen the image before, hidden within the forged painting he'd rescued from the dealer's studio.

He said as much.

"The three spheres represent *Jing,* the body essence, *Chi,* life force, and *Shen,* spiritual force, in the teachings of Taoism. They can also be thought of as embodiments of compassion, frugality, and humility."

"I'm not going to ask how you know this stuff, Vic. You are an enigma, my friend. Instead I'll ask, do you ever get the feeling that you are in way over your head?"

"Every day," the big man said with a wry smile. "And I wouldn't have it any other way."

The gates were closed.

There was no sign of any intercom or gatehouse.

Rye got out of the car to try the gate; it was locked, and no amount of rattling would open it up.

He noticed a surveillance camera mounted on the wall. It watched him intently, though if anyone was watching it on the other side of the feed it was impossible to say. He waved at the lens, trying to draw someone's attention in the hopes that his dance would be greeted by a deep resonating click as the magnetic lock disengaged.

No such luck.

He went back to the car, but didn't get in. Vic wound down his window. "I'm going over the wall. If I can open up from the other side, I'll let you in, otherwise I'll head up to the main house and see if there's a way to trigger the mechanism from up there."

Vic killed the engine and sat back, waiting while Rye walked the line of the wall looking for the best way over. Even with the glass-lined top, the eight-foot wall presented little challenge for a man of his particular skill set. He took off his jacket and used it to cover an area of broken glass, then used one of the yew trees to brace himself and climb up to an overhanging branch. Thirty seconds later he dropped down on the other side of the wall and reached up to retrieve his jacket. It was as easy as that. He walked back to the gate, looking for something to release it. There was a panel set into the stone beside the gatepost. One of the buttons was worn smooth. Taking an educated guess, he pressed it a couple of times, and a moment later the huge gate began to open inward.

Vic started up the engine and drove slowly into Guérin's estate.

The grounds went on and on, immaculately landscaped with miles of hedgerows and topiaries trimmed into an exotic menagerie. It was stunning and must have needed an army of gardeners to maintain. The lawns stretched as far as the eye could see, rising in gradual tiers until they reached the huge fountain before the chateau. It was imperial in its grandeur. It stank of the kind of privilege that led to a great queen proclaiming "*Qu'ils mangent de la brioche.*" He could only imagine the kind of security Guérin had in place. The driveway ran parallel to the hedge maze for two hundred yards, then curved around a crystal-blue lake with a glass butterfly house in the center. Everywhere he looked Rye saw the kind of ostentatious wealth that was out of the reach of mere mortals. Pathways wove around the lawns. Flower beds offered splashes of color to offset the thousands of shades of green. Several paths led to statues, but they were too far away for him to make out any details.

Peacocks strutted across an immaculate croquet lawn as they pulled up in front of the house. The black slate roof had seven conical towers of varying sizes, some with windows promising rooms up there, others without. On one side, away from the main building, stood a fortified tower that was attached to the main building by an elevated walkway. To the other was a chapel, though again the architectural ambition gave lie to the name; he'd seen cathedrals in poor countries that struggled to match the building's beauty. Granite steps rose toward the huge iron-banded oak doors.

They got out of the SUV and walked toward the main house expecting someone to come out to challenge them at any moment, but no one did.

Rye looked up at the imposing house. "I've got a bad feeling about this."

Vic didn't disagree with him.

He walked up to the main door and pulled on the bell-pull to announce their arrival. The chimes resonated throughout the entire building. They waited. Still no one came to answer.

Rye moved to the side, pushing through manicured rosebushes to peer in through one of the lower windows.

It was dark inside, but he could just make out the lines of a chiaroscuro world of light and shadow. Deep within the darkness he caught a flicker of light that might have been a candle or a reflection from the sun behind him trapped in the glass.

"Ring it again," he told Vic.

Again, he saw the flicker of light, but there was no other obvious response.

"No one's home," the big man said, stepping back from the door to peer up at the rows of windows.

The place didn't feel empty, but it was hard to explain why.

"So, what do you want to do?"

"We've come all this way," Rye said. "It'd be rude not to go in."

TWENTY-ONE

Getting inside was easier said than done, even without any obvious security.

Rye walked the perimeter, looking for an uncomplicated point of entry that wouldn't demand too much creativity on his part.

The windows on the lower floor were locked, many barred, some shuttered. He tried every door without joy. The second story was no better, and with no fairytale Rapunzel to let down her hair for him, scaling the side of the tower wasn't a great option. Doable, probably, but there were better angles to climb if that was his only alternative.

Rye checked the chapel, not sure what to expect. The main building was round rather than rectangular, which dated it to post-Crusades. He'd read somewhere that these round chapels didn't begin to appear until after the Templars returned from the Holy Land. The cross had been carved into the wall, alongside what appeared to be a weeping knight, both hands wrapped around the hilt of his huge greatsword, what looked to be a serpent or dragon slain at his feet. The craftsmanship that had gone into the carving was staggering. He could feel the warrior's pain.

Rye opened the door. Inside was small and cold. A number of graves had been laid into the stone floor, the memorials in a language he couldn't read.

He walked across the dead.

There was very little in the way of ostentation in here, no elaborate carvings in the stonework, no decorative flourishes. It was a simple place of worship. Even the altar was a single block of stone, though he noticed runnels had been carved into the flat surface which, he realized, meant that old stone had almost certainly seen sacrifices.

To one side, he saw a worn-smooth font filled with holy water, and to the other a small iron-banded oak door.

There were Bibles on every seat, which he took to mean the chapel was still in regular use. The only concession to modernity was a blackboard that appeared to display hymn numbers and Bible verses.

Vic entered the chapel behind him.

He crossed himself before the altar.

"What are you thinking?" The big man—who seemed so much bigger in the cramped confines of the medieval chapel—asked. He walked the line of small wooden pews, fingertips lingering on the backs of the seats as he passed.

The sun filtered through the stained-glass windows. A kaleidoscope of light spread out across the stones at the foot of the altar. It was beautiful and simple at the same time. There was a crack in the glass, he realized, which had caused a dark fissure to run through the center of the kaleidoscope like a crooked smile.

"I'm not sure," Rye admitted. "Maybe there's a passage that joins this place to the main house."

"Not impossible," Vic said. "The chapel almost certainly predates the chateau by a couple of hundred years by the looks of things."

He tried the door. After some initial resistance, the iron latch lifted, and the heavy old door groaned like it bore all the weight of the world on its rusty hinges.

Inside was dark.

Vic pulled a Maglite from his pack and lit the way.

Stone stairs led down to a vault, which contained a single stone sarcophagus. They approached it cautiously, their footsteps loud in the eerie silence. The lid of the grave bore the same detailed likeness of the weeping knight from outside the chapel. At another time it might have been interesting, but they weren't here to rob any graves. Vic shone the light around the dank chamber picking out the mouth of a deeper darkness—a tunnel leading off in the direction of the house. The stone around the tunnel was damp with the cold. The tunnel walls weren't constructed from bricks. Bleached skulls were stacked on top of each other, thousands upon thousands of them, to create the low arches of the catacomb. The beam of Vic's Maglite roved across the walls and arches, only settling long enough to confirm that they were all fashioned from bones.

"Cheerful," Rye said, not wanting to touch anything.

"We could break a window if you'd rather?" The big man nodded up in the direction of the fresh air.

"This is better," he said, not sure who he was trying to convince, himself or Vic. "Right now, Guérin has no idea we're onto him. The longer we can keep it that way the better. Broken glass all over the floor tips our hand."

"This way," Vic said, nodding his agreement. He shone the way as the bone passageway branched out into two, and then into two again. Thousands upon thousands of people had died to make this tunnel—or been stolen from the cemeteries of Paris postmortem. He didn't ask how Vic could possibly know which tunnel to follow, he was too busy looking at what he hoped was a garter snake curling itself around an eye socket a few feet from his face. They had made their nests inside the skulls. The light drew them out.

He followed Vic through several more twists and turns, not looking back once, before they came to a stone staircase, six short steps that led up to a door.

Vic reached out for the handle.

It twisted, but the door didn't open.

The big man put his shoulder to the door and, leveraging his weight, hit it once, twice, three times, and the wooden frame around the lock gave way.

"So much for covering our tracks," Rye said, picking at the splinters of wood where the lock plate had come loose.

"It's still better than a pile of glass on the floor upstairs," Vic said. "And we're inside, which is what counts."

"We can only hope that Guérin doesn't spend much time down in the servants' quarters."

Vic stepped through the open door. He looked back at Rye. "Coming?"

TWENTY-TWO

The door opened onto a pantry that appeared to have been stocked to survive the apocalypse.

There was all manner of canned goods, their labels faded beyond recognition, lining the shelves. He took a can down and saw the smudged numbers printed on the aluminum. Not apocalypse, Rye realized. Holocaust. Row upon row of canned goods, all decades over their Use-By Date. There was enough here to survive occupation, but of course at the time the room had been stocked that's exactly what this little idyllic slice of France had been facing. Canning went back to the Napoleonic Wars, the process perfected not a hundred miles from where they were. Tomatoes, sardines, tuna, vegetables. Peaches, pears, and ham. The pantry was filled to bursting with all of that and more.

There was a second door that led out into the servants' quarters below stairs, and off to the left, the kitchens, which by rights ought to have been the heart of the house.

They went through.

It was as though that one simple step had taken them back a couple of hundred years.

Nothing down here had changed in forever.

Rye looked around the kitchen. The thick patina of dust and cobwebs told their own story: no one had prepared a meal here in a very, very long time. The range, which should have been permanently warm, was ice cold. One of the far walls had a cream refrigeration unit with a weird, almost robotic head on top of it with a single temperature dial that offered no reading.

He tried a couple of the drawers, which were stocked with ivory- and bone-handled knives and other cooking utensils. The prep surface was a huge oak block deeply scored from years of cooking, stained with all sorts of juices and fats.

They moved through the kitchen, looking for the servants' stairs that would lead into the house proper.

The place was vast.

They could have walked through the warren of passages and rooms that made up the below-stairs portion of the house for hours; there were over fifty rooms that had obviously been set aside for the full contingent of staff that a place this size needed to keep functioning smoothly. None of the beds had been slept in for years. There was a musty quality to the air that suggested the place had been mothballed, like some weird museum to a better life. There was a newspaper folded up beside one of the beds. Rye couldn't read a word of the headlines, or anything above the fold, apart from the date, which marked the paper as over seventy years old.

Things were no less confusing—or strangely dilapidated— upstairs.

The back stairs offered a passage all the way to the top of the chateau, joining the various floors, ballrooms, and dining and reception rooms. The wealth amassed within these four walls was incredible, but that wasn't what caught Rye's eye. One of the great rooms had been transformed into a gallery. Several works of art hung on the walls. "Metzinger's *En Canot,*" Vic said, pointing at one. "Van Gogh's *The Lovers: The Poet's Garden IV.*" He pointed out another. He shook his head as though he couldn't quite grasp the enormity of what they'd stumbled upon. "And that one is Otto Dix's *The Trench.* Incredible."

They just looked like paintings to Rye; good paintings, sure, but aside from the Van Gogh, he didn't recognize the artists' names, and didn't think any of them were incredible, but he didn't say anything for fear of betraying his ignorance. Art wasn't his thing. As far as he was concerned, a picture was just a picture.

"All three pieces were declared degenerate art by the Nazis and thought lost," Vic said, continuing his commentary. "And here they are."

"Worth a pretty penny?" Rye asked.

"Priceless."

"Our boy Guérin gets more and more interesting by the hour," he said.

TWENTY-THREE

They found the body in the library.

It had been a long time dead.

Much of the black skin had ruptured and shrunk away from the bones, leaving a skeleton sitting in the old leather armchair. There was no sign of putrescence. The dead man's hair had fallen out, and the fingers clutching at the armrests had no nails. The dead man's chin had collapsed to rest on his chest—a chest that was open to the air where the internal organs had swollen and ruptured, finally tearing the skin apart.

Despite the mess, the cause of death was obvious, even without going close to examine the corpse: a bullet to the back of the head.

The hole was dime-sized in the top of his skull. Where it still clung to the corpse, the dead man's skin was like leather, puckered and rigid, and harder than it had ever been in life.

As Vic lifted the man's head up, Rye saw the harrowing expression that had been frozen in place. "I think we just found the real Sébastien Guérin," Vic said, looking the dead man in the eye cavity. The seventy-year-old newspapers, the musty trapped air of a mausoleum that clung to the old house, the photographs with Guérin posed side by side with the Führer's inner circle, all of that added to the fact the man they were chasing should have been one hundred plus, and it wasn't an unreasonable assumption to make.

"But if this is Guérin, who are we chasing?"

"Someone else," the big man said.

"Don't take this the wrong way, Vic, but I'm seriously beginning to wonder who the fuck you people are. This shit is off the charts. I signed up to play courier, pick up a map, go home. This is a whole other level of fucked up."

"That it is, but in my defense, it isn't always like this," the man said.

He didn't believe him. Not even for a minute.

Vic rifled the dead man's pockets, looking for anything that might confirm his identity. He found an old leather billfold stuffed with colorful banknotes.

Rye didn't recognize them at first.

They weren't Euros. They were French francs, a fairly large denomination, utterly worthless now as it had been nineteen years since the franc had gone the way of the dodo. These notes were older, all dated between 1927 and 1938. There was a driver's license, but it was so old it predated photo ID and was a single folded piece of paper on pink stock. It was Guérin's license, dispelling any notion that the body in the chair could be anyone other than him.

Putting the cash back, Rye walked across to one of several grand bookcases lined with leather spines and gilt lettering. There were several photographs on display, but one caught his eye. It was of a monastery set high on a mountainside. It looked oriental in design, certainly not Christian in origin. The snow had slid down from the steep pitch of the roof, leaving red clay tiles exposed. The building seemed to grow out of the sharp angles of the mountainside. The monastery wasn't the focus of the photograph. There were a dozen men in high-altitude climbing gear with guide ropes strung between them, fur-lined hoods covering most of their faces. One of the men appeared to be smoking a bone pipe, which was an incongruous detail that caught Rye's eye. The sleeve of his thick coat bore the familiar Nazi swastika, though rather than being the stark black he was familiar with, it appeared to be two-tone with four spheres in the spaces between the arms of the swastika. One of the other men in the photograph had the silver spread-winged eagle atop the swastika on his arm.

He took the old black-and-white shot out of the frame and slipped it into his back pocket, putting the empty frame back on the shelf.

Beside it, there was another photograph; in it, Guérin appeared to be measuring the face of a Tibetan native with a pair of calipers. He didn't need to be an expert in Nazi atrocities to know what was going on in the photograph.

Rye moved from the photographs to the books themselves, realizing quickly that the subject matter ranged from the esoteric to the astrological. There were countless books by names he recognized—*The Voyage of the Beagle* and *Origin of Species* by Darwin, *Philosophiae Naturalis Principia Mathematica* by Newton, *Dialogue Concerning the Two Chief World Systems* by Galileo, *De Revolutionibus Orbium Coelestium* by Copernicus, *Physica* by Aristotle, *Relativity: The Special and General Theory* by Einstein—and more by names he didn't recognize. There were religious texts and doctrines side by side with star charts and so much else in this strange room. There were texts by von List, and Lanz von Liebenfels on "Theozoology" and "Ario-Christianity," both terms he had never encountered before. Another spine was labeled *Das Geheimnis der Runen,* which, if he was right, translated roughly to something like The Secret of the Runes. He recognized a couple of the Armanen runes that had been co-opted onto SS flags and uniforms.

There was plenty in this room linking Guérin to the Nazis.

There was even an entire section given over to Hörbiger's Glazial-Kosmogonie, the "cosmic truth" of the World Ice Theory, which had been Hitler's favored cosmology as it counterbalanced the perceived Jewish influence on the sciences.

He had a quick skim through, though his understanding of the original German was thin at best. As far as he could tell, the basic idea was that the solar system had its origins in a collision of two stars, one gigantic, the other considerably smaller, dead, and waterlogged. The impact caused a huge explosion that saw fragments of the dead star spin out into space, where they froze into vast ice blocks. A ring of these formed the Milky Way. The planets slowly spiraled inward, along with ice blocks. The proof of this seemed to be in the form of shooting stars and meteors—ice moving through space.

One passage he read claimed that the rock strata of geological eras was actually the result of impacts of these ice satellites.

It was absolute nonsense, of course, but it sat side by side on the shelf with some of the greatest thinkers of all time, giving the idiocy a level of credibility that it couldn't possibly deserve.

There were several other pieces that referenced the Nazi expeditions into Karelia, Bohuslän, Val Camonica, New Swabia, and Tibet. There were several handwritten letters detailing the search for lost Dacian kingdoms, one rubbishing the notion of Atlantis, and several that seemed to document the search of mythical holy relics.

"What on earth was this guy involved in?" Rye said, mainly to himself.

"This," Vic said, holding up something he'd found.

Rye couldn't see what it was until Vic put it in his hand, and even then, he wasn't exactly sure what he was looking at.

It appeared to be a photograph of some sort of half-consumed body, flesh clinging to the bones. The face was unmistakably Guérin's. There were strange oily umbilici attached to various parts, including a thicker one at the neck that looked like a cord of rope or a power cable in the grainy photograph.

"I'm sorry, dude. This is just too fucking freaky. There's no way the guy in that chair is the guy in that photograph."

"And neither of them are our murderous thief," Vic agreed.

"I'm not loving this."

Rye crossed the room to leaf through what looked like hundreds of star charts piled one atop another on a ring-stained coffee table. The first half a dozen were of no constellations he had ever seen before, causing him to doubt his first guess that that was what they were. Halfway down the pile he found a pencil sketch that appeared to be some sort of prayer wheel. There were seven sections to the drum, each pockmarked with different constellations, including the ones he didn't recognize at the extremities. The stars were aligned across all seven segments of the drum.

The word ཟླ་བ was inscribed on the top—or at least he assumed it was a word, though it was in no language he'd seen before.

"What do you make of this?" he asked Vic.

Vic leafed through the first few pages. "It's Tibetan," he said. "Two characters, *la-ma,* you might recognize the word?"

"Lama? As in the Dalai Lama?"

"The one and the same. It means teacher, though I'm not sure how that can relate to star charts. These are no sky I have lived under," Vic said with a confidence that suggested a deeper familiarity with the stars than Rye possessed.

He nodded.

"What about the star-drum? Any ideas?"

The big man shook his head. "Some sort of pillar? I don't know." He shrugged again. "The drawing is quite detailed, but to be honest it could just as easily be a doodle as the key to the kingdom."

Rye nodded. Even so, he folded the sheet and put it in his pocket.

"It doesn't really change anything," Vic said. "We're still looking for the same man. He's obviously stolen a convenient identity, so the threads are going to lead back to him, even if he isn't who we think he is. He can't hide."

"I don't think he's trying to," Rye said, looking out of the window.

He saw a silver two-seater Mercedes sports car, still more than five hundred yards away, crunching along the winding driveway as it approached the chateau. The driver was in a hurry.

Vic joined him at the window.

"I think things are about to get *interesting,*" the big man said, but it was the way he said that final word that sent a chill right into Rye's heart.

TWENTY-FOUR

"How do you want to play this?" Rye asked, looking for somewhere to hide in a building so vast a hundred cloned versions of him could have hidden out for a hundred days without being stumbled upon.

The silver Merc approached rapidly. They had maybe a minute, a minute and a half, before the driver was out of the car and walking up the steps to the house.

"Right now, he doesn't know we are in here," Vic said, thinking aloud. "And even with the hire car out on the main road, there's no reason to suspect anything. We were behind him in Stockholm; if you're him, you don't expect to be overtaken when you're being hunted, you expect to be chased. He still thinks we're behind him. Probably getting closer, but definitely still behind him." Rye couldn't argue with any of that. "We didn't come through the front door. No broken windows. So, we either hide, and hope he leaves again, conveniently leaving the real painting out on a table somewhere, or we get proactive, take advantage of the situation."

"You mean hit him on the back of the head, tie him up, and ask questions when he comes to, that kind of thing?" Rye asked, and Vic couldn't quite tell if he was joking or not.

"A cruder version of what I had in mind," Vic said, "but yes. Take him down, ask some hard questions. We've got about sixty seconds to decide. What do you want to do?"

"It's your rodeo. I'm just along for the ride," Rye said.

The big man nodded.

Moving quickly and quietly, they took up positions in the grand foyer, out of sight of the door in the deeper shadows that offered concealment, and waited for the thief to enter.

They didn't have to wait long.

Rye heard the key in the lock, and the heavy *click* of the ancient tumblers falling into place. The door opened and light slithered in. The door closed, feet scuffed on the mat. Keys rattled in a metal bowl. All the sounds of the little rituals of homecoming.

Rye didn't move.

He listened.

He waited some more.

He could see Vic reflected in a huge gilt-edged mirror. It took him a moment to realize the dark shape in the man's hand was a weapon. A heavy silver candlestick. He bit back on a bark of a laugh at the reflection, his mind quickly and inappropriately conjuring the dapper and dangerous Colonel Mustard, in the library, with the candlestick. Vic bounced the candlestick off the side of his thigh, tense, ready to explode into violence.

The man came into view. He was talking on the phone, walking into the heart of the house, without looking around. He was dressed in jeans and a casual deep blue linen shirt with sleeves rolled up and one button too many undone to reveal a thick tangle of black chest hair. His words were rapid-fire French. Rye couldn't make head nor tail of them, but there was no mistaking the urgency behind them.

The man stopped between them, his argument spiraling.

Vic made his move, launching out from the shadows beneath the curved stairs. The sudden flurry of motion drew the man's eye, and even if he didn't know what he was seeing, he reacted instinctively to the danger, dropping the phone and bringing his hands up defensively to ward off Vic's clubbing blow. He took the full weight of the first wild swing on his forearm and blocked the immediate follow-up with his other arm. As Vic drew back his fist for a third huge haymaker, the man stepped in close and rammed the heel of his hand into Vic's jaw, snapping his head back. In close, he countered with three brutal body blows—left, right, left— in dizzying succession. The sheer force of each openhanded punch folded the big man up, diminishing his huge physical presence with shocking ease. A forth blow slammed into his chin, driving Vic's head back. His legs buckled beneath him and he started to topple with all the grace of a felled oak.

Rye knew he was there to be seen in the mirror. He couldn't duck out of sight without risking the sudden movement catching the man's eye and couldn't just stand there, either. Without dwelling on what he was doing, he launched himself at the man's back, the sheer momentum of his linebacker-challenge sacking the man.

They went down together, sprawling across the hardwood floor.

Rye saw the glint of silver off to his left—Vic's candlestick—but couldn't break his grip on the man for fear he would squirm out from under him, so he concentrated on trying to subdue him.

There was no holding the man.

He writhed and bucked about like an electric eel beneath Rye, struggling frantically to dislodge him. He grabbed a handful of the man's hair, tangling his fingers in the stuff, and slammed his face into the parquet.

He did it again.

And again.

When he pulled the man's head back a fourth time he saw the blood.

Gasping, he loosened his grip, and in that moment Vic swung the candlestick, a crunching blow to the side of the man's head that put an end to any thoughts he had about fighting back. The stiffness went out of the man's muscles. He lay on the floor in a whorish sprawl.

Leaning against the wrought-iron balustrade for support, Vic offered Rye a hand.

He took it and stood.

"That could have gone better," the big man said, the blood on his teeth ruining his smile.

"Oh, I don't know," Rye said. He leaned down over the unconscious man and turned him over to get a better look at his face.

A froth of white foamed from between his blue-tinged lips.

The man shuddered in his arms.

And then he was gone.

TWENTY-FIVE

Rye looked down at the dead man, trying to understand what had just happened.

"I'm sticking with my first thought," Vic said. He gripped the dead man's jaw and pried it open to reveal a wooden peg tooth in the molars at the back of his mouth, which had come loose, spilling its contents. Vic fished the wooden tooth out of the dead man's mouth and held it between two thick fingers.

"Is that—?"

"A false tooth," he confirmed. "Whoever this guy was, he really didn't want to talk to us."

Rye retrieved the dead man's phone.

He put it to his ear. The line was still open. "*Que ce passe-t-il? Parle moi. Yanis? Que ce passe-t-il?*"

"He's dead," Rye said, looking at the dead man. "You might as well talk to me."

"*Qui est-ce?*"

"Who is this?"

The line went dead. He looked at the handset, thumbing back through the call log. There were dozens of texts he didn't understand.

"Anything?" Vic asked.

"You speak French?"

"Some," he said.

"Then maybe." He handed the phone across.

Vic navigated through the texts. "There's only one number. He hasn't made or received a call from any other number. No name in the contacts list. All of the messages relate to the theft of the painting. The second to last is a kill order."

"For us?"

"No names, but it's a reasonable assumption," Vic said.

"Okay," Rye said flatly. "So, the pressing question, does someone like this work alone, or is the guy on the other end of those

texts just going to send another assassin after us?" Rye asked, thinking aloud.

"They send someone else," Vic said. "Every time."

"Well, there's tonight's motivation then. Okay, let's think smart.
Give me the phone," he said to Vic, and a moment later was thumbing through the apps for some form of fitness tracker, anything
that might be GPS enabled and show where their would-be killer
had been over the last week or so. They were all disabled. "Well,
that didn't work . . ." But that wasn't the only kind of tracker out
there in the modern world. "Stay here."

"Where are you going?"

"To the car."

He didn't waste time explaining any further. He knelt beside
the corpse and rifled his pockets for his car keys. They weren't
there. He remembered the rattle of the metal bowl and found the
Mercedes sport's keys lying side by side with the house keys. He
scooped them up and rushed across the parquetry floor, out from
beneath the shadow of the grand staircase, and through the main
doors that the man they'd just clubbed to death had entered
by. He took the few stone steps down to the gravel forecourt and
crunched across the driveway to the car.

The driver's-side door was unlocked.

It was important to keep focused on the matter at hand and not
get lost in the minutia and let themselves get derailed. They'd come
looking for the painting, not the man, so it stood to reason it was
in the car.

He opened the passenger's-side door, bringing the overhead
light to life. There was nothing on the seat, or on the bench seat in
the back, and nothing in the footwells.

He tried the bench itself to see if it could somehow lever upward to reveal additional storage space, but it was set firm. He tried
the trunk, but the only thing in there was the spare and the tire
jack. Meaning the man didn't have the painting on him.

Which made no sense . . . unless he'd made a stop along the
way?

Rye went around to the other side of the car and slipped in
behind the wheel.

He checked the dash for some sort of built-in GPS, finding the disabled handset in the glove box. It had been reset, all of the previous journeys wiped from its memory.

The car was fastidiously clean.

The driver was someone used to leaving no trace of his existence behind, which, all things considered, shouldn't have come as much of a surprise.

He rifled through the contents of the glove box, but there was nothing in it to indicate where the car had been: no gas station receipts, no paper bags from one of the patisseries of Paris or other convenient clue that jumped up and down shouting: over here, look at me.

The only possible thing of interest was the rental service sticker on the manual, and that wasn't giving much away other than the fact it wasn't from one of the regular car rental firms.

Rye took his phone from his pocket and called through to Jeremiah Byrne back in the States.

"I need you to do something for me," he said.

"I'm not sure we're quite at *that* stage of our relationship yet."

"Funny boy. I'm in a deluxe car rental, the GPS has been scrubbed, there's nothing but the name of the private hire company. But I'm hoping they'll have some sort of tracking device on it, given it's a fifty-grand car. I need to know where it's been. More precisely if it's made any stops in the last twenty-four hours."

"Give me the VIN."

He opened the door again, and read the seventeen characters of the Vehicle Identification Number that were unique to the car he was sitting in. It was better than a license plate. A couple of seconds later, Byrne confirmed, "The registration's held by Taranis Inc., a small private hire company. They list twenty-four vehicles in their fleet. Shouldn't be too difficult to find a way into their network. Give me a few and I'll get back to you."

"Good man." Rye killed the call and headed back into the house, where Vic was in the process of cleaning up the scene. He'd moved the body through to one of the kitchens.

"The painting?" Vic asked, blood still on his hands.

Rye made a face that didn't need a translator.

Before Vic could ask a follow-up question, Rye's phone rang.

"What have you got?" he asked.

"We got lucky. They use LoJack on all of their cars. Yours was rented out to a Tenzin Dawa yesterday. He made a single stop after leaving Paris, an after-midnight visit to an address in Bussy-Saint-Georges, an hour east of the city."

Guérin's estate was an hour south, so worst case they were two hours away from where they needed to be; less, assuming the auto-route avoided the congestion of the city.

"Do we know what's there?"

"We do indeed, if by *we* you mean *me*. Bussy-Saint-Georges is a relatively new city. Dawa visited an area of the outskirts of the place nicknamed the Esplanade of Religions. It's a sort of holy quarter, which, given the secular nature of France, is something of a miracle in itself. There is a mosque, a Laotian Buddhist pagoda, the largest Taiwanese Buddhist temple in Europe, a Jewish synagogue, and overlooking them all on a grassy hilltop, a Roman Catholic church."

"Where did he go?"

"Dawa made one stop, which lasted forty-two minutes. The Tibetan monastery."

He thought about it for a moment. "A Tibetan assassin?"

"Assassin? Way to bury the lead."

"Did I forget to mention that not content with getting the painting first Dawa was dispatched to kill us? Yeah, that. It would be really nice if the boss would tell us what the fuck is going on."

"He will," Byrne reassured him. "But it's a face-to-face conversation. Trust me."

"It doesn't look like I have a lot of choice in the matter," Rye said. "Okay, text me the address. Let's go and get this painting, and I can get my life back."

"Don't pretend you're not enjoying this. I can hear it in your voice. You're just as damaged as the rest of us."

More so, he thought, but didn't answer him.

He killed the call.

"Okay, we've got an address," he told the other man. "Let's

finish up here and—" The roar of a car engine firing up in the courtyard stopped him midsentence.

Rye reached the door in time to see the silver Mercedes churn up the gravel as its rear end swung around, a dead man at the wheel. Vic was ten steps ahead of him, running uselessly after the car as it tore up the long driveway back to the country roads beyond the gates.

He stopped, doubled over, hands on knees, watching it disappear.

TWENTY-SIX

Tenzin Dawa's corpse was gone, but there was plenty of blood.

"I thought he was dead," Rye said.

"Obviously not," Vic contradicted him, coming up the stone steps to join Rye at the chateau's door. "The question is: did he hear us? Because if he did, he knows we know where he hid the painting."

"Meaning we've got to beat him to it."

A slashed tire put an end to any thoughts of a high-speed chase. It would take at least ten minutes to change the wheel out, and that was ten minutes they'd never make back on the road no matter how fast Vic pushed the big Volvo SUV. Now, had they been in his Vanquish or Vic's Lavoisier it might have been a different story, but the SUV topped out at 132 mph against the Mercedes's 198 mph. If it came down to a footrace, they didn't stand a chance in hell.

But they weren't alone.

Vic called Rask.

He could only hear half the conversation, but it was obvious that he was bringing the rest of the team into play. It wasn't their race anymore. Success or failure would be down to Zima and Carter Vickers, who were half a day behind them. Half a day meant they should be touching down at Charles de Gaulle in the next hour.

It was going to be close.

All they could do was replace the ruined tire and follow as quickly as they could.

"No, no, no, Jesus I'm an idiot," Rye said. They'd been on the road to Bussy-Saint-Georges for no more than twenty minutes, meaning Dawa was probably halfway there if he was pushing the Mercedes to the limit. He fished his cell phone out of his pocket and hit redial. Byrne answered a couple of seconds later. "Don't tell me, you need me to do something for you?" he said. "It's all a bit one-sided, this new relationship of ours."

"The LoJack," Rye said, like that explained everything going on inside his head.

"Do you want to elaborate?"

"Can you trigger the LoJack so it starts sending its stolen car signal to all of the local receivers?"

"I like the way your mind works," Byrne said. "You know I can."

Every Gendarmerie car within a five-mile radius would pick up the signal, their tracking units showing the make, model, and registration of the stolen car, including the color, and an approximate distance and direction, painting a target on Dawa's back. Arial support from police helicopters would pick up the signal, too.

"With a bit of luck, having to dodge half of the police force in Paris will slow him down, even if it doesn't stop him completely," he said.

"And slowing him down might just buy us enough time to make a difference."

Vic didn't need telling twice, he pressed the pedal flat to the floor, gassing the engine and pushing the Volvo up into the red line.

TWENTY-SEVEN

The church looked down from the hill, its catholic guilt dominating the skyline of Bussy-Saint-Georges.

Vic drove the length of the holy quarter. The Tibetan temple was easy to see, even among the many pantheons gathered along the strip. There were three cars parked in the lot outside, none of them the silver Mercedes. Vic pulled up alongside another nondescript people carrier and killed the engine. Three people emerged from the other car: Iskra Zima, Carter Vickers, and Olivia Meyer. The thief carried a backpack slung across one shoulder.

There was no sign of Rask, but when did someone like him ever get their hands dirty?

"Anyone inside?" Vic asked across the top of the SUV.

"Place is locked up tight," Ice said. It was hard to imagine her as the ex–Soviet intelligence agent Rask had introduced her as, she just seemed so *normal,* but that was all part of the deception, wasn't it?

He nodded to the thief.

Rye asked, "So who's going in?"

"You and me," Carter Vickers said.

"Okay, so what do we know about this place?"

"Here," the thief said. He handed Rye a small earbud and inserted an identical one in his own ear. Rye followed suit. "Push it in deep," the thief told him, and he heard the faint click of the comms coming online.

"Nice of you to join us," Byrne said in his ear.

"Oh god, he's everywhere," Rye said.

"You get used to it," Carter said. "Even if he likes to think of himself as the voice of god. Okay, several points of ingress: the front doors, which are pretty much a no–no; there's a tiered roof garden around the back, which looks a lot less like a Walmart." It was hard to argue with his comparison, though perhaps the temple had more in common with a state penitentiary than a supermarket.

"Several windows on the ground, second, and third stories. There's a service door you can get to from the ceremonial gardens over there." He nodded toward the neatly trimmed rows of green and the last lingering flowers of summer. The true explosion of color came from the temple gardens, which were watched over by white elephant statues and three grinning Buddhas that looked like they ought to be carrying signs for General Tso's chicken. "My vote is for the balcony through the temple gardens. Nine times out of ten, security is laxer when you leave ground level. Hence where your expertise comes in."

"Works for me."

"Guuleed, that means you, Olivia, and Iskra are our eyes and ears out here. Let's get this party started before we have any unwanted visitors. We have to assume the Gendarmerie won't keep Lazarus busy forever. We want to be out of here before he shows up."

"Agreed," Rye said.

They ran around the side of the temple building and stepped back to get a good look at the balcony. Unlike the Thai temple across the holy road, where the red-tile swoop of the multitiered roof and the decorative arches created the kind of temple he'd imagined, the Tibetan temple was, from this side at least, a square concrete block, although one entire side of the building had been given over to a trellis of climbing plants that cascaded down the wall like a brightly colored waterfall. Everything about the place was purely functional as opposed to aesthetic. At first, he assumed the rear of the temple was broken up into half a dozen smaller, staggered tiers that descended from the roof garden, but from this angle he realized it was actually an optical illusion and the drop was considerably less. Still, the roof garden was the easiest way down, and the trellis offered a short traverse to the balcony running along the side of the tier of stairs.

"Do what I do," he said, and a couple of seconds later had started the climb down.

He was agile, and moved with practiced grace, scaling the trellis hand under hand.

Rye carried on all the way down to the concrete terrace rail, and leaning back slightly, reached up to curl his fingers around the tangle of climbing plants, knowing they would only hold him for a few seconds before his weight tore them away from the wall. Moving fast, Rye swung his legs around, until his foot found the concrete railing. It took his weight, but was impossible for him to simply step off, so he was forced to lean back then pull himself forward, fast, in a crude jump over the balcony, letting go in the process.

He landed hard, rolling forward and dropped into a crouch. He waited for Carter to follow him down.

Carter was considerably less graceful, but he made it across the gap onto the balcony.

"Over to you," Rye said, making room for the thief. He scanned the outline of the glass door, looking for alarm sensors. In this day and age of religious intolerance it stood to reason the temple was protected in some manner, but they'd seen no guards outside, and there was no indication the doors were alarmed, so Carter took a small diamond-headed single suction cup glass cutter from his pack and set to work.

He placed it alongside the handle and locked it into place on the glass. Less than ten seconds later the thief had scored a perfect circular hole in the glass and lifted the fist-sized piece away.

"Here goes nothing," he said and reached through the hole. He looked at Rye as he felt around for the lock, then withdrew his hand and stepped back.

There were no alarms as the door swung silently open.

"Hi honey, I'm home," the thief said, as they went inside, closing the door behind them.

Rye raised a finger to his lips, indicating silence.

There were several small lights glowing in sconces along the long galley they'd entered, all of them above curious paintings that weren't at all what he'd expected. He wouldn't have called any of them works of art. Some looked like they might have been dancing women, others possibly giant elephants made of cloud. There were statues in alcoves, Buddhas in various poses.

He heard movement down below.

His eyes darted toward the staircase at the far end of the gallery, but there was no sign of anyone coming to join them.

Glass cases in the middle of the gallery contained several older relics, though in truth none of them looked particularly old or holy.

There was no sign of the painting they were looking for, and the longer it took them to find it, the greater the chance of discovery.

He moved quickly from case to case, checking them, then turned to see his partner in crime shaking his head. "You got any better ideas?" he whispered. His voice carried alarmingly loud in the silence. Carter crossed the gallery to join him.

He nodded. "If Dawa left it here, it's only been here for a few hours, no way it's on display yet. There has to be some sort of safe where they store their treasures."

"I'm not sure they have any treasures," Rye said. "Look around you."

They moved from the gallery into the contemplation suite behind it and the various rooms that served the needs of the monks. Without any real clue where Dawa might have stashed the painting, they were reduced to a room-by-room search, which turned up nothing of any interest.

"We need to be smarter about this," Carter said, his obvious frustration growing. He pressed a finger to his ear, "Byrne, we're coming up blank. Any ideas?"

The third man's voice crackled inside Rye's head. "Thought you'd never ask. Okay, according to the blueprints filed by the architect there's a repository built into the basement that goes deeper underground. It appears to be some sort of natural cavern. Odds-on that's where you'll find it. Aren't you glad you asked?"

TWENTY-EIGHT

They stopped on the stairs, listening.

Someone was moving about in the darkness below them.

The last thing Rye wanted to do was hurt someone, least of all a monk. But the road to hell was paved with those kinds of intentions.

The orange-robed holy man shuffled by, head down.

Rye willed him not to look up. To keep on walking.

He held his breath.

They were six of the longest seconds of his life, but the monk kept his head down, oblivious, saving himself a beating that Rye didn't want to have to dish out, so they were both happy, even if one of them didn't know they were meant to be.

"Come on," Carter said, when the monk was out of sight.

They ran deeper into the temple complex.

It was a curious building, to say the least, with a gift shop, an altar draped with shiny baubles like a Christmas tree, and the Tibetan equivalent of a fast-food restaurant all under the same roof. None of those interested the thief. He found a service stair and followed the concrete steps down. They made no attempt at stealth. Their footsteps echoed up through the curves of the stairwell.

The basement level appeared to be mainly storage, but beyond the man-made twists and turns of the cellar rooms, they found a doorway that had been hewn out of the natural rock itself. Rye followed Carter as he moved through the arch into a much older, deeper part of the temple. The air down here was so much colder, a good ten degrees or more below the outside temperature. The fine hairs along the length of his arms bristled as he saw the same three spheres surrounded by an aura of flame that had been rendered in the metal of Guérin's gate.

Jing, the body essence, *Chi,* life force, and *Shen,* spiritual force.

"We're in the right place," he said, but Carter was already two steps ahead of him, and had found what looked for all the world like an old-school bank vault with capstan wheel lock and all. The entire thing was set into the bare rock.

"Guess we know where the painting is," he said. "Can you open it?"

"Without bringing half the temple down on our heads? Probably not."

"So, what do we do?"

"We bring half the temple down on our heads," Carter said, with a smile. He swung his pack off his shoulder to retrieve a shaped charge.

He set it around the huge hinge where it was bolted into the rock, working it into position before he set the short-fuse timer. There was no finesse to it. He gave them five seconds to get the hell out of the way and dragged Rye back behind cover before the whole thing blew.

The explosion sent shivers through the bedrock.

The shriek of tortured metal sounded like the gateway to Hell opening up before them.

Smoke and rock dust filled the claustrophobic air.

The cacophony still rang in his ears as he struggled back to his feet. His eyes stung. He reached out blindly for support, stumbling over fallen rubble. Licks of flame curled through the smoke ahead of him. Rye covered his mouth with his left hand, not that it made any difference, and walked back into the aftermath of the explosion.

There was no denying it got the job done.

The flames offered light to replace the bulbs the explosion had shattered, but it was a fitful light that kept shifting and throwing shade over the interior of the huge walk-in vault.

They went inside.

The thick steel door had shielded the contents from the worst of the explosion, but even so, there was no escaping the fact that the huge fissures that had opened in one side of the wall undermined the entire vault's integrity.

Rye could hear the rock straining under the incredible pressures acting on it.

He looked around for some sort of tube that might contain the stolen painting. Most of what was in the vault looked like worthless junk, but what was junk to one person was heritage to another. The Tibetans had suffered horribly in recent years at the hands of China, and that had culminated in monks burning themselves alive in protest, causing outrage across the world. Against this backdrop of brutality, the holy men had been forced to smuggle their treasures out of their homeland for fear that they'd be lost forever. And now, there in the smoking ruin, heritage became junk. He didn't have time to worry about the niceties of it all, he needed to find the painting and get out of there before the vault came down around him.

He took one side, Carter the other.

Near the back of the room, Rye saw a black leather tube propped up against the wall. It had a twist-off lid and a canvas strap; the kind of thing art students carried.

"Got it," Carter said.

He turned to see him holding up an identical tube.

"Me too," Rye said, showing him.

"Then we take both and worry about which is which once we're out of here."

But Rye wasn't about to walk out of there without knowing for sure they had recovered the Blavatsky painting, so he uncapped the tube and teased the canvas out.

It only took a couple of seconds for visual confirmation. It was the stolen painting. But it was never going to be as easy as that. Carter showed him his. There was no denying the fact he was looking at a perfect copy of the painting in his tube, meaning Tenzin Dawa had collected at least one of the fakes before he'd stolen the original from the dealer in Stockholm.

Meaning there could be more tubes in here.

"Knife?" he asked.

Carter shook his head. "Next best thing?" He offered Rye a small electrical screwdriver from his pack.

Rye used the tip to peel away a small patch of paint from the corner of his painting. Beneath it, he saw the same faint grayscale shadow that had proved the first one a forgery. He didn't waste time peeling away more and instead held out a hand for Carter's.

This time the flakes of paint came away to reveal a tiny patch of bare canvas, not the faint grid of the copy, meaning his was the original.

"Okay, we've got what we came for. Let's get out of here," Carter said.

Rye nodded. "I'm right behind you."

But he wasn't. He waited until the thief left the vault before he pulled the switch.

He folded the original in two, not caring if it damaged the surface, and stuffed it down the front of his shirt into the waistband of his jeans and walked out of there with the tube containing the forgery in his hand.

TWENTY-NINE

Getting out was easier than getting in, but no less stressful.

They charged up the concrete stairwell, only to be confronted by frightened-looking monks at the top. Three robed men blocked their route to the front door. Rye looked at Carter, then remembered the earbud and pressed down on it. "A second way out wouldn't hurt," he said, earning a chuckle from Byrne.

"You don't ask for much, do you?"

"You don't ask, you don't receive."

"Sadly, I'm fresh out of miracles. Your only way out is straight through the middle of them."

"Ah, well, thanks for nothing."

Carter was grinning. That was more alarming by far than the sight of the three unarmed men on the landing above them.

"I hope you're not thinking of doing something stupid," Rye said.

"Depends on your definition of stupid," the thief said, reaching into his pack. "Cover your ears."

"What?"

Rather than answer, he threw something up the stairs, and ducked, covering his ears and closing his eyes even as the flash-bang went off. The blinding flash of light blazed pure white across the monks' eyes as it burned out the photoreceptors and rendered them temporarily blind even as the concussive blast bowled them off their feet.

Smoke streamed out of the stun grenade, choking the stairwell. It was impossible to see.

The smoke stung Rye's eyes.

The bang of the detonation was worse, though. It was so loud, even with his hands cupped over his ears, that the shrill whistle carried on long after they had negotiated the tangle of bodies at the top of the stairs and were running for the door.

Coughing, Rye reached the glass doors a couple steps behind the thief.

Carter rattled at the locked door, not seeming to understand why it wouldn't open for him.

On the other side of the door, Iskra Zima wasn't messing about.

She wasted no time at all with the niceties of breaking and entering, and they stood aside as she put three bullets into the glass, shattering the door.

Rye followed Carter Vickers out into the fresh air of the French night.

The first thing he saw as the fresh air hit him was Olivia on one knee laying down covering fire as he and Carter staggered out of the smoking building.

"Let's get out of here," Carter said.

They raced across the blacktop to the SUVs.

Eyes still watering, Rye thought he caught a glimpse of the silver Mercedes in the distance, but when he finally managed to focus there was nothing to see.

He clambered into the front passenger seat, tossed the tube with the forgery into the back, and belted up.

Beside him, Vic got in behind the wheel.

Olivia got in the back.

Carter and Iskra got into the second car.

"We've got the painting," Vic said. For a moment Rye thought he was talking to him and was about to say he wasn't stupid, as he patted the original pressed close to his chest, but then the big man said, "We're sixty minutes from the airstrip," and he realized he was on the comms with Rask.

"Make sure the plane's ready to take off as soon as we roll up. I don't want to stick around any longer than necessary."

Vic checked the mirror before gunning the engine.

As soon as the car peeled away from the lot, the security lights came on, flooding the rearview mirror with light.

Vic didn't slow down.

They drove quickly along the Esplanade of Religions, the second car behind them. Vic didn't ask what had happened in there, so Rye didn't tell him, but he could see that Olivia was itching to ask. Vic took them through a series of turns, then pressed the earbud and said, "Carter, you guys go ahead, we'll meet you at the landing strip."

"Problem?" Rye heard the other man's reply.

"Nah, just low on gas. I saw a gas station near the cloverleaf where we came off for the city."

"Gotcha."

The second SUV maneuvered around them and accelerated toward the main autoroute back into Paris.

Rye checked the mirror.

There was no one else on the road.

They turned into the Total France forecourt and drew up alongside the pumps.

Rye got out to stretch his legs while Vic filled the tank. He walked across the parking lot to the grass embankment and looked down at the lights rushing by on the freeway like some living time-lapse photograph. The engine roars dopplered away from him as he stood there.

He had a decision to make. His deal with Rask had been to collect the painting, and as soon as he turned it over to him, that was that. Job done. All he had to do was put it in his hands and he could go back to real life and all it entailed. But did he want to do that? Right now, there was an air of unreality to everything that staved off the grief and gave him something else to focus on. He knew he was running away from it, but what happened when he stood still for a moment and allowed it to catch up with him?

Rye didn't want to think about it for too long, even in the glorious not-quite Parisian night.

A semi pulled up beside the diesel pumps.

It wasn't carrying a trailer.

He saw Vic standing beside the car waiting for him to return, and Olivia walking across to join him on the embankment, so rather than hurry back, he lingered, savoring the fresh air.

"So, thinking about calling it quits?" the woman asked.

"I'm not sure this is me," Rye admitted. "You know what I mean?"

"I do," she said, like she was accepting the weirdest proposal. "All too well. Very little of this is me, either. I'm more at home with my head stuck in some dusty old books wrestling with Olmec, Akkadian, and other dead languages. You said you took some photographs?"

Rye nodded. "Yeah, a few. Mainly for *National Geographic*. You know the sort, spectacular landscapes, incredible creatures."

"And none of this is very *National Geographic*."

Rye smiled at that. "Understatement of the year."

He turned back to look at Vic, and over his left shoulder saw the unmistakable lines of a silver Mercedes sports car parked on the side of the road. Rye started walking toward it, but even before he was halfway it was obvious there was no one in the driver's seat.

He turned back to scan the forecourt, but there was no sign of Dawa.

He was jumping at shadows.

The semi gunned its huge engine and pulled away from the pump.

Shrugging to himself, Rye wandered back to the SUV where Olivia had joined Vic.

"Everything okay?" Vic asked.

He nodded and clambered back into the SUV. "Come on, then. Let's go give the boss the precious."

THIRTY

They drove around the edge of the cloverleaf, merging with the main stream of traffic heading back toward the big city, and followed the autoroute for twenty miles before leaving it for more suburban streets. Traffic lights went from green to red, red to green, as they drove in the long shadow of the great iron tower. It was a city of contradictions, of old and new, with wonderful old apartment blocks, with their iron balconies like something out of a Truffaut movie, side by side with the hard lines of newer functionalist cubes. Wide boulevards ran in rings around the narrow alleyways with their cobbled stones and enchanting names.

They drove through the arrondissements, each with their own unique personalities.

Vic slowed, bringing the SUV to a standstill at a wide crossroads and yet another set of lights.

Rye looked out of the window. He'd always meant to visit Paris with Hannah. It was one of those bucket list places. Enjoy the sunset at Butte Bergeyre, have a lazy breakfast at La Palette, share a lovers' picnic at Canal Saint-Martin, stroll along the banks of the Seine to Les Bouquinistes, and do everything else that lovers did in this City of Light.

His mind wandered toward the life he'd never get to live now, and to Hannah, and it was hard to imagine what came next. But, for a few hours more at least, he didn't have to worry about it.

The lights seemed to take an age to change, but when they finally did, Vic pulled out.

Olivia leaned forward in the seat, her hands on the shoulders of the two front seats as she started to say something she never got to finish.

The SUV made it as far as the middle of the intersection when the world around them exploded in fear and fury. And so much noise it sounded like the earth was being ripped to shreds. It was brutal. And so incredibly *fast*. The impact was horrific, the side of the car concertinaed inward as the huge cab of the semi crunched into the side of the SUV. Momentum spun them as the airbags deployed. The world rushed past, everything beyond the glass a blur. Steel screeched, rubber burned on the blacktop, and above it all, the screaming. The stench of scorched talcum powder, corn-starch, and explosives filled the SUV as the airbag slammed Vic and Rye back in their seats.

Paris spun and spun endlessly around them.

And then it stopped.

The SUV toppled onto its side, metal screaming as it slid across the road, spinning in a graceless ballet with the semi as the momentum carried them across the intersection. They finally stopped spinning, blocking off the route south.

Metal dug into Rye's side.

He couldn't move his legs.

But there was no pain—which terrified him.

He tried to call out to the others, to check they were okay, but couldn't hear the words if he actually managed to say them.

It was impossible to focus. Tears stung his eyes. He wanted desperately to reach out, take hold of Olivia's hand, and just let her know it was going to be okay, but the airbag wouldn't let him. He was pinned in place. He twisted his head, which he prayed to a god he didn't believe in meant his neck or his spine weren't broken, and saw that Olivia was unconscious and bleeding. The entire right side of his face was lacerated with broken glass, and he could see angry-looking burns from the airbag around his hands and neck. But he was alive.

Olivia Meyer's body lay in an impossibly twisted sprawl, bones at angles they were never meant to bend into. There was surprisingly little blood compared with Vic, but Rye saw the spur of metal from the trunk that had pierced the back seat and pinned her through the kidneys. Olivia's eyes were dead. She wasn't in there.

Rye felt his grip on consciousness slipping.

Then he heard rescuers pulling at the door, trying to get to them.

The pain arrived in slurs as he tried to beg for help but couldn't form the words.

The last thing he saw before blackness took him was Tenzin Dawa reaching over Olivia for the tube with the rolled-up painting.

"You should have killed me properly," he told Rye, but Rye was already lost to the world.

THIRTY-ONE

Rye came around in a strange room.

Vic sat at the side of the bed, a brown paper bag with a picked-clean bunch of red grapes in his hand. The right side of his face was a mess of cuts and bruises, and his eye was bloodshot, but he wasn't wearing a hospital gown, which meant they must have discharged him.

"Olivia?" He already knew the answer but needed to ask anyway.

Vic shook his head. "She didn't make it."

Rye couldn't look at him, not with so many emotions swelling around inside him. It brought it all crashing back: Hannah, the shooting. "Is there someone?" Meaning did she have someone? Was there a Rye to her Hannah?

Vic nodded. "We've told her family."

"Good. Good. Shit . . . Did you see him? Dawa. It was him, wasn't it? I wasn't imagining it."

Again, the big man nodded. "I saw him."

"How is it even possible? We killed him. He was dead. You saw that, didn't you? I'm not just imagining it. He was dead."

"He was dead," Vic agreed. "But he was dead in that chair and in those photographs, too."

It was hard to argue with, but how could a man die three deaths and still keep haunting them?

"I'm struggling, Vic. How does a dead man run us off the road in a stolen semi? What the fuck is he, some sort of zombie?"

"Rask has a few theories. Unfortunately, we lost the painting."

"No, we didn't," Rye said. "It wasn't in the tube. That was the forgery."

Vic looked at him.

"What did you do with the original?"

"I had it on me."

"So, when they cut your clothes off, they destroyed it. It's still gone."

"They didn't destroy it," a voice said from the doorway. It was Carter Vickers. The thief had the rolled-up painting in his hand. He tapped it against his cheek. "We need to get this to Byrne so he can get to work unraveling its secrets. I'm beginning to think you might just have a future with us, Ryerson McKenna."

"Not if Dawa knows he's been played," Vic said. "Then he's coming back here to make sure that's exactly what you don't have."

"Aren't you just the glass-half-empty soul this morning," Carter said, taking up the room's spare seat. "So, what's the prognosis? You look like shit."

"Funny, I feel fan-fucking-tastic," Rye said. "But he's right, Dawa's coming back."

"Way ahead of you," Carter told him.

"What are you thinking?"

"Do you trust me?"

"Not in the slightest," Rye said. It hurt to smile.

"Smart man. Okay, here's the deal, I figure we dangle you in front of him like a tasty morsel we know he won't be able to resist, and when he comes, we take him down. No muss, no fuss."

"You make it sound simple."

"The best plans are. Shit only gets complicated when you make it complicated. Get the guy in this room, he doesn't walk out of it. Even Jesus didn't come back from the dead twice."

Rye laughed. He really shouldn't have. It was a short snort of a laugh that sent a sharp runner of pain from his ribs to his brain, every pain receptor firing along the way.

"I don't like it," Vic said.

"You don't have to like it," Carter told him. "The boss agrees with me. Dawa needs to be taken out."

"That is murder," Vic objected. "I will have no party to it."

"It isn't," Rye said, surprising both of his visitors. "It's retribution. We're not doing this because of some stupid painting. We're doing it for Olivia. She was part of your family. That, right now, makes her part of my family. So, I'm in. What do you need me to do?"

THIRTY-TWO

A slice of silver moonlight ghosted across the hospital room.

It came through a chink in the blinds, creating a nighttime landscape of shadows and strange contours conjured from the familiar furniture and not-so-familiar medical apparatus. The door was closed. The only sound in the darkness was the regular beep of the monitor reading Rye's heart rate. He lay absolutely still, listening for the slightest noise out of place, just as he had for the last three nights.

And still the assassin didn't come.

He'd started to think that Dawa never would.

The ward was quiet.

It would be another hour before the night nurse did her rounds, bringing medication to those in need. It was the perfect time for the assassin to make his move, assuming Dawa had been watching the place.

Somewhere beyond the door he heard a faint murmur of voices. It was just the nurses at the station, Rye knew. His would-be killer wouldn't waste time talking. Even so, his heart rate monitor picked up the slight increase in his pulse.

He closed his eyes.

And kept them closed even though he heard the faint *click* of the latch disengaging and the door opening ever so carefully.

The footsteps were so soft he didn't hear a sound until Dawa stood over the bed, looking down at him just as he had in the SUV four days earlier.

It was only as his hand closed over Rye's mouth that he opened his eyes.

"Where is it?" Dawa whispered. The words were strange on his lips. English wasn't a language Dawa was comfortable with, that much was obvious from those three little words.

Rye struggled against his hand, bucking beneath him. He needed his eyes on Dawa and only Dawa, so it had to be convincing. Real. And that meant selling the fear, which was no great stretch as he was absolutely terrified looking up into the assassin's dead eyes.

Rye yelled into Dawa's hand. The assassin's cupped palm stifled the sound, but that didn't stop Rye from bellowing like his life depended upon it.

The assassin waited for him to run out of strength, pinning him to the mattress until he stopped fighting before he repeated the question. "The Blavatsky painting, where is it?"

"Not here," Iskra Zima said from the shadows.

The Russian didn't waste time with niceties.

She didn't give him a chance.

As Dawa turned toward her hiding place, she pulled the trigger, putting the bullet through the middle of his face.

The weapon was silenced, so the shot sounded more like a *whump* of rushing air than any gunshot Rye had heard on TV.

The blood spatter sprayed across his cheek, leaving a smear as the dead man's hand fell away from Rye's mouth. The impact twisted Dawa away from the side of the bed, and for a moment he stood there, frozen impossibly in place, before he stumbled back into the heart monitor which flatlined in sympathy as his fall dislodged one of the many trailing wires.

The Russian wasn't taking any chances; not after all the talk of how Dawa had come back from the dead at the chateau. She crossed the room and, standing over him, put a triangle of bullets into his face with ruthless efficiency. There was nothing left where his mouth and nose had been.

"It is over," she said, talking to the rest of the team via the earbud. "And before you ask, he won't be getting up again, believe me. I don't care how miraculous you think he is, when I kill someone they stay dead." She looked at Rye. "We need to get out of here." Iskra twisted the silencer off her weapon and stowed it in the holster at the base of her spine, pulling her black sweater over it so that the weapon wouldn't be accidentally visible to anyone they passed on the way out.

"Thank you," Rye said, swinging his legs out from beneath the white sheets. He was fully dressed, just as he had been for the last three nights.

The Russian looked at him, confused. "No need to thank me. You're one of us," Iskra said, going through the dead man's pockets. Satisfied there was nothing that would lead them to whoever had sent him, she stood up. "I would kill for you. I would die for you. That is the promise I made to Rask when he gave me a second chance. It is what being part of this team means. Of course, I would prefer not to do the second one. Now, give me a hand."

Quickly, they gathered the dead man into their arms and lifted him up into the bed.

He was heavier than he looked.

Rye checked the thick vein at the side of his throat for a pulse he knew couldn't be there, not willing to take anything for granted.

"I told you he's dead," the Russian said, pulling the white sheet up over Tenzin Dawa's ruined face.

It was the most effective hiding place they had; a corpse in a hospital bed was not an unfamiliar sight. So, with a little luck, it would buy them the hours they needed to get wheels up and out of this damned country.

She tapped her earbud, and told the man on the other end, "I need you to make it look like our boy was never here."

"Already on it," Byrne said in their ears. "Give me a few minutes and it'll be like Rye doesn't exist."

It hurt to walk.

He was forced to lean on the Russian, favoring his wounded side as he limped painfully toward the bank of elevators.

Before they were halfway there, a grinning Carter Vickers appeared around the corner steering a wheelchair toward them. "In you get," he told Rye.

He wasn't about to argue.

THIRTY-THREE

Vic waited for them at the main entrance.

He sat behind the wheel of an SUV identical to the one that Dawa had totaled. The thief and the Russian helped Rye into one of the rear seats, then took up their own positions, one in the front, one in the back with him.

Vic drove the thirty-three minutes out to the airfield like a man possessed, barely slowing for any of the lights, weaving in and out of traffic, always alert, his eyes darting to the rearview and wing mirrors obsessively as he somehow found gaps in the traffic that Rye was sure weren't there to be found.

The mood in the car was as dark as the night outside of it.

Rye finally broke the silence to say, "I still don't understand how it could be the same man."

"Imagine if he comes back a third time," Carter said. The guy was relentlessly happy. That could wear thin real quick.

"Not happening," the Russian said, ending the conversation before it could get started. "Whatever Rask believes, there are no such things."

"Things?" Rye asked.

"Demons," Iskra said, making a show of just how distasteful her practical mind found the idea. "Aliens. I don't care what he thinks they are. It's not my delusion. But then I'm not the one dying."

Rye said nothing.

"I think you owe it to the boss to at least give him the chance to explain for himself, Ice," Carter said, using the nickname Rye had given her. "Rather than filling Rye's head with your own prejudices."

"Not prejudice, common sense. There's a difference. We live in a rational world."

"Says the woman who just killed a man for the second time," the thief observed. "That might be enough to at least make you wonder."

The Russian didn't argue. Instead she closed her eyes and settled back for the rest of the short drive to the waiting Gulfstream.

Rask was already on board.

He looked bone weary. He raised a scotch to the newcomers as they came up the stairs into the luxuriously appointed cabin.

"We shall be pushing back in a few moments," the pilot informed them over the PA. "Anything you need, the lovely Kevin will be happy to see to your needs. Flight time to Bucharest is estimated at two hours and fifty minutes. Conditions up there are good, so it should be a nice smooth flight."

Kevin, the one-man cabin crew, closed the door and engaged the seals that would keep the plane pressurized at thirty thousand feet.

"Romania?" Rye asked, taking a seat across from Rask.

"The National Museum of Art has one of the best conservation departments of any facility in Europe. A friend there has agreed to examine the Blavatsky canvas for us out of hours. Their equipment is state of the art. With luck we'll know what lies beneath the original painting soon. But enough about that, how are you feeling, Mr. McKenna?"

"Sore, but alive," he said, "which is more than can be said for Olivia."

"I know," Rask said. "It is a tragic loss. She was a very special person. Quite brilliant. The amount of knowledge that passes with her doesn't bear thinking about. Arrangements will be made," Rask promised. "I have already instructed my legal team to see that a scholarship is set up in her name at her alma mater."

"Which sounds like a rich man's way of appeasing his conscience," Rye said, more bitterness in his voice than he had expected, given the fact he hardly knew the dead woman.

"Perhaps it is," Rask agreed. "So, how about you? Are you thinking of leaving us, too?"

Rye surprised himself by shaking his head. "No. Not anymore. I was. But things change." There was no need to say what things. "I want to see this through to the end. Whatever end that might be."

"I'm glad. May I ask you a question?"

"Go for it."

"Are you a man of faith, Mr. McKenna?"

He laughed at that. "I wasn't religious before Hannah was murdered, I'm sure as hell not now."

Rask looked at him. "That's not what I asked, though, is it? I asked if you were a man of faith, not if you were religious. I have no time for any sort of god if we are made in their image. I mean, look at the world: Would you want to worship something capable of all this horror?"

Rye couldn't argue with that. The same thought had crossed his mind a hundred times a day over the last few months. "Did you know there are over four thousand belief systems in the world today? They can't all be right, so, to believe in one god you reject thousands of others. It all seems a bit desperate to me."

Rye considered Rask's words for a moment. "This is all fascinating." The way he said it suggested it was anything but. "Still, I have to ask how this relates to a forged painting?"

"Patience. Another question, first: Have you heard any of these words before? Shambhala? Cintāmani? Syamantaka? Agartha? Thule? The Ahnenerbe?"

"Yes some, no to others."

Rask nodded.

"Few people have, fewer still remember them. I would like to tell you a story, if I may?"

"Knock yourself out. We're on a plane, it's not like I can go anywhere."

Rask smiled.

Rye felt the Gulfstream rock on its wheels as it began the slow taxi toward the runway.

"Centuries ago, a chest fell from the sky," Rask said, his gaze shifting involuntarily upward. "It contained a stone of incredible power; they named it the Cintāmani. The stone was a gift from the Sun God. Such was its might that the stone was split into three fragments: One third was given to Solomon, the king of Jerusalem, and set in his famous signet ring, which of course was lost to antiquity after it was stolen by the Knights Templar. Legend has it that the seal allowed him to summon and speak with demons. The second fragment, the Syamantaka, was said to protect the land from natural disasters: flood, drought, earthquake, and famine. It was set into the Seal of Muhammad, the ring worn by the Prophet. This, too, was lost, this time in Medina. The final fragment was put in the hands of monks from the Dzyan Monastery. It is believed that brotherhood of holy men serve, even now, as the protectors of Shambhala, an ancient, lost city hidden somewhere beneath the surface of the earth, where the Cintāmani is kept safe, away from the world. Where the seal of Solomon could translate languages and Muhammad's was capable of controlling the elements, this fragment offers the gift of healing."

"And you're sick," Rye said, finally understanding where this quest Rask had them all on was going.

"And I am sick. Very sick. The stone is almost certainly the origin of the Holy Grail legends and, of course, the philosopher's stone, but I believe it is more than that. I don't believe in magic or the supernatural," Rask said, earning a grunt from the Russian in the seat across the aisle.

"Glad to hear it, because then I really wouldn't be able to help you."

"There is a phrase, I don't know if you've ever heard it, but the notion is that any sufficiently advanced technology is indistinguishable from magic. The mind can't grasp how it works so chooses instead to believe in the miraculous."

"I'm not following. You're talking about a rock. How can a stone be any sort of technology, even if it fell from the stars?"

That brought a wry smile to Rask's thin lips, and in it Rye saw again the shadow of the reaper waiting in some close tomorrow. "Aside from the idea that a stone proved to be the key to deciphering Egyptian hieroglyphics and ushered in a new age of understanding, opening up the history of the world to us, I believe you're being too literal in clinging to the word *rock* rather than the idea of the powers it imbues. If we study the Terma—the holy teachings of Tibet—one of the first things we learn is that many of the great wisdoms fell from the sky. Think about it: wisdom falling from the stars."

Demons or aliens, that was what Iskra had mockingly said. Now the dying man was making his pitch.

"I have spent much of the last year chasing shadows in the search of the stones, finding my own fragments of tantalizing truths, and believe me, as skeptical as I was when I began this treasure hunt, it is becoming harder and harder to ignore the truth."

"Well, it is out there, right?" Rye said, unable to help himself.

"You are a very cynical man, Mr. McKenna. I rather like that about you."

"Not being funny, but I tend to believe in what I can see, touch, taste, and feel."

"Which is generally a good trait in a person. Now, it shouldn't surprise you to learn that I believe the miraculous powers the stories promise *are* otherworldly, yes, but not supernatural. I believe the contents of that chest, the Cintāmani, represent some form of alien technology. Technology capable of healing the sick. Technology capable of manipulating weather patterns. Technology capable of deciphering languages. And bringing together these three fragments once more will unlock their awesome potential. I'm willing to bet my life on it."

Rye nodded. "Which is a great story. But, not to sound insensitive, what have you got to lose, right? You've already said you've spent stupid amounts of money chasing miracle cures that aren't there. What's a cure falling from the sky if it isn't a mythical kind of extraterrestrial snake oil?"

"What if I told you that through an artifact auction conducted on the Dark Web I recently recovered a single page from the Book of Dzyan, the ancient holy book of the Brotherhood sworn to protect the stone? In that text there is a partial description of the two men who arrived at the court of King Lha Thothori Nyantsen bearing the Cintāmani, and they are entirely alien. And by that, I mean *our* interpretation of alien. Picture, if you will, a towering hairless figure with a disproportionately large head and featureless face lacking ears or nose, but most peculiarly of all, possessing opaque jewellike eyes."

Rye shook his head. "I know you don't want to hear this, but I'd say you've been had."

"Perhaps, but there is no denying that the description, written in a form of ancient Sanskrit that hasn't been used for more than fifteen hundred years, bears a remarkable resemblance to more modern descriptions of alien life-forms, not least H. G. Wells' Selenites, moon dwellers who were used as food for the Martians he wrote about, and Gabriel Linde's Unknown Dangers, of which he said, 'What was most extraordinary about them were the eyes—large, dark, gleaming, with a sharp gaze.' Chariots of the Gods, and then of course there are the Roswell aliens and Betty and Barney Hill's Zeta Reticulans. Strieber's alien visitors, which he compared to the Sumerian goddess, Ishtar. The same imagery appears in film and television again and again and again, even now. It has to come from somewhere."

"Then that's where your description comes from," Rye reasoned. "From all these books and TV shows."

"You assume it is a forgery, despite the fact the language of the text is a dead one?"

"I do, and so should you. You could read it, or at least get it translated; stands to reason someone else could do the same thing to make it. Especially when there's a lot of money on the line."

"Olivia was one of the only people in the world capable of deciphering that text," Rask said.

"And she wouldn't lie to you. I get it. It's about faith. I don't know you, Rask, at least not very well, but I appreciate what you've done for me, and I'm guessing everyone else on this plane, and I'm willing to see this through to the end purely because I owe you for Matthew Langley. I can understand that you are desperate for a happy ending even when there isn't one. Any old miracle will do, right? It's your life. In your place, I think I'd be the same, or I would have been before Langley. But that doesn't change the fact that your desperation makes you gullible, and if there's one lesson every rich man from Walt Disney on has learned, it's that money can't buy you more life, even if you cryogenically freeze your head. It doesn't work that way."

"Or," Rask posited, "you could argue that this is a description that is deeply rooted in our collective psyche, and these artists are merely tapping into those recessive memories."

"There are a lot of crazy people out there," Rye said, the inference being that Greg Rask was one of them.

"It is a relatively easy process to authenticate the age of something, and this page dates back over thirteen hundred years, which is around the time that the Dharma was introduced into Tibet."

"So, before *The X-Files* then."

Across the aisle, Iskra Zima snorted. "I think I like you, Rye."

Rye inclined his head a little, offering a slight smile.

"Very much so," Rask said, not rising to the bait.

The idling engine sounds changed as they gathered power, ready to roar along the runway and into the night sky.

"I believe that the man you encountered, Tenzin Dawa, was part of the Brotherhood, and the reason that he did not die easily is that he is one of the Asuras that protect the secrets of Shambhala. The Asuras, like the stone, descended from the stars, though in our simple mythology we named them demons—"

"I did warn you," the Russian interrupted, raising her own glass to Rask's particular brand of crazy.

"—which of course goes a long way to explaining the demon-summoning powers of Solomon."

"If you believe the stories," Iskra said.

"Even if you don't, there is no denying that the Brothers of Dzyan will stop at nothing to protect their secrets."

"An occult brotherhood obsessed with their ancient secrets, I can get behind," the Russian said. "That makes sense. That's all about power. *That* I understand."

"I'm so glad you approve," Rask told her.

"And the painting is the key?" Rye asked.

Rask nodded. "I believe it contains a map to their lost city, yes. Though I doubt very much that it will be as straightforward as an X-marks-the-spot kind of thing. Find Shambhala, find the first of the three fragments of the Cintāmani. And, the fates willing, some clues to the location of the other pieces."

Around them the engines strained. The entire structure of the plane shook as the explosive power of the Gulfstream fought against its brakes, and then surged forward, racing down the runway.

"Can I ask you something?" Rye asked, as they climbed toward cruising altitude.

"Of course you can."

"What happens when we fail to turn up your miracle?"

"Then we look elsewhere."

"Which is what I'm worried about. Even if we go searching all the way to the ends of the Earth, it's got to end somewhere."

"It does. With me in a box. I am not naïve enough to think that this is anything but a lost cause, but it's a lost cause I'm willing to bet my life on, which is my right."

"Can't argue with that," Rye said. "Okay, let's find us some starry wisdom, shall we?"

THIRTY-FOUR

When Rask said he had a friend in the museum, what he really meant was a guard he'd paid handsomely to look the other way for a few hours.

The National Museum of Art wasn't as majestic as many of its counterparts across Europe. It was a rather austere four-story building with impressive wings to the left and right that were considerably more spacious than the main colonnaded building itself. There were two sets of wrought-iron gates and, in the middle, a small tree-filled lawn with a bronze statue standing guard. It was right on a busy main thoroughfare offering little in the way of cover for any sort of breaking and entering, even with the guards looking the wrong way.

But Rask had them covered. His money had bought an open door through the gift shop. Rye, moving gingerly, followed Carter and Iskra Zima inside, while Vic kept a lookout from the street. They were all connected through the earbuds Byrne monitored from his nest back in Rask's HQ in the US. There was a slight delay as the signal was relayed back through Rask Industries own satellite, but nothing compared to what it might have been. It meant that Byrne, who never had to leave home, was a serious re-source for the team.

Iskra opened the door. She looked up toward the ceiling as though expecting to trip the alarm despite Rask's assurances, and when it didn't go off seemed almost disappointed. She led the way with a high-density flashlight. Getting from where they were to where they needed to be meant traversing several galleries as well as negotiating a maze of corridors.

The galleries contained precious—if not priceless—works of art and were all heavily alarmed. No amount of bribery from Rask would have silenced *those* alarms. So, they were forced to proceed with caution, touch nothing, brush up against nothing, just in case.

Several shadows appeared to be reaching out, clawing at the darkness around the statues casting them.

It was an unnerving trick of the light.

Rye just walked on, eyes front, listening for any indication they might have company.

Most of the passageways were in semi- if not complete dark-ness, while the galleries were still spotlit, meaning the art itself was often the only thing they could see in any of the rooms.

They climbed a set of white marble stairs to the second floor. The middle of each step had been worn smooth by the passage of art-loving feet over the last hundred and more years.

On the landing, with a choice of left or right, with a thick red rope cordoning off half of their options, they pushed through glass doors marked THE IMPRESSIONISTS and hurried through banks of loose brushwork and light palettes and all of those split seconds of life the artists had so brilliantly captured.

Beyond two more smoky sets of glass doors the distant lambent glow of computer screens cast some light, guiding them deeper into the complex.

Every turn had several bilingual signs pointing the way.

Art Restoration was up in the farthest reaches of the place, iso-lated from the hubbub of the museum's day-to-day existence.

In this case, that isolation was a godsent as it meant they were unlikely to draw unwanted attention.

The Russian checked her watch, then pointed in the direction of another elaborate marble staircase that wouldn't have been shamed in Versailles.

They climbed the stairs in silence.

Even in the darkness there was an incredible sense of space and emptiness that was probably some sort of artistic metaphor for the relationship of the viewer to the artist's creation or some such bullshit, Rye thought, smiling wryly to himself. It was the kind of wise-ass remark Hannah used to make all of the time. And again, he was hit by a pang of loss, realizing something so simple was gone from his life for always. What he would have given for just one more dumb remark from her.

Through another set of doors—these wooden, not glass—and a final vacuum-sealed door before they reached a different part of the museum. Even the air in this section felt different, as though it was processed to remove the pollutants and chemicals that might otherwise cause the art to deteriorate.

A wall of offices, each one specializing in some specific stage of renovation or other, and a larger "clean room" dominated this level. The fifth and final room up here was given over to the spectrography and deep X-ray equipment the department used to examine every layer of a painting before beginning work on its restoration. All the rooms on this level had one thing in common, they looked more like science labs than an artist's studio.

Rye laid the canvas out on the flatbed of the graphene scanner even as Carter powered it up.

He didn't really understand how the thing worked, and without the time to get to grips with stuff, they had to rely upon the magic of a different piece of technology to get the job done.

"Okay, we're in place," he told Byrne through the earbud.

"Model?"

"It's a Treelogic graphene scanner."

"Okay, give me a second and I'll talk you through it," the voice in his ear said, supremely confident that in just a few seconds the mysteries of the machine would be cracked wide open. "It's really pretty cool stuff. The graphene inside the scanner acts as a frequency multiplier which allows it to generate terahertz frequency deep scans which can actually penetrate all the way down to the gesso layer and varnish itself, which used to be impossible. We're talking superfine details all the way down to the brushstrokes, even pigments and hidden defects within the canvas without damaging the art itself. The technology is incredible. Way more detailed than anything X-rays or reflectography could manage. And because it's all done at terahertz frequencies it doesn't heat the canvas up at all. It's still pretty much prototype tech, but if this bad boy is half as good as the inventors promise, it's going to offer the Blavatsky's secrets right up."

"Thanks, Wikipedia Man," Carter Vickers said, grinning as he stood up. The immense scanner hummed into life. "That's all fucking fascinating, but can you use it? Otherwise we're looking at the world's most expensive lump of metal."

"Pretty sure that's downstairs," Byrne said, deadpan. "Right, do what I tell you, exactly."

THIRTY-FIVE

It took two hours for the canvas to give up its secrets.

The ghostly images on the screen changed imperceptibly as layer by layer the scanner looked deeper into the painting. There was nothing even remotely maplike to be seen, and that didn't change as Byrne guided them through the intricacies of the software. They isolated areas of the painting, homing in on brushstrokes magnified so much they looked more like the white caps of a raging sea. They shifted their search. They looked deeper into the paint, seeing shadows and shadow shapes that in turn became nothing as the graphene scanner penetrated the next layer of Blavatsky's creation.

It was looking increasingly obvious that, despite all the rumors and promises, there was no map.

But Greg Rask wasn't about to give up, no matter how long the odds.

In reality, they would have needed weeks, if not months, to properly analyze the painting, but they didn't have that luxury, so if nothing was immediately obvious they moved on, and on, and on, until Rye said, "Wait. What's that?"

It was a single spot, smaller than a piece of punctuation left by a pencil, but it was obvious that it didn't belong on the canvas. His mind raced with the clichés of microdots and other spy paraphernalia he'd seen in countless half-baked movies, but it wasn't that. Sometimes a spot was just a spot, and they were damned.

Or so it looked until Carter noticed a second peculiar dot and Iskra tapped the screen isolating two more.

"This has to be it," the Russian said, indicating a third.

"But what *is* it?" Carter Vickers asked the room, knowing none of them had the answer. So far, they'd isolated no more than half a dozen of the peculiar dots. "Some sort of braille?"

"A star chart?" guessed Rye, pointing at three dots which looked vaguely like Orion's Belt.

"Not sure about that," the thief said, isolating a couple of others which looked out of place. "But I'm no astronomer."

"Can you scan the layer where these spots are," Rye asked, "and isolate them from everything else? Maybe it's like some sort of join-the-dots thing hidden beneath the picture or something."

"Sure, give me a couple of seconds to calibrate the software," Carter said. He was getting used to the basics of the machine now, even if he wasn't exactly proficient in its intricacies. Good to his word, a minute or so later the scanner began to scour the layer between the gesso and the varnish, picking up all sixty tiny imperfections on the surface of the canvas. He printed them out and, using the networked software, sent a copy back to Byrne in the US.

"What am I looking at?" Byrne asked.

"We're kinda hoping you'd tell us," the thief said. "You know, using some of that Wikilike genius of yours. Maybe it's some sort of Morse code? Or some sort of dot code?"

"Helpful as ever, my light-fingered friend," Byrne said in their ears. "First thought is Rye might be onto something with a star chart—after all, that's a traditional form of navigation, and we're supposedly looking at a map—so while you lot get yourself to the rendezvous point, I'll run it against all of the star charts I can find and look for points of similarity. Maybe we'll get lucky."

But it was never going to be that easy.

· THIRTY-SIX

The rendezvous point was Kathmandu's Tribhuvan International Airport, a twelve-hour flight from Romania.

It was a major hub servicing over twenty airlines, connecting with Budapest, Rome, Vienna, Istanbul, Frankfurt, and countless other destinations.

They used the time to catch up on much-needed sleep, though Rask spent much of the flight in conference with Byrne back in the US. The video link provided Rye with his first look at the young tech's lair. It looked like something Bruce Wayne would have been proud of. Byrne barely made eye contact with the camera. He talked obsessively as he worked, mostly saying "No. No. Shit. No." in a running commentary of disappointment.

He pulled up every star chart imaginable, going through them grid by grid as he tried them from every conceivable angle and rotation, switching them for northern and southern hemisphere orientations as he tried to match the mysterious dots against astronomical objects and planetary position tables, and still came up blank.

It took several increasingly frustrating hours to realize they were getting nowhere fast.

"Face it, folks, it's not written in the stars," Carter said, from his seat.

He had his feet up on the leather of the seat across from him and a can of Coke perched on the armrest.

"Sixty dots. Ten of which are slightly more pronounced than the others. It's got to be significant. Maybe we're looking at them the wrong way," Rye offered, thinking of an old movie he'd seen.

"Maybe it's not meant to be flat, but rather side on, like musical notes on sheet music?"

No one laughed at the suggestion, but if it was music, it was no lost concerto. They played flat tuneless tones with absolutely no musicality to them.

"Braille?" The thief suggested, but there was no rhyme or reason to the clusters of dots even when condensed to a more readable scale.

"It's not Morse code, it's all dots, no dashes," Iskra offered. It was the first thing the woman had said since they'd boarded the plane. "But that doesn't mean it isn't a code. There are hundreds of codes we would never crack without a cypher." Which was painfully true, but a truth Rask didn't want to acknowledge.

Up on the screen, Byrne shook his head. "I've got nothing. Seriously, it's garbage. There's no map here. But there has to be a way of reading this," he said, doing well to mask his frustration. "Otherwise they wouldn't have sent assassins after you."

It wasn't a terrible assumption—why risk discovery, coming out into the open in a very public attack on them, instead of staying in the shadows if the map wasn't decodable?

"We need to remember when this was made. It's not some sophisticated computer-generated code, it's over a hundred years old, and it's a map, not a key. If we remember that, these sixty points of reference have to correspond with something in the region."

"Mountains," Rye said.

"What are you thinking?" Rask asked immediately. He leaned forward.

"It's when you said region. What's the one thing that comes to mind when you think about the landscape of Tibet, Nepal, Bhutan, and those areas?"

"The mountains."

"And they're not just mountains; we're talking about the Himalayas, the most extreme mountain range in the world, with sixty peaks over twenty-three thousand feet, and ten over twenty-six thousand."

"Good. Good. Now you're thinking. Jeremiah, can you overlay the scan on a map of the mountain range?" Rask asked Byrne.

"Already on it," he promised, but it didn't take more than a few seconds to hit the first stumbling block. The ten more pronounced markings didn't line up with any of the highest mountains on a topographical map of the region, which seemed to negate the theory.

But Byrne had an answer of sorts for that. "Remember, this is what I do, or at least a version of it. Bear with me. Now, when Blavatsky wrote the Secret Book of Dzyan, that was back in the 1880s, and maps of the region were crude at best. They only listed something like forty peaks above an elevation of eighteen thousand feet, not the sixty we know today. Any sort of exploration of the territory was a perilous undertaking." Rye nodded even though Byrne wasn't looking at him. "It wasn't until well after World War II that ground photogrammetry and satellite reconnaissance was sufficiently advanced to create an accurate map of the mountain range. Then we started using aerial photographs and plotting glacial erosion in the changing landscape. Back in the 1880s, we're literally talking about the very first climbing expeditions into the region."

"So, the map could be wrong," Rye asked.

"Put bluntly, yes. The question is *how* wrong, and if it's reconcilable to the more modern maps. It's safe to assume she never went to the region, so she was working off secondhand information, including the relatively crude 1850s-era maps compiled by d'Anville, the French cartographer. One of the things d'Anville was renowned for was removing what he considered largely fictitious features from his maps, like Shambhala. Not that we were ever likely to find a simple *X* marks the spot."

"What if we find a map from before his?" Carter suggested. "Try and line them up? See if the dots reveal a secret entrance to the lost city or something?"

"Theoretically, not a horrible idea, *but* the only known map of the mountains that predates d'Anville was drawn up by a Spanish missionary several hundred years earlier and is essentially worthless. We're talking a Here Be Dragons sort of thing. What I can do is look at the current satellite imagery for any telltale changes in the light spectrum that might indicate the presence of hidden chambers or caverns or something underneath the surface, but even the most advanced remote sensing is going to struggle with the terrain. There's so much we don't see with the naked eye, frequencies outside the visible spectrum, that actually have an impact on the land above and the vegetation, so we might, just might, get lucky. Remember, unlike 1880, there are millions of satellite images of the Earth being taken every day. All sorts of changes can show up across them if you know what you're looking for. It's just time-consuming."

Rye, though, was still thinking in three dimensions. He couldn't shake the idea that the dots might somehow align in a more simplistic manner to the landscape and they were just overcomplicating things. "Humor me," he said, thinking aloud. "But what if we're overthinking it?"

"How so?"

"Well, first up, they didn't have any scientific means to measure the height of the peaks back then, but they did have their eyes. So, what if we're looking at something really obvious, like the view from the doorway into Shambhala, would that work? Each dot corresponding to the highest points on the landscape, marking the mountain peaks from where the map was drawn. Something like that? Maybe that's why some are shaded differently, either because they are the ones that can be seen, or can't be seen, from where the map was drawn?"

"It'd be a unique topographical map, visually accurate to a single place on the planet," Rask agreed.

"Not bad," Byrne said. "I might be able to work with that. If the dots correspond to elevations that might even give us a place to start looking. Okay, leave it with me. This won't be fast, I'm afraid, even if we know the general area we're looking in, the range itself, the Greater, Lesser, and Outer Himalayas runs fifteen hundred miles, with climates ranging from tropical at the base to perennial snow at the highest elevations. We're talking grassland, shrubland, coniferous forest, tropical and subtropical broadleaf forests, and glaciers. All in one search radius. That, and the fact that it's still susceptible to an incredible amount of tectonic upheaval means this isn't going to be as easy as just looking at a few old photographs. It could take years to do a proper detailed study of a region that size. And then there's no guarantee we'd find anything. Those mountains don't like giving up their secrets."

"Ah," said Rask, smiling. "But it doesn't have to be that broad, does it? We know the route Ernst Schäfer's expedition into Tibet took. It's documented. We know there are links between Hess, Edmund Kiss, the occult expert, and Guérin, the man we've been chasing. We know they were influenced by Blavatsky's theosophical beliefs and attended the Thule Society as honored guests. But none of that compares to their membership in the SS Ahnenerbe, the occult division of the SS. That's the mother lode. That expedition is where we start looking. We examine the topography of the mountain ranges along Schäfer's path through Tibet. We follow Himmler's search for the Holy Grail, because now we've got the key. I have total faith in you, Jeremiah," Rask said. "Is there anything we can do on this end to help you?"

"Not really," Byrne said. "Like I said, this is why you pay me the big bucks."

"Very well. Then I suggest we take advantage of the remainder of the flight to catch up on our rest, so we can hit the ground running." Rask killed the satellite linkup without another word, leaving the screen dark.

THIRTY-SEVEN

They landed in the heart of the rainy season.

It was hot and muggy, the air humid.

The ground was still dark from the last rain, but for now at least the sky was blue.

The buildings themselves presented a wall of color not unlike the gaudy streets of Newfoundland, each block of crumbling concrete offering a wall of reds and greens, yellows, faded blues, and other vibrant lies that wrote over the poverty beneath them. They were so tightly packed the sense of place was claustrophobic, while up on the hill the spire of the monkey temple looked down, separated from the tragedy of Kathmandu by a lush layer of forest.

Rye made his excuses to Vic, explaining that they were going to need equipment if they were serious about venturing into the mountains, and as the only climber among them, he volunteered to take point on procurement, checking out what the city had to offer. His shopping list was fairly basic but necessarily comprehensive, and he had no idea how much of the stuff would be readily available in the city:

Fifty-five-liter climbing packs, minus-forty-rated sleeping bags, ultralight inflatable sleeping pads, water purification tools, knives, ice axes, forty feet of pre-tied Prusiks (to save fiddling with them in the extreme environment), climbing rigging, full carabiner systems (large and small wiregates, a large pear-shaped locking screw carabiner and a smaller auto-locking one), alpine climbing harnesses and belay devices, trekking poles, ascenders, and twelve-point crampons with anti-balling that would withstand the sheer amount of walking they had to do as well as the climbing itself.

It needed to be quality stuff, though, because out there on the mountains their lives were going to depend on it, so there was nothing to be gained by shaving off a few bucks here and there for the sake of safety.

Then there was the clothing, which was all specialist stuff. Ideally they wanted high-altitude all-in-one boots and separate hiking boots; some decent heavyweight wool socks; base-layer pants; long-sleeved and short-sleeved merino wool shirts; heavy base-layer climbing pants, preferably Polartec; snug, formfitting lightweight fleeces with hoods for over the base layer; trekking pants; softshell pants and jackets—no zip-off stuff, that was too light for the terrain; fully waterproof non-insulated hardshell pants and jackets; twenty-six-thousand-feet-rated down parkas and pants; gloves and liners; climbing helmets and ski hats and face masks or a balaclava system, head flashlights and glacier glasses.

All this stuff was core; without it, they were going to struggle out there, and given the city was a major staging post for assaults on the peaks, he was banking on the fact that capitalism would have reached this far, but just in case, he duplicated the list for Rask to source and fly anything in he couldn't find locally.

Rye checked in with the concierge, who recommended several high-end climbing shops in the city, including a place in the bazaar that sold unused secondhand gear people had traded in when they'd done their visit to base camp and decided they'd scratched their adventurous itch.

"Do you think we'll be able to source this stuff?"

He showed him his list.

"Of course. People come to Nepal for two reasons, to find inner peace or climb the mountains. Everything you need for both is readily available."

He gave Rye directions to the bazaar.

He headed out of the cool air-conditioning of the hotel lobby into the humid afternoon.

He hadn't been walking fifteen minutes before the fabric of his shirt clung to his back. In the distance he heard the banging of drums and decided to follow the sound. The drumbeats led him to voices, and he rounded a corner onto a large-scale protest with hundreds of monks in their saffron robes walking down the middle of the road. The monks, he realized, were protesting Chinese rule. This kind of demonstration was prevalent in the region, though reports in the West had diminished. It was hard to discredit the holy men as cranks or traitors, so the soldiers had little choice but to allow them to walk through the city, their voices raised in defiance of their would-be masters.

One man walked at the front of the line.

Across the street, Rye saw a face that looked impossibly familiar, but before he could be sure, the man turned away, and everything about the street scene changed.

It took Rye a moment to understand what was happening, and by the time he did it was too late to do anything to change the course of the monk's death.

The voices lulled into a heartbeat of silence as the protester reached into the folds of his robes for the lighter he carried hidden in his pockets, and then rose again as the monk touched the naked flame to the oil-soaked undergarments.

The flames were voracious.

They spread across his body in the silence between one heartbeat and the next, engulfing the man in fire.

He carried on walking—one step, two, three—his hand reaching out as he fell to his knees.

Rye took a fourth into the road, instinctively moving to help, but before he could take a second felt a hand on his shoulder.

"Best not," a voice said, close to his ear. The accent was cultured British, but not native. A second-language speaker raised on Austin Powers movies and Keira Knightley.

People along the sides of the road screamed their anguish while others ran to try and help the burning man, but the flames consuming him were so fierce none of them had a prayer of getting close enough to him to try and smother them. No, Rye realized with horror, they weren't trying to get close enough to put out the flames, they were forming a protective cordon around the burning man so that the police couldn't get to him. They were helping him die.

The woman behind him agreed. "They won't move until the other monks have performed rituals of rebirth, to give his soul a better chance of a beneficial resurrection. If the police get hold of his remains the monk will be cremated, which is a secular rite, and as such denies his sacrifice any sort of progression on the wheel of life."

Rye turned to see a well-groomed, middle-aged woman in chinos and a white cotton blouse. She looked like a 1930s photograph of an explorer. "They will keep him safe until the rites are complete, and then take him back to the temple where they will feed his corpse to the birds, honoring his life."

"Jesus," Rye said, trying to wrap his head around what he was seeing.

"Not quite," she said. "But close enough. Cressida Mohr." She held out a hand. "German embassy."

"Ryerson McKenna. Rye to my friends. Uncouth American tourist."

She met his smile with one of his own.

"Well, Rye, if you're not averse to a little well-intended advice, I suggest we both get the hell out of here before things turn nastier than they already are. The police want that body and the crowd won't surrender it without a fight."

She was right. Rye saw batons coming out as one man was beaten to his knees even as others crowded around him.

He didn't want to watch.

As Rye followed the woman away from the main street, Cressida explained the basic politics of what he'd stumbled into. "It's a sadly common form of protest against the Chinese government who try to ignore the basic unrest in the region. This self-immolation is brutal, but it helps the monks avoid the wide-scale violence that would generally erupt through more traditional protests and marches. A burning man is a message that can't be easily brushed aside." It was hard to argue with that. "The key is that the monks cause no damage to property or other people in their freedom protests. Self-sacrifice is a noble death rooted deep in the traditions of Buddhism," the German woman explained, leading Rye onto a third street, all the while putting distance between them and the protesters. "Remember, there are countless teachings of the Buddha doing similar, perhaps the most famous being the sacrifice where he surrenders his flesh to a dying tigress so she might feed her cubs. You see? Self-sacrifice is noble."

"But burning yourself alive?"

"Indeed. It's hard to imagine, isn't it?"

Rye nodded, though he didn't have to imagine too hard at all.

"A lot of it is against forced resettlement of nomads and rampant mining and exploitation of the environment," Cressida said, crossing the road. She didn't look either way, obviously familiar with the traffic patterns of the city. A car horn blared its protest. She held up a hand in thanks and carried on walking. "Of course, the undercurrent is still autonomy from China's rule and the issue of status, but that is much harder to win in a fight like this."

Before they were three parallel streets away, the sounds of violence erupted behind them.

"Where can I take you?" Cressida asked.

"Nowhere. But you can walk with me to the bazaar if you've nothing better to do," Rye said, grateful for the company.

"It would be my pleasure."

THIRTY-EIGHT

He couldn't shake the feeling that he'd seen that man in the crowd before, more than once, and that each time it had ended in death.

Tenzin Dawa.

But that was impossible. The man had died twice. And the second time, Iskra had made damned sure he wasn't getting back up again with three bullets to the face.

But that didn't change the fact Rye had seen him, or at least someone with more than a passing resemblance, which meant they knew they were here.

They.

The Brotherhood of Dzyan.

If Cressida noticed he kept looking back over his shoulder, she didn't comment on it. She led him through a dozen streets, side streets and back streets, until the road before them opened up into the sweeps and swags of the stalls' brightly colored canopies. The bazaar was crowded with tourists and locals alike, with people pressed in around them haggling over the price of overripe fruit and bags of dried spices. The noise was overwhelming and, as a direct counterpoint to the fighting half a mile away, so much more intimidating. Life most definitely went on as usual in the city. He watched a small boy, no more than five or six years old, pocket an orange and scamper off through the crowd, somehow finding a path between all the legs and disappearing before the stall holder could set off after him. He couldn't help but smile.

Another stall had a small transistor radio playing out a tinny and barely recognizable version of Madonna's mindlessly chirpy eighties' pop.

The climbing gear was in a shop across the street from the bazaar itself, with racks of high-end boots on display outside. In the window were faceless manikins dressed in fleeces and down jackets, modeling the wares. There were half a dozen people inside, going through the racks.

With one last check to see he wasn't being followed, Rye crossed the marketplace to the store.

This time Cressida did notice, "Looking for someone?"

"Not sure," he said. "I thought I saw someone I recognized back there."

"Ah," the German woman said, as though that explained everything. "You know, when I was in Italy last time, I bumped into three different people I knew, including my ex-husband. Most disconcerting." The way she said it made him laugh, and the fact he laughed made it impossible not to sound flirtatious, even if that was the furthest thing from his mind.

"Well, this is me," Rye told her, meaning this is where we part ways.

"It's been a pleasure, Rye McKenna," she said, offering him a crooked smile. "And if you intend to be in the city for a while, I would very happily serve as your tour guide."

"I'm more likely to need a Sherpa by the time I'm done in here," he said, inclining his head toward the store.

"Well, the offer is there. Might I ask where you are staying?"

"You might," he said, giving nothing away.

"Ha. Allow me to rephrase that. Where might an interested lady find you, say around sevenish tonight?"

"In the bar, I suspect."

"And which bar might that be?"

"The hotel bar," he said helpfully.

"Give a girl a break. I'm trying to ask you out for a drink."

"Hotel Moonlight."

"It's a date," Cressida Mohr said.

"I wouldn't go that far," Rye said.

"If you're looking for a way to kill time later, I highly recommend the monkey temple, it really is quite something."

"Yeah, I think I'll take a hike up there when I'm done."

"You do that," she said, and with that left him to his shopping.

The climbing shop was a veritable treasure trove of traded-in equipment, with more than enough quality gear to satisfy their needs. He gave an eager-faced assistant his shopping list, and after an hour of picking and choosing, arranged to have everything he needed delivered to the hotel before breakfast the next day.

Done, he headed back out into the city, not sure what to do with himself. With Byrne promising it would still be hours, if not days, before he got a hit on his end of things, he had time to kill.

Alone, the tourist thing was the most obvious way of killing time.

Rye had never been to Kathmandu, though again they had talked about it, one of those bucket list destinations for when they ran out of urban challenges and decided to tackle honest-to-god mountains again.

The white dome of the monkey temple, Swayambhunath, dominated the skyline.

It was a fairly easy walk up a long flight of stone steps, with rhesus monkeys waiting at the top, but even so, at 4,500 feet above sea level, the air made it heavier going than it might otherwise have been. Still, he was fit and healthy, and took the time to enjoy the climb, following the brightly colored semaphore of flags as they zigzagged up the hill to the white temple at its peak.

He turned frequently to look back down across the rooftops of the city.

Even though he was more than used to looking at the world from this kind of elevation, Kathmandu was an awe-inspiring sight. It wasn't so long ago that a brutal earthquake had savaged the UNESCO heritage site, and the signs of it were still there to be seen, with several damaged walls and exposed brickwork where the plaster façade had crumbled.

It took him more than twenty minutes to walk up the hill. He smiled to every brightly dressed local and every considerably more restrained tourist he passed on the ascent. He couldn't help but think about the German woman. There was something charming about the whole slightly too-stiff thing the Germans had going on. And thinking about Cressida, he realized that Hannah would have hated her.

That made him smile, too.

Most of the flashes of memory he'd had since her death in the Sheridan Meadows had been decidedly sanitized. It had been all of the good stuff, condensed. But the truth was she could be a sanctimonious cow, just like everyone else. It was nice to remember the real woman, not the Hollywood version of her.

Half a dozen monkeys climbed across the rooftop of the first building, while two more ran and leapt, splashing into what was probably a sacred pool. They were having such obvious fun it was contagious. Tourists watched as they swam back and forth, then clambered out dripping wet, to climb to another high point and launch themselves once again into the water.

Rye watched them for a full five minutes, enjoying the sun on his skin.

An overweight tourist struggled up the stairs, her laboring breath promising an impending cardiac arrest. Red veins stood out against Pillsbury Doughboy skin. She took a bottle of Coke from her pack and chugged it down like it was the elixir of life. She didn't stop drinking until the plastic bottle buckled, empty. She wiped her lips and then her brow with the palm of the same hand, then lurched off with a rolling gait toward the holy shrine.

Rye wasn't about to judge her; she was out, conquering the world, not at home conquering the couch.

He took a sip of water from his own bottle, then followed her.

There were countless golden statues of the Buddha, and bells suspended on frames, all of them segregated by chest-high hedgerows that grew mazelike across the summit. White-domed buildings were painted with eyes and eyebrows, giving them the vague appearance of the chubby holy man. And everywhere there was so much bunting, all the colored flags fluttering endlessly in the breeze. If the bright colors were meant to suggest prosperity, this place was wealthy beyond counting. Rye smiled.

He followed the other visitors into a main square with a few tourist shops bedecked with Tibetan masks of demons and elephant gods and selling CDs of Tibetan incantations and music. He saw a statue of Kali, the Hindu goddess of Time, Creation, Destruction, and Power amid the dozens of other small figurines on display with the gaudy handbags and postcards.

In the center of the square were row upon row of very different monuments. Without a tour guide to explain what, exactly, he was seeing, Rye could only guess. They looked like miniature reproductions of much grander temples and shrines.

Several times he turned, a flurry of movement drawing his eye, only to see more of the monkeys that gave the temple its name scurrying and scampering around, leaping from roof to roof around the square, lords of all they surveyed. They were fascinating creatures, utterly disinterested in the people trampling around their home. He noticed a couple of tourists trying to tempt them with food. One came forward to take a slice of fruit from an outstretched hand, then scampered back to the safety of the shadows.

Everything here was so peaceful it stood in direct contradiction to the burning man. He couldn't reconcile the two faces of Kathmandu he'd been shown, but then all cities had aspects they didn't want to show for fear of losing the tourist dollars.

He found a life-sized statue of the young Buddha with red wax staining the middle of both of his hands like stigmata.

There was a red cloth and two chalices of water beside the statue. The visitor he'd followed into the square bent awkwardly to pick up the cloth and then struggled to kneel. He watched her wash the statue's feet while a malnourished cow wandered around the square behind him.

The whole scene was so incredibly alien to him, he struggled to take it all in.

He saw a woman burning candles behind what looked like a grill and another lighting lanterns all around the stupa—the main shrine of the monkey temple. He made his way toward the golden door. It was guarded by statues of lions. The rattle of a prayer wheel being spun caught his attention and caused Rye to turn instinctively toward the sound. He thought for just a second that someone had been watching him—they'd disappeared around one of the corners out of sight—but knew he was seeing ghosts where there were none and put all thoughts of the dead man from his mind. He knelt at the steps of the stupa and offered a prayer for Hannah to whatever deity might have been listening.

As he stood again, he saw him, and this time there was no mistaking the face of the man.

It was him.

Tenzin Dawa.

The man who had already died twice.

A chill chased down the ladder of his spine.

It couldn't be him, of course, his rational mind screamed. Men didn't come back to life after you put bullets in their face. It couldn't happen.

He looked around, trying to remember the curious layout of the monkey temple and how best to get out of the place without leaving himself exposed or putting others at risk. He didn't want to turn his back to Dawa, either. So, he backed up a couple of steps, struggling to rationalize the enormity of what his return meant. Could the man truly be the demon Rask believed? What had he called them?

Asuras.

Demons descended from the stars. . . .

Beside him another pilgrim rattled a prayer wheel.

THIRTY-NINE

He didn't have a lot of choices, but that in itself led to indecision. Narrowed down to left or right the wrong call became a toss of a metaphorical coin. Rye zigged left.

He should have zagged right.

The dead man followed him, coming fast.

He ducked into a shaded area that might have been a smaller shrine among the more obvious holy places on the hill. He kept trying to picture the long stair down in his mind and get his bearings even as he ran. People were looking at him. He couldn't think about that. He darted across an open alleyway between two of the shops and was confronted by a grinning Buddha and the same binary choice, left or right. He chose left again, knowing it would bring him around toward the white-domed stupa. He was deliberately trying to work his way back toward the main square and, from there, to the pool with the bathing monkeys and down. He had no intention of taking the stairs, though, not with the anonymity of trees promising him somewhere to hide as he descended.

But first he had to get past the dead man.

And that wasn't going to be easy.

Dawa stood in the alleyway ahead of him. His face, half in shadow, looked remarkably bullet-hole free.

Rye's heart hammered in his chest.

His hands were clammy with sweat.

He clenched the right in a fist, not sure what good knuckles would be against a man who could survive bullets.

He shuffled one step back as Dawa took one step forward, matching him again as he took a second and then a third step toward him.

The pilgrims in the next street sounded a million miles away.

He backed up another step as the dead man flew at him.

Rye needed to use his head—and his natural talents—if he was going to get out of this alive. That meant thinking on the fly. He ran, arms and legs pumping furiously, but with his head up, looking for a different kind of path out of the monkey temple.

Monkey see, Rye do, he thought madly, as he ran at a stucco-covered wall, planted his foot, and pushed himself up.

He reached toward the roof, his hands slapping against the edge of the overhang and slipping on the clay tiles.

For one horrible second, he thought he'd misjudged it and was about to come crashing back down to earth in a helpless sprawl, but his fingers found purchase on the wooden timber at the edge and, kicking out, Rye hauled himself up and levered his body over the edge, so he lay on his back looking at the sun. He didn't have the luxury of time to think about what he was doing. He pushed himself to his feet and ran across the red clay tiles, then launched himself into the air like one of those rhesus monkeys, arms and legs pinwheeling as he tried to squeeze every inch of distance out of his wild jump, and came down hard on the roof of the next building, staggered forward two clumsy steps, and then was up and running again, not looking back.

He ran across the rooftops, climbing to greater heights as the buildings before him rose, dropping to a single story above the ground, never slowing down, never looking back. The monkeys took interest in him, running along beside Rye, hooting and screeching as they mirrored his leaps from building to building, and making it obvious to anyone below which way he was running.

Which was a problem.

So was the fact he was running out of rooftops to run to.

He was twenty feet above the ground when he reached the edge of the last roof and had no choice but to gamble he'd guessed right.

Rye took a huge leap of faith, using all of his momentum to hurl himself forward and upward, kicked out to try and claw extra precious inches from the jump, praying to the monkey gods that the sacred pool was waiting for his splashdown.

He came down hard, slapping against the skin of the shallow water. It felt like concrete beneath him as he went sprawling. The shock of pain was agonizing. The impact shivered up the twin bones of his forearms as they took the full weight of his fall.

When he looked up, still on his hands and knees in the shallow pool, he saw the dead man looking down at him.

FORTY

"You shouldn't be here," Dawa said. "Go home. Forget about the Cintāmani. Only death awaits you in the mountains—"

Before he could say anymore, or Rye could question him, one of the monkeys launched itself at the man, clinging to his hair and clawing at his face as it hung on for dear life as Dawa twisted, trying to shake free. A second and third monkey latched onto his legs as he struggled, and for a moment it looked almost comical until the side of the dead man's head exploded in a spray of blood and bone.

He stood there for a moment, the look of shock on his face half-obscured by the blood-spattered rhesus monkey on his shoulder, then he pitched forward, falling into the sacred pool.

Rye splashed back, trying to get away from the dead man as his blood spread out around him in a watery halo.

The blood pulsed out, turning the sacred pool red.

Someone screamed. That one voice brought more screams. The monkeys joined in the cacophony, their howls echoing across the hillside.

Still on his hands and knees, Rye saw Iskra Zima walk up to the pool's edge and hold out a hand for him to take.

"We need to go. Now," the Russian said, closing her hand around Rye's wrist as he reached up.

Iskra hauled him up to his feet.

Several monkeys were already in the water, splashing about in the blood. More joined them. They moved like piranha in the grips of a feeding frenzy as they descended on the dead man.

Rye stood at the edge of the pool, trying to unravel what had just happened.

"How did you know—?"

"Where you were? That you were in trouble? That the dead just won't stay dead?" She tapped her ear. "Byrne tracked you." It took Rye a moment to realize the Russian was actually tapping her earbud. The Russian joined him in the pool and went through the dead man's pockets looking for some form of ID. "It's not the same man," she said, rolling him over. "Look at his face. It's similar, frighteningly so, but it isn't him."

She was right.

The resemblance was uncanny. Genetically, they probably shared familial DNA; there was more than a passing resemblance between them. But it wasn't the same man they'd killed in the hospital, which quite possibly meant it wasn't the same man they'd killed in the chateau.

Rye stepped out of the pool as a pair of the site's guards came to investigate the screams.

"Now we really do need to go," Iskra said, pulling him toward the tree line.

They ran down the embankment, pushing off between the crowded tree trunks like pinballs ricocheting off the bumpers, half-hurdling, half-stumbling over protruding roots that tried to drag them down, and they didn't slow down until they were at the base of the hill with the entire city opening up before them.

A siren wailed out, but they were long gone before the police descended on the scene.

The trick was looking innocent as they followed the main tourist thoroughfares back to the hotel, and that meant talking like they didn't have a care in the world, which wasn't easy given the fact they'd left a sacrifice up on the temple steps.

"That's the second person I've seen die this afternoon," Rye said.

"Lucky you," the Russian said.

"Not really, the first one burned himself alive."

"Last time I was here I watched a policeman cut a monk's tongue out. The stuff you don't hear about," Iskra said, and shrugged like she didn't have an answer for the woes of the world after all. "Don't let it get you down."

Rye checked her watch. It was almost 5:30, meaning he had ninety minutes before he was due to meet Cressida in the hotel bar. The last thing he felt like doing was wasting an evening making small talk. But he didn't want to go to sleep, and maybe for once alcohol would be a decent solution?

It took them fifteen minutes to walk back to the Moonlight.

Iskra went to report in, but the first thing Rye wanted to do was get out of his wet clothes and take a long hot shower. He set the spray running so hot it steamed up the mirrors of his luxurious bathroom, and stripped. Even if he spent every minute from now until Cressida Mohr arrived under the spray, there was no chance he'd even begin to feel clean.

FORTY-ONE

She sat in a soft leather armchair by the huge window that over-looked the view that gave the hotel its name. The gibbous moon hung silver over the hillside, casting a radiant gleam across the treetops. It was reflected perfectly in the still waters of the swimming pool.

"It really is quite beautiful," she said, not looking up at Rye. She saw his reflection in the glass and smiled through it at him.

The German woman nursed a single malt. There was a folded copy of *Bild* on the table beside her bearing today's date. Once upon a time, getting a foreign newspaper abroad was an expedition in itself, but globalization had made the world so small it hardly warranted a raised eyebrow now. The fact that the hotel bar twelve thousand miles from home was piping in a lounge act rendition of Adele's latest proved, if anything ever could, that the West had won the war of hearts and minds across the world.

Rye took the seat across from her. A keen waiter was already at his shoulder, white towel draped across his forearm. "What can I get for you?"

"A gin and tonic," he said.

"We have William Chase, Tanqueray, Bombay Sapphire, Hendricks, Hayman's, and Beefeater. Do you have a preference?"

"The Chase," Cressida answered for him. "Trust me on this." The smile was self-deprecating, but the fact she'd taken the choice away from him was a refreshing change. He liked a woman who knew what she wanted out of life, even if it was something simple like a drink order. He wasn't old-fashioned. He was happy to bow to her greater experience. Right now, he just wanted to forget about the day he'd lived through, and the gin would help with that, whatever label it had on the bottle.

"I'll take your word for it," he said.

As it turned out, she was right. The drink was rich with juniper, apple, and elderflower, but subtly undercut with a citrus tang.

It came served with a slice of apple, which he had never seen before.

"So, Uncouth American, if I may be so bold, what brings you to this colorful and not so pleasant land?"

"The mountains," he said, without missing a beat. They hadn't talked about any sort of cover story, so it felt easiest to stick as closely to the truth as he could without admitting they'd come in search of a lost civilization's magical space rocks.

"Ah, yes, they are rather spectacular. Everest, I presume? Most visitors seem to want to make the pilgrimage to base camp these days."

"In part," he said. "We're looking at the Khumbu region and the Everest massif: Everest, Lhotse, Nuptse, and Changtse. And if the weather allows, moving west to see Pumori and Cho Oyu."

"That's quite the trek," Cressida said. "You intend to make the climbs?"

Rye nodded. "It's something I always promised my wife I would do."

"Ah, you're married?"

"Widowed," he said.

"Oh Lord, I'm so sorry. I didn't mean—"

"It's fine. It's still raw. I'm not sure I've even started to process it yet."

"Might I ask what happened? Was it an illness?"

"No," Rye said, without elaborating.

"She was a climber, I assume?" He nodded. It was easier to let the woman think it was an accident than admit to the truth. He didn't want a long conversation raking over what it felt like to pay to listen to the love of your life being gunned down. "So this is a pilgrimage?"

"I suppose it is."

"Forgive me if this sounds indelicate, but are you thinking about scattering her ashes in the peaks?"

"It crossed my mind," he admitted, without explaining why it would be impossible to do so. Instead, he raised his glass in a silent toast to Hannah and took a deep swallow, emptying the glass. He caught the waiter's eye and raised a finger to ask for one more.

The waiter nodded, and a moment later was back at their table with a fresh drink. "You'll forgive me if I don't really want to talk about it."

"Oh, of course. Absolutely. I'll be honest, I'm just trying to avoid talking about how you feel after watching a man burn to death this afternoon, because frankly I'm a little. . . ." She shrugged, not finishing the sentence.

"I can drink to that," Rye agreed, and found himself polishing off that second gin with all the eagerness of an alcoholic embarking on a three-day bender. "So, tell me, German embassy, what's life like here, you know, besides self-immolating monks and the police cutting protesters' tongues out to silence them?" She furrowed her brow at that. "Something a friend told me."

"Well, to be honest, it's all a bit 'last days of the Raj.' It can feel like we're the last bastion of civilization some days, what with the constant tension between the Chinese and the Nepalese, and the protests of the monks. But I must confess I rather like the turmoil. It keeps things interesting. Life would be so very dull if we were all just friends." There was a mischievous undertone to the "just friends" line that left him in no doubt that she wasn't talking about the geopolitical trials of the locals.

He ordered a third drink.

She showed no interest in matching him, but rather savored the flavor of hers, making the one glass last through three of his.

"We should eat," she said. "Assuming you are hungry?"

"I could eat a horse."

"Well, much of the food is more Westernized, pizza, burgers, fries, and sizzling steaks," she said, with a slight smile. "But if you've got your heart set on horse, we'll just have to see what we can do. Failing that, I do know a wonderful Thakali place that does a wonderful daal baht."

The place was hidden behind a curtain. There was nothing on the door from the street to indicate it was a restaurant, and inside it was dark to the point of being conspiratorial, lit by a few tea lights in brass table lanterns. There were no menus. The waitstaff greeted Cressida like an old friend, matching her *namaste* with a warm smile and "*Namaste* Cressida-ji." Within a few minutes, they were seated with drinks in front of them. There was no flatware on the table.

"You eat with your right hand," Cressida explained. "The left is meant for wiping yourself after." She inclined her head toward the rear of the small restaurant, where he assumed the toilets were. "Using your left hand for anything is the height of bad manners."

"And hygiene," Rye assumed.

"Well, yes, exactly."

The food, when it came, was served on a silver platter. He wasn't entirely sure how he was meant to eat it with his fingers, but followed Cressida's lead as she took the daal and other condiments and added them to the rice, kneading the mixture into a neat ball with her right hand, and pushed it from her fingertips into her mouth without it touching her lips.

Each mouthful was delicious.

They talked through the meal, running the gamut of first-date conversations, trading stories about where they grew up and the oddities of their lives that had led them to this point in time. They didn't talk about Hannah or burning men or his relic quest. She was the perfect dinner companion. He, sadly, wasn't. But if she noticed, she didn't let on.

It was late by the time she walked him back to the hotel doors. She made no move to go inside.

"It's been a rare pleasure," she told Rye. "But this is where I must wish you sweet dreams."

"Are you always so . . ." He caught himself before he could finish the thought. The gin had loosened his tongue, which wasn't always a good thing.

"So?"

"Prissy," he said, earning a proper gut-laugh from the German woman.

"Ah, my Uncouth American friend," Cressida said. "Would you care for a nightcap?"

"No," he said, taking her hand and leading her toward the bank of elevators. "Right now, all I want to do is fuck and forget about everything."

FORTY-TWO

She was gone before he woke up, but the memories of the night were still written on the sheets in the tangled outline of their bodies.

Rye was in no hurry to get up.

He lay there hating himself. Part of him wanted to reach over to the minibar and drown the guilt he felt, but he knew that was a bad idea. Instead, he forced himself into the shower and stood under the stinging spray for as long as he could bear, trying to wash every trace of the German woman from his skin. He was fucked up and he knew he was. The last time he'd lathered up, sex had been the furthest thing from his mind. The act of soaking had been a purge, sluicing the day from his body like a second skin. But standing outside the hotel it had felt right. Sex and death were intrinsically linked. It was more about the burning man and Dawa than it was about Cressida Mohr, but that didn't change the way he felt now. He lathered the soap up and worked it into his skin, and when it washed away under the spray, lathered up more, staying in the shower.

He emerged, wrapped himself in a towel, and went through to the room. He used the television to put some music on, not wanting to be alone with his thoughts, and sat on the edge of the bed.

Something on the carpet caught his eye.

He got down onto his hands and knees and fished it out from beneath the desk. It was Cressida's slim card wallet. It must have fallen out of her pocket during their frantic undressing. He remembered throwing her up against the wall and her willingly giving in to his aggression. And there was no mistaking that he was the aggressor. She surrendered to his lead at every stage of the seduction—though that was far too nice a word for what he'd done. The belt had come undone before the shirt had come off, and even as he'd pressed his palm against the flat lines of her stomach, her trousers had fallen from her hips. Somewhere after that, as she'd kicked them off her feet, the wallet must have fallen out of her pocket.

He looked through the contents.

There was nothing particularly interesting in it, a few credit cards, her driver's license, a colorful fold of Nepalese rupees, and a slip of paper with his name and the Moonlight's address on it. There was no husband's photograph, no smiling children to look out of the billfold, or anything else incriminating.

He tossed the wallet onto the bed and crossed the room to the hotel phone. Zero dialed down to reception. "Hi, can you connect me through to the German embassy?"

"Of course, sir. One moment."

After a couple of rings, a very crisp, clear Germanic accent told him, "Good morning. You've reached the German embassy in Nepal. How may I direct your inquiry?"

"Hi," Rye said. "Could you put me through to Cressida Mohr, please?"

"I'm sorry?"

"Cressida Mohr? Dresses like she stepped out of the 1930s?"

"We have our fair share of those," the receptionist said, and Rye could hear the smile in her voice. "But I'm afraid we have no one called Cressida here."

He didn't ask for a third time.

Rye hung up.

He pocketed the wallet and went in search of the others, not sure exactly what he was supposed to tell them.

He found Carter Vickers in the bar sipping a latte. He waved as Rye approached. "And where did you get to last night, young man?" he mocked, doing a passable impression of a wiseass parent catching his son creeping into the house after curfew. "You dirty stop-out."

"We may have a problem," he told him.

His demeanor changed instantly. "What?"

Rye explained the one-night stand and the fact his mysterious paramour wasn't who she said she was. "It doesn't need to be anything," he said.

"But it could be," Vickers finished for him. "Okay, we better tell Rask."

Which wasn't what he wanted to hear but was what he knew needed to be done.

They found the man in the middle of treatment; it was the first real sign of just how sick he was. Greg Rask sat immobile, tubes in his arms, eyes closed. Thelonious Monk's soft jazz filled the room, but there was an extra set of notes playing free-form around his melody. They came from the machine. Rye didn't understand what the machine was doing, though it appeared to be some sort of dialysis, where it took his blood from his body, purified it, and returned it to his veins. Rask looked properly sick for the first time.

Rask didn't open his eyes.

"Mr. McKenna, Mr. Vickers, what can I do for you?"

"We've got a problem," the thief said, but Rye amended it to, "Maybe."

"Go on," Rask said, still not opening his eyes, so Rye told his story again, explaining how he'd met the well-mannered German woman in the street and how she'd steered him away from the burning monk and helped him procure their equipment at the bazaar, and how her parting suggestion had been that he visit the monkey temple, then how they'd met again, later, drank a little too much, and ended up in bed.

"Which is all very human, and I can understand why you might feel some shame, or at least guilt, given your situation, Mr. McKenna, but hardly a problem," Rask said.

"I found this." He showed them Cressida's wallet. "I tried to return it via the embassy where she said she worked, only they have no record of a Cressida Mohr on staff."

Rask said nothing.

"It could be nothing," Rye said. "A woman who picks up tourists, spins them a line to get laid, then moves on."

"Or it could be something," Carter said.

"She was asking questions," Rye conceded. "Stuff like why was I here, were we heading into the mountains. It could all have been completely innocent. Faking an interest. It wouldn't be the first time someone's tried to get someone else into bed by pretending to give a crap about what's going on in their lives."

"Or it could have been a fishing expedition," the thief said, again offering counterpoint, which felt more and more believable the more Rye thought about it.

"Hence, we're here. What do you want to do?" Rye asked.

Rask thought about it for a moment before making his mind up. "I will send Guuleed to find out who your nighttime caller was, and if necessary take care of her. In the meantime, we need to make arrangements to move. Assume the worst, hope for the best. If this German woman is part of this, that means she sent you up to Swayambhunath with the intention of seeing you dead. That possibility cannot be ignored. We must act accordingly until we know otherwise."

"What do you want me to do?" Rye asked.

"Pack. Be ready to leave in a few minutes. I will have Iskra meet you in your room."

"Where am I going?"

"Somewhere else. Right now, Cressida Mohr knows where to find you, that puts us at a distinct disadvantage. Once you are resituated, we shall regroup. With luck Mr. Byrne will have news for us before long."

FORTY-THREE

And he did.

The call came through before Rye had left his room. Iskra Zima knocked once on the door and told him Rask requested his presence upstairs. He carried his few possessions with him, leaving the tangled sheets for the cleaners.

In the time he'd been gone, the medical paraphernalia had been packed away and a projector had been set up utilizing the room's largest wall as a screen. Byrne's face was a dozen times larger than life as it looked down on them. Carter Vickers was already lounging in one of the room's plush armchairs. Vic was the only member of the team not in place.

"Proceed, Mr. Byrne," Rask told the man as Rye took up a seat.

"Well, it wasn't easy, but I got a hit eventually. I did what you suggested and followed the routes of the SS Ahnenerbe's expedition from Sikkim, a border region, into Tibet itself. They traveled from Gangtok, through the Teesta River Valley and north, venturing into Lhasa, heading for Gyantse. What I found particularly fascinating about this leg of the expedition was that it was dedicated to the exploration of the ancient deserted capital, Jalung Phodrang, which immediately made me think of what we were looking for, a lost city. So, I focused my search here for a while, but came up empty. Records show the Ahnenerbe ventured on to Shigatse. But again, I came up empty-handed. As far as I can tell, the first expedition was purely an anthropological one, but what I didn't know was that the SS had two concurrent expeditions running in the region at the time, and the second, a mountaineering one, headed by Heinrich Harrer, was set on the exploration of the Nepalese mountain ranges."

"You found what they were looking for?" Rask asked.

"I did, indeed. The thing about the region is that even as recently as the '80s it was still incredibly poorly mapped. The heights of summits were wrong, locations of mountains themselves misplaced by cartographers. But the Germans had near perfect maps made, and that proved a better starting point than randomly trying to overlay the reference points from the Blavatsky painting onto satellite imagery and photographs of the region looking for a match. What I found was that if I divided the Blavatsky dots into two, the ten pale ones and the other more pronounced ones, I got two separate matches. The ten match the approximate summits of various peaks in the range around Gangkhar Puensum—which isn't in Tibet at all, but lies on the border between China and Bhutan, and is the highest unclimbed mountain in the world. The name means White Peak of the Three Spiritual Brothers. I would have missed the connection without the old maps. The White Peak wasn't measured until thirty-three years after Blavatsky's death, and was so badly misplaced by those original maps the first expedition into the region couldn't even find the mountain. To give you an idea about how bad those early maps were, some showed it miles away from where it actually is in Bhutan, placing it in Tibet. It has never been surveyed, and mountaineering is completely forbidden. Before the ban, no expedition succeeded in making the climb, either because of impassable terrain or freak weather conditions, almost as though the mountain didn't want to be climbed. Legend holds that the secrets of the white peaks are protected by phantoms that oppose and ultimately block any attempts to climb them. It's a key location in numerous yeti sightings, ghostly apparitions of dead climbers and lost travelers; the recorded expeditions all claim to have experienced weird magnetic anomalies, seen strange lights in the night sky, and there are reports of numerous disappearances over the last century."

"Which all make it perfect in terms of what we're looking for," Rask said.

"As does this," Byrne said, and his face on the screen was replaced by a photograph of the mountain. "You see that?" he asked, and a ring appeared around a discoloration on the mountainside.

"What am I looking at?" Rask asked, leaning forward.

Byrne magnified the image. It lost some clarity, pixelating in the process, but it was obvious what they were seeing. The red-tiled rooftops of a monastery built on one of the highest ridges.

"Now this is where it gets interesting," Byrne said, flipping the image and overlaying the darker dots of Blavatsky's painting on the landscape. They lined up almost perfectly with the jagged edge of Gangkhar Puensum's spine. "I'm willing to bet we won't find a closer match anywhere in the one and a half thousand miles of the mountain range. This is where the map's leading us. I'm absolutely sure of it. The deviations are just down to the fact that Blavatsky painted the mountain range without having ever been there. It's remarkable, really."

"And this is what the Ahnenerbe were looking for?" Rask asked.

"I'd say X marks the spot," the space archaeologist said. "Now I know where to focus my attention, I shall analyze every frame of satellite footage I can find and look for any kind of clue as to what might be hidden beneath the mountain."

"Good work, Mr. Byrne. Very good work."

"Which is all well and good," Rye said, "but you're forgetting about the whole forbidden mountain thing. We can't just walk up to it."

"Ah, but that's exactly what we *can* do," Rask said. "Break the rules, then apologize later. It's always easier that way."

"Especially when someone is chasing you," Carter added helpfully. "You notice the name? Three spiritual brothers. You think it's a coincidence? We've killed the same man three times."

"Not the same man," the Russian corrected him. "Just someone with a very strong resemblance."

"Like, oh, I don't know, brothers? Three of them?"

"It's not impossible," said Rask.

"Says the man who thinks they are creatures from outer space," Iskra Zima said, though this time it was gentle chiding, delivered with an almost tender smile.

"I am open to the possibility," Rask said. "Especially when we are hunting for wisdom fallen from the stars."

It was obvious this was an argument they had had many times, and would, god willing, have many more times. It was equally obvious that the Russian cared for Greg Rask. There was genuine affection in her gentle mocking. For his part, the dying man took it in the spirit it was obviously intended and was quite happy to play his part.

"So, we're off to the mountains," Rye said.

"You're looking at almost thirty hours by car from where you are to the staging post at Jakar," Byrne told them, changing the image on the screen again. "Then several days' trek through inhospitable country to Bampura. There's also a site—I'm going to call it a temple but that's not really what it is, at least according to the few notes I've been able to find about the place. It was constructed by the Ahnenerbe. I'm going to send through coordinates. You might want to check it out. There are some pretty interesting stories about the place. And given its links to the Thule Society and Blavatsky, I've got a feeling the detour could pay off. It's closer to Jalung Phodrang than the mountains, but not so far out of your way."

"Want to enlighten us?"

"Not really. I don't want to oversell the place. Better you see it for yourself."

Rye nodded. "Given the fact we'll be climbing to serious heights and risking serious altitude sickness if we ascend too quickly, it's probably worth taking it slow and checking the place out. It'll give our bodies more time to adjust."

"Why can't we just air drop you in?" the thief asked.

"To put it at its most basic, altitude sickness is no joke. The higher we climb, the less oxygen there is in the air around us. Once we're up around the two-and-a-half-thousand-meter mark we're in dangerous territory. If we ascend more than one thousand meters a day, we're risking some serious problems; in the mildest cases it's like having a hangover: Loss of coordination. Trouble walking. Headaches, nausea, dizziness. Aching muscles. Confusion."

"Doesn't sound so bad."

"That's the mildest case. You're at risk from high-altitude pulmonary edema, which is a buildup of fluid in your lungs from the reactions of the air pressure on your body. With the fluid in your lungs, it becomes harder and harder to breathe. Your breathing gets wheezier and wheezier as you fight for each breath, until you're coughing up a pink froth of sputum. This is life-threatening. Your blood can't get the oxygen it needs. And normal medication isn't going to help you. This is bad shit."

"Got you."

"The worst-case scenario, cerebral edema," Rye said. "Fluid in the brain. That happens, you're not coming back from it."

"And this is all because we go up too quickly?"

"Yep. The only way to combat altitude sickness is acclimatization."

"There's no way to just fly in, grab the stone, and get out before it all goes to hell?"

"Do you know where the stone is?"

"Good point. Slow it is."

"Wise move. But it doesn't solve every problem we're going to face on the mountain."

"For some reason I didn't think it would," the thief said.

"Hypothermia is a very real possibility given the hostile weather. We're going up through so many different temperate zones, that temperature drop is steep."

"And that's ignoring the spirits protecting the mountain," Carter Vickers said.

"And the Bhutanese military, which are likely to shoot us in the back for trespassing on their holy mountain," Iskra agreed.

"Sounds like a whole heap of fun," the thief said.

No one argued with him.

FORTY-FOUR

Vic returned while they were packing up the equipment into the back of one of the two off-road vehicles Rask had sourced that morning. There was no denying the fact that money made the world go around, and Greg Rask stood slap-bang in the middle of its axis.

The big man had his fists buried in his pockets and a face like thunder.

As he approached Rye, he took his right hand out of his pocket and Rye saw his bloody knuckles.

"Defending my honor?" he asked, not too keen on hearing the answer.

"I was jumped in an alleyway near the embassy. Three of them. They should have brought more," he said soberly. He flexed his fingers. "It got ugly." The blood was proof of that. "They brought weapons, but weren't prepared to use them properly. It was a warning rather than a murder. When a man isn't prepared to end a fight but turns up with a weapon, it makes him vulnerable rather than strong. He is restraining himself. He isn't fighting for survival. Now one of them, at least, won't be able to chew his food for a very long time, and the other two will not forget our meeting in a hurry."

"Thank you," Rye said.

Vic shook his head, as though denying his thanks. "This place is ugly, Rye. There is an undercurrent here that reminds me too much of the country I left behind. It isn't a civilized land, no matter what it looks like on the surface. That is just a veneer of civilization. There is a darkness here. Step out of line and it will drown you, no questions."

Rye nodded. The fact that a man had to set himself on fire for his argument to be heard underlined just how barbaric so-called civilized society was in this place. "Did you find her? Cressida?"

"No, but I found the answers I was looking for even without finding her. The mugging wasn't some random act of violence. They have our hotel under surveillance. They watched me leave the hotel, followed me, and waited until I was in a place where they could move without risk of being seen—or stopped—by passersby to make their move. It was professional. A lesser man would be in the ground now." Rye didn't doubt him for a moment. "I don't know who your German woman is, but I have been around enough violence in my life to know that someone is playing with us. Word will get back to her that her men failed. The sooner we are away from here and in open terrain where we can see her coming, the better. I have no great fondness for pretending to be someone's prey, but neither do I particularly enjoy hunting killers through streets crowded with women and children."

"I'm sorry," Rye said.

"Don't be. It is not your fault. You are the victim here. The only person to blame for anything that has happened to you is the German woman. And I will make sure she faces the consequences of her actions, even if she is a woman, you have my word." He raised his hand to his heart, his ruined knuckles emphasizing his promise in a way that went far beyond words.

"You're a good man, Vic."

"Not many people would call me that," he said, with a grin, and stooped to lift the heaviest of the sacks with his bloody hand and heave it into the open tailgate. "Have the others left you to do all the hard work?"

"You don't expect Carter to get his hands dirty, do you?"

"No," the big man said.

"I heard that!" the thief called from somewhere not too far away.

"You were meant to," Rye said, looking around for him. "Come on, it's your stuff, too."

It took ten more minutes to load the cars, distributing the equipment evenly across them, by which time Rask had emerged from the hotel. He leaned heavily on his nurse's arm. Before Rye could ask, he raised a hand to forestall questions and told them, "Don't worry, I am not foolish enough to try and make the journey with you. Mr. Byrne has assured me our communication lines will remain intact during most, if not all, of your journey, as they are satellite linked. I have merely come to wish you god's speed, my friends. My life is in your hands, and I couldn't ask for a finer bunch to fight in my corner. I'll hold the fort while you go find me a miracle."

"We won't let you down," Rye said. It was a stupid thing to say. An impossible promise. But he had every intention of keeping it.

Even if it meant going to hell and back.

FORTY-FIVE

Rye rode with Vic. Carter and Iskra shared the second car.

They had been on the road for hours, not pushing themselves because no matter how far and how fast they drove there was always farther to go. They'd already passed through several climate zones, moving from the oppressive humid heat to bullet rain into heavy mists that obscured the dizzying drop down the mountainside where the narrow road ran far too close to the cliff's edge for comfort. Vic didn't elaborate on what had happened outside the embassy, though every now and then he did take his hand from the wheel and flex his fingers as if trying to work the circulation back through them.

Rye noticed he had a habit of checking the rearview mirror to see if there was anyone back there that coincided a little too regularly with the hand flex for it not to be connected deep down in his reptile brain.

They couldn't go the obvious crow-flies route into Bhutan because of the mountain range, and the Chinese had completely closed down the remaining land border into the country, so Byrne had found the only viable route.

"Doesn't look like Bhutan is big on visitors." Byrne was on the speaker.

"What do you mean?" Vic asked, straining forward to see through the still-thickening mist. Visibility was down to no more than thirty feet and, given the drop to the left was considerable, he was taking no chances.

The sound of the road was insulated from the off-roader's cab.

"Just looking at the hoops they want you to jump through. All sorts of visas, and get this, they charge you an arm and a leg every single day in visitor's fees just to *be* in the country. Two hundred and fifty bucks a day. Looks like they've discovered the free market."

"So how do we get in?"

"There are two overland border crossing points: one is from West Bengal into Phuntsholing, the other is Samdrup Jongkhar in the southeast. I've made arrangements at the Phuntsholing border for you to pass through. With luck, it should be pretty uneventful."

"Famous last words," Rye said.

"Palms have been greased," Byrne said. "Bhutan, it seems, is fluent in the universal language of greed. Once you're in, do try to bear in mind you're totally illegal. No visas, no embassy help. And there's no telling how long it will take us to get actual practical help to you on the ground, so try not to get into any trouble."

"Why are you looking at me like that?" Rye said to Vic, earning a chuckle from the speaker.

"Don't even joke about it," Byrne said.

On either side of the road now were tea plantations that rose in tiers up the sides of the hills, the lush greenery glistening with moisture, though occasionally they were afforded glimpses of the Toorsa River. Always ahead of them, the darker outlines of the mountains towered over the land. When the mists finally thinned, the white peaks stood out starkly against the too-blue sky.

They saw women in saris collecting fresh drinking water from bore wells, and emaciated goats walking along the roadside.

It was a six-hour drive down to the border. They talked. How could they not. Most of the conversation was about nothing, sharing odd memories that offered unconscious glimpses into their psyches. One thing that became obvious to Rye was how little he knew the others. The drive back from Matthew Langley's jail cell, then the mess of Stockholm, meant he'd forged a bond with Vic, but he knew next to nothing about Iskra or Carter, and whenever he tried to ask his companion about them, all he would say is that theirs were not his stories to tell. Rye had to respect that, but going into the mountains they would be putting their lives very firmly in each other's hands, and it felt odd trusting people he didn't know so absolutely, but what choice did he have?

The last few miles descended through a heart-in-mouth series of switchbacks toward the town of Phuntsholing. They were beyond exhausted at this point, having been on the road for what amounted to thirty-six hours, plus breaks, and having slept badly in the cars. Rye was starving. There were only so many protein bars you could eat before your stomach rebelled, so the plan was to find a hotel, rest up, eat, and move out fresh in the morning. But even that was optimistic.

It took another hour, with traffic of mainly VW camper vans overflowing with people and luggage backed halfway up the hillside, and what felt like a thousand-meter decline, before the flat plains of Phuntsholing opened up before them. They crawled on, a few precious feet at a time. The plains were called the Duars, a mangling of the original Doors, as in the Doors to the Himalayas, and the view, even with the endless snake of cars through the middle of it, was nothing short of spectacular.

They'd been operating under the assumption that they were ahead of the enemy, and that whoever Cressida really was, she had no choice but to give chase. That was predicated upon the fact that they'd left Kathmandu ahead of any pursuit. But that was false logic because the limited border crossings made them predictable, even without knowing their destination beyond the mountains. If she was somehow connected to the Brotherhood of Dzyan and its devotees that had already tried to kill them more than once, then she knew their destination better than they did, and that took the guesswork out of where they would cross the border and made intercepting them a simple case of mathematics. They could only travel so fast in the ever-changing conditions, even if they spelled each other with the driving. Meaning the biggest risk of ambush was this side of the gate. And that had them all on edge. Watchful.

"I'm tired of being the gazelle," the big man said out of nowhere. "It's time to think like the leopard. Do you trust me?"

He didn't have to think about his answer.

"Implicitly."

"That helps. We know they are looking for us. We have an idea why, but in truth we're just running blind. We've done this entire journey with one eye on the mirror to see if there's anyone back there. We know they're coming. I want to draw them out."

"And that involves my trust how?"

"I'm thinking we use you as bait."

"Never a word a guy wants to hear."

"We put you out there in public, make a show of the fact you are on your own, and see how long it takes for them to bite."

"Simple enough. Not too many moving parts. So, million-dollar question: What happens if it goes wrong?"

"We'll be watching," he promised.

"Watching?"

"From a safe distance. But you'll be on your own out there. We can't risk any sort of signal they could track or register on a bug sweep, nothing that might give away the fact it's a setup." Which made sense. It wasn't reassuring, but it made sense.

"What could possibly go wrong?" Rye said.

"Plenty," the big man said truthfully. "You'll just have to trust me when I say I won't let it."

"Okay. So, what are you thinking?"

"You have a gift for getting in trouble," Vic said, offering a smile to take the sting out of the words. "We find somewhere to stay, then you go sightseeing, maybe grab some food, sit out in the park, wander around a temple, just be very visibly alone and very much in public, not hidden away in hotel bars. I want you on the street. There aren't going to be many tourists here, so with luck you'll stand out like a sore thumb."

"With you. We paint a target on my back." Rye nodded. "And what if they don't bite?"

"Then we push on across the border. But they're going to make a move. Trust me. They have to. They know we're getting closer to whatever it is they don't want us to find. That's going in our favor. They don't want us making it to their mountain. The trail of bodies they left trying to stop us getting our hands on that map proves that." It was sound logic, but there was a body-shaped hole right in the middle of it. His body.

"How do we know they won't just take me out as soon as they see they've got a shot?"

"We don't, but we have to assume if they wanted to kill you your paramour could have done it easily enough when you were asleep beside her." He had a good point, but it was one that was dependent upon the idea that Cressida Mohr was part of some grander conspiracy and not just a liar who made a game out of fucking tourists. "And strategically speaking, if they're trying to stop us from getting to their mountain, they want to do it here, as far away from it as possible, in case something goes wrong. The closer we get to the mountain, the less room they have to maneuver."

"I think it's a great idea," Byrne said across the airways. Rye had completely forgotten the other man was listening in. "Think of it like a team-building exercise, you know, a trust fall. You let yourself go, rely on the other guys to catch you."

"And if they don't?"

"I'll have eyes on you, don't worry. I'll reposition the satellite on Phuntsholing. Don't worry. We've got this."

"If you keep saying don't worry it's going to have the opposite effect. Okay, I'm in. Just do me a favor, try not to get the new boy killed."

The crossing was on the northern edge of the town.

It was essentially a long wall with a single gateway that looked very much like one of the many Tibetan shrines he'd seen in the monkey temple. It was guarded by soldiers in two different uniforms, and locals seemed to be passing beneath without even showing identification. The difference between the divided city was stark: on one side it seemed vibrant and full of life, with shoppers bustling around, while on the other it was more urban, with the buildings appearing to be homes rather than havens of commerce. The Bhutan side of the gate was considerably quieter, with fewer cars on the roads. From their approach, a single road snaked up the hill on the far side of the city. It was the road to Thimphu, the capital.

They found lodging, avoiding the luxury that marked their previous hotels. It was a small deceit, but if their hunters were looking at past behavior to predict future choices, it was the kind of small deceit that might just buy the few precious seconds that made all the difference.

At only a thousand feet above sea level, the air was normal, if incredibly fresh in Rye's lungs. The lack of pollutants almost made it harder to breathe, not easier, so conditioned was he to the impurities of city life. He found a street vendor selling *momo,* pale white dumplings stuffed with so many spices his mouth exploded with the flavors as he bit down into them. He dipped the *momo* in chutney as he sat in the park in the heart of the town center. A couple in their eighties sat on the bench facing him, alternatively feeding the birds and themselves with mouthfuls of *momo.* They were so obviously in love Rye couldn't help but smile. It was good to be out in the fresh air after so many hours cramped in the car, even if he was being dangled like a big juicy worm on a hook. The park itself was incredibly peaceful. Across the way he saw monks walk in and out of their temple. His mind flashed back to the burning man falling to his knees, dead before his body could understand the full extent of what was happening to it. These men, by contrast, seemed so utterly at peace with the world.

On the far side of the park were market stalls, where the locals went about their daily shopping. He heard voices haggling and amused laughter. He heard what he took to be the stall holders trying to entice custom with outrageous promises about their wares.

Rye watched them, eating his *momo* and smiling as another elderly couple walked up the temple steps to spin the prayer wheel. He wondered what they were wishing for.

While he sat there, a pigeon settled near his feet. Then another. He broke up one of the *momos* with his fingers and scattered the crumbs for the birds to eat. Within a minute there were a hundred birds crowding around. And then a hundred more. He scattered his last *momo* and watched them fight over the scraps with unexpected savagery. In the sky he saw easily another thousand black specks as more birds circled the park.

He used the birds as an excuse to look around, trying to make out where the others were. But they were good. He had no idea where they were hiding.

Rye walked back toward the hotel.

As he entered one of the narrower alleyways across the street from the lush greens and bright blossoms of the park, he caught a flicker of movement in his peripheral vision, which on any other day he would have dismissed as nothing, but already on edge, he looked and realized just how much trouble he was in.

Rye reached up to activate the bud in his ear, only to realize it was on the bamboo nightstand back in the seedy hotel room.

A car—a rusted old Ford with a broken headlight and busted radiator grille—blocked the alleyway. There were three men in it; another appeared to be an Indian border guard leaning in to talk to the driver through the open window—no doubt telling him he couldn't loiter there. There was a suppressed *whump* of sound followed by the guard's sudden lurch upright, hand reaching out to the open window for support as his legs betrayed him. The guard fell, a bloodred rose flowering in the center of his chest.

The driver had seen Rye, as had his companions in the car.

He backed up a step but couldn't look away as the driver opened the door and clambered out. The driver stood over the guard while he bled out. There was nothing rushed about his manner. He knelt beside the fallen man, put his hand over his mouth, and clamped finger and thumb across his nose, hastening his demise.

The guard's body barely bucked, his left leg kicking twice at the ground before the life went out of him.

The driver watched Rye while he killed the man.

Rye turned, knowing he had to get out of the confines of the alley, and fast, only to see a fourth man blocking the way.

He couldn't see Vic or the others, and the overhanging rooftops obscured at least a portion of the street from the sky.

He'd been stupid.

Stupid got you killed.

The fourth man read his mind and aimed the Uzi at the middle of his chest.

"Don't go getting any ideas," he said in perfect English. "Get down. On your knees. Hands behind your head."

With no other way out of the alley, he had no choice but to do as he was told.

Rye shook his head. "No."

That threw his attacker. "Don't make me hurt you."

"In about thirty seconds I'll be saying the same thing to you," he said with a confidence he didn't feel.

"I don't think so," a voice said, behind him.

Rye didn't turn to see who it was. He took a side step toward the alley wall, trying to put something solid behind him, still unable to take his eyes off the Uzi.

"Down," the gunman repeated, his patience wearing thin.

"Fifteen seconds," Rye said, hoping to hell that the others were out there.

He felt a crunching hammer blow to his kidneys and dropped to his knees.

"Hands behind your head," the gunman repeated, jabbing the muzzle of the Uzi at his face.

"Ten," Rye said, interlacing his fingers behind his head, and continued the countdown. "Nine."

He clung to the belief that if they wanted him dead, he'd be dead by now.

What he tried not to think about was that sometimes dead was better.

"Eight."

"You're a funny man," the gunman said. As far as last words went, they weren't the most profound. They didn't offer him any insight into himself that he didn't already know. Before Rye could say "Seven," the man's jaw exploded in a spray of blood and bone.

"Guess I was wrong," Rye said, the dead man's blood on his face as he turned to look at the driver. "He didn't live long enough to beg. Now, where were we?"

"Seven," Carter Vickers said helpfully, walking into the mouth of the alleyway.

"Seven," Rye said, nodding. "Good number."

The driver dropped to his knees. The two other men did the same. Neither had said a word. They were locals, he realized, looking at them properly for the first time. There was no guarantee they even spoke his language. Still, violence was universal. The two men had absolutely no loyalty to the driver that hadn't been paid for with his rupees, and whatever it had cost, it was pretty much spent now. Rupees didn't buy the kind of loyalty that left half of your jaw splattered across an alleyway.

"I want to hear you say it," Carter told Rye.

"Okay, just for you." Rye turned to the driver. "Don't make me hurt you."

"Nice," the thief said approvingly. "Got some gravitas going on there, man. I'm impressed. I completely believe you'd hurt him, and you know, it sounds like you might even enjoy it. You'll fit in nicely. Say something else. Say, give me an excuse. Go on, give me an excuse. Make trigger fingers like you're going to put a bullet in his temple."

"I'm not saying that," Rye said.

"You don't have to pull the actual trigger," he said helpfully. "And it's not as though he's innocent. There's a dead guard over there. That's on him. He's a man of the world, he knows he's not walking away from this. All we've got to do is keep him here until the rest of the guards show up and they'll pull the trigger for us."

FORTY-SIX

The first thing Rye heard when he put his earbud back in place was Byrne's warning, "You've got company coming in fast. Another unit of four, coming two by two. They should be with you in under a minute."

He looked around for Iskra, but the Russian was nowhere to be seen.

"We've got to bug out," Vic said. He didn't waste time with any niceties. Instead, he cuffed the kneeling driver around the side of the head hard enough to fracture bone, and as the man dropped, grabbed him by the arm and dragged him toward their own vehicle, one block over.

"What do you want to do about these two?" Rye asked.

"Are they going to be a problem?"

The two men looked back blankly at him.

"I doubt it."

"Your call then. Put a bullet in their foot so they don't come after us."

Rye didn't have a gun, and the idea of shooting someone, even in the foot, was anathema to him. But he didn't have time to bargain their freedom either, so he grabbed the first man by the shoulders and told him to run. He didn't need to repeat himself. He lurched away from Rye, staggering three steps before his feet found a rhythm through the fear. The second thug bolted after him, arms and legs pumping frantically as he ran for his life.

"Thirty seconds," Byrne said. "Coming in hot. Get out of there. Now!"

Rye followed Carter and Vic as they dragged the driver beyond the rusting Ford to the corner where their SUV was parked, engine running, Iskra behind the wheel.

They were closing the doors as the first shot ricocheted off grille and the second put a spiderweb through the windshield. "Down!

Down!" the Russian barked, hitting reverse and flooring the accelerator to get them out of there fast.

It took Rye a second to realize that Vic hadn't got into the car with them when he'd bundled the driver into the back seat. He looked around for the big man but couldn't see him.

Another bullet tore into the soft fabric of the interior, inches from Rye's shoulder.

He didn't dare move as Iskra threw the SUV into evasive maneuvers, tires spinning up smoke as they laid down streaks of black rubber on the road. She whipped the tailgate around so violently Rye was pressed up against the window as more bullets tore into the black metal, and then they were powering away from the gunmen, losing them in the labyrinth of back streets between the ambush and the hotel.

Not that the Russian had any intention of pulling up outside their base.

She had another destination in mind, on the outskirts of the small town. The smell as they approached was sickening. Smoke billowed out of the stacks. Those chimneys were the source of the stench. Rendered fat.

She'd brought them to a slaughterhouse.

They slid to a halt, tires spitting gravel as the SUV slewed across the parking lot, and she was out of the car and had the driver by the scruff of the throat, dragging him toward the huge steel doors before the others had even exited the vehicle. The man kicked out, fighting her every step of the way. Rye felt a curious sense of relief at that, as he'd feared the worst after Vic had pistol-whipped him.

The Russian hammered twice on the huge doors and waited.

They opened an inch, then wider.

Vic was already inside.

Rye had no idea how he could have beaten them here. Iskra didn't wait for the big man to open fully. She propelled the driver through the dark slash of the doorway. Vic stepped aside as the driver went down hard, sprawling across the concrete floor on his hands and knees.

Rye and Carter stood side by side, both looking at the doorway like it was the gateway to Hell without Cerberus to warn them off. "You sure you want to do this?" the thief asked. "I know what's going to happen in there."

"We're in this together," Rye said, with considerably more calmness than he felt as he stepped through into the darkness.

FORTY-SEVEN

On the other side of the door, the building's true nature was inescapable. He was confronted by metal troughs along the walls and hoses conveniently placed to wash away the blood. There were meat hooks suspended from the ceiling and runnels in the tiled floor, which gently sloped toward the troughs so that the animal blood wouldn't congeal on the tiles and make a mess of the sterile environment. It would work just the same for human blood.

Vic worked pragmatically, no real thought for what he was doing as he winched down two of the meat hooks until the barbed metal reached torso height, then with Iskra's help went about securing their prisoner's wrists to each one. Neither of them talked as they worked, which made it all the more unnerving.

Vic tested the right wrist, then the left, to be sure they would hold, before he returned to the winch and began turning it. Each revolution of the crank lifted the man's arms up maybe ten or twelve inches more, so for the first three turns very little pain was exerted on his body as the meat hooks transformed him into a living, breathing embodiment of Da Vinci's Vitruvian Man. The fourth turn brought a wince, the fifth a gasp of pain as muscles and joints were forced into positions they were never meant to experience.

He broke his silence.

Rye had no idea what he'd said: it may have been nothing more revelatory than a prayer to his god, or more damning than a pox on Vic's line.

"Who hired you?" Vic said finally.

He walked around the hanging man slowly. He didn't touch

him, but every step was close enough that their prisoner would be able to feel his breath on his skin.

"I want a name. Give me that and it doesn't have to hurt."

The hanging man spat, though there was very little anger behind the gesture. It was nothing more than token resistance. He wasn't about to offer his name, rank, and number. It wouldn't take much to break him. When it came right down to it, he'd been paid to do what he did, this wasn't some holy crusade for him, and that meant he was always going to talk. It was only ever a matter of time.

But they didn't have the luxury of patience. So, Vic clenched his fist, and from behind, drove a brutal punch into the hanging man's kidneys, spinning him around on the meat hooks as he cried out in pain.

"I'll ask you one more time," Vic told him, "but I won't ask a third, so it's important you decide just how much you want to hurt. Who hired you?"

The man bit down hard on his lower lip, gritting his teeth against the inevitable agony of Vic's second punch. This one was so savage it lifted him two inches on the chains. He came down hard, the barbed hooks slicing into his wrists. Vic simply stared at the man, waiting, while the blood trickled down his forearms.

Rye couldn't bear to watch: the symbolism of the slaughter-house, the body on the meat hooks, the first blood dripping into the runnels in the tiled floor. He knew what happened next. "Tell him," he said, begging the man to do the smart thing and save himself. "Please, just tell him what he wants to know."

True to his word, Vic didn't ask a third time.

His third punch left the man spitting blood.

The front of his sweat-stained shirt was a mess as Vic patiently worked him over, tenderizing his body. For a full thirty seconds, he delivered blow after crunching blow, each one doing unseen damage as they weakened their prisoner's resolve. The man twisted and writhed against the crucifying chains, but without so much as a muted cry of pain.

Vic stepped back and let Iskra turn the hose on him.

The pressurized spray of ice-cold water hit their prisoner almost as hard as Vic, driving his head back as she focused the intensity of it on his gasping mouth. He couldn't spit the spray out fast enough to draw a breath.

He was drowning on dry land.

Rye couldn't watch. He turned his back and walked toward the door. The sound of the jet spray changed, no longer hitting meat but instead bouncing off the metal troughs behind the hanging man as Iskra gave him the chance to save himself.

He heard three words before he walked out. "The German woman."

FORTY-EIGHT

Outside, he saw Carter Vickers leaning up against the side of the rental car. He was smoking a hand-rolled cigarette. He didn't want to know what kind of tobacco he'd sourced since arriving in the border town. Some things were better left unknown. He flicked the half-smoked stub away when he saw Rye coming.

"Pretty grim in there?" he asked, though it didn't sound like much of a question.

"Just get me out of here," he told the thief.

"That bad? Roger that." He opened the driver's-side door and leaned over to pop the lock on Rye's. He clambered in. "Where to?" the thief asked. His first impulse was to say a bar, intending to get so drunk he didn't remember those three mumbled words he'd just heard, and didn't have to think about what Vic and Iskra were doing to the man in there. With enough alcohol inside him he might—just might—be able to convince himself that all was fair in this particular round of love and war, but it wasn't. It was anything but fair. He'd allowed himself to be vulnerable, choosing to forget about Hannah for a few hours, and the world had fucked him.

Well, fuck the world.

That seemed like a fair response.

"A bar. Any bar. I'm not picky."

"Your wish is my command."

"Then drive, Genie."

It took the thief five minutes to find a gaudy-looking sign that promised oblivion. He pulled up outside the door. "You want company?"

"What I want is to get shit-faced," Rye said.

"Are you sure that's such a good idea?"

"It's a terrible fucking idea," he agreed. "You know what? I've changed my mind. Wrong Disney cartoon. You're not the Genie," Rye said. "You're Jiminy fucking Cricket." He opened the door. "You can stay out here and keep watch if you are worried about me getting into trouble."

"Probably a good idea," Carter said. "All things considered."

"Just try not to let me see you. I want to forget about this shit for a while."

A while turned out to be less than an hour, and not long enough for him to get seriously drunk, despite going about it seriously. He had three empty glasses lined up on the bar by the time Vic joined him.

Vic held up a hand, said, "Two more," to the barman and waited for him to decant the spirits before he asked Rye, "What the fuck do you think you are doing?"

"I could ask you the same thing. I didn't sign up for torture and murder, Vic."

"Neither did I. I escaped torture and murder in my homeland. I have no interest in bringing it into the new world with me."

"Easy to say, but I saw what you did back there."

"We did what had to be done, nothing more. And, I might add, we did not bring him into this. You did."

"So now you're blaming me? It's my fault that you had to torture that guy?"

"Yes," Vic said matter-of-factly. "That is not up for dispute. You got drunk, exercised poor judgment, and slept with a woman who, it would seem, is looking for the same thing that we are. You did this, Rye, not me. Not Carter or Iskra or Rask. But that doesn't mean it wasn't a good thing in the long run. Until a few minutes ago, we had no idea how close this second party interested in the

Cintāmani stones are to discovering the whereabouts of Shamb-hala. Now we do, so we can act appropriately."

"So, it's my fault, but it's good I took one for the team? Great. Guess I don't need to feel guilty about you killing him then." He downed the liquor in one swallow and let out a gasp as he shook his head. The sting brought tears to his eyes. Or at least he wanted to believe it was the sting.

"Who said anything about killing him?" Vic downed his own drink, though there was no smacking of the lips or shaking of the head in his case. "I merely convinced him it would be in his best interest to forget all about the German woman and her money and return to his village. I convinced him that I am the devil, and if he should break his word and try to contact Cressida Mohr I would hunt him down, his parents, his wife and children, his favorite primary school teacher, his long-lost kin, and anyone else he's ever given a shit about, and I would cut their throats while they slept at night. I think he believed me."

"Shit. That's brutal."

"Better than killing him," Vic said, and Rye couldn't argue with that.

"So, what happens now?"

"We carry on as planned. We hole up here for the night, then go over the border tomorrow, try to get a head start on anyone else who takes it into their head to follow us. Check out that Ahnenerbe temple Byrne found. These people ruined one of the vehicles, so we need to source a replacement today, if we can. Other than that, drinking is as good a plan as any, as long as you don't bitch about the hangover in the morning."

"Thanks for the permission."

"You need to get this—whatever this is—out of your system, Rye. I don't think it is about what you saw in there. I think it is because you look at me now and you see the same man who killed your wife. I am *not* that man. So, if that means you need to get drunk tonight to banish that vision, then do it. I would rather you didn't, but I am not going to tell tales. None of us are. But once we're over that border tomorrow, our lives are going to depend upon your skills, so you don't bring your ghosts with you. Understood?

They stay here. Tomorrow is a different country. Tomorrow you need to be the best you you can be."

"But tonight I get to be a self-pitying drunk? Okay, I can live with that."

"Carter will wait outside. He will see you get back to the hotel safely."

"Has anyone ever told you that you take all of the fun out of life, Vic?"

"My wife, god rest her soul."

"I didn't know you'd been married," Rye said, and in that moment looked at the big man beside him very differently, aware of the kindred bond they shared.

"Why would you? I didn't tell you. There is much you do not know about my life before Mr. Rask saved me, and that is as it should be."

"How did she die?"

"What does it matter?"

"I'm just trying to understand you."

"She died because I could not save her."

"I know that feeling."

"I know you do."

"So that's why you spend the rest of your life trying to save us?"

"That would be too easy, but if that is what you want to believe, then yes. That is why I spend my life trying to save Mr. Rask, you, Iskra, Carter, and the others. And why losing Olivia hurt so much. Because every time I save you I make up for not saving the woman I loved." There was genuine bitterness behind his words, the kind of raw emotion Rye had not heard from him before. It was disconcerting, to say the least.

"I'm sorry," he said, not sure what else to say.

"You have no need to apologize, Rye," the big man said, pushing back his barstool.

He left twenty American dollars on the bar, which more than amply covered his tab, and left Rye to drink himself unconscious.

Rye pointed at the empty glass.

FORTY-NINE

Dawn brought only pain.

Rye rolled over in the tangle of sheets, reaching for his cell phone. The clock on the display told him he'd been in bed less than five hours. Those five hours had dragged like fifty, sweating the alcohol out of his system as the temperature in the room never dipped below twenty-five Celsius.

The shower didn't work, which meant he was going to stink of alcohol all day. He washed himself down using the bathroom tap; the water was a muddy brown, but it was cold, and splashed across his face it brought him back to the semblance of life. He knew that everything he'd done yesterday after hearing the hanging man say "the German woman" had been self-destructive. Dangerously so. He couldn't help it. Self-destruct was his default setting since he'd listened to Hannah die. He was resigned to the fact that it would be for a long time to come, no matter what Vic wanted from him.

It was too soon.

He cleaned his teeth with the brown water, and sprayed more body spray than was good for the environment, before he bagged up his stuff and headed down to the car.

The others were waiting.

None of them said anything as he dumped his bag in the trunk. He realized that the second car Vic had sourced wasn't a car at all, and in no better condition than the shot-up SUV it was replacing. It was a flatbed truck with wooden slats for sides. The back was filled with their gear. They threw a tarp over the top and fastened it down.

The morning was bright, the air clear but humid, the threat of rain imminent.

They divided up between the cars, Rye in with Carter Vickers this time, Iskra and Vic in the SUV. The cab of the flatbed lacked the luxury of air-conditioning, though the wooden beads draped over the seats stopped his skin from sticking to the leather. The radio didn't work, but given the fragile state of Rye's head he wasn't complaining—a little silence and the rhythms of the road would be just fine for now.

They buckled up and moved out.

Long before they reached the border gate, the voice of home chirped in his ear, Jeremiah promising them that five hundred US dollars should be enough to see them over the border without the proper visas. "The joys of capitalism," the thief said, but Rye noticed he wasn't himself this morning. When he questioned Carter about it, the thief just brushed his concerns off, saying, "Just tired, don't sweat it."

But that wasn't it.

He was hypervigilant, eyes everywhere at once, scanning the buildings and rooftops for possible threats, checking each corner and parked car for potential bogies. This was a different side of him.

Carter pulled down the sun visor and took the vehicle registration papers down from where they were secured with a thick elasticized band. He handed them to Rye as he rolled the window down.

They drove around the main temple square, following the flow of traffic toward the gate.

There were six guards checking the papers of the locals coming and going, though they didn't appear to actually look at any of the documentation they were shown.

Behind them, monks filed out of the temple.

Rye marked at least six tourists near the huge prayer drums. With them was a young boy who seemed less than impressed with the whole thing. It took Rye a moment to realize the thing he took from his backpack was a can of spray paint. He couldn't quite believe the idiot was going to tag the temple, but he shouldn't have been surprised. "Welcome to the modern world," he said to himself. Carter made the mistake of thinking Rye was talking to him and answered as though they were disembarking from a flight.

"Thank you for flying with Tibetan Airlines, flight why-do-we-have-to-get-out-of-bed-so-early. We would like to thank you for choosing to fly with us, and hope you'll enjoy your stay in the modern world. Flights back in time are available upon request."

"Shut up," he said.

"That costs extra," Carter told him, and he could well believe that.

It took them a quarter of an hour to reach the front of the procession of cars and trucks, the sun rising markedly in the sky in that time so it cast a hot band of light across Rye's thighs. It worked like a magnifying glass on his skin; thankfully he wasn't an ant ready to burn.

One of the border guards banged on the roof of the truck's cab, and another gestured for them to pull over out of the flow of traffic. Both men, he noticed, were armed with semi-automatics, though they looked more like schoolboys playing dress-up rather than soldiers. That, in part, was down to their racial characteristics, he realized, and he didn't like the way generations of preconceived ideas still filtered through his mind despite the fact he liked to think of himself as a prejudice-free modern man.

There was, of course, no such thing.

We were all the sum of our experiences, our environment, and our best efforts to be our best selves, but we were always going to fall short of perfect.

That was the essence of being human.

The human condition.

To try and to fail, only to try better and fail harder.

"Papers?" the guard asked, that one English word uncomfortable in his mouth.

"Of course," Carter said, reaching into his pocket for a billfold which contained the five hundred bucks they'd set aside to bribe their way beneath the gateway into another country.

The guard took it, rifled through the notes as though counting them, then asked, "What is this?"

"Our paperwork," the thief said. "It's all there, count it."

The guard's brow furrowed, as though he didn't grasp the fundamental concept of being paid off to look the other way.

"American?"

Carter nodded, "Good old USDA prime."

"You people make me sick. You think you rule the world. You throw your money around like it is the answer to everything, no thought for just how insulting it is to those of us on the receiving end. You think our integrity can be bought so cheaply? This is our country, we are as proud of it as you are of your apple pie. You want to come in, you want to climb, you will follow the proper procedures, apply for your visas and permits for the mountains you intend to climb, and wait for them to be granted."

"We could do that," the thief agreed. "But our colleague was assured that these five hundred dollars would be more than enough compensation to pay for your troubles."

"Then you were misled."

"How much will it cost?" Rye asked.

The man sniffed and said something to his companion, who pointed at the black SUV, no doubt reminding his friend that there was a whale to be gutted here. They traded a few more words in their native tongue, then the guard leaned back into their window and said, "This much, each. There are four of you. Two thousand should be enough to secure the proper paperwork from my office."

"Two grand? That's daylight robbery."

"Yes it is, but that doesn't change the price."

"We don't have that kind of money on us."

"That is unfortunate, but it is not my problem. That is the price."

"How much have you got on you?" Rye asked him.

"Another couple of hundred, and my Amex." He turned to the guard. "I don't suppose you take plastic?"

The man shook his head. "There is a bank in town. It opens in an hour. Go there. Tell them I sent you. They will allow you to take the money from your card, for a fee. I will keep your truck here as insurance until you return."

"Jesus, what a con." Carter turned to Rye. "Will you be all right in the truck?"

"You stay here, I'll go," Rye said. "I could do with the walk to clear my head."

"Knock yourself out." The thief reached back for the handle that would recline his chair and closed his eyes.

"Where's the bank?" Rye asked the border guard as he clambered out of the battered old truck. He pointed the way, offering rudimentary directions, and told him his name as though it was the key to the kingdom, which maybe it was in this corrupt little junta.

Rye pressed the earbud to activate it.

"You realize how ridiculous this is? We work for a billionaire and we can't afford to pay a miserable little bribe?" he told Byrne through the earpiece. That earned a laugh in his ear.

"It wouldn't matter if we'd had the cash, they'd have found an excuse to send us to this bank of theirs, and charged us to exchange it, or deposit it; it's all about working the angles. They're embracing capitalism."

This time it was Rye's turn to laugh.

The bank wasn't a bank at all.

It took him ten minutes on foot, and he was sure he'd walked the wrong way somewhere along the route when he faced a big wooden door that led into a courtyard. It looked more like an apartment than a bank, and his impressions of the place only got worse when a kid on the bottom step begged loose change off him. He went inside. The floors were marble, and the iron balustrade on the staircase was worn free of varnish in places from years of people running their hands across it as they climbed and descended. It was easily ten degrees cooler inside than it was out. Rye climbed the stairs. "This place is weird," he told Byrne. "I feel like Hansel wandering off into the worst enchanted wood, ever."

"If he offers you candy, you might want to run."

It was good to know the other man was there.

He went up.

There were two doors on the next landing, one with a brass plaque above the mailbox. He couldn't read what was written on it, but at least it looked official, so he knocked on the door and waited.

It took a moment before a fat man answered.

He wore a linen suit that looked as though he'd slept in it for the last week, and which came replete with sweat rings beneath the armpits and what appeared to be blood on the collar from where he'd cut himself shaving. "What?" he asked in English. Rye had no way of knowing if he'd guessed based on his complexion or, more likely, if the guard had called ahead to warn him Rye was coming, but the fact he'd not even attempted a hello in his native tongue was telling.

"Metok sent me. He told me you were a bank?"

"How much do you need?" the fat man asked, without actually opening the door wide enough for him to see inside.

"Two thousand US dollars."

"That is a lot of money. What makes you think we hold that much?"

"He said you would be able to help."

"Well, yes, but it won't be cheap. We have to make a living, after all."

"Of course," Rye agreed. "How much?"

"What type of card is it?"

"American Express."

"Ah, that is unfortunate. It is the most expensive card. Mastercard or Visa would have been better. But for you, I can do it for thirteen percent of the transaction fee."

It wasn't like he had a choice, and he knew full well had he said Visa or Mastercard it would have been just as unfortunate, and the same thirteen percent. "That's fine," Rye said.

"Good. Good. Come in."

The fat man stepped aside to allow him into the apartment. It appeared to be a single room, with one chair and a desk in the center, no other furniture, no decorations on the bare white walls. There was another door at the far side of the room, which presumably went through to the strong room.

"Sit. Sit," the fat man said, gesturing toward the chair, while he took the other seat, behind the desk. "So, what brings you to our beautiful country?"

"We're climbers," Rye said, sure the man must have heard the same thing with every shakedown.

"Ah, off to conquer the great peaks? You must be excited. Surely a once-in-a-lifetime experience for someone like you?"

"Something like that," he said, taking his wallet from his back pocket. The whole situation was a bit surreal, but he handed the card across.

"Ah, straight down to business. I can appreciate that," the banker said, taking a portable card reader from the desk drawer. He put Rye's card into the machine and punched in the sequence of numbers, turning it to him to put in his pin number. The screen said the charge was 2,260 USD, which, if his mental arithmetic was right, was thirteen percent. The fact he hadn't used a calculator to check his math convinced Rye the border guard had called through and he was in on the sting. Well, it wasn't his money, and it wasn't as though Rask couldn't afford it, so he punched in his four-digit pin, and a few seconds later the machine spooled out a receipt.

"Wonderful," the fat man said, tearing it off and offering him the top copy. "My assistant will be through with your money in a moment. Can I get you something to drink? Tea? Coffee?"

"I'm good," he said, not wanting to prolong this peculiar experience any longer than he absolutely had to.

It took another uncomfortable minute of silence before the door behind him opened and the boy Rye had seen panhandling downstairs came through carrying a wad of notes.

He gave them to the fat man, who counted them out.

They looked like they'd been spent fifty times over and were close to worn out, but they'd spend just fine and that was all that mattered. "Two thousand dollars," he said, laying the last note down on the desk. "A pleasure doing business with you." He pushed the well-used notes across the desk to Rye.

"It's certainly been an experience," Rye said, standing up. "This has to be the strangest bank I've ever been in."

"Oh, is that what Metok called it?" the fat man said with something approaching a grin. "That's an interesting choice of words."

Isn't it just, Rye thought, but didn't say out loud.

He assumed the man's primary business was drugs, or at least contraband, which made sense, given his close ties to the border guard.

The fat man showed him to the door, but didn't follow him down the stairs, "You'll forgive me," he said, by way of good-bye, "but this body of mine wasn't made for climbing." He laughed like he'd just said the funniest thing in the world.

It took Rye half the time to get back to the border crossing because he knew where he was going. He caught himself looking over his shoulder more than once to be sure he wasn't being followed. The thief's paranoia was contagious.

Carter was leaning against the side of the truck, smoking and talking with the guard.

The others were still in the SUV, parked up on the other side of the gate.

"I trust you had no problem finding the bank?" the guard said as he approached. Rye noticed that his companion had his own semiautomatic in his hands and was watching him carefully. Having a gun pointed at him wasn't a feeling Rye ever wanted to get used to.

"Fine," he said.

"You have the money?"

"I have the money."

He handed over the thick wad of used notes.

The man couldn't hide his smile as he counted through it to be sure Rye hadn't skimmed any off the top. "That'll do nicely," he said, a parody of the old advert, and slipped the dollars into his pocket. He nodded toward his companion, who disappeared into the gatehouse and a moment later emerged with a stamped visa and various permissions for a climbing expedition into the region.

"Your paperwork seems to be in order," he said, handing them over.

FIFTY

They crossed the border into Bhutan.

The farther they drove on the Lateral Road, the more obvious it became just how unstable the geology of the region actually was. Rye saw the stark evidence of landslides along the roadside, with great boulders broken up onto smaller shale by the road crews who had been brought in after the monsoons to clear the debris. There were vast stretches of cliff face that had been propped up with timber from the endless forests of the region.

None of it looked particularly permanent.

The climb was gradual, but the thinning of the air was obvious.

More unnerving than the unstable slopes towering over them were the frequent one- and two-thousand-foot sheer drops where the roadside fell away into nothing. In places the distance between the truck's wheels and the drop was down to a matter of inches. Carter drove in absolute focused silence, eyes never leaving the narrow road, never risking more than twenty or thirty miles an hour, and often coming down as slow as five or six when tight switchbacks demanded.

The views were breathtaking, the drops never less than dizzying.

Rye realized he had spent the last forty minutes gripping the fake leather hand grip above the open window as though his life depended upon it. It offered a curious illusion of an extra layer of safety, as though if he held on tightly enough it could stop him going over the edge—or at the very least pull the truck back from the edge. He was good with heights, naturally so. He'd clung onto some of the highest structures in the world with nothing more than his fingertips between him and the drop and it hadn't fazed him, but this was different. It wasn't down to his skill, it was all about someone he barely knew and hardly trusted not taking them off the road.

He didn't like it.

Up ahead of them the mountains loomed.

As they neared, it grew more and more obvious that the road was leading them toward a ravine. The asphalt had been replaced by an immense iron two-way girder that had been set into the mountainside itself.

"We're going over that?" he asked.

"Just don't look down," the thief told him.

"It's okay, I kinda like heights," Rye reassured him.

"I was talking to myself," Carter said, and actually managed a glimmer of a grin.

"Of course you were."

The sound of the wheels on the road changed as they went from stone to metal. Rye looked down. There was something incredible about looking down upon the world from such a height: The tops of the bamboo forest far below them looked like blades of glass rippling in the breeze. The shades of green and brown were all subtly different, like the weave of a beautiful rug left out in the sun to fade.

It took them less than five seconds to traverse the pass. "That wasn't so bad," Carter said as they reached solid ground again.

All along this stretch of road Rye saw colorful prayer flags strung up like bunting. "I asked someone about those, back in Phunt-sholing," Carter said, following the direction of his gaze. "Travelers string them up in thanks for their safe arrival. They are all over the region. They are supposed to bless the mountains. The different colors mean different things. There are five colors, each represent-ing one of the five elements, and the five pure lights."

"It's as good a faith as any," Rye said.

"Better than some," Carter agreed. He didn't need to say which he didn't consider worth believing in. Or perhaps his disdain was for all of them. It was hard to tell.

The next pass was considerably worse; first, because of the angle of elevation, with the truck tackling an almost sheer gradient and, second, because they weren't on reinforced iron girders this time, but rather a single-wide wooden bridge that seemed to be balanced precariously on top of felled trees held together by hemp ropes. It was more than five times the span of the iron bridge, too.

The width of the pass meant a fierce wind blew all around them.

"I'm not loving this," Carter mumbled, coming down low in the gears. The old truck was stick shift, which forced a greater control on him, but meant he was constantly aware of the engine's responsiveness beneath him.

The seemingly makeshift bridge held, but Rye couldn't help but imagine the same precarious traverse during the true monsoon season, with the wood slick with rain and the winds whipping the downpour into the windshield faster than the wipers could sluice it away. The mountains would have been impassable.

He looked in the rearview mirror and saw Vic driving the SUV. He seemed at ease with the treacherous conditions, though, like Carter, wasn't pushing the car, content to get to their destination whenever they got there.

More and more frequently a burst of static in his ear would signify the loss of connection back to Byrne in the US. And the more remote their route, as the road took them through twists and turns up and down the mountain ranges, the harder any sort of sustained communication with the space archaeologist became until it was finally pointless. Rye took the earbud out and pocketed it as they crossed another pass. This time the forests down below appeared to be some sort of orange plantation, the fruit ripe for the picking.

"The temple's got to be somewhere around here," he said, looking for some sign of a road or track leading off the one they followed.

"Another hour or so," Carter said. "I've got the coordinates logged in the GPS. It should ping before we pass it."

During the next hour the drive became more and more grueling, the demands on Carter's concentration incredible. But he didn't complain—unlike the old truck's engine, which did nothing but bitch and moan its way up and down the steep roads. "I don't mean to point out the obvious," Rye said, tapping the fuel gauge, "but that red line, that's a bad thing given the fact I can't remember the last time I saw a gas station."

"I'm painfully aware of it," the thief said. "There's a couple of gas canisters in with the gear in the back, but right now we're looking at fumes long before we reach our destination, even without the detour to the Ahnenerbe temple. Byrne's calculations didn't account for the demands the constant ascent and descent would put on the engines. Worst case, we get out and walk a bit sooner than we planned."

Rye couldn't tell if he was joking, though the landscape promised to transform a bit sooner into something approaching days of punishing trek if they were forced to abandon the vehicles.

Off far, far in the distance, a white horizon foreshadowed the glacial peaks of their ultimate destination. They were still a full day's drive and more from their intended base camp.

FIFTY-ONE

The temple was half a mile off the road.

The short trek was a taste of what the hostile environment had to offer them. With the thin air, it was more debilitating than it would have been under ordinary circumstances. The small temple was the only building for miles around, sheltered in a cleft in the valley several hundred feet down the mountainside from the road.

As they approached, Rye couldn't see what was supposed to be so remarkable about it. It looked like nothing more than a small round chapel set in miles of grassy tundra. It wasn't until they were much closer that he began noticing some of the more macabre details of the façade, including curious little gargoyles and more demonic faces that seemed to peer out through the stonework.

The way the sun reflected against the walls emphasized the dark hollows of their empty eyes.

"I guess this is what Byrne meant by saying we needed to see it," Rye said, as the thief tried a heavy iron-banded door that hadn't been opened in half a century.

"Not even close," Carter Vickers said as he went inside.

Rye followed him in, needing to duck slightly to negotiate the low lintel. Inside was dark, but the dusty light filtering in through the three windows along the side wall revealed a vault that appeared to have been fashioned from bones. Rye moved deeper inside. Not just bones, he realized. Children's bones. They were so small, nowhere close to fully formed. There were femurs and tibias, jaws and skulls, and so much more. The ceiling was a latticework of discolored femurs that formed an oppressive ivory crisscross vault overhead, while the walls were row upon row of tiny skulls piled one on top of another. None of the skulls were broader than the span of his outstretched fingers. Children. Several were missing jawbones. The fontanel of others had been caved in, bearing the wounds of whatever had killed them.

The altar had been constructed from rib cages, the brittle bones interlaced to create a stronger support, with more of those skulls, many misshapen, Rye saw, used as ornamentation.

But what stopped him dead in his tracks was the insignia, which he described for the benefit of the Byrne, who was back listening in his ear. *"Irminsul,"* the other man said. "Irmin was an aspect of Wodan. Odin to us. In Old Norse it means Jörmunr, and linguistically, Jacob Grimm believed that Irminsul meant The World Tree, or The Great Pillar of Odin. It was the emblem of the Ahnenerbe."

It was only then that Rye noticed more Norse runes had been incorporated into the construction of the place, including the life rune, another sigil with strong links back to the Germans' obsession with the occult.

"It's an Aryan temple," Rye said.

"It's ghoulish is what it is," Carter contradicted him.

"It's a reminder that we are walking in the footsteps of men and monsters," Vic said from the doorway. And that was hard to deny. "There is no distinction between the two to be made."

"These were people obsessed with the idea that this stuff, the Ark of the Covenant, the Spear of Destiny, the Holy Grail—they believed they were literal treasures that could be found, their powers harnessed," Byrne said in their ears. "Remember, the Ahnenerbe believed that Aryans were a creation of the Black Sun—this superior race was descended from aliens. They were searching for the divine, and in this case, the divine, more often than not, originated in a galaxy far, far away. They came here looking for their Aryan forefathers, in hidden cities like Shambhala and Agartha, as well as for the fossilized remains of giants to prove the World Ice Theory. Is it any wonder they build a temple in their honor?"

"From dead children," the thief said.

"It just gets more and more batshit," Rye said, shaking his head as he crouched down beside a peculiar construction of bones that had caught his eye. There appeared to be several rather crude triangles carved into four of the bones; a triangle divided into two horizontally, the point facing up, another identical divided triangle inverted so that the narrow tip pointed down into the ground, and two simple equilateral triangles, again one tip pointing to the ceiling, the other the ground. There was a fifth bone with what looked like a crude wheel with eight spokes.

"The elements," Vic said, seeing what he was looking at. "Earth, air, fire, and water. The wheel represents the spirit. They come together in the traditional pentagram. Together they are the essence of all things, including the physical body."

Around the small chamber they found several other similarly carved bones, some bearing runes, but if there was any doubting the identity of the temple's builders it was dispelled by a single splash of light illuminating the black sun hidden within the floor tiles, the black sphere radiating jagged streaks of black lightning.

"This place is seriously creepy," the thief said, holding up a baby's skull. It was vaguely deformed, suggesting the plates of bone had been damaged during a forceps birth and had never managed to settle back into place. It looked almost alien in nature. He put the skull down. Iskra hadn't said anything since she set foot in the place. The quiet Russian had found something.

"Did you know about this?" she said finally. She wasn't talking to any of them. She had her finger to her ear and was talking to Byrne, who answered, "I told you, you needed to see it for yourself."

"See what?" the thief asked, then saw what the Russian had found. "That can't be real."

Trapped within the middle of the wall, half hidden in shadow, was a complete skeleton that stood a full three feet taller than Rye, with huge elongated phalanxes and phalanges, massively oversized fibulas and tibias that were twice the length of an average man's, a spinal column that seemed to contain a dozen more vertebrae than was human, and curved exaggeratedly at the top as it supported a massively distended mandible on its axis. The head was like nothing Rye had ever seen outside of a cinema. It was more reptilian than human, a bulbous dome with slanted eye sockets and an enormous cavity in the center that was lined with fine filaments of crab-like bones where there should have been teeth.

"They called it Vril," Byrne said, giving the thing a name. "They believed it was proof of alien life and the link between their ideals and the so-called Übermensch, the Aryan superman. The Shrine of the Black Sun, which is what you are standing in, was constructed to hold the bones discovered by Edmund Kiss on his first expedition into the region. Kiss claimed that even in death the bones of Vril contained an essential energy we lack the ability to harness, so call it magic in our ignorance. Blavatsky had another name for the thing. Writing almost half a century before Kiss found proof of its existence, she named it Asuras."

Rye said, "This thing is Rask's demon?"

FIFTY-TWO

They didn't mention the Vril as they returned to the vehicles.

It was too much to think about—certainly too much to give credence to. But all Rye could think was that they had just witnessed a colossal fraud. The bones couldn't possibly be real. There was no such beast, demon, or whatever the fuck that thing had been. There couldn't be. There was no place for that in any sort of evolutionary history of the world. The Nazis had built that thing to perpetuate some grand hoax. That was the only thing that made any sort of sense to him. Though why do it so far from civilization? And why, eighty years on, hadn't any of the locals torn the place down? There were signs very much to the contrary that suggested some made pilgrimages to the strange little bone shrine, offering their devotions to the eerie skeleton.

For the next couple of hours they were the only two vehicles on the road.

Until they weren't.

Carter had pulled over to the side of the road and was busy siphoning gas into the tank from one of the two canisters, when Rye marked the three black, ant-like smears against the green of the mountainside. He watched them for a full minute and more, shielding his eyes from the sun. It was hard to be sure. They were a long way back.

"Do you see them?" he asked Carter as he finished and wiped the mouth of the canister with a rag. The thief joined him at the hood and followed the direction of his finger as he pointed the tiny staccato smears off in the distance.

"Not sure," he said. "What am I looking for?"

"Three cars. At least I think that's what they are."

It took him a moment, and in that time the front car navigated a switchback, the sunlight reflecting off its windshield, confirming what they were looking at. "I see them. It doesn't mean they're following us."

"Three cars, close together, driving faster than we dared. It doesn't mean they *aren't* following us, either."

He reached into the cab for his earbud, hoping he'd be able to raise Vic on the comm-link. He slipped it into his ear and pressed down on it to wake the little device from sleep, only to be greeted by a harsh burst of static. "Shit," he said. Carter didn't have to ask what was wrong.

"Come on, we've got to catch up with the others. We're not letting them pick us off one by one."

"Assuming they are following us."

"You know they are as well as I do," he said. And he was right. Rye knew they were. He watched them a little while longer, wishing he'd thought to add binoculars to their kit. In terms of weapons, ice axes against Uzis didn't feel like much in the way of a fair fight.

They drove faster than was safe on the narrow road.

Rye didn't look out of the side window. He didn't want to know how close they were to the edge. The engine whined frequently as Carter burned through the gas, closing the distance between them and the SUV. It took them ten minutes of reckless driving and one eyes-closed moment as the thief negotiated another girder bridge, before they saw the black SUV on the road up ahead of them.

Carter flashed his lights, but the afternoon sun killed any chance of Vic seeing them from that distance. He was reluctant to hit the horn because he had no idea how the sound would travel and the last thing he wanted to do was let on that they knew they were being followed. It was their only slight advantage in the grand scheme of things, so he wasn't about to waste it. Instead, he pushed his foot flat to the floor, gassing the engine again, and changed up through the gears. The old truck rattled as though it was struggling to hold itself together.

They could hear the groans of the wooden sidings inside the cab as well as the tormented shrieks of the chassis as the suspension struggled to cope with the rutted road.

Carter flashed the lights again as the distance closed between them.

This time Vic answered with a flash of his own, or rather three sharp flares of the brake lights as he slowed. There wasn't room for the two cars to pull up side by side, so Vic slowed to a halt in the middle of the road and clambered out.

Carter pulled up behind him.

Rye was out of the cab before the truck had stopped moving. "We've got company," he called, all thoughts of alien bones forgotten as he pointed back over his shoulder. He walked toward Vic. "Three cars. Coming fast."

"How far back?" the big man asked.

"Maybe fifteen miles behind us, it's hard to tell." It sounded like a long way, but in reality that meant they were no more than twenty minutes behind them, and if he was wrong it could be a lot less than that.

Vic rubbed at his scalp, thinking.

The chase had taken them around the curve of another peak,

meaning there was no way for Vic to confirm his guess. "Three cars?"

Rye nodded. "Four people per car, that's a likelihood of twelve guns being pointed at us in the next fifteen minutes or so." Vic turned his attention to the road ahead. Rye realized he was looking for a choke point, somewhere they could turn the savage terrain to their advantage. Four against twelve wasn't great odds, but they were hardly insurmountable if they turned the mountain to their advantage.

He tried to look at the mountainside the same way, but he wasn't a strategist and had no experience of combat in any way, shape, or form, not even on the PlayStation.

It was hard to see anywhere that wasn't horribly exposed, and impossible to see anywhere they might hide the two vehicles.

He wished he knew what Vic was seeing.

"There," Vic said, pointing.

Rye wasn't sure what marked that particular spot out from the rest of the road, or why it was preferable for what could well be their last stand, but he nodded like he could read his mind. Vic seemed to be pointing at yet another stretch of road where the rock was being reinforced by a timber wall. "We have ropes and hooks in the truck?"

Rye nodded again.

"Then let's go and bring down a mountain on their heads."

FIFTY-THREE

They retrieved a fifty-foot-long coil of high-tensile rope, a metal carabiner to lock it off, and two of the ice axes.

The makeshift retaining wall was constructed of tree trunks, most of them so large Rye wouldn't have been able to interlace his fingers if he tried to wrap his arms around them. They towered over him, easily twice as tall again as he was.

He didn't want to imagine the wall coming down on top of them before they got out of there.

The trunks were bound in place by a chain-link wire fence that worked like a safety net, pinning them against the loose rocks behind them.

Ideally, they would have used wire cutters to clip through the fence but, forced to improvise, Vic hacked away at several of the links with the ice ax while Rye and the thief worked the climbing rope behind the thick bole of a tree trunk. It wasn't easy, but by dint of the natural materials they were working with they found a part of the wooden barrier that didn't fit flush to the cliff. Rye fed the fused nylon end of the rope behind the wood inch by inch, willing it to keep going even as it butted up against the stone. He worked it, teasing it up and down and up again, looking for the kind of angle that would force the hard head of the rope to go sideways because it couldn't go forward.

No one rushed him, but he was conscious of the seconds ticking and what each one meant.

It took more than two minutes for him to finally work the rope around the trunk and lock it off.

Moving quickly, Carter tied off the other end around the truck's tow hook.

"How's it going with the fence?" he asked the big man as he labored with the ice ax. Vic had fallen into a rhythm, no longer just hacking savagely at the chain link. He rocked back on his heels, raised the ax, turned his shoulder, and stepped forward into the swing, metal hitting metal, rocked back on his heels, raised the ax again, turned his shoulder, and stepped forward into another swing. He didn't break rhythm, answering on the backstep. "Painfully slowly," he admitted. "But hopefully there are enough broken or weakened links that the metal will sheer beneath the sudden weight."

It was fine in theory, but they didn't have the luxury of testing the hypothesis; their pursuers would catch up with them in less than ten minutes. Which wasn't long and definitely not long enough.

Rye laid a hand on Vic's muscular shoulder, causing him to break the rhythm finally. "It's got to be enough. We need to go."

He didn't argue. He handed Rye the ice ax, but instead of

walking back to the SUV, Vic took another step up to the cliff and gripped the chain-link fence with both hands, curling his fingers around the metal links. He breathed deeply, once, and straightened, drawing his shoulders back before putting every ounce of strength he could muster into one savage pull, trying to tear the fence apart by sheer force of will.

Rye heard several of the links give, the metal snapping beneath the strain.

Satisfied, Vic clambered back into the SUV.

Iskra had taken over driving duties.

She was already moving before the big man slammed the passenger door.

Rye tested the rope, then rushed around to the driver's side. It was his turn to spell Carter, who was already in the passenger seat waiting. He gunned the engine, easing down on the gas. The truck rocked forward, taking up the slack. The rope locked tight, and for a moment Rye worried the engine wouldn't have the torque to do the job. He gave it more gas. The engine strained against the sheer weight of the tree and the resistance of the chain-link fence. Then suddenly a vicious snap cut across the engine's whines and the truck lurched forward, bringing the tree and half of the mountainside with it.

Half a dozen of the retaining timbers tore away from the cliff wall as the center piece was pulled free.

The wire fence buckled beneath the incredible weight, and within seconds the massive tree trunks had spilled out onto the narrow road, leaving it impassable.

Huge boulders—the smallest still bigger than his head—spilled out behind the trees as the years of monsoon undermining the slope's integrity gave way to gravity. Tons of rock and mud slid onto the asphalt, tearing more trees away from the retaining wall as the safety net ripped apart.

The noise of the landslide was a huge elemental scream of the land crying out.

Rye gave the truck more gas, dragging the tree trunk clear of the debris before he killed the engine and hopped out to cut the rope free. By the time he was back in the cab, Vic's SUV was five hundred yards away. He looked back at the debris blocking the mountain road. It might not stop them, but it would slow them down.

A lot.

That was preferable to going into a gunfight with an ice ax.

He coiled the climbing rope up and put it back with the rest of their gear.

They had a long road ahead of them, and none of it was meant for driving on.

FIFTY-FOUR

The next town was more than six hours' drive, and it was more like a shanty town, with buildings of plywood, bamboo, corrugated metal, and sheets of plastic, than anything like a permanent town. There were no satellite dishes or other signs of the modern world. They approached from above, the temporary settlement spilling out across a valley floor where the small river provided the stuff of life. Rye saw yaks grazing in the fields and, a little way removed from them, a campfire with a number of people gathered around it, either cooking or warming themselves. It was impossible to tell from that distance.

Their original plan had been to rest up at one or two of these temporary villages on the way to base camp, but with Cressida Mohr's mercenaries behind them, the idea of standing still felt like suicide.

Rye did see cars, though: not many, but enough to convince him they'd be able to source more gas for the remainder of their journey.

He followed the SUV into town.

They passed children playing barefoot in a stream. Childhood was hardly the same everywhere in the world, but the essence of fun was. An old man with a face weathered to resemble a wrinkled prune watched the children play while his wife scrubbed away at trousers in a steel bucket. Her backbreaking work had got the soap lathered. A younger man came out to join the older man, taking up a seat on a stool beside him, and together they smoked something herbal. This was life, so different from the one they'd left behind Stateside, but essentially so familiar just the same.

They saw more people as they drove deeper into the shanty dwellings, but there was no sign of any gas station, makeshift or otherwise.

Rye slowed, pulling up alongside a group of men sitting roadside. He wound down the window and asked, "Do any of you understand English?" to blank stares. "Gas?" Then he tried, "Gasoline? Petrol?" And patted the outside of the truck's door, miming driving. It was crude, but seemingly effective as one of the old men pointed farther along the road. He nodded, encouraging them to go. Rye nodded his thanks and rolled on deeper into the shanties.

The place reeked of humanity: bodies unwashed, or at least lacking the perfumed deodorants and those other masks he associated with cities—everything from the unique signatures of gas and exhaust fumes to the fusions of every cooking style imaginable and coffee and beer and everything he took for granted. The smells coming in through the truck's window were far more natural: manure from the yaks in the fields, the aromas of meat cooking in a fire pit, and the sweats and natural oils of every man, woman, and child living together in these lean-to houses.

Several, he noticed, hadn't bothered with roofs, making him think that come the monsoon rains they'd be long gone, moved on to some other valley floor out of the path of the rains.

Without being able to speak Dzongkha or Nepali, Rye had a feeling they were going to be shit out of luck. Still, he drove on, slowly, looking for anything that might pass as a gas station. Off to the left he saw a larger building, still very much temporary with walls of corrugated steel, but as he drove past half a dozen kids came streaming out of the door. A younger woman followed, lingering on the threshold. She was dressed in a white blouse and jeans. She had blond hair and a tanned but very European complexion. Rye leaned out of the window and called, "Excuse me?"

earning a smile and a wave from the woman. She came over to the truck.

"Do you speak English?"

"I do. So do all of the kids. It's the language of school lessons here. Are you guys lost?"

"I hope not," Rye said with a smile. "We're looking for somewhere we can get gas," and seeing the confusion on the schoolteacher's face added, "petrol."

"Ah, you need Sonam, he's on the edge of town. His place looks like a scrapyard. You can't miss it, just keep on down this road until you're leaving town. There's a huge red corrugated iron wall—it's rust, not paint—that's Sonam's place. Don't let him fool you, he speaks English perfectly well. I should know, he's my greatest achievement." She grinned, but her pride was obvious.

"That's great, thanks. Can I ask how long you've been here?"

"Here, six months; with the tribe, closer to six years now. We're nomadic. We move two or three times a year, depending upon the severity of the seasons. I came over on a mission and ended up falling in love with the place. I'm not sure I'll ever go home again. Or at least back to Sweden. This is my home now."

"Nice."

"What about you guys? Trekking I assume."

"Climbing, up to the north in the glacial peaks."

"Good luck with that," the young teacher said, shaking her head. "Even getting to those peaks is an absolute nightmare. They reckon it's the toughest trek in the world. And then you intend to climb? You're braver souls than me."

"Thanks for those inspiring words," Carter said, leaning across to flash a cheeky grin at the teacher. "If this doesn't work out you should think about motivational speaking."

She laughed at that. "Now that's a thought. Anyway, Sonam can sort you out. And if you want, you're welcome to come back and join us. We've got a stew on the fire pit. Lhaden is a wonderful cook. She's been working on the stew all afternoon. It's lentils, rice, and vegetables spiced with chili peppers and yak's cheese, with chunks of meat." She didn't say what meat.

"We wouldn't want to impose."

"Nonsense. It would be good for the children to practice their English. It'll give them an excuse to show off."

Rye looked at Carter. They needed to eat. But that had to be offset against losing ground to the chasing pack.

"We won't be able to stay long," Carter answered for him, "but who can resist the lure of mystery meats?"

"It's a date. The kids are going to love you guys," she promised.

They followed the road through the rest of the shantytown, seeing more of the same, with older men watching while their women worked, until finally a long rust-red wall of corrugated iron came into sight. Rye couldn't see over it, even from the truck's elevated seat. He flashed his lights at Iskra in the other car, before he swung through the wide gap in the iron wall that served as a gateway. He could see what the teacher meant about a junkyard. There was scrap metal everywhere, with bits of car chassis and bodywork in various states of decay lined up to one side where a young man in his early twenties was working on them.

He watched them as they rolled to a stop.

Rye saw that he had a welder's torch in his hand, but no mask to protect his eyes. He killed the engine and clambered out of the truck, raising a hand in greeting as he did.

Carter got out the other side as Iskra brought the SUV into the junkyard behind them.

"We need gas," Rye called. "We were told you were the man we needed to speak to?"

He set the torch aside and walked over to them. Close up, he was a good-looking kid, but it was obvious he was closer to twenty than thirty. Rye scanned the junkyard, noting what appeared to be the body of an old Shell gas tanker up against the side of an office structure where Sonam made his home.

He said something to them, which Rye assumed was an "I don't understand" in his native tongue, so he answered, "Your teacher warned us you'd try that. She also said you were her best student."

"She's a terrible liar," Sonam said. "But she's sleeping with me, so she had to say that."

That earned a wry smile from the thief.

"So, you can help us out?"

"Sure, we've got gas." He pointed toward the huge cylindrical drum. "But like all good things, it comes at a price. Supply and demand, you Americans call it? I have something you want, and only I have it."

"That seems to be the way the world works," Rye agreed. "So how much?"

"For both vehicles?" Rye nodded. "Not cheap. We won't get another delivery before it's time to move out, so whatever I sell you I can't sell to my own people. It could be the difference between a couple of families making it to the next camp or not, so how do you put a price on that?"

"I'm sure you can manage to somehow," Rye said.

"It depends. Are we talking American dollars, Indian rupees, or Bhutanese ngultrum?"

"American," he said.

"Ah, see, then I need to get it changed into money I can spend, so that will be more."

"Of course it will," Carter agreed. "Just as if we'd said ngultrum, you'd have said American would be better."

"You are a cynical man," Sonam said, but he was grinning like he'd just been found out.

"How much?"

"Two full tanks? So, we're looking at what—forty gallons? Three hundred dollars."

Carter didn't even argue; he stripped three hundred in notes from the five hundred he'd got in his pocket and handed them over. "You should have said five hundred."

Sonam grinned, palming the notes. "Did I say three? I meant five."

"Nice try," Carter said, "but given your girlfriend has invited us for dinner tonight I figure three hundred's a more than adequate day's profit. Hell, I doubt you see that much money in a week."

"A month." Sonam's grin just grew wider, stretching into a proper Cheshire Cat smile. "Move your truck over to the tank and I'll take care of it."

They filled the truck first.

There was no pump mechanism to speak of, just a hose with a shutoff valve that worked by a system of basic fluid dynamics. Sonam fed one end of the hose into the truck's gas tank and opened the valve, letting it flow until gasoline bubbled out from the overfull tank. He shook off the end of the hose and wiped down the side of the truck with a rag before recapping the tank.

He repeated the procedure on the SUV.

It took no more than five minutes to fill both vehicles.

In that time, Rye decided to explore the junkyard. Sonam had a mongrel chained up to one of the stripped chassis. The animal showed no interest in him. It had a plastic ice cream container as a water bowl. The container was empty, the plastic stained brown around the side with a crust of something unpleasant. He took some of his own water and poured it into the container. The dog came forward hesitantly, not sure it could trust him, until its thirst got the better of it and the animal began to lap at the water.

"That was kind of you," Vic said, behind him. "I am learning more about you, Rye McKenna, every day we spend together. An explorer and an animal lover."

Rye knelt, holding out a hand for the dog to come forward and sniff in its own time. It didn't take long for the mongrel to creep forward a couple of tentative steps, and then he felt its wet nose nuzzling against the palm of his hand. Learning him. "Who's a good boy?" Rye said.

The dog quickly lost interest in him and returned to the shade beneath the metal struts of the chassis and settled down.

The thief had negotiated with the nomad to throw in two extra gas cans at no charge, meaning they at least had enough to reach Tangbi Mani, which would serve as the base camp for their trek to the world's highest unclimbed peak.

They'd worry about the whole "getting back again" when the time came.

They put the metal canisters in with the rest of the gear and secured the back.

Rye checked his watch. It was three hours since they'd brought the side of the mountain down. He had no idea how long it would take twelve men to clear the road, assuming they could without any specialist equipment.

They could be through already for all he knew.

"Come, then, my new friends. Let us go back to school and feast on Lhaden's stew."

"I don't know about you, but I'm so hungry I could eat a yak," Carter said, falling into step beside Rye.

"Funny you should say that," the tribesman said with that wicked grin of his fixed firmly in place.

"Don't tell me that," Carter told the other man, "you know the deal: what I don't know won't hurt me."

"There must be a lot that doesn't hurt you," Rye deadpanned, earning a belly laugh from Sonam.

The five-block walk back to the makeshift school building took no more than five minutes. It felt good to stretch their legs and work some blood through the muscles after so long cooped up inside the cars, but Rye couldn't shake the feeling that it was five minutes too long and they were going to regret not having the vehicles close by when they'd finished the meal. He'd tried to put it out of his mind, but caught himself looking back up the mountainside in the direction they'd come from, looking for any sign of those three black cars.

The road was empty.

Everything the Scandinavian schoolteacher had said about Lhaden's stew was true. The old woman truly was a wonderful cook. The simple flavors were a revelation, but besides the sheer amount of taste within the relatively simple dish, the real kicker was just how spicy it was.

"The chilies," Sonam said, licking his fingers as he wiped a piece of flatbread around the rim of his metal bowl. "The woman is a fiend with them. I swear she has no tastebuds left, so she puts enough in until she can finally taste them."

Rye didn't doubt it for a minute. But Hannah had been the same. She'd loved a good curry, the spicier the better as far as she was concerned. Thinking about her made him turn his gaze toward the higher peaks all around them. She would have loved this place.

Everywhere you turned there was a summit beckoning. There was so much good climbing to be had he could have lived in this high valley for a month without repeating a route.

"Penny for them?" Carter asked, coming to sit beside him.

"I'm not sure they're worth it," Rye said.

"I'm a rich man, I'll risk it."

"I was just thinking how much Hannah would have loved it here."

"How are you doing? I mean really."

"Coping," he said, which was the truth. "Mainly because I'm trying not to think about it. It feels like we've been running non-stop; it's only when we slow down I start to remember."

"I can't imagine. Honestly. But you need to know, we're basically family now. You're one of us. That means I'm the pain-in-the-ass little brother. Anything you need, if I can help, I will. You've just got to ask."

"I appreciate it," Rye said, and realized he did. The one thing he needed right now was somewhere to belong, and if Carter Vickers wanted to make out that Rask had put together some sort of dysfunctional family, well that was fine by him.

It was better than being alone in the world for the first time in his life.

"Hey, I'm not just the pretty face around here, I'm the heart and soul of the team. Vic's the muscle, and Iskra, well, she's just a fucking enigma, to be honest. She's not exactly talkative. She's been with us for two years. I know less about her now than I did the day she walked through the door and Rask introduced us. I'm not sure what her deal is, but she's saved my life half a dozen times already, and that's good enough for me."

"Mine too," Rye agreed, thinking back to the temple in Kathmandu. "But when we move on, who's going to look out for these people?" He inclined his head slightly toward the group of kids who had gathered around Vic to listen to him tell a story of his homeland. They hung on his every word. Rye couldn't help but wonder if he was the first black man they'd ever met, because every now and then one of them would reach out to touch his skin, like they thought the color might rub off.

"They aren't alone. Two or three hundred people live in this place."

"Against twelve armed men?"

"You can't let yourself think like that. The people chasing us aren't indiscriminate killers, they're hunting us. They want what we want. They're not looking to rack up a body count."

"You can't know that."

"Maybe not, but I have to believe it. And so do you. We can't be responsible for everyone."

But he wasn't listening to the thief. Rye pushed himself up to his feet and wandered across to join the schoolteacher at the fire pit.

The young Swede was perched on a log, leaning forward to heat something in the dwindling flame. "I need to tell you something," he said, sitting down beside her.

"If you're going to complain about the food, you need to take it up with the chef," she said, then saw Rye's expression and immediately changed. "What is it?"

"There are some very bad men chasing us," Rye said, knowing he sounded stupid, but knowing he had to warn the woman.

"How bad?"

"They killed people back in Phuntsholing."

"And knowing this you brought them to us?" There was no escaping the betrayal in the young teacher's voice. "We've got children here."

"It's not like that. They are after the same thing we are. They are ruthless, but they're not monsters. I don't think they'll hurt you, but they're going to want to know where we've gone, and how far behind us they are."

"What do you want me to tell them?"

Rye thought about it. "We're going to Tangbi Mani up in the north, tell them we're heading west, toward the Chinese border. Tell them we're going to climb Jomolhari. Or tell them nothing, simply tell them you don't know, that we didn't talk about it."

"Why are they chasing you?"

"It's a long story."

"Then at least tell me if you are the good guys or the bad guys," the teacher said.

"Doesn't everyone think they're the heroes of their own life?" Rye told her.

"If they ask, I'll lie for you. But if they hurt the children—"

"Then you tell them the truth. You do whatever you have to to protect those kids."

The Swede nodded.

He hadn't realized that Sonam was standing behind them, listening. "I will help you," he promised.

Rye shook his head. "It's too dangerous."

"Which is how I like it." He grinned, but Rye could tell he was terrified and this was his bravest face. "I will gather the hunters. We shall buy you time."

"I don't know how to thank you."

"Just tell your friend to buy the gas for five hundred on the way back."

FIFTY-FIVE

The hunters were tooling up as they left the shantytown.

There were thirty of them in total, most of them made up of the old leathery-skinned men Rye had seen sitting around watching their womenfolk do the work, but there were half a dozen young, incredibly lithe, muscular men, who looked like they could run for miles without breaking a sweat. They carried a mixture of makeshift weapons and farming tools, none of which would be a match for a bullet, but Sonam assured him they weren't about to do anything stupid like end up in a showdown. "We know what we are doing," he said. "This is our land. We hunt it every day."

"They aren't antelopes or wild pigs you're dealing with."

The tribesman laughed. "Last week we brought down a black bear and a snow leopard."

"Neither of which had submachine guns," he pointed out.

They made their farewells.

This time it was Carter's turn back at the wheel. The plan was four-hour shifts, driving through the night. With any luck they'd reach Tangbi Mani before dawn. Part of the journey would see them join the Trongsa-Yotongola Highway, which would be the first real road they'd drive since crossing the border.

They left the shantytown, pushing the truck on the open road to take advantage of the relatively good conditions to make time before they returned to the meandering twists and turns of the climb up ahead. The road ran parallel to the river for half an hour. Before long, mists had begun to gather in the basin around them, thickening quickly until, after another half an hour or so, the valley floor had been swallowed by thick primordial fog. Even with the truck's lights on full beam they could only see twenty feet beyond the hood, and with the sun going down it was uncannily like they were driving into another world.

"Do you think they'll be all right?" Rye asked eventually.

"You warned them what was coming. That's more than I would have done," Carter admitted.

"But do you think they will be okay?"

"I have no idea. But it's their choice. You didn't force anyone to play hero. If they buy us an extra few hours, that might be all the difference we need to find this place, get what we came for, and go home," he said optimistically. "And I'm all for that."

"You do realize it's all relative, right? We've got eight to ten days walking ahead of us once we reach Tangbi Mani, and we're talking six to eight hours walking a day, a fairly monstrous ascent, up into the glacial peaks, and then we've got to find this place, assuming it's there to be found.

"All we've got to go on is a view of some mountain peaks and some guesswork from Byrne based on satellite telemetry. This is the most grueling trek in the world, and let's not forget the sacred mountain is off-limits to climbers. We have no idea how the Bhutanese or the Chinese on the other side of the border police this place, if they even do, but one thing is for sure, we are entering nightmare territory in terms of physical endurance. You heard what Byrne said about those two Nazi expeditions; despite the shrine back there, we have to assume they didn't find what they came looking for, and they turned back empty-handed.

"And all of those stories about the haunted slopes, and everything Rask was saying about the demons supposedly protecting the place. The Asuras. You saw those bones as clearly as I did. If the Brotherhood are protecting this place, and they've got those demons for backup, I'm thinking it's safe to say it doesn't want to be found."

"And yet we are going to find it," the thief said confidently, "because we've got one thing all of those other explorers didn't have: we've got the map and Byrne."

"That's two things," Rye said, but he knew what Carter meant. He just wished that his enthusiasm for the hunt was as infectious as he thought it was. "I'm just saying that, even if we get a full day's lead on Cressida's crew, there's no guarantee that's enough. We could be in those peaks looking for a way into Shambhala for weeks—and that's assuming we actually find it, or that it's even there to be found."

The mist continued to thicken as the sky darkened, like his mood. Without the ambient light of civilization to counter the absolute black, everything around them lost shape and form as it was swallowed by the night.

They were forced to slow down even more as visibility reduced to almost nothing, trusting that the road would eventually lead them up above the mist.

Rye felt the gradient begin to increase. It was a gradual thing, but within half a mile they had climbed high enough to break out of the low-lying fog. The headlights transformed the drop-off from the roadside into a rippling blanket of white as far as the beams could see. The SUV climbed the road ahead of them.

They drove beneath the shadow of a mountaintop monastery, the sweeping rooftops of the nine towers lit by the silver moon. The place was so incredibly remote, the mountainside it was built onto so perilously steep it was hard to imagine the builders making the climb with all of those materials slung across their backs, but somehow it had been built, and now it offered the monks the ultimate in contemplative solitude. Or so it felt for at least three more miles, until they saw the lights of a restaurant up ahead, promising great burgers. There was a hotel a little farther on down the road and a sign that promised the Bank of Bhutan was only five minutes away. They were moving into the outskirts of Thimphu, the last major settlement before they reached base camp.

Rye saw the stark blocks of a huge hydroelectric plant that braced two peaks off in the distance lit up like Disney's Magic Castle, feeding the power back into the town. The plant generated every kilowatt of electricity used by Thimphu, keeping the lights on. It was an incredible sight after the seemingly endless mist and darkness, coming down again into what looked like a modern town.

The moonlight gradually lent more clarity and definition to the golden rooftop of the capital's incredible temple fortress. But for the engines, they were in a silent world. The temple was part of the core urban sprawl that was taking over the city. Rooftops, like parasols in the moonlight, spread out down the middle of the valley, the buildings very much confined to the geological possibilities the place offered.

The river split the city in two.

Rye was struck by the sheer size of the temple, with four immense corner towers like some medieval castle. A larger central tower behind the perimeter buildings was easily the tallest building in Thimphu, rising over all others. Houses clung to the sides of the valley. Even in the moonlight Rye realized the east and west sides of the valley were composed of forms of vegetation, with the river cutting through the middle seeming to demarcate two completely different temperate zones.

As they drove farther into the city, following the main highway that itself followed the river, the first thing he noticed was a distinct lack of traffic lights. He didn't see a single one all the way into the central business district.

Nightlife in Thimphu was almost quaint in comparison to Kathmandu, but he did notice a handful of bars along the roadside. He was watching a group of young male revelers negotiating the traffic, drinks still in hand, as his cell phone began to vibrate to an incoming message. Six texts came in quick succession as they came into range of the cell tower, all of them from Jeremiah Byrne.

Beside him, Carter's phone matched the vibrations as the same string of texts landed.

The thief checked his screen, then told Rye, "Earbuds in," as he retrieved his own from the glove box and popped it in.

Rye pressed down on his, hearing three short beeps inside his head as the connection was established. The next thing he heard was Byrne's voice.

"About time," he told the family's fifth sibling.

"I could say the same thing. You're way behind schedule. You should have been in range over four hours ago."

"They're not exactly country roads back there," Rye said defensively. "Some of those stretches were barely single lane, and you're looking at a thousand-foot drop if you put a wheel wrong. So, whatever Google Maps says, we weren't getting here any faster. Plus, we had company." He filled Byrne in about what had happened since they'd last talked at the shrine.

"I've seen the damage," he said.

Rye was about to ask how, but remembered Rask's private satellite. Byrne was a literal eye in the sky.

"I've sent you through maps and GPS stuff to help once you're out of the cars. I've got no idea how long we've got before we lose the signal again, given half the homes in this place don't even have running water, never mind flushing toilets, and I'm not hopeful, so listen up. Bad news first: the rain is coming. You're maybe twenty klicks from the edge of the storm, and the weather front is stretching all the way through Punakha into Gasa, though by the time you get far enough north the elevation means snow. We are talking full-scale Snowmaggedon. It's looking evil out there."

"Fan-fucking-tastic," Carter said beside him. "So, what's the good news? And don't say at least you packed your snow shoes."

"Man, I've missed you, Carter. These few hours of radio silence have been positively desolate. I was going to say, the good news is that I used the time productively. I've had the satellite over the White Peaks of the Seven Brothers, and there's definitely something going on there. There's marked variations in the vegetation coverage and color where it's below the permafrost, and subtle differences to the topography and geology of the main mountain itself. It's enough to suggest there was a settlement of some sort there."

"Was?"

"It's hard to say with any certainty without actual hands-on digging, but there's enough in terms of surface anomaly to assume we're looking in the right place for Shambhala, though whether it was ever the city Rask hopes it was remains to be seen. There's an area of spotting—I've sent you a scaled-up image—which looks to be looting holes, which makes me think the Nazis weren't far off when they were digging, but there's no evidence I can find yet to suggest they found a way down into the subterranean city. I've been running the satellite's hyperspectral camera and have found something I think *might* be worth exploring—that's the third image I sent. It would seem to be a large hominid fossil bed."

"A what?"

"An ancient graveyard," Rye said, translating for the thief.

"Not necessarily all that ancient, of course, given the extreme conditions of the mountain, but a hominid burial ground would suggest civilization at some time or other, so it is another marker that we're in the right place."

"What are the other files?"

"I thought you'd never ask. One is a hand-drawn map; now what's interesting about this is it's not supposed to exist. It predates d'Anville's map of the Himalayas, and seems to have been drawn during Napoleonic times, meaning it also predates the Blavatsky we're working with, but is considerably closer to d'Anville's than the Spanish missionary's fantasy thing replete with monster sightings."

"Where did you find it?"

"I didn't. Rask bought it off a private collector."

"How on earth did he know to even look?" Rye asked.

"Remember the names of the buyers our forger had sold copies of the Blavatsky to?"

"Someone else looking for Shambhala?"

"Someone else at least interested in the theory behind it. A legend hunter. A deal was done, money changed hands, and a facsimile of the original drawing was procured, and is now on your cell phones thousands of miles from where it has been locked away for the best part of seventy years. I still haven't told you the best part."

"Spill."

"The drawing's previous owner? One Edmund Kiss, the occult expert connected to Hess and Himmler, and most notably, Sébastien Guérin. The same Kiss who was part of the Nazi expedition into Tibet you're walking in the footsteps of. He was a key member of the Thule Society and the SS Ahnenerbe, his primary obsession was the Holy Grail, and according to our collector, Kiss believed this drawing to be the key to finding that fabled chalice."

"Forget Rome," Carter said, "it's like an internet argument, all roads lead to the Nazis."

"Eloquently put, Mr. Vickers." Vic's deep basso-profundo voice filled their ears, reminding them they weren't alone. "And the final attachment?"

"A satellite photograph, it shows differences in moisture levels in the underlying soil in the valley in the shadow of Gangkhar Puensum. Normally I'd look at plant life, try to see textual differences in the spectral imagery from their root systems. Stunted roots would suggest something down there, but given the glacial layer, it's almost impossible, but I have marked on it a pink fissure which runs almost half a kilometer through the valley bed and seems to lead to the unnamed monastery the satellite imagery threw up. It may or may not be anything, but I wanted to flag it up for you."

"Excellent work, Mr. Byrne," Vic said. "Truly excellent. One final question: Can you tell how far behind us our hunters are?"

"Do you have any idea what sort of vehicles I'm looking for?"

"They are black and driving in close formation."

"I'll look for them. It's dark, there are no streetlights, and the fog is thick back there. It might take a minute."

They continued to drive through the center of Thimphu toward a golden spire that appeared to be some sort of shrine.

Byrne came back to them. "They're still back at the roadblock, you brought half the mountain down. It's pitch-black out there, but they're working by headlights trying to get it cleared. It's hard to put a time on it, but I'd figure the next hour or so."

"And then they've got to deal with Sonam's hunters," Rye reminded them. "So, we're looking at being a good half a day ahead at least."

The first fat drops of rain hit the truck's windshield.

FIFTY-SIX

The rain carried on through the night.

They spelled each other behind the wheel, each taking turns to sleep for a few hours, though the old truck's seats were hardly built for comfort. More than once, eyes closed, Rye heard Carter curse out some animal crossing the road ahead of them. The rain made the road treacherous, and combined with the near-absolute darkness, lethal. The wipers couldn't keep up with the rain streaming down the windshield, and the headlights couldn't push on through the downpour, so they couldn't see where the road was taking them. The first time they crossed one of those precarious girder bridges Rye felt the wheels sliding away from under him as the truck aquaplaned across the slick surface. Thankfully the deluge meant he couldn't see the drop, and before he could think about it, the truck was on the other side and the sound of the wheels on concrete replaced the eerie *shwoosh* of the slide.

Beside him, the thief didn't so much as stir.

Either he was a lot cooler than Rye, given the circumstances, or he'd fallen asleep with his head up against the glass of the passenger window. The second time he felt the wheels lose their traction on the road, he steered into the skid and narrowly avoided ending up in a ditch.

And still the rain got worse.

The incessant drumming on the metal roof threatened to drive

him out of his mind, and with no radio he couldn't try to drown
it out with other noise. It wasn't restful, like listening to a summer shower on an old tin roof. It was frantic, filled with panic and
urgency. It was relentless, driven by an elemental madness.

It just kept on and on.

In several places the already-treacherous road was in danger of
flooding. The truck's high-riding suspension meant there was
good clearance between the underside of the vehicle and the gathering pools of water. Cars that rode lower were going to be in
trouble. And it was only going to get worse. Vast stretches of the
road were going to become impassable.

Rye finally grasped what the rainy season truly entailed—and
it was unlike any weather he'd experienced in his life.

Still, he drove on through the night, always going forward,
slowing down sometimes to a crawl that took them closer to base
camp every minute of every hour until dawn.

The first glimmers of sunlight brought golden fields to life all
around them.

They were stepped in tiers, with farmers driving teams of yaks
across them, already hard at work in the paddy fields. Incredibly,
if he craned his neck he could actually make out the first dustings
of snow farther up the same slopes. These wetlands were full of
wildlife and lush colors. Where the trees gathered in close to the
roadside, he saw a Tarai gray langur and its mate sheltering from
the torrential rain. The monkeys skittered away from the edge of
a branch as the vehicles ploughed by. Rye couldn't hear their hooting, but their agitation was obvious. The greenery of the mountain around them was too vivid, too lush, and too false, as though
a child had colored them with a crayon and only had chlorophyll
green in their box of colors.

And still Carter Vickers didn't stir.

The man could sleep through the end of civilization without
so much as a groggy, "What was that?"

Rye checked the coordinates on his phone. The battery was
running low. He had maybe five or six hours left before it would
need charging. Carter had turned his off, so that when Rye's died

they'd still have his. Likewise, Vic and Iskra had turned theirs off. With luck, that would give them enough battery life in one device to make it all the way to Gangkhar Puensum.

Not that he felt lucky.

The GPS on the phone wasn't tracking properly, and they'd lost Byrne hours ago with no promise that they'd be able to get him back.

"Time to go analog," Rye told Carter, who mumbled something about a waste of good sleep, but reached into the glove box for the map book. It took him a moment of thumbing through the pages and tracking the road from Thimphu toward Tangai Mani and Bampura to work out roughly where they were, and another few minutes of peering out into the rain to try and find some sort of landmark capable of proving his guess was right.

He led Rye from the main highway to a much smaller road and eventually a track that was in the process of turning back into mud.

The SUV had no problems negotiating the deteriorating surface, but the truck, with the extra weight and weaker engine, labored. The rain showed no sign of easing off.

"We're supposed to go out in that?"

"And walk for a week," Rye said cheerfully. "But worry not, it'll be snow soon enough."

"You're a strange man, do you know that?"

"I've been called worse," he said, following Vic toward base camp.

He didn't know what he expected, to be fair. But the reality was they followed the muddy road as far as they physically could, and then they had no choice but to go on by foot. They pulled off the track and parked up.

Vic clambered out of the SUV and ran over to them.

It would have been pointless to try and keep himself dry, so he didn't bother.

He rapped on the passenger window and gestured for the thief to wind it down. "We can't leave the cars here, they're a signpost for anyone following us."

"What do you propose?" Rye asked the big man.

"About two miles down the road there was an outcropping of rock, and beside it a bamboo copse."

"I saw it."

"I'm thinking we come off the road there and try and hide the vehicles."

"And walk two more miles in the biblical flood," Carter moaned.

The extra distance aside, it was smart thinking. They didn't want to simply abandon the vehicles by the roadside, as they were their only way out of here, but it wasn't like they could just park up outside some quasi-official trek company's yurt and join a tour, either. So, it was a compromise, extra walking for an improved likelihood their followers wouldn't immediately see where they'd left the cars and neutralize them. A few slashed tires out here would be the end of any hopes of escape should things go south. It didn't need to be any more spectacular than that.

Rye reversed, struggling to put the flatbed truck through even the most basic three-point turn, and headed back the way they'd come. It took the best part of ten minutes to reach the bamboo copse, though looking at it properly now—and knowing their purpose—it was hard to imagine it being a good hiding place. The cover it offered was thin at best. But it wasn't like they had a lot of choices, so he took the truck off the road, aiming for the channel between the rocky outcrop and the first shoots of the climbing trees, and kept going as far as he could with the wheels churning up mud and spinning, struggling for purchase.

"I need you to get out and push," he said, looking back over his shoulder toward the road. "We're getting no traction."

Carter nodded and climbed down into the rain.

He ran around to the back of the flatbed, slipping and sliding in the thick mud, and put his shoulder to the tailgate, banging twice on the car to tell Rye to ease down on the gas. The truck lurched forward a few inches, the wheels spraying mud, then rocked back into the deep grooves they'd cut.

He saw the thief rooting around in their gear and realized he was looking for something to brace the wheels long enough to get them out of the deep grooves. Carter settled for two of the wooden siding panels, which he worked free, and laid down in front of the wheels to give them something to bite onto as the truck lurched forward. This time when he pushed, Rye managed to get them moving again. Not far, but hopefully far enough.

Carter rooted around in the gear some more, retrieving one of the ice axes, which he used like a machete, to hack down some of the thinner bamboo to weave a makeshift screen to camouflage the truck. By the time he'd finished, Vic had parked up and Iskra had set about doing the same to hide the SUV.

It took them the best part of thirty minutes to weave halfway decent screens, and in that short time Rye noticed the effect on his breathing. He was a fit man. Thirty minutes of exertion wouldn't normally leave him breathless, tight-chested, and light-headed, but this did. It was the first real test of the altitude, and it felt like he was failing it.

They changed into a top layer of waterproofs inside the vehicles. There was no room for modesty. Rye didn't bother trying to turn his back as he stripped down and layered his clothing for the trek, stacking several thinner fabrics to allow heat to trap within the layers, and pulled the waterproofs on. He laced his hiking boots and climbed down out of the truck. He noticed Iskra Zima watching him.

They divided the kit up, each person responsible for their own gear and rations, with the group gear, like the camping gas burner that would act as their stove and the two tent frames, divided evenly between them.

An hour after they'd pulled off the road, they were ready to move out. The journey of a thousand miles begins with a single step. The walk facing them was considerably shorter, but with the rain lashing down, and the promise that as they climbed it would become a blizzard made it no less daunting. There was a reason this trek to the valleys around the White Peaks of the Seven Brothers was considered the most challenging in the world. The conditions were extreme, and the threats facing them along the way nothing short of deadly.

"Ready?" Vic asked.

Rye did a mental run-through of the equipment checklists to make sure he had everything. "Ready."

"Ready," the others echoed.

With that, they took that first step.

FIFTY-SEVEN

By midday on the second day the rain still hadn't stopped.

By the time they made camp on the third night, Rye was seriously beginning to doubt it ever would. Three solid days through the driving rain had reduced the world to two absolutes: rain and pain. Those three days had seen them climb over three thousand feet in altitude, reaching heights of thirteen thousand feet.

The third day was the worst, as the saturation of oxygen in their blood thinned out to the point Rye felt his breathing adapt, coming in slower, deeper breaths as his heartbeat quickened trying to absorb more and more oxygen with every breath he took.

It was a fatal trap.

The first stages in altitude sickness, as his body put all of its natural reserves into blood function.

Ideally, they would have had four days at this altitude before pushing on, to give their bodies time to adjust and adapt through long-term acclimatization. Rye knew the science behind what was happening to him: his body was slowing down nonessential functions, suppressing the digestive system among other things, to dedicate its energy on cardiopulmonary reserves until full hematological adaptation was achieved with the red blood count plateauing.

He did the math in his head. At this elevation it would take forty-six days for that to happen.

Forty-six days.

That wasn't going to happen. Not in any way, shape, or form.

He tried to convince himself it was the dehydrated trail rations that were tying his stomach up, but that was explained by the science, too. And over the next four days it was only going to get worse as they reached extreme altitudes nearing the death zone.

That twenty-six-thousand-foot threshold was higher than anything around them, but only just.

The summit of Gangkhar Puensum rose ahead of them, the entire mountain range forming an impassable wall across the horizon.

He was cold. He was wet. And he was miserable. But he was stubborn, and he was determined. They'd walked fifty miles from base camp in three days, through the worst nature had to throw at them.

Or so he thought.

As he sat on a boulder staring up at the slice of moon above the mountain, he felt the first snow against his face and knew it was about to become worse.

The altitude made sleeping difficult, too, which in turn made them tired, so each mile walked was harder than the mile before.

Carter emerged from the two-man tent they shared, to join him under the canvas awning.

"I've been checking out the map. That fissure Byrne found is maybe a day, day and a half from here, and the fossil graveyard looks to be half a day closer. That's the good news."

"I love the way you suggest a day and a half climbing into the glacial zone is the good stuff. Can't wait to hear what you imagine is bad."

"There's a choke point between where we are and where we want to be that, unless I'm mistaken, is little more than a rope bridge over a very fucking scary chasm."

"And we've got to cross it."

"How's your head for heights?"

"A lot better than yours, I'm guessing," Rye said.

"Not being funny, but everything hurts."

"And like Bon Jovi said, we're only halfway there."

"You do know that when Jon Bon sings he's being optimistic, right?"

"I just focus on the living on a prayer bit, that's my day-to-day these days." Rye grinned at the thief.

"I know I've said it before, but you are a very strange man, Rye McKenna."

"Can I ask you something?"

"Sure."

"Why did Rask pick you?"

"You mean, aside from my good looks and devil-may-care charm?"

"Yeah, aside from that. Why did you deserve a second chance? Why you and not some other thief?"

"That's a big complicated question, Rye. The short answer is luck. I didn't do anything special, or particularly worthy of notice. I'm a Brooklyn boy. I grew up with a group of friends who looked a lot like me, if you go in for stereotypes. The narcos did. There wasn't a crime that happened in our borough that they couldn't pin on one of us. Guilt didn't matter, and truth was relative. Basically, my takeaway was that even if we hadn't done this particular crime we were good for something else, so it just saved everyone a lot of time to lock us up before we could. You don't really need me to tell you what it's like being a young black kid growing up in gang territory. You're either some low-level grunt working the street corners to peddle their dope to broken people looking for an escape from the projects or you're one of the broken people trying to escape. I did things I'm not proud of. You're not looking at some gentleman thief, Rye. I've done some seriously bad shit in my life, and ever since Rask found me in Rikers I've been paying back for my luck."

"What did you do?"

"You don't need to worry. I've been straight for two years now."

"I'm not worried, and that's not what I asked," he said.

"I know, but it's the only answer you are getting. Maybe when we know each other better. But, honestly, all I want to do is forget about that other life. It's not who I am."

"Fair enough," he nodded.

They sat a while in silence, warming themselves on the last embers of the campfire. Rye kept his eyes turned to the wall of mountains waiting for them. He fancied he could hear the low whistle of the wind through the peaks, even from here, and wondered if this was the cause of the supposedly ghostly calls reported by climbers.

He caught a flicker of movement across his eyes: a shadow moving through the tree line. When he turned to better see it, there was nothing to see.

The sudden shift of balance as he leaned forward was enough to have Carter ask, "What is it?"

"I'm not sure. An animal probably."

"Yeti?"

"More likely a snow leopard," he said.

"Now, that's a comforting thought."

He kicked out the last remaining embers of the campfire, and when the thief looked at him, Rye just told him, "Better safe than sorry," which, all things considered, was hard to argue with.

With nothing but the moonlight to see by, he didn't see the creature again, but he was sure it was out there, watching them. Finally, with a long day waiting for them on the other side of sleep, Rye turned in.

FIFTY-EIGHT

He woke in the middle of the night to the sounds of the big cat attacking the tents.

Rye crawled out on his hands and knees in time to see Vic and the Russian lashing out with what looked to be one of Vic's thermal undershirts wrapped around the head of an ice ax, burning. It was crude but effective in terms of keeping the creature back. The problem was that its mate prowled the darkness a safe distance from the makeshift firebrand as Vic lashed out in big sweeping arcs.

The cloth wouldn't burn for much longer.

When it went out the snow leopard would pounce.

The big cat moved around the dark perimeter of the camp, so much pent-up strength in its body—but for it to have risked venturing so close to the tents the poor creature must have been starving.

Iskra, he saw, had a second brand balanced easily in her hand, ready to launch herself at the big cat if hunger got the better of it.

Carter emerged behind him and surprised Rye by immediately making a lot of noise and flapping his arms about like he was pretending to be a gigantic bird. It would have been comical but for the fact it was drawing the big cat's attention, which made it suicidal. "What the hell do you think you're doing!" Rye yelled at the thief, but in the moment the big cat had turned its attention to him, the Russian leapt into her attack.

Humans weren't meant to fight great beasts like this, armed or not. But Iskra's speed and skill with the fire defied reason. She was in so close before the creature could react to her threat, and had the wild cat by the jaw, every ounce of strength needed to prevent the snow leopard from turning those huge teeth on her before she thrust the burning brand at the creature's face, close enough to sear the fur. She held firm for a few seconds, then allowed the creature to bolt. It took off at a pace, scaling the side of the slope with shocking speed.

Iskra rose from her tight crouch to her feet and held the burning torch beside her, watching the snow leopard's mate as it howled, trying to decide whether to brave the fire or not.

It stayed back beyond the small circle of torchlight protecting the tents.

The few charred threads that remained of Vic's thermal vest fell away from the ice ax, those last orange embers rising into the dark sky as they burned out, and suddenly the only light was Iskra's.

"Shit." Rye heard Carter stumble in the darkness, followed by a deep-throated growl so filled with menace it chilled his deoxygenated blood and had his heart tripping.

Iskra moved toward where Vic had been, the four of them gathering to stand back to back, circling and watching the night for the deeper darkness of the big cat prowling around them. "This is wrong," the Russian said, surprisingly calm, given the situation. "The snow leopard isn't an apex predator. It should run. It should never attack."

"Do you want to tell it that?" Carter said. "Because it sounds hungry."

Rye wasn't listening to him. He heard a peculiar *chuffing* sound in the darkness beyond Iskra's torchlight, not a roar, not quite a growl. It was unlike any sound he'd heard. "There's a flare gun in the kit," he said, and without waiting for Vic to tell him no, Rye scrambled back toward the tents and their backpacks. The sudden movement didn't draw the cat toward him, which was a mercy. He crouched down on his hands and knees, rifling through the pack for the gun, which had worked its way down behind his clothes, but he found it and crawled back out of the tent. His eyes adjusted to the night. He could see the three of them, ten feet away, shuffling their feet as they scuffed the faint dusting of snow that had gathered beneath their feet, and beyond them the rippling in the darkness that was the snow leopard circling them.

Rye gripped the flare pistol in both hands, and aimed it close to the creature, but not so close as to risk burning it as the flare ignited and fired.

The flare whistled out of the muzzle, scorching across the ground as it blazed a trail across the campsite in the direction of the wild cat. The flare spat red flame and burned off a thick miasma of smoke.

The animal recoiled from the flame, startled and afraid. Mewling, tail between its legs, the snow leopard bolted away from the still-sizzling flare, following its mate up through the strata of rock that made up the rock face they'd sheltered beneath with the natural grace and dexterity of a creature born to these slopes.

Rye didn't dare move until the flare had burned itself out and, even then, it was only to retrieve the flashlight from his pack and inspect the damage. The big cats had shredded the side of the other tent, effectively rendering it useless in terms of protection against the elements.

Iskra got a fresh fire going.

"Something caused that poor creature to betray its base nature and attack us," the Russian said.

"I'm glad you didn't kill it," Rye said, seeing the wicked knife the Russian was using to split the kindling down.

"It is a majestic creature," Iskra agreed, "but that doesn't mean there won't be killing tonight. Whatever scared it is still out there."

"We take no chances. We sleep in shifts until first light," Vic said.

No one argued with him.

"You sleep," Iskra told them. "I will take first watch."

FIFTY-NINE

First light brought with it more horrors. These ones, of an elemental kind.

There was little that could be practically done to patch the second tent, meaning they were going to be forced to share the two-man berth in a roll-on roll-off rotation. That, at least, would mean someone would be taking watch through the night. But that was a problem for later. They struck camp and moved out.

The climb was much harder today, the conditions necessitating a change of gear into the heavy-duty kit. The temperatures had dropped starkly over the last forty-eight hours, with early-morning cold tipping the scales at minus fourteen, with a windchill making it feel closer to minus twenty. The biting wind chapped the skin around Rye's cheeks and lips, but the worst of it by far was how it felt going into his lungs: like an icy hand reaching down his throat to claw his insides out.

Every breath came at an increasing cost.

Every step took more strength from his legs than the one before, with the buildup of snow on the ground making it hard going. His calf muscles and thighs ached from dragging his boots out of the virgin snow time after time after time. The thin air and his shallow breathing had him convinced his heart was on the verge of seizing every time he drew in another icy breath.

There was no banter between the team.

The conditions demanded their full focus.

The savage terrain was only made worse by the snowstorm as the blizzard gathered in around them, the wind driving the flakes into Rye's face whenever he lifted his head to see where he was going. Most of the morning was spent looking at his feet and the yard or so of snow-covered ground ahead of him as he trudged wearily on.

His pack felt heavier with each mile.

It was as much about will as it was endurance.

All four of them shared the same core stubbornness that kept them moving forward. Always forward. But it wasn't easy. Visibility was reduced to nothing, the churning snow whipping up into their faces all the time. They knew that the twin peaks of the pass that Carter had identified as a choke point were up ahead, but where was anyone's guess.

All they could do was walk on.

Carter turned to look at him, the sun reflecting off the oily surface of his sunglasses. He didn't look happy. He said something, but the wind whipped away his words. He gave up trying to communicate, and leaned into the storm, trudging on.

There were no signs of the snow leopards on the slopes, or any other creatures.

The sense of isolation was absolute.

They might have been the last four survivors of a broken world.

An unblemished blanket of snow rolled out before them. Behind them, their footsteps were the only scars on the white landscape, carving a line of least resistance from where they'd started the day toward where they were going to end it. The fresh fall would erase all signs of their passage soon enough.

Over the next hour the winds worsened, making it a physical effort to move forward. Each breath became more and more labored. Rye couldn't feel his face. Any skin exposed to the elements had frozen to the point that it felt as though it was burning beneath the chill. He put his hand over his mouth, letting the warmth of half a dozen exhalations thaw his cheeks, but the second he took his hand away the bitter cold stole in worse than before.

They needed to find shelter.

There was no way they could keep forcing themselves to go on, not when somewhere up ahead was a wire rope bridge over a gaping chasm, where, in these conditions they'd be dead before they were halfway across.

Not that they'd make it halfway across.

Rye scoured the endless white for anywhere they might be able to take shelter: ideally a cave set into the side of the sheer slopes but failing that some sort of overhang they could shore up with part of the ruined tent to offer shelter to see out the worst of the snowstorm. Of course, that was working on the theory that it couldn't last.

Maybe it could.

This high up, the mountains didn't just have their own ecosystem, they had their own climate and weather patterns.

Reading his mind, Vic pointed off to somewhere he couldn't see because an icy blast whipped up a snow devil that swarmed in a gyring tornado-like vortex as it churned a path across the mountain before it blew apart, scattering across the rocks.

Head down, Rye forced himself to walk on, following the general direction of Vic's arm until he saw what the big man had seen; a slight hollow in the cliff face. It wasn't much, but it was better than nothing as part of the rock would shield them from the worst of the wind. Out there on the mountain the wind was the killer.

He dumped his pack, and along with the others, used them to build a windbreak that extended the natural shelter the rock offered. Vic took a pair of the walking poles and drove them into the frozen ground, using them as struts to support the ripped tent cloth, and within five minutes, with a lot of improvisation and no little frustration, they'd erected a very crude lean-to shelter.

Iskra used some of the bamboo she'd hacked away from the forest down below, and firelighters, to get a small fire going. The heat from the flames barely touched their skin, but as with the bags and the tent sheeting, it was more about building a barrier to keep the elements at bay than it was about building a proper fire.

The close confines forced them to huddle together, but that also allowed them to talk for the first time in hours.

"How far to the bridge?" Vic asked, rubbing at his cheeks to get the blood circulating through them properly.

The thief shook his head and shrugged a "how long is a piece of string?" shrug. "We're well out of my element here, big guy. I'd guess it depends how much ground we've covered this morning. Gut feeling? We might not make it all the way before nightfall."

"I don't want to be stuck on this side of the chasm when the sun goes down, given what happened last night. The more distance between us and the snow leopards' hunting ground, the better."

"It would have been much easier if we could just fly in," Carter agreed.

"Bubbles in your bloodstream, brains leaking fluid, choking on the shit in our own lungs, yep. Easier. But dumb."

"I know, I know, but still, a boy can dream. You'd think there'd be some sort of tech Rask could buy. I dunno, a big decompression chamber or something?"

"It only works if we know where we're looking and can get in and out fast. We've got no idea where the stone is. It could take us days up there to find it, and we wouldn't have the time to look. Fly in without acclimatizing and every minute you spend at extreme altitude the risk of edemas and embolisms increases to the point of certainty. I don't know about you, but given the choice between this and that, I'll take the discomfort of a long cold walk through a blizzard every time."

"You'll not catch me arguing with that," the thief agreed. "And seeing as we can't fly, let's be realistic. We could push on, but there's not much to be gained by breaking our necks in the process." Carter offered a surprising voice of reason. "We can't see where we're putting our feet, and somewhere out there there's an accident waiting to take one of us. I say we wait out the worst of the storm, eat now, and hope the conditions improve in a few hours."

"Pretty boy makes a lot of sense," the Russian said from the edge of the shelter. She had her back to them and seemed to be peering out into the heart of the storm. She was watching their back for followers—but who or what could follow them through that? *Nothing and no one,* Rye thought.

He hunkered down and pulled a ration sachet from the pocket

of his pack, rehydrating it with snow that melted quickly in a pot. The meal tasted like shit and had a basic consistency of congealed mashed potato. Whatever the packet promised, it was not steak and fries. But it filled a gap, and the four of them ate, waiting out the storm.

They didn't talk about what they'd found in the Shrine of the Black Sun. It was almost as though by deliberately not talking about the unearthly skeleton it simply didn't exist.

For two hours the blizzard showed no signs of relenting. Indeed, if anything, it worsened. The howling winds tore across the savage frontier. The closeness of their bodies and the shelter of the packs lessened the windchill; sitting still for so long brought their core body temperatures down far more than the relative drop of the windchill factor, meaning the cold wormed its way into the layers of air beneath their heavy-duty gear, the sweat turning cold against their skin.

They needed to move every few minutes to keep from freezing, but they were dressed for the elements, thick down-filled parkas and quality fleeces meant minus twenty wasn't any great hardship once the snow wasn't being driven relentlessly into their eyes and mouths as they struggled to breathe and battled for each step.

Long before the storm abated, they needed to move on. Rye found it hard to argue, least of all because they couldn't make a proper camp here no matter how alluring the seductive embrace of the shallow overhang was. They had to pray they would find better shelter closer to the pass. Even if they didn't brave the wire rope bridge, they needed to get as close to the choke point as possible before darkness came.

The uncomfortable truth was that the cold was sapping away their strength, and every day longer on the slopes reduced their chances of coming home again. They were on limited resources, with enough ration packs to get them through twelve days in the mountains, six out and six back again.

That was the cold hard math of the situation.

And that wasn't factoring in a lot of time for the search itself.

But desperation wasn't getting them through that pass before nightfall.

They followed another narrow gorge carved by glacial creep millennia ago. Where the snows had fallen away from the steeper sides red raw rock had been exposed.

The endless rise of the last few days into the snowcapped peaks was broken by a sudden sharp decline, which promised to take them down a thousand feet or more in a tight corridor of rock that went so far down the fresh scents of jasmine rose up to meet them again.

The climb down took them below the most ferocious teeth of the storm, the highest peaks sheltering them more effectively than the lean-to had.

As the snow thinned enough for them to see a fair distance, the twin peaks of the pass were a jagged cut across the fading sun. The red sky revealed a number of channels and gullies cut directly into the cliffs, each offering a different way to die—even though they promised the same ultimate end: a body broken against the bed of stones all the way down by the riverbed, thousands of feet below.

Rye stood as close to the edge as he dared, looking down at the rushing waters. The bridge was five thick wires stretched taut across the five-hundred-foot-wide chasm. Thin slats of wood had been threaded between the wires to form steps, though the distance between each slat was an uncomfortable stretch from the last, with the river raging away quite visibly between every step. Two thicker cables were strung across the gorge to form guide rails for them to cling to as they traversed the wickedly swaying wire bridge.

Below the bridge, an expanse of bare rock caught Rye's eye. A honeycomb of two dozen small caves appeared to have been hollowed out of the rock. The sunlight didn't penetrate more than a foot or so into the hive of caves. The mountains weren't about to willingly surrender their secrets—at least not so easily.

"What do you think?" he asked Vic as the big man joined him at the edge.

"Home sweet home," Carter answered for him.

Iskra joined them at the edge.

"Assuming we can make it to the other side."

"And there's a good half mile of almost vertical climbing waiting for us if we do," Rye said.

"You really know just what to say, my friend," the thief said.

"So, who's going first? I would say ladies, but I don't want to get slapped for my casual chauvinism."

"Age before beauty," Iskra suggested.

"So, you then? Great."

SIXTY

The first step was the most daunting.

The wooden plank gave slightly as Rye put his weight on it. The entire wire structure lurched wildly beneath him as his weight unbalanced it. The amount of sway, even this close to the anchor points, was terrifying. He didn't want to imagine what it was going to be like out in the middle.

Unfortunately, he wouldn't have to.

The second step put all his weight on the wire cords.

"What's it like?" Carter asked from the safety of terra firma.

"Why don't you come and find out for yourself?"

"I'm good. I'll just wait to see if you make it all the way across first," the thief said.

Rye knew he was joking, but that didn't help much as Carter's smart mouth pretty much echoed his own internalized sarcastic bastard who had plenty to say on the matter. An internal monologue ran through his head, concentrating mostly on stuff like *nice and steady, watch where you're putting your feet, don't trust the wooden slats, they're too thin, gently, gently, it's not a race,* and other gems of a newly frightened mind. Ten steps out into the gulf, too far to leap back if something went wrong, he hesitated. That hesitation turned into paralysis. There was nothing in it. A couple of seconds. But suddenly, he couldn't put his best foot forward.

He was frozen.

You know why, don't you? that internal bastard mocked, like he knew a secret and he couldn't wait to tell. *It's the first time since Hannah. That drop, it's nothing. A thousand feet at best. You've been higher. But this is the first time since her murder that you've had to face your fears. New fears. But they're yours just the same. You can't do this.*

"I can," he said, but what he really meant was he had to. That was different.

"You okay?" Carter called.

He looked down at his hands.

They were locked around the steel wire.

You're going to have to answer him, the bastard mocked. *If you don't, he's just going to come out here after you, and two people's weight on the cables changes the dynamic. Every step becomes a swing, every swing becomes a curve that snakes all the way back to the mountain, working away at the anchors. Enough swings and it'll be like you're trying to cling onto the back of a writhing serpent. And eventually something's got to give. He'll put a foot wrong, or you will, and if you're lucky you catch your balance, if you're not you slip between the cracks, and then what? By some miracle you manage to grab onto his hand and you're holding him, you're the only thing between him and that thousand-foot drop to the rocks and the raging river below. And we all know what happens then. So, answer him. Tell him you're fine. Tell him you're admiring the view. Tell him anything, just don't let him come out here.*

"Loose plank," he called back. "I'm good."

And he realized he was. All it took was one step to break the paralysis, and he could do that. Couldn't he? One step?

Yes.

He could.

Rye forced himself to let go with his right hand, transferring his weight onto his front foot, and stepped out across the two-foot gap to the next wooden slat. It was supple under his weight, threatening to give way, but it would hold. It might be different for Vic, he probably had fifty pounds on him. That might make a difference. "This one's rotting," he called back, "so watch yourself."

The next one was better.

By the time he reached the middle, they had maybe thirty minutes of sunlight left before darkness, and they all needed to be across.

The thing about the Himalayan night was that it fell, it didn't creep in like back in the cities.

It went from light to dark in a matter of minutes, and when that darkness came, it was absolute.

No one wanted to be tackling the wire bridge by flashlight. No one.

SIXTY-ONE

There was a narrow ledge stepping down the side of the cliff to the honeycomb of caves.

Rye led the way, moving carefully, his back pressed to the rock wall as he descended.

Again, the thoughts kept running through his head: Who would build such a construction? Because one thing the narrow steps proved beyond any possible coincidence, was that these caves were a man-made feature of the mountain. There was only one option that made any sense, and given what the last construction they'd done entailed, he was in no hurry to see what Kiss's expedition had left behind in the mountains.

"Careful," he told himself as much as the others as the sole of his boot scraped across loose shale. His head whipped around reflexively, making the beam from his head flashlight rove out across the chasm.

It was hard to believe they'd only been on this side of the divide for five minutes and already the night was absolute.

He took the last three steps down to the ledge and edged his way inch by inch into the first of the caves.

It was cramped, but still considerably bigger inside than he'd expected, and went deeper into the mountain than his flashlight could properly illuminate.

He moved inside to allow Vic to follow him in.

The air was a little warmer in here than outside.

He put that down to the lack of wind. Rye pushed his hood back.

The interior was maybe thirty feet across, a little over six feet high, meaning Vic had to stoop. At first, he thought the cave was empty, but toward the rear there appeared to be three wooden boxes.

Curiosity got the better of him.

He crouched beside the first one and tried to work the lid off. It had been nailed shut. He unclipped the ice ax from his belt and worked the blade into the crack where two panels of wood met. The wooden side of the box splintered at the first sign of pressure, cracking the container open like an egg—though it wasn't a yolk that spilled out.

Rye wasn't immediately sure what it was, but as he cleared away the debris it became obvious that he was looking at some half-mummified skeleton of a deformed child, though that deformation was almost certainly exacerbated by the way its tibia had fused to its rib cage making it appear almost fetal.

"What you got?" Carter said from behind him.

He realized that none of them could see the child's remains, so he held the body up. He knew he must have looked like some weird shamanic priest offering up a human sacrifice, but the image made damned sure and certain that the others didn't mistake what was in his hands.

"There are two more," he said by way of explanation.

"What is this place? Some sort of prehistoric burial chamber?"

"More modern than that, judging by the nails they used to seal the coffins."

"And there are two dozen caverns like this carved into the cliff face. That's a mausoleum. An entire tribe could bury their dead here. Generations of them, even."

Rye nodded.

"This isn't right," Carter said. "Hold on." He dropped his pack from his back and rooted around inside for his cell phone. It took him a moment to power it up, and then find the images Byrne had sent through, but when he did they confirmed his misgivings. "The burial site he's marked is still half a day from here."

"Well, we've got the bodies to prove it," Rye said. "Plenty of them."

"I'm not arguing that, I'm just saying it's not the burial ground Byrne identified. That makes a lot of dead bodies up here."

Rye nodded, putting the half-mummified child back in what remained of its box. "These have been here a long time. The man-made caves suggest some sort of ancient burial rite, not Christian maybe, but there's a definite reverence for the dead. So, who built these caves? It's not the Nazis, the bones are too old. So, the same people who build the bridge? Their antecedents?"

"The ghosts under the mountains," Carter offered helpfully.

"The demons," Iskra Zima said, shutting the pair of them up.

Carter knelt beside the second box and ran his glove across the surface of the lid as though feeling out for the life force of who-ever was inside. "Want to open another one?"

Rye turned to look at him. "Why on earth would you want to do that?"

"Knowledge," the thief said.

He didn't believe him for a second.

"We aren't tomb raiders," Vic said, echoing his doubt. "There is no need to make this worse than it already is."

"What do you take me for? Sheesh. Honestly. We're looking for some mystical treasure hidden away in some of the world's most inhospitable mountains, and we've stumbled across what looks to be a—what?—century, two centuries, old mausoleum, and you don't want to crack every damn coffin open just in case there's something in there that ends up being the difference between us finding what we're looking for and going home empty-handed? Shame on you. Seriously. I say we don't leave any stone unturned. We tear the place apart looking for proof of Rask's demons."

He didn't wait for permission.

He took his own ice ax to the side of the slightly larger con-tainer, prying it open. The nails were red with rust, meaning they were iron. He stood up and stepped back, pushing the lid aside. "Well, fuck me," the thief muttered, looking at the contents of the box.

It was another body, but this one had been bent, bones broken to fold it up so that it fit into a coffin the same size as the dead child's despite the fact it was a fully grown adult male. The man's skin was black, not the pigment of an African American but rather blackened by exposure to the freezer burn of the elements without the natural decay that would have caused decomposition back down in the valley. The man was naked, and given the way his bones had been broken to fit him into the box, there was no obvious cause of death. The shriveled state of his skin made it impossible to age him.

"What's that?" Iskra said, looking into the casket. She reached in, teasing something out of the leathery folds of skin around the man's neck. It was a teardrop-shaped pendant, though the curves of the drop were fashioned to resemble flames.

Rye had seen the image before—or at least something very like it.

And he remembered where: woven into the ironwork of the gate into Sébastien Guérin's chateau. The engravings within the teardrop resembled three spheres shrouded in flame. The three forces of life: the *Jing,* or body essence; the *Chi,* or life force; and the *Shen,* or spiritual force.

"Aren't you glad we opened the box now?" Carter said, recognizing the pendant. "These tombs—or at least the bodies in them—link back to that chateau in Paris and our immortal assassin, Dawa. See, me, I'd say that's knowledge worth defiling a grave for."

"You seriously want us to open every single coffin?"

"You got anything better to do?"

"Fine," Rye muttered, turning his ax on the cave's final box. This one was a woman, or so he thought at first, seeing the smooth scalp and smoother genitalia. Closer inspection corrected his misconception. The man in this box had been gelded.

"A eunuch?"

"Brutal," Carter said. "Why do that to someone?"

"Lots of reasons, culturally speaking," Vic told him. "Eunuchs fulfilled many roles in society, from courtiers to singers, religious adherents or royal guards. Castration removed the hormonal drive that might otherwise make them unreliable or unsuitable for certain duties. Eunuch priests featured heavily in several religious cults, predating Christianity, including several Indian, Tibetan, and Nepalese sects. They call them *Hijra*. In many of the lands in this region the *Hijra* are recognized legally as a third sex. It's about being neither man or woman, meaning they are of a special caste."

"So, you think this is a holy thing?" Carter asked.

"It makes as much sense as any other answer as to why we have three bodies here, a man, a Hijra, and a baby. It isn't exactly a traditional family unit."

"It's not like we are ever likely to know," the Russian said, offering a pragmatic solution, "so why should it matter? They are dead whether they were lovers or holy men. They still ended up in a box."

"I'm inclined to agree," Vic said. "It isn't as though Tenzin Dawa buried these people here, even if they worshiped the same demons. At best, it means that we are getting closer to Shambhala."

For once it was Rye that disagreed with Rask's Number Two. He wasn't sure he wanted to admit it out loud, but Carter had a point. There was knowledge to be had from interrogating the dead, even if it wasn't the kind of knowledge anyone might have been comfortable learning.

He pushed himself to his feet, the light from his head flashlight turning on each of their faces as he looked from Vic to Iskra to Carter. "God help me, but I think he's right. I think we need to explore at least one more cave. That pendant links this body to our search—which just gives us more questions than answers. And I want to know. I want to know what we are walking into. I want to know if we're being hunted by religious zealots who practice genital mutilation to prove their purity and faith. I want to know if he's the only one or if every cave is filled with eunuchs. And if so, I want to know why. What does it mean? What's the significance to the Asuras or the Brotherhood of Dzyan? Because that's what I think we've stumbled upon here, the Brotherhood's death house."

Vic nodded slowly, considering his words. "It is possible," he said after a moment.

"And if this is their mausoleum," Carter offered, "where is their temple? Carved deeper in the mountain? Is one of these caves the front door? Fuck it, I'm in, let's explore."

"I'm in no hurry to eat another bowl of reconstituted mulch," Iskra said. "I vote we explore."

"That's three to one," Rye said.

"This isn't a democracy," Vic told him, but despite that, he agreed. "But I do think Mr. Vickers makes a strong argument. You explore. I shall see about building a fire and preparing the campsite here, assuming no one objects to sleeping with the dead?"

"It's better than joining them because we froze to death out there," Carter said.

SIXTY-TWO

Over the next two hours they moved from cave to cave, working their way across the cliff face. Every cave contained at least two boxes, every box contained more bones. Adult male bones, male child bones, *Hijra* bones, but in all of those boxes in all of those tombs, there wasn't a single female corpse.

Rye didn't know what to make of that, but Carter had a theory. "Eunuchs and men. It's a religious thing. A cult. It's the Brotherhood. It's the only thing that makes any sense when you think about all of it, big picture. They castrate the boys, train them, turn them into hunters like Tenzin Dawa, and bind them to this secret. Without hormones raging through their bodies, the boys can focus with deadly concentration on learning what it takes to become priests of the demons or ghosts or whatever it is that haunts these mountains, and they dedicate their lives to protecting their secrets. This is where they bury their dead."

"So how do they recruit more boys into their ranks if there are no women in their number?" Rye asked, but he knew there were a hundred ways around that, starting with the most basic and obvious solution—they took children from the neighboring tribes and children of the nomads, and put them into servitude. They made slaves of them before they castrated them and transformed them into spiritual warriors.

Each fully grown adult body wore the same teardrop pendant around its neck, which only served to support the religious monk-warrior argument. And all the bodies seemed to have reached the same level of held-off decomposition and begun a natural mummification process, but without the right equipment there was no way of knowing for sure how long they'd been buried in this place.

In several of the caves, Rye found crude paintings on the walls, and though these didn't depict the tribal hunter-gatherer stories of the Lascaux cave's famous paintings, there was a basic sense of narrative to them.

One, in the tomb of four adult males and one *Hijra,* was of a roughly outlined man sitting cross-legged, arms open wide. Where his head should have been blazed the three spheres of the forces of life, the *Jing,* the *Chi,* and the *Shen,* and his skull had been replaced by the flame-wreathed teardrop of their pendants. In another, the three spheres were borne on the back of a beast of burden, the ethereal flame of the *Jing, Chi,* and *Shen* rippling across its back. In a third, the sitting man had his own head, though it was disproportionately large—like the head of the skeleton they'd found in the Shrine of the Black Sun—set on narrow shoulders, and in each upturned palm the three spheres burned as though he juggled them. In his left hand they burned blue; in his right, red.

The two caves that had the most mundane images were farthest from the stone stair.

In the first, a sphere with illegible script running around its circumference contained a triangle, the three points touching the edge of the sphere, and within the triangle, the three familiar burning globes of the *Jing, Chi,* and *Shen.* Rye couldn't decipher any of the writing, though he assumed it must be some form of esoterica linked either to the Dzyan Brotherhood's arcane beliefs, or to Blavatsky herself.

The second cave contained a variant symbol, with a much grander sphere, though instead of writing curling around the circumference, the three burning globes of the *Jing, Chi,* and *Shen* had been separated and split the circle equidistantly around its circumference. Again, within the circle was an equilateral triangle, its angles touching the inner edge of the grand circle. Inside the triangle this time he saw a many-armed goddess, much like the one he'd seen back in the temple just before Tenzin Dawa attacked. Though this one, with red-pigmented skin, looked more demonic than the idol of Kali he'd seen there.

SIXTY-THREE

First light on the fifth day they pushed on.

The sky was clear blue, the air colder than it had been in all their time on the mountains. The clear skies offered a view that stretched on for miles. Far off in the distance Rye could see the familiar spine of the White Peaks of the Seven Brothers. Gangkhar Puensum was maybe thirty miles away. Mercifully, they weren't climbing the holy mountain, but even so there were several peaks up above the fifteen-thousand-foot range.

There was something about the mountain itself that caught his eye, an anomaly in the snowcapped peaks within the permafrost.

He couldn't see what it was properly from this distance, but something on the mountainside kept catching the sunlight and glinting like a precious jewel.

It had to be the temple Byrne had turned up on the satellite imagery.

"This way," the thief said, leading them toward the shallow declivity that Byrne had marked as a potential burial site. Rye followed him over the edge and started down the slope. The way down was far from easy, most of it being a huge boulder field. The rocks were loose. They shifted under his feet as he scrambled down the slope.

Above him, Vic slipped, causing a sudden slide. Hundreds of smaller stones skittered down the slope around him, forcing Rye to crouch and reach out with his right hand for balance against one of the bigger boulders. The noise increased tenfold as the sound waves bounced back upon each other, amplified by the curious acoustics of the valley's walls.

He turned back to see Iskra Zima silhouetted against the brilliant blue. The Russian didn't move to follow Vic until the last of the rockslide had settled, and when she did, it was with a grace that was a match for Rye's own. The woman moved from boulder to boulder, descending in a quick zigzag down the slope. She didn't lose her footing once, and barely scuffed up loose shale.

The boulder field went on for more than five hundred feet, bringing them down to a sheltered valley where some stubborn vegetation still clung to the mountainside. There were a few juniper bushes and several patches of thick grass showing through the snow.

"It should be here," Carter called over his shoulder as he reached the bottom.

"It is," Rye called down from his vantage point. There was an area thirty or forty feet from where the thief stood where the snow was discolored, something obviously beneath it.

He pointed.

Carter followed the direction of his hand, picking out the subtle changes in the white once they were pointed out to him, and nodded. He scrambled across the scree that Vic's clumsy descent had dislodged.

The rumble of the rockslide still echoed around the valley, the sound seeming to roll on and on long after the last stone had settled.

Rye followed Carter to the discolored snow, reaching him as he crouched, brushing his glove across the surface to dust away the finer snowfall. At first there was nothing to see, but the more insistently he brushed away the snow, the more the ground beneath his glove darkened until the back and forth exposed cloth.

There was a body under the snow.

More than one.

The discovery only caused Carter to work harder at clearing the snow that crusted the corpse. He uncovered a hand. The skin was remarkably well preserved. There was no sign of decomposition, or the dried-out leathery hide of the bodies back in the mountain's mausoleum. A thin crust of ice had preserved the vitality of the corpse, so much so it was almost possible to believe the meat was still fresh.

Carter brushed away more of the snow, exposing more of the dead man's uniform.

Standing over him, Rye recognized the insignia on the dead man's lapel before the thief did: written in a runic script the words *Deutsches Ahnenerbe* circled a sword and ribbon, and over his right breast Rye saw a silver pin with a circular swastika embossed upon it, marking the dead Ahnenerbe officer as a member of the Thule Society.

"These aren't ancient bodies," Carter said, recognizing the Nazi emblem for what it was.

"Nope. I think we just found some of the Nazi expedition."

"Some, or all of it," Carter agreed, looking at the vast plain of discolored snow around them.

The Russian reached them before the more cautious Vic, who was very careful now about where he put each foot down. Iskra skirted the ridge, scanning the discolored snow back and forth before she said, "At least fifty. Maybe more."

Rye moved deeper into the Bone Garden and set to work clearing away more of the snow. He uncovered two bodies close together, both belonging to the expedition's Sherpas. There was no obvious sign of what killed either of them, but it didn't make sense that so many men should have chosen this valley high up in the sacred mountains to simply drop dead. The fabric of their furs had crusted hard and turned brittle in the process. They'd been left with the kit bags they'd been carrying.

The photograph he'd found in Guérin's chateau could have been taken on this very spot.

It didn't make sense.

He hated things that didn't make sense.

"They're not all SS," Rye called across to the others. "These two are natives. Sherpas. They've still got their kit bags strapped to their backs." He shook his head.

Iskra confirmed another dead member of the Thule Society, though he was not wearing the uniform of a soldier. Instead, he was wrapped up against the elements in layers of woolen sweaters and a thick sheepskin greatcoat. When she cleared the snow away from his hands, she found a death's-head ring on the dead man's ring finger.

The SS-Ehrenring was a personal gift bestowed by Himmler, marking the dead man as someone of some rank. To the right of the skull there was a small rune framed by a triangle, not dissimilar to the cave painting.

"Got something," she called, drawing the others over.

She showed them the ring. "It's an honor ring," the Russian explained. "They were only given to Himmler's chosen few, and under normal circumstances, if the wearer died the ring would be returned to Himmler himself. I guess this one never went home to the Third Reich. Help me get it off him."

The metal had contracted under the extreme cold, making it impossible to pry free. Carter didn't waste time trying. He used his ice ax to cut the corpse's finger off and picked up the ring where it fell in the snow.

He handed it to Iskra, who looked inside the silver band, reading the inscription. "Markos Vogel. Third of September 1938," she said, naming the dead man.

She tossed the ring to Carter.

"A keepsake."

They checked a few more dark shadows, uncovering more Nazi officers among the dead.

"This didn't make it into the history books," Rye noted, more to himself than anyone else as he found another Thule pin.

"Why would it?" the Russian said. "My people understand the power of propaganda. You do not record your failures, only your triumphs, and if you lose men along the way you turn them into part of the grander lie, the greater triumph. You do not dwell upon something as inconvenient as the truth. No one cares, anyway. If the Nazis lost half of their expedition here, what does it matter in the grand scheme of things?"

"It hardly proves the superiority of their so-called master race," Carter said, palming the ring.

"No race is genetically superior," Iskra said. "We are all just as–

pects of divergent evolution. We adapt to our environment. We are all inherently the same. That is the only truth worth knowing. None of this superior species bullshit. Someone evolved to survive these altitudes would cope better with the thinning oxygen. Someone evolved to live under the baking desert sun would develop pigment protections against UV rays. Because we as a species are survivors. We always have been."

It was the most he'd heard Iskra Zima say since they'd met, and Rye agreed with every single word of it.

He'd traveled the world, he'd climbed in every city imaginable, and the one thing that had remained inherently the same in all those places was the people. Race, creed, or color, it didn't matter, their basic concerns were the same. "Amen," he said quietly. Turning his head slightly to better see the Russian, Rye's eye was caught again by the reflection of something on the side of the mountain on the other side of the range.

Only this time when he tried to focus on it, he saw more than just the light reflecting off the jeweled surface.

This time, because of the lower angle, he could make out the darker base of some sort of angled structure that had been built in sight of the holy peak. "There," he said, directing the others attention to the structure. "Is that what I think it is?"

"The Brotherhood's temple," Vic said, shielding his eyes against the glare of the sun.

Carter shrugged his pack off his back and crouched, teasing his right glove off with his teeth and holding it in his mouth while he rummaged around in the pack's pockets for his phone to check the images Byrne had sent through along with the maps, including the Blavatsky.

It was hard to see the screen for the glare, but with full brightness on, he swiped through the images until he found the shot he was looking for.

"Look at where it is. Look at the angle. That"—he pointed to the temple perched preciously on the mountainside—"is where Blavatsky's map was drawn."

As best he could tell from here, Carter was right.

"Then that's where we need to be," Rye said.

They set off across the Bone Garden.

The snow rippled around their feet as they walked, the crampons biting on the ice beneath the fine dusting of fresh snowfall. It was slow going, but at least they weren't walking into the eye of the blizzard anymore.

It was a small mercy.

But, as the saying went, the Lord gave with one hand and took away with another.

SIXTY-FOUR

They were halfway across the Bone Garden when they heard the distinctive *whump whump whump* of an attack chopper's blades cutting through the air.

"Move!" Vic yelled, already running across the ice.

Rye didn't need telling twice.

He started to run.

The first few steps were slow, the fresh snow compacting beneath his feet as his weight crushed the layers of air out, his feet sinking two inches for every step, which made his gait clumsy and progress across the snowfield much slower than he needed it to be if he was going to reach some form of shelter before the chopper reached them.

But that didn't stop him from giving it his all.

Vic, being the heaviest, struggled the most, but he was also the most powerful, and drove himself on, covering ground fast. He looked back over his shoulder once, scanning the blue skies for the chopper, then turned and ran, head down, arms and legs pumping furiously. He was breathing hard. Rye could hear each labored gasp from five steps behind him. His own breathing wasn't much better. Iskra brought up the rear, but not because of fitness or conditioning. She moved lightly across the snow. She was making sure Carter didn't fall behind.

The *whump* of the chopper blades grew louder.

Rye could feel the displaced snow churning up around him.

He half turned, still stumbling toward the building twenty-five miles away, to see the first of the men rappelling out of the chopper.

In five ragged steps three more men had come down on their own ropes.

He could see the shape of their AK-47s—a jagged silhouette against the base of their spines as they swung out over the Bone Garden.

They were followed down by four more men before they'd released their harnesses.

The first wave hit the ground running.

They moved with well-disciplined precision.

The second wave hit the ground thirty seconds after the first, with the final wave following them down.

Rye ran for his life.

He drove himself on, gritting his teeth against the burning ache of his thighs and calves as he struggled with the terrain. Head down, he covered the ground expecting to hear the first crack of gunfire at any second.

Behind him, he heard Iskra urging Carter on.

When he looked up again, Vic had gone.

The field of snow was empty up ahead of him, broken only where jagged rocks pierced the drifts. He looked left and right, but aside from more of the boulder field he couldn't see anywhere the big man could be hiding: and none of the closest boulders were big enough to hide a man of Vic's size.

Vic threw a look back over his shoulder, but Vic wasn't back there, either.

Rye couldn't think about it.

Vic knew how to look after himself.

He needed to concentrate on keeping himself alive.

And that meant running until he dropped, then picking himself up again and running some more.

But he needed somewhere to run to, because there was no way he could outrun bullets across twenty-five miles of mountaintops no matter how stubborn he was.

Behind him, the chopping of the helicopter's blades changed

subtly as it swept across the valley, cutting low over his head. He felt the downdraft from the rotor batter him as he stumbled forward.

It was no more than fifty feet above his head as it flew down the center of the valley, and then it was a comet blazing a trail across the sky.

The distress flare had arced over his head, into the open side of the attack chopper, the pilot wrestling frantically with the controls even as the interior caught fire.

It took less than a minute, the red phosphorus tearing through the leather interior.

Huge plumes of black smoke engulfed the helicopter as it veered erratically across the sky, banking away toward the side of the high valley.

The impact sent shock waves through the length of the valley, the concussive blast of the explosion powerful enough to hurl Rye from his feet as he tried to run away from it.

Unarmed, Vic had carefully and methodically brought down an attack chopper single-handedly. Rye had absolutely no doubt it was his flare, or that he'd had the presence of mind to seek out higher ground from which to make his attack. The man was a hunter.

Rye picked himself up and forced himself to move, no looking back this time.

Carter overtook him, running like his ass was on fire.

He grabbed for Rye's sleeve, hauling him onto a new path. He realized what the thief had seen: an optical illusion of the rock face around him. There was a narrow cleft in the valley's side that was all but invisible from their angle of approach. It was barely narrow enough for him to run down without tearing the outer shell of his parka as it dragged along the sides.

A moment later he heard the staccato burst of gunfire and a cry.

He couldn't think about it, he kept running, chasing the thief deeper into the fissure, praying he wasn't leading them into a dead end.

Another round of shots ripped through the deathly quiet of the mountain, echoing all around them and seeming to get louder and louder instead of fading.

Ahead of him, Carter stopped running.

Rye saw why immediately.

There was nowhere to run to. Literally. The ground fell away beneath their feet down a treacherous drop, three hundred feet on a seventy-degree slope. The thief looked at him. Then looked behind him. For a moment, Rye thought Carter was going to turn around and run back toward the gunfire: but it was a short moment. Carter crossed his arms over his chest like they showed in the airplane evacuation movies, and stepped out as though onto a slide, and dropped away down the sheer ice sheet, howling as he fell.

Rye hesitated, knowing each second he wasn't moving was a second closer to one of the hunters coming up behind him.

"Fuck it," he said, and followed the thief over the edge.

He dropped like a stone, feeling each and every jagged spur of rock beneath the too-thin blanket of snow, which did absolutely nothing to protect him from the battering his body took on the descent.

He plummeted faster than any roller coaster without the safety of the rails to stop him being hurled bodily into the rock face beneath him.

Carter slid out of control, his legs kicking out as his body twisted, and Rye realized he was at risk of being turned around and going down the rest of the descent headfirst, but somehow the thief managed to right himself, and then he was rolling and sliding uncontrollably into a dead stop, and Rye realized why he'd been fighting the last hundred feet of the descent so desperately— there was a gorge between the slide and the rock wall. It could just as easily have been five feet deep or five hundred, there was no way of knowing at this angle, but the momentum he'd built up from his rate of descent wasn't going to be enough to see him sail over it safely with the weight of the pack on his back.

But he couldn't stop himself from falling, and all he could think in that long-sliding second was: *I don't want to die. . . .*

And in that moment, that desperate slide, his heartbeat froze, time dilating as the mountain raced away beneath him, and he thought about how he was going to survive this.

Hannah used to say that screaming was a waste of thinking time, and certain death, whereas not screaming bought you maybe two or three seconds more thinking time.

It might not save your life, but it might make all the difference.

And it did.

Rye grabbed for the ice ax still clipped to his belt and hit the release, even as his body started to twist away beneath him—and he understood why Carter had suddenly lost control of his descent—and as his momentum took him onto his stomach, gripped it with both hands and slammed it into the sheet of ice as he slid uncontrollably down it.

Rye felt rather than heard the rip as the side of his backpack tore on a razor-sharp barb of protruding rock, slicing through the heavyweight nylon fibers. The rent in the fabric ran the length of his arm, wide enough to spill the contents across the slope. There was nothing he could do about it: he was falling faster than he could hope to control. It was all he could do to resist the impulse to reach out to try and grab onto something to arrest the momentum of his descent. All that would succeed in doing was wrench his arms from their sockets and leave him in agony as he continued to fall.

He couldn't help himself, this time he screamed.

And used that scream to fuel another desperate swing of the ice ax.

This time the head of the ax bit, but the snow rippled away around it, the blade grinding as he slid relentlessly on.

He kicked at the ground, trying to dig his crampons in, but as the small metal spikes bit they jammed, and his legs twisted, his body coming away from the ground.

He slammed the ax down again, hitting bare rock so hard the handle nearly twisted out of his grip.

He was losing it.

Snow plumed up all around him.

Every erratic spur of rock cut at his belly.

There was blood on his front where rocks had torn through the parka to cut him open and burns where friction from the slide had melted the material, leaving black scars across the colorful padded jacket.

The ax bit into the slope, but his momentum yanked it clear before it could slow him more than a little.

He bounced and slid, tumbling wildly out of control, losing sense of what was up and what was down as his weight threatened to carry him out over the edge.

All around him the contents of his pack skidded and spilled, burrowing into the snow.

Rye put everything he had into a final frantic swing of the ice ax, knowing he was out of time.

His body plummeted down the ice slide, his wild descent faster in these last few feet than at any other time during the desperate slide. He plowed on, body skimming the planes of snow, bouncing and juddering and being battered every inch of the way as the edge of the slope and the sheer drop down into the gulf opened up before him.

The point of the ax hit home, burying the blade into frozen mud beneath the sheet of ice. The sudden jarring stop wrenched the handle from his grasp, and even as he dug his feet in, his weight carried Rye over the edge and there was nothing he could do to stop himself from falling.

SIXTY-FIVE

In those few precious seconds between the edge and oblivion he learned how to fly.

But that miracle didn't last anywhere near long enough. Rye slammed into the sheer side of the gorge's far wall, the ruined pack on his back taking the brunt of the impact.

It was enough to save his life for at least a few seconds longer.

The impact drove shockwaves of pain through his body, radiating out from each point of impact in ever-increasing waves that became one with every screaming nerve-ending and synapse. The collision sent Rye tumbling, hands and head down, like Superman flying through the atmosphere in those first awkward flights as he seemed to bounce and hit everything. The added weight of the pack tipped him, and for one sickening second Rye thought he was going to hit the ground flat on his back—which would absolutely shatter his spine and leave him paralyzed at best, or dead. But then, maybe dead was better?

A rock splinter gouged into the side of his face, tearing a second smile from above his right ear to just below his nostril. There was a lot of blood.

He couldn't see the bottom of the gorge and had no way of knowing how far he had left to fall.

There was a limit to what was survivable, and without the ice ax to slam into the rock there was precious little he could do except fall.

He'd fallen thirty feet in what had felt like minutes but could only have been seconds.

His mind raced.

He seemed to be capable of thinking a million things at once, none of the thoughts taking up more than a fraction of a second outside of his head.

He grabbed at the pack's thick shoulder strap and pulled it off his shoulder, moving instinctively. It wasn't as though he could use the pack as a parachute, though. It was hardly going to arrest his fall.

Rye didn't flail or kick out, he simply fell, twisting and rolling as he went.

He'd fallen sixty feet in the few seconds since he'd slammed into the wall.

There was no surviving a free fall of sixty feet.

And he was only going to fall faster the farther he fell, assuming the crevice didn't abruptly end in a base of scree and built-up snow.

The pack tore away from his shoulder, ballooning open as it created enough drag to jerk his body physically backward despite being in free fall.

He saw his chance.

It's a million to one shot, Jim, but it might just work, that sarcastic bastard in his head heckled, quite probably for the last time.

The drag factor threated to tear the pack out of his hand as he clung onto the one remaining shoulder strap. He needed to get this exactly right. There wasn't a millisecond's room for maneuver. Beneath him, coming fast, Rye had seen a protruding rock— like a gigantic crooked finger—and he had one shot at hooking it with the pack.

Whatever happened after that was in the lap of the gods.

He dropped his shoulder, slipping out of the strap, and lashed out with his right arm in a single motion, the ripped front of the pack catching and tearing on a boil of the rocky finger. For one sickening second, he thought the cloth was going to shear all the way through, but the reinforced stitching of the main seams held, and suddenly he was hanging, not falling.

Rye clung onto the strap, painfully aware that the material simply couldn't and wouldn't hold for more than a few seconds.

He needed to find a handhold or foothold, something to take the strain.

His heart hammered in his chest, and yet, despite the flood of adrenaline coursing through his system, Rye was remarkably calm.

Looking down, he still couldn't see the bottom of the crevice, but that was as much because the gorge narrowed to the point where it was little more than a fissure in the rock and there was no way for light to penetrate deep enough to reveal the true extent of the drop.

The shadows were a mercy.

There was no telling how far that fissure split the mountain. It could run all the way down to hell for all he knew.

The nylon tore another juddering inch. Rye dropped, the strain on his shoulder almost too much to bear. With his free hand he reached out for the wall in front of him, feeling out desperately with his fingers for even the slightest lip in the rock he could use to his advantage.

The crevice narrowed as it descended, becoming a chimney. So, if he could climb down to that point it would be easy to brace himself hand and foot on either side of the chimney wall and crab down to the bottom.

If.

The wind moaned eerily through the upper reaches of the crevice.

He looked up to see Carter leaning out over the edge. But before he could call down, another burst of machine-gun fire tore through the air. Rye saw the puffs of snow where the bullets buried themselves into the side of the fissure, and splinters of stone rained down into his eyes.

Rye flailed at the icy wall of stone, and his toe caught. The steel crampons made it impossible to contemplate trying to climb with any kind of grace. It was all about strength, and with luck, some crude hand- and footholds big enough to accommodate the teeth of the crampons.

The problem was that he couldn't climb with his gloves on, and without them he was going to freeze, but short-term necessity had to supersede long-term need. One toe braced against the wall, one hand tangled around the strap of the backpack, Rye teased his right glove off with his teeth and let it fall away into the darkness beneath him.

He didn't hear it hit the bottom.

With his fingers free, he felt like he had a chance.

He twisted slightly, finding another toehold.

That changed everything.

Two points of contact meant he was going to survive.

He felt out with his fingers for a third before he let go of the strap.

The pack hung over his head, dangling from the hooked finger of stone, as Rye worked his way down the fissure until it narrowed enough that he could span it side to side, taking his weight on his feet.

Foot by foot, he crabbed his way down another ninety feet of rock chimney until he stood on solid ground again, still very much alive. Breathless, high on the adrenaline coursing through his system and dizzy from the lack of oxygen in his blood, but alive.

He'd lost everything in the fall.

And he couldn't hear anything from up above.

The only reason he could see anything was because he still had the head flashlight on, and the only reason he still had that was because he'd put it on his hat last night when they'd gone to explore the caves and hadn't bothered to take it off this morning when they set out walking. It was nothing but luck that he hadn't. Ninety-nine times out of a hundred he would have stashed it back among his kit last night, but the half-mummified corpses and the cave paintings had weirded him out.

And saved his life.

Now, as he looked around, the narrow beam showed Rye just how few options he had. The fissure seemed to run a long way, which put him in mind of the pinkish line Byrne had highlighted on his topographical satellite shots. He tried to recall the exact path it ran, but without his phone to confirm his memories, all he could do was follow the fissure to wherever it ended, hoping that if it didn't reach the temple it at least offered a reasonable escape.

He had to trust that the others would keep going without him and hope to rendezvous somewhere around the Dzyan temple.

SIXTY-SIX

Not knowing what was going on with the others was torture. Not knowing where he was going or when he might find food and water again, hell. A very different kind of hell to the brimstone and lava hells of Christian mythology, but much more real for its earthly nature.

Rye walked on.

There was no light up above here, meaning at some point the fissure had failed to split the rock all the way to the surface and now he was in an icy tunnel network, walking blindly toward where he hoped he'd find a way out.

He wasn't feeling great about his chances.

The ravine narrowed around him, so tight in places Rye was forced to shuffle sideways to keep moving forward. The stone was sheened with moisture. When he reached out to touch it with his fingertips he realized it had frozen into a thin skin of ice. After a minute of shuffling, he discovered that the ravine had widened again, presenting him with a different challenge.

It looked for all the world as though he had reached a dead end, though looking up Rye realized the reality was that whatever tectonic pressure had formed the fissure had broken the rock more than twenty feet above his head but not down here.

He had no choice but to scale the obstruction.

The crampons made it considerably more difficult than it needed to be, but bouldering was one of the climbing exercises he'd always enjoyed for its discipline. It wasn't about getting to the top or being the fastest or the most daring, it simply allowed Rye to focus on the rock and moving with grace and precision.

The edges around the fissure where the stone had sheared were sharp enough to offer easy handholds.

He looked up, tracing the route with his flashlight, and began to climb.

It only took a few minutes, and the shelf itself ran less than fifteen meters before he was forced to descend again.

He moved lightly, on the balls of his feet, and continued on.

What he hadn't expected was to be presented with choices. Up ahead the ravine opened up, and he saw not one but four paths diverging before him, each going deeper into the mountain, and the widest of them was simply no guarantee it would run the farthest or ever reach open ground.

He struggled to orient himself, but he'd been turned around a dozen times in the fall and had no easy way of gauging which shaft went where he needed to go. So, he had no choice but to pick one and push on, trying to hold the map and the pink line of the fissure in his mind.

But it was pointless.

Down here every twist and every turn was disorienting, and there was nothing to say that the path he was on was the right one, or that it wouldn't simply dead-end around the next curve. All he could do was follow it.

He heard an eerie sigh as the wind lost its hold on this place, blowing out to nothing.

He realized he was moving awkwardly, favoring his left side. He'd hurt something on the way down; how badly, he had no real way of knowing, but it was interfering with his freedom of movement, which wasn't good.

Rye felt out his side, pushing and probing as best he could through the thick parka, but it was impossible to isolate the source of the pain. As long as it was a dull ache rather than a sharp stabbing pain he could live with it.

The flashlight's beam picked out the dark contours of cracks and crevices along the walls.

The scrape of his crampon's metal teeth grated in his ears as he walked on, the sound made deafeningly loud by the tight confines and weird acoustics of the tunnel.

He wouldn't be sneaking up on anyone.

More jewellike seams glittered in the flashlight's glare.

Time quickly became meaningless as he lost any sense of how long he'd been down there. He'd climbed five similar blockages in the shafts and been forced to bridge two more where the cave floor disappeared beneath him. In that time, he'd found another dozen or so possible passageways leading off what he thought of as the core fissure.

He'd covered no more than half a mile in that time. With at least twenty times that to go, there was no way of knowing just how many paths he'd have to ignore and how many more they could in turn lead to before he reached the end.

Rye realized, as he walked on, that the ground beneath his feet was on a gentle decline, taking him deeper into the Seven Brothers, and presumably away from where he needed to be.

He tried to think.

Had he been turned around by the choices, and somehow branched off the main passage without realizing that was what had happened? Or, more distressingly, given his predicament, was it in his head? His mind playing tricks on him in the dark?

He stopped.

Somewhere in the blind distance he heard the *tink, tink, tink* of water dripping from the ceiling, improbably loud. A peculiar moss clung to part of the rock wall. It possessed a weird luminescent quality, not in any way enough to offer illumination by itself but caught in the flashlight's beam it seemed to glow, adding to the light in the tunnel.

You do realize that's going to run out, don't you? His sarcastic savior chirped up, reminding him that batteries didn't last forever. *You'll be lucky if you get another couple of hours out of it. No way it's going to last while you stumble around in the dark for ten miles.*

"It's not like I've got a choice," Rye said, his voice chasing away through the honeycomb of tunnels. He was painfully aware of just how much shit he was in. The weight of the mountain pressed down metaphorically on him as he wrestled with a whole string of bad choices looking for a least-bad option. He knew he had no realistic alternative but to carry on, and hope it took him close to the rendezvous point, because he wasn't getting up the side of the ravine where he fell; not without the right equipment. And there was no telling what would be waiting for him up top even if he tried.

Twelve heavily armed hunters looking to end his life wasn't a particularly enticing incentive when it came to making the climb.

This way at least there was the illusion of a chance.

But with no equipment, no rations, no water—though there was ice on the walls, which meant he wouldn't die of thirst—and no real clue where he was, it could only ever be an illusion, and no amount of stubbornness and promises that he didn't want to die could change the outcome if he didn't find a way out of this place. And soon.

Before his flashlight died.

He needed to think smart.

He pulled off the crampons and used one to score the rock, marking his passage.

He repeated the mark at every choice in the warren of tunnels, marking the one he chose so that he could easily double back and change his route under the mountain without getting lost.

But it was hard.

There was no life down here, and every crack and crevice looked like it could have gone on for miles beyond the flashlight's narrow beam.

It didn't help that every time he turned his head the motion caused a hundred tiny shadows to jump around and trade places like capering fools trying their damnedest to turn him about and about again.

Rye listened for anything out there, any possible sound that could suggest someone was coming to find him, but beyond the *tink* of droplets of water and the faint hum—which in all probability was the echo of the blood in his own head—there was nothing.

Up top, ten miles was two and a half hours. But that was going in a straight line and keeping to a steady pace. Down here a mile could take an hour with all the obstacles he had to navigate. Depending upon the cells in his flashlight, he could reasonably expect it to last for four or five hours.

He wished he knew what was going on up there.

If Vic and the others were all right, or if they were sprawled out across the snow, cold.

He needed to believe the three of them were more than a match for a dozen mercenaries, armed or not. The little he knew of Vic's story and the stuff he'd been through in Africa was enough for Rye to back him in any fight, no matter the odds, and he'd seen Iskra in action firsthand in the monkey temple. But Carter wasn't a fighter, not like the other two, and that meant they were looking at dealing with six each, which outside of Hollywood was a hellish challenge. Unarmed, it ought to be impossible.

But Vic had brought an attack helicopter down, so who was to say what was really impossible?

After another hour in the darkness, Rye began to feel his injuries. The adrenaline had worn off, leaving him battered and raw. There was more of the peculiar moss on the wall. It gathered where the ice melt ran down through the cracks. It lent the tunnel an ethereal, haunted quality that was exacerbated by the low resonating hum he'd noticed a while back. It didn't get any louder, though it showed no signs of fading either. When he rested his hand against the stone, Rye felt the very slight vibration running through the mountain.

He crouched, putting his hand flat to the stone floor.

It was warmer than he had expected.

He wasn't entirely sure what that meant, but given the fact he was still probably close to fifteen thousand feet above sea level, with several hundred feet of rock above him, it should have been colder.

Much colder.

He stood slowly and walked on to the next possible fork in the tunnels, scoring his choice into the stone before he took it. Ten paces into the tunnel, he crouched again to feel out the stone floor, and again it felt warmer to the touch than he would have believed possible.

All sorts of reasons ran through his head, one of which was some sort of weakness along the collision edge from where the two tectonic plates had come together to fold the land into these incredible mountains. But the crust here was so thick, thicker than along any of the fault lines, there was no chance of superheated steam or volcanic eruptions penetrating the rock. There wasn't a single volcanic weakness, active or dormant, throughout the entire Himalayan range, with the two nearest being the Barren and Narcondam Islands. But, deeper down, it was possible, surely? With subduction and the gradual melting of the northern collision edge of the Indian tectonic plate? But even if it was happening, any sort of volcanic activity would be way too far down for it to have any residual heating effect on the stone around him.

And yet the rock was undeniably warm to the touch.

He felt a shiver thrill through the stone beneath his fingertips.

The mountain range may not be volcanic, but it was most certainly a very active seismic zone and prone to devastating earthquakes.

Was that what he was feeling here? The buildup of seismic forces that would eventually blow and send shock waves throughout the region?

Rye pushed on, letting his fingers trail across the stone, as though by being connected to the low-frequency vibration he could somehow hope to decipher it.

The sound made no rational sense. But that didn't stop his mind from racing. He knew very little about the practicalities of geology and what something this deep in the mountain itself signified, but could only assume the vibrations intensified the closer he got to their source, and dissipated the farther away he got, but did that mean he was walking toward some sort of breaking point? A place where the fissure was in the process of tearing itself wider, or even collapsing the side of the mountain itself? Were the vibrations the rock's response to something more seismic beneath him? Deeper down in the mantle, was the crust tearing itself apart under the incredible strains on the mountain range? Or was the source aboveground? An avalanche bringing one of the Seven Brothers to its knees?

And if it was, what happened then?

Did he die down here, slowly, starving to death, another corpse for the mountain to call its own?

Those kinds of external forces dictating his survival weren't worth worrying about. If an earthquake brought the whole mountain down on his head, it brought the whole mountain down on his head. It wasn't as though he could influence the outcome by worrying about it, or even planning for it.

Over the next mile or so, the quality of air changed. It was hard to say what was different, but he felt his breathing become more and more labored, each breath nourishing him a little less than the last.

All he could do was walk on, letting the tunnels lead him wherever they would.

The echoes and silences grew.

There was another sound down here, he realized, unsure of how long he'd actually been listening to it before he was aware of what it was: the steady *dubdub-dubdub* of a heart beating.

Again, when Rye put his hand against the tunnel wall, he felt that echo in the vibrations, making them less like the cold stone of Gangkhar Puensum and more like the belly of a huge, hungry beast.

And still he walked on, the flashlight beam moving endlessly ahead of him, the shadows it cast in a permanent sense of agitation. Heavy shadows picked out a marking on the cave wall. At first, he assumed it was just some sort of deformity in the rock formation, a scar left over from the shearing of the fissure, but as he moved closer to investigate, he found it was much more man-made than that.

The now-familiar tripartite image of the three burning spheres of the *Jing, Chi*, and *Shen* had been chiseled into the tunnel wall, each flame intricately rendered with clean lines that defied any crude hammer and chisel but rather suggested the kind of precision cutting tools of the modern age. The delicacy of the work was exquisite.

Studying it closely, Rye realized it was subtly different from the image he had seen on the Nazi pendants. The three spheres overlapped slightly, like a Venn diagram, and in those points of overlap there was a symbol he didn't recognize. He wished he had his phone or some way to record the carving. The fact that it was so close to what they were familiar with, but different, felt important.

He traced the flames with his fingertips.

An electric thrill shivered through him, the charge strong enough to cause Rye to pull his hand away from the carving.

He tried it again and was immediately shocked by the charge.

Rye looked down at his hand, seeing the very slight welt where he'd been burned by the rock and the echo of the flame's outline on his fingertip.

He kept on walking, hearing the *dubdub* of the mountain's heartbeat increasing, scoring the wall with his crampons every so often to mark his passage, feeling the chill creep into his blood and the hunger gnaw away at his gut.

He began to doubt he'd ever find his way out of this place.

It was hard to imagine some lost city down here, harder still to believe there could ever have been a civilization that would choose to build its so-called paradise in such a place.

But that was what Rask was banking on; a whisper of legend,

the idea that there was a faith based around wisdom that somehow fell from the stars.

Rye knew that the man was clutching at straws.

He'd admitted as much himself.

But the notion that something here could somehow save him had never felt more ridiculous.

Magic stones? Magic beans more like, that inner voice chimed, but for once the doubter was only saying what Rye had felt all along. There was no such thing. This was a world as devoid of magic as there could ever be, and the idea of some superior technology feeling like magic was just wishful thinking.

He scored another deep gash into the tunnel wall, and as the shriek of metal echoed out, felt the wall give beneath his weight.

SIXTY-SEVEN

The seam where the two sections of rock met was near perfect, but the flashlight revealed a thin dark line of shadow. Rye pushed and pressed around the seam, trying to replicate the sensation of the rock moving inward against his touch, but it wasn't happening. He was beginning to think he'd imagined it, when his fingers found a series of slight imperfections in the rock—little pinpricks in the rough surface that he would otherwise have missed—but once he noticed two or three of them he couldn't help but notice more, until he felt out a whole constellation of imperfections in the rock wall, and knew that was exactly what he was feeling out. His fingers brushed up against marks that represented the swirl of the Milky Way, which felt like a galaxy of braille beneath his fingers.

As Rye pressed and pushed at the imperfections he heard a heavy *clunk* deep within the rock as something disengaged. A moment later he felt the entire wall move inward to reveal a stone stair leading up. The mechanism was crude. The wood behind it had rotted in several places, but the release still worked. Putting his shoulder into it, Rye pushed the heavy stone door aside.

The steps were crudely carved into the bedrock.

They rose into darkness, but he noticed several places where iron rings had been driven into the wall. He assumed this was where reed torches were set to light the way.

He started to climb, not sure what he expected to find at the top. The steps rose several stories without showing any sign of ending, before he saw a wooden door bearing the familiar three burning spheres of the *Jing, Chi,* and *Shen*. He pushed open the door and crossed the threshold into the lower reaches of Dzyan temple.

There was a chill about the chambers that made them feel un-lived in, and it grew worse the more he explored.

Rye moved throughout the lower level, listening for signs of movement above, for any sign of brothers sworn to keep the secrets of Shambhala, or anyone else, including Cressida Mohr's kill squad.

Nothing.

The place was desolate.

The cold was unbearable. Worse, even, than outside, as though the walls worked as some sort of insulation that kept the icy chill inside them.

But that didn't stop him going through the entire structure. He walked the narrow hallways, checking each chamber. He found empty cots and prayer mats. There was precious little in the way of personality about the place, and no ornamentation bar the repeated sigils of the *Jing, Chi,* and *Shen* on several of the walls. He moved from room to room, finding another bare kitchen. Unlike Guérin's chateau, there was no stockpile of canned goods in the pantry, either.

Leaving the kitchens, he climbed another set of stairs, following the light. The hallway opened onto a gallery that looked down over what must have been the heart of the ancient temple. On the wall, a giant rendition of the three burning spheres engulfed what could only have been the Vril whose bones they had found built into the walls of the Shrine of the Black Sun. It was an imposing creature, utterly alien in its nature. The Vril's bulbous head and distended jawline were accentuated by haunting deep-set black eyes that looked impossibly large in the already impossibly large skull.

Rye couldn't take his eyes off the thing.

A biting wind blew in through the empty frame of the enormous central window. The window looked out over the imposing landscape. A rime of frost and ice clung to everything in the room. Rye didn't have the Blavatsky to compare, but he was willing to bet Rask's life on the fact that he was looking out over the reality behind the occultist's crude drawing.

He couldn't see a single spire or rooftop, but why should he? It wasn't as though the earth was simply going to surrender its secrets because he had found the place where X was supposed to mark the spot. Life didn't work like that.

According to Rask, the city, if it had ever existed, was the genesis for several of the Hell legends every bit as much as it was the source of so-called Paradise tales. It was never going to be there, like some mountaintop nirvana. The treasures—and horrors—of Shambhala lay beneath the mountains, buried down in the deep places of the earth.

Rye leaned out over the gallery to get a better look at the space beneath him.

He counted a dozen pews lined up to face the broken window.

There were six people down there.

One sat, head down in prayer, on the first row of pews. There were four more, all wearing the same shades of red vestments, all with their heads bowed in prayer in the other pews. The last man was on his knees before the Vril idol, forehead pressed to the floor. The frost rimed the creases in the fabric of their robes, giving them a peculiar glittering luminescence as the sunlight shimmered across them.

It was unnaturally quiet in the chamber, not even the mumbled whisper of a prayer reaching him.

They hadn't noticed him.

Rye watched for a full two minutes, not daring to breathe.

They didn't move.

They didn't say a word.

Rye looked down at the last of the Brotherhood of Dzyan, the caretakers of this strange temple, and knew that the line had died out in this room.

At the far side of the gallery, he found a stair leading down to the main floor. Each step was frosted with a layer of ice. The descent was treacherous. He went down with care, holding the handrail until he emerged on the temple floor. From here both the window and the Vril were considerably more daunting than they had been from the higher vantage.

Standing in the shadow of the Vril, Rye looked at the downturned faces of the monks in the front few pews. Their skin was a dark freezer-burn black, leathery and heavy with deep creases that marked them as ancient. Ice crystals had frosted around their lips. The hairs of the one bearded monk had frozen into a thick white mask. Every brittle hair was encased in ice.

Rye moved closer, unable to take his eyes off the dead monks.

The wind cried around him, a haunting elegy as it whispered across the prayer floor and climbed up to the gallery.

Rye reached out, touching the dead monk's face. The crust of ice crackled beneath his fingers. As the ice flaked away, it took with it a layer of tissue, exposing the bone beneath in one horrifying second. The ice shattered on the tiled floor, the fallen flesh cracking into a dozen shards.

He backed away from the dead man.

He stood over the monk who was on his knees with his forehead pressed to the floor. He could see the wound that had killed him. The bullet holes in the base of his skull, mirroring the pattern of the *Jing, Chi,* and *Shen.*

Standing over the dead man, he heard someone bark, "Freeze!"

SIXTY-EIGHT

"Jesus Christ, I nearly shit myself," Rye said, laughing at the sight of Carter Vickers' amusement. He leaned against the pew, shaking his head. "What the fuck is wrong with you?"

"Nothing a good stiff drink wouldn't cure," the thief said, walking toward him. "What the hell is this place?" The chiaroscuro of shadows made his bruises look even more impressive. Vic and Iskra were behind him and looked equally battered.

"All that remains of the Brotherhood, I think."

"Six people sitting in their pews praying, all mysteriously die at the same time?"

"Not so mysterious," Rye said. "Bullet to the back of the head. Looks like the expedition found its way this far and put an end to the monks' line."

"Signs of torture?"

"Not that I saw, but honestly. Double-tap to the back of the head, that'd make most people talk." Rye raised an eyebrow at that. "Okay, not the person being shot, but you know what I mean."

"It's pretty grim," Iskra said, walking the line of dead penitents, shaking her head as she checked each one for bullet holes.

Each of the bodies slumped in their seat as she passed.

"I'm not sure how a bunch of monks are meant to defend against a Mauser or an MP 40."

"They aren't," Vic said. "They took the secret of Shambhala with them to the grave."

"How can you be so sure?"

"Because the expedition failed," the big man said.

Rye nodded. It made sense.

"What happened to you, Carter?"

"Your girlfriend's thugs weren't too happy after Vic blew up their helicopter," Carter said. "Let's just say that after you fell down that hole things started to get interesting."

"It was convenient they chose to attack in what was already a graveyard. Saved us the effort of burying them afterward," Iskra said.

Rye quite liked this new, more talkative woman, even if her sense of humor veered to the macabre end of the spectrum.

"Then pretty boy here told us what had happened to you, so we shadowed the fissure as long as we could, hoping to find a point of entry where it leveled out. It didn't. So, we went on to the rendezvous point, and here we are."

"And isn't this just the creepiest fucking place in the world," the thief said. "An abandoned temple in the middle of the most inhospitable mountain range in the world, looking at six executed monks. Rask should be paying us danger money."

"He does," the Russian said. "So, how did you get in here?" she asked Rye.

"I followed the fissures and ended up at a crude stairway that led up from the tunnels."

She nodded. "Given we need to descend, that feels like a good place to start looking for the lost city."

No one argued.

He took them down to the tunnels.

"There's something you should see," he said, as they emerged from the man-made stair.

"What am I looking for?"

Rye led them to where the familiar symbols of the *Jing, Chi,* and *Shen* were carved into the wall, and told the Russian, "Touch it."

Iskra laid her palm flat against the rock, then recoiled. "Okay, that's just wrong. It feels . . . alive."

That was the same word that had occurred to Rye. *Alive.*

"Doesn't it just? Which makes me think we are in the right place. The problem is I don't see where we go from here? I'm not seeing a lost city. I don't know about you but I kinda hoped we'd find a second stair, or maybe a gaping maw into hell or something down here. There has to be *something.*"

"You mean like this?" the thief said. He shone his flashlight down a crack so thin Rye had missed it.

The problem was that there was no way they could possibly squeeze through the crack, but the flashlight's beam teased a darker descent on the other side.

"I didn't see that," Rye said.

"That's because it wasn't there until Iskra put her hand on the sigil."

"Are you sure?"

"Positive. I saw it open with my own two eyes. Vic, put your hand on it, see what happens?"

The big man moved forward, deliberately placing his palm flat against the rock on the third sphere in the design.

Rye felt rather than heard the deep rumble in the mountain and looked at the others for confirmation they'd heard it, too. "Landslide?"

The big man shook his head. "It felt like it came from deeper down, not above us, more like the rumblings of an earthquake."

He was right.

It was in the rocks around them as much as it was above and below them, like they were in the belly of the beast.

Rye moved to peer in through the crack.

It hadn't mysteriously widened in response to Vic's hand on the rock. There was no way any one of them could squeeze through, but there was definitely something on the other side. He could see the distinct shadows of a stair, the steps themselves so well defined they had to be man-made, like the ones leading down from the temple.

The thief stood behind him, close enough to peer over Rye's shoulder. "Are you seeing what I'm seeing?"

"A way down?"

"That's the one."

"But there's no way we're getting in there." He pointed out the obvious problem.

"You say that," Carter said, smile grinning, "but I know something you don't know."

"God, you can be an annoying bastard," Rye said. "Spit it out."

"Follow the moisture on the ground," he said, shining his light down at the small slick of moisture that ran away to the right, away from the hidden stair.

Rye did.

What he found was a deep shaft that dropped deeper than his flashlight could shine, but about halfway down was a stone gallery that, if his sense of direction was right, ran back far enough to link up with the stair.

"What do you think?"

"I think it's a long way down."

"And *I'm* the annoying one?" Carter said. "I mean do you think you can climb it?"

"Sure, and I can rig up ropes so you can, too."

"That won't be necessary, honestly. One person scouting out an area is fine," the thief said.

"I wouldn't want you missing out on the fun," Rye said, already looking for somewhere that could work as a belay point to secure the ropes as he began setting up a line down.

Vic was the first into a harness.

Rye worked the line while the big man descended, walking slowly down the wall of rock a step at a time as he played out the line. When Vic reached the gallery, he unclipped the harness so that Rye could pull the rope back up for Iskra to follow him down. As Rye was setting up the line for the next one to go, the big man disappeared from sight, taking his light from the gallery. A moment later he returned, leaning out over the edge to shout up, "He's right, it leads through to the stairs, but there's a problem."

"Problem how?" Iskra called down, stepping out over the edge.

"Best you see for yourself," Vic said, stepping back from the edge so she could walk down to him.

It took another ten minutes to get Carter Vickers down to the ledge, and for Rye to stow the ropes and free-climb down the shaft, working his way down the narrowest of cracks and holds without being able to see where he was going most of the time. He worked his way by feel.

Vic leaned out and shone the flashlight against the last few feet of his descent, then gathered him in, lifting Rye lightly off the wall. In that one moment, as he swung in to the ledge, he really appreciated just how incredibly strong Vic was.

"What do I need to see?"

Rye walked through the narrow tunnel between the shaft and the stair and saw the problem long before he reached the first step. The descent was dizzying, again disappearing into darkness far beyond the edge of his flashlight's beam, but in between where they were and where they needed to be was a gulf where a huge section of the stairway had caved in.

"Well, it was never going to be easy, was it?" Carter said, coming to join him.

Again, that deep bass rumble shook through the mountain. Loose shale on the steps fell away, spinning down into the black.

He didn't hear it hit the bottom.

"Are we even sure we're going the right way?"

Rye looked at him like he'd just said the stupidest thing he'd ever heard. "Seriously? We are hundreds of miles from civilization, almost directly beneath a monastery that isn't visible on satellite images, directly in line with the mountaintop points of a unique view that couldn't be replicated anywhere else in the world, and we've found a man-made stair leading down into the heart of the mountain that is signposted by a mystical sigil we've been following from France . . . and you wonder if we're going the right way?"

"When you put it like that," Carter said ruefully. "So how do we get down?"

"Same way we got this far: we climb," he said.

"I knew you were going to say that."

It was harder to set up the ropes this time; Rye was forced to hammer in the belay pins as he free-climbed his way spiderlike across the gulf, threading the rope as he went. It was a thirty-foot gap across an unknown drop. He was comfortable making the climb, but for someone like Vic it was asking a lot of him, despite his strength.

Vic fastened his harness onto the guide rope and crabbed his way across the gap. Halfway, a chunk of rock flaked away from the rock face and, unbalanced, he lost his grip and fell.

The sudden weight on the rope nearly pulled Rye off his feet as he struggled to brace himself against the steps to arrest his fall. Even so, Vic dropped twenty feet like a stone, his cries deafening as they echoed down the stone chimney.

Every muscle in his body tensed, straining against the pull of Vic's weight as he swung there helplessly, the beam from his flashlight roving wildly across the shaft as his head whipped around frantically looking for somewhere to cling onto.

Rye caught a glimpse of something in the shadows of the roof of the deep shaft that he couldn't explain, something he'd seen before somewhere else. . . .

In that Blavatsky painting.

It was one of the core images of the esoteric painting—the peculiarly unnatural tree of glass wrapped in pastel-shaded angel wings and lit by a triangle of three gloriously golden suns—one ablaze—and it was carved deep into the stone, like a demon watching over the descent.

It was creepy as hell.

It disappeared into shadow as Vic's gaze turned downward.

Rye felt the belay pin slip an inch as Vic's weight pulled it free of the rock.

"I need you to find a foothold," he called down to Vic. "You're going to have to take some of the weight off the pin, or it's coming out of the rock and we're both going down," he said bluntly, no time for softening the message.

Vic grunted, and Rye felt his weight shift beneath him as he turned in to face the wall of rock.

"Any time you like," he called down.

The big man scrabbled about the rock face trying to find something, anything, to take his weight. The twist of his body against the rope was enough to pull the pin free with a ping of tortured metal, and he fell another ten feet, Rye's grip on the rope the only thing stopping him from falling a lot farther.

There was no way he could hold him.

The rope slipped inches through his grip, burning across his palm as he struggled to hold his balance.

But he refused to let go.

"I've got you," he promised, even as the pendulum of Vic's weight threatened to pull him over the edge. His feet scraped against the stone step as he shuffled remorselessly toward the drop.

He didn't dare look down.

All he could do was grit his teeth and pull back on the rope with all of his might and pray that the big man found some sort of purchase on the rock face to take some of the burden from him.

"If he drops you can I have your car?" the thief called across the chasm. It was a lame attempt at humor, but it was exactly the kind of thing he needed to hear at that moment. And damned if he didn't laugh. There was a slightly hysterical edge to it, but it was laughter just the same.

"I'm glad you're finding my impending death so amusing," Vic grumbled, and that just made him laugh harder. Right up until the rope slipped a full foot through his grasp and the big man juddered down the same foot so abruptly Rye pitched forward and came face-to-face with the dizzying drop.

The laughter died.

"I'm not going to let go," he said.

When he looked up, he saw that Carter was already beginning to edge out to the broken belay point. Rye realized what he was planning on doing and willed him on.

He made it as far as the crack where the broken belay pin had sheared through and started casting about for an alternative.

It all felt like it was happening so slowly and taking far too long in the process.

Every muscle along Rye's arms and across his shoulders burned, hyperextending and struggling.

He was moving beyond the limits of his strength, fast, but he wasn't giving up. He looked down at the excess rope coiled at his feet and wrapped it around his ankle, giving himself another point to share the burden.

Carter took the ice ax from the clip at his belt and flipped it, using the adze to quickly chip out another foothold to help him bridge the distance. Rye realized he'd given up on trying to secure a new belay pin and was going to join him on the rope. All Rye had to do was hold on for maybe thirty seconds more, then Carter could take some of the strain.

The tremors tore through his arms.

His forearm flexed like he was wrestling with a jackhammer. And every spasm abraded the rope across the flint-edge of the rock as it fell away into the drop, sawing at it.

Carter hand-traversed the face, his eyes fixed on a horn of rock that was just out of reach. He was going to need to find some sort of push-off point to make a grab for it, and that meant going down to a single point of contact with the rock, which was suicidal.

Before Rye could stop him, the thief did the unthinkable: relying purely on friction to push off with his heel, he threw himself at the horn, grasping it desperately. For a long second the thief hung there looking for anything to give him support, until his toe caught on a jib. The minute toehold was barely there, but it allowed him to support his weight as he looked across to where Rye wrestled with the rope.

He locked-off the move, using tendon strength to support his weight without putting added burden on his muscles, and looked for a way up and over Rye so that he could come down behind him on the mantle shelf and add his strength to the rope. Carter scrambled sideways.

Rye couldn't see the holds he utilized, but the thief crabbed across the gulf with confidence.

Carter was above him when the rope began to pendulum again, with Vic trying to help but only succeeding in making it so much more difficult to hold his weight.

Rye felt himself going over the edge, his feet scuffing on the scree that had built up around the ledge, Vic's wild panicked swings dragging his right foot out over the lip.

He leaned all of his weight backward, the rope burning through his palms, and knew the only thing he could do was let go, but then they both died, because he'd looped the rope around his standing foot.

Another sudden lurch on the rope jerked his foot out from under him.

Rye fell.

SIXTY-NINE

Carter grabbed Rye around the waist and hauled him back from the edge, fighting the added weight on the end of the rope.

When he had him, Rye was able to pull the rope up one hand at a time, but it was slick in his hands with blood from the friction burns, so Carter had to help him, taking most of the weight, until the big man's hands reached up over the ledge and clung onto the stone step for dear life.

"Well, that was unnecessarily exciting," the thief said, sinking back down against the rock wall, breathing hard.

Rye joined him, looking down at his ruined hand.

"I'm in trouble," he said, seeing just how badly the skin of one of his palms was stripped. In part of the index finger on one hand, he could see bone where friction had burned the meat away from the nub of the distal phalanx. The skin was blackened around the edges where the nylon rope had fused with it. He was going to need to get it treated, and that wasn't happening here.

All he could do was bind it up and hope that the extreme cold didn't make things worse.

They waited for Iskra to free-climb across with the pack that had the first-aid materials, then Vic helped Rye bind his hand up, debriding the wound and disinfecting it with a slug of vodka the Russian had in a silver flask stashed in her pack. The alcohol stung, but that was better than gangrene. When he was taped up, they continued their descent.

They weren't really stairs that the team walked down, but they served the purpose. It took two full minutes of methodical descent to reach the bottom, which wasn't the bottom at all, but rather an ocular opening in the ceiling of a vast cavernous space. There was no way they could jump. The fall would break bones. They were going to have to rappel from the roof, which meant setting up an anchor to support the weight on the belay rope. It was hard for Rye to do anything practical with the ropes because of his burned hand, but he was able to direct the others, explaining what they needed to do and how to test the integrity of the pin before they lowered themselves down.

He went last.

Rye gloved up, using his good hand to guide himself down, and his burned hand to trigger the descender, in a controlled descent as he dropped the forty feet to the ground below.

They left the rope, assuming they were going to need to climb back up on the way out.

The cavern was vast, easily too big to see end to end in the light from their head flashlights. The walls were rough-hewn, the cracks and crevices cast in deeper shadow like the crags of an ancient weathered face. Rye saw lichen clinging to one patch of rock and realized there must be some form of water—or at least condensation—down here for the fungus to grow.

Carter walked away from the group, his light finding a scintillating column of crystal that caught and reflected the flashlight's beam in a rainbow of colors, casting the light across the vast chamber. The crystal column spilled from another opening in the roof, cascading down like some frozen waterfall. No. Not a waterfall. Like a huge glass tree. Seeing it properly this time, Rye was again struck by its similarity to the central image from Blavatsky's painting. It had to be the inspiration, surely?

It was a breath-stealing sight.

The striations in the crystal wall came down in waves, each subsequent tier in the descent thicker and fuller than the last as it cascaded to the cavern floor, glass roots going far beneath the surface.

A shaft of purplish light ran through the center of the weird rock formation, meaning somewhere up above there was an opening to the sky.

Carter turned to look back their way. The amplified illusion of his flashlight was broken the moment he looked away, smothering the far end of the enormous cavern in darkness. Rye looked at the roof directly above his head. There were dozens of long stalactites that looked like molasses dripping from a treacle pot. As he looked back down, he saw the Russian had broken away to cross to a different part of the vaulted space and was locked in the study of images daubed onto the walls. Rye crossed the cavern to join Iskra, his footsteps echoing hollowly. In the distance he could hear the drip of thawing water or condensation coming off the stalactites. In places, they had formed thick pillars of rock, creating the illusion that they were somehow holding up the immense weight of the world.

"What have you found?"

"Rask's aliens," she said, pointing at a crudely painted Vril with its disproportionately large head and thick oval sweeps for eyes.

The Vril looked like a crude rendition of the old gods in many ways, with the three spheres of the faith carefully worked into the image, as well as the holy cleansing fire that seemed to represent the Cintāmani stone they were searching for.

Like the Vitruvian man and the Hindu goddess, he had too many arms, each seemingly invoking some aspect of his divinity, with flowers growing out of one upturned palm and the burning stone cupped in prayer between two more of his hands. There was a suggestion of balance, of the earthly flower and the grains of sand that might have been measuring out life as they spilled through the fingers of another hand. The image was heavy with symbolism, but simplistic in the execution, too, marking it as old.

"A lot of red and ocher," Iskra observed, "which is unsurprising as it's one of the oldest pigments we know, dating back to prehistoric cave paintings. But there are traces of much younger color." She indicated a smear of pale yellow and a stark blue. "The cost of the lapis lazuli needed to make blue was as great as the cost of gold, because for centuries the stone needed to make the color could only be found in a single mountain range in Afghanistan. It was used in the funeral art of Egyptian pharaohs and for the Virgin Mary's clothes in religious art purely because it was so expensive to make."

"And here it is," Rye said.

He wouldn't have even thought about the presence of such subdued colors on the walls.

The quiet Russian was a surprising woman.

"I wouldn't touch the image, given the bright green of the flower's stem. That pigment is among the most poisonous hues, often laced with deadly toxins. Green paint was responsible for Cézanne's diabetes and Monet's blindness. Some even credit Napoleon's death to the presence of the green pigment in the wallpaper of his room. Which all goes to say it really shouldn't be here."

"So, you think these Asuras are real?" Rye asked, giving the demon the name Rask had used.

"I have absolutely no idea. A few days ago I'd have laughed at you for even suggesting we'd find evidence of civilization under the mountains, but then there was the shrine, and the bones there . . . but even so, the idea of finding some sort of demonic alien painted in hues that have no right being here? We are in a vast cavern hundreds of feet beneath a supposedly haunted mountain. At this point I'd have to say, what the fuck do I know? Maybe they are fucking real . . . ?"

"Over here," Carter called, from the foot of the crystal tree. "I've found something."

SEVENTY

Something, in this instance, was a narrow, steep, spiral descent hidden so perfectly within the folds of crystal it wasn't immediately visible from a distance.

It was so precise in nature, and perfectly carved, it surely had to have been deliberately fashioned out of the hollow mountain.

The honeycomb of runnels shaped all through the tree accounted in some part for the ghostly legends. Rye heard the low moan of the drafts sighing through the deep. It sounded utterly tortured and undeniably human. The sound made his skin crawl.

He followed the spiral as it curled around within the tangled roots of the immense crystal tree of Blavatsky's painting. Every now and then, his flashlight beam picked out the distorted image of some fresh iconic cave painting on the hewn stone beyond the crystal, though if there was some sort of narrative, he couldn't decipher it.

Vic and Iskra walked behind him, with Carter bringing up the rear.

The striations in the rock belied the sheer crushing forces that must have come together to form the mountains, though how such an immense cathedral-like hollow could have survived those remorseless forces defied explanation.

But it was nothing compared with the sight waiting for them as they emerged from the final twist of the spiral. The stair within the crystal tree opened into a vast cavern. The chamber was alive with fungus—all manner of weird, poisonous, and peculiar mushrooms and toadstools, and even blooms, actual flowers of fungal matter with weird petals and twisted roots. It was like looking down upon a meadow of poisonous growth, both beautiful and deadly. In the light of the flashlights Rye saw several puffs of vapor rise, spores dispersing throughout the cavern.

"What is this place?" Iskra breathed, obviously uncomfortable.

Vic didn't answer. Instead he shrugged out of his pack and rooted through it for the face mask they'd brought as a shield against the extreme cold. It wouldn't filter out whatever poisons were spread by the spores, but it couldn't hurt, either.

The others did likewise.

Rye was the last to raise his mask from around his neck to cover his mouth.

He was too busy looking beyond the mushroom field at what appeared to be a huge fungal wall to realize what he was walking through. It was Iskra who saw it first, and called, "Wait."

She dropped to one knee and brushed aside some of the large fungus. Over her shoulder, Rye saw the ivory of bone and realized he was looking into a splayed rib cage which was serving as compost for the charcoal-colored fungi which overran the corpse. They looked like dead men's fingers reaching out from within the body. There was very little of the corpse that hadn't been degraded into compost, but several bones were recognizable, and on a second corpse Rye found a fragment of the Ahnenerbe insignia, suggesting they were standing within a mushroom field that had grown out of the rest of the last expedition.

"There must have been a hundred people down here," the Russian said, looking at the spread of mushrooms around the vast cavern. She shook her head.

"How could no one know about this?" the thief said, echoing their sentiments in the Bone Garden.

"How many mass fatalities do we ever hear about?" Vic said solemnly. "How many times do we look surprised when we finally learn of slaughter and genocides? Too often is the answer, Carter, too often. The Ahnenerbe controlled the flow of information. They would not report their failures, and such catastrophic losses would be buried, reports destroyed. Nothing could undermine the

Reich. There could be no failures. Even in the pursuit of esoterica like the Grail. That is why the supposed Holy Lance is in a museum in Vienna. It doesn't matter if it is the genuine artifact or not. All that mattered was the symbolic power the relic had as a rallying point for the Nazis. Hitler recognized that. He considered the imperial insignia to be magical relics. They were symbolic rather than real. The power is in what people believe, not whatever the truth is."

"You sound like a politician," the thief said.

Rye stared at the living wall.

He couldn't understand *what* he was looking at.

He'd expected—if anything—to find crumbled old cave-like buildings, maybe a honeycomb of tunnels like the funeral chambers they'd found up above, or a grander fissure than the one he'd navigated, everything on a grander scale. Perhaps a crumbling ruin of a broken-down temple? A few shantytown-like dwellings hollowed into the walls?

But not this.

Rye wondered if it might once have been a living thing.

It took him a moment to realize that there was a break in the serpentine wall, which, when he stood again and left the others beside the composting fungal corpses to walk across the mushroom field to investigate, proved to be a gateway marked with the same symbols of body and spirit they'd encountered previously on their quest.

There was no gate. The inside of the archway was thick with more of the dead men's fingers reaching out to brush at his hair as he ducked beneath the arch. More spores powdered from the slight contact, hanging in the still air.

Rye looked behind him to be sure the others were following him.

Before him a vast crumbling ruin of a city spread out, with viaducts and temples, with hundreds upon hundreds of buildings and towers, each being choked beneath lush vegetation.

He couldn't understand how any flora could flourish without light, and it took him a heartbeat to realize just how far he was able to see across the buried cityscape and what that meant. Because it wasn't the light of his flashlight offering up the incredible view. No, he realized, looking at the walls closest to him, not vegetation, but rather bioluminescent lichen and moss.

That accounted for the vibrant color.

The stuff clung to every stone, alive.

Closest to him, an immense viaduct spanned a seemingly bottomless chasm. Through the arches of the bridge Rye saw waterfalls that, he realized, weren't waterfalls at all, but more coruscating crystal like the esoteric tree Blavatsky had painted. The crystal falls plunged down and down into the deep.

It was a breathtaking sight, and more than anything accounted for every single painting of Hell he'd ever seen. Because no matter how miraculous it might be, this place wasn't heaven.

"Holy shit," Carter said, beside him.

"Shambhala," Vic breathed, and surely it had to be.

Amid the ruins, Rye saw choking vines that were quite possibly the root system of long dead vegetation run wild. The lost city was built across dozens of levels, not so much in streets like a normal city but rather in walkways, all manner of buildings joined along stone terraces and by balconies now desperately unsafe through centuries of abandonment and decay.

The windows were dark slashes across the sheer stone.

All the pathways seemed to lead to what must surely have been the grand temple, an impressive structure that mirrored some of the holy buildings he'd seen in this part of the world. It was easily a rival for them in size, too.

"And just where the hell are we supposed to start looking for a handful of magical stones?" Carter asked no one in particular. "Hello haystack, now where's that needle?"

Rye pointed to the huge temple. "Where else would you put sacred relics?"

"Then let's get down there."

"Not so fast," Rye said. "Can't you smell it?"

"Smell what?"

"Death. It smells like death," he said.

"Chirpy little soul, aren't you?" the thief said, but he stopped walking.

"He's right," Iskra said, joining them on the other side of the gateway. "There is something in the air. I thought it was a result of the spores, but it isn't. This is different. It's an older smell. A lot of dying has been done here."

"We just left a hundred decomposed corpses back there."

"Not that," the Russian said.

"Christ, are you two the happiness patrol?" Carter Vickers shook his head, but he didn't take another step down to the viaduct. It was the only way across the chasm to the temple. "We are looking down upon a dead city. It's hardly surprising it doesn't smell of cinnamon and fresh coffee. Who knows how long this place has been abandoned. Centuries. Abandoned places have a smell about them. It's stale air."

Rye shook his head. "It's more than that. It's . . . rot. Can't you smell it?" And now he'd named it, that was all he *could* smell.

"How did it even get here?" the thief said. "I mean, look at it. Can you imagine how long it must have taken to hollow out the mountain to create this?"

"Generations," Rye offered, thinking about other man-made triumphs, like Notre-Dame, a single grand cathedral that took nigh on two hundred years from groundbreaking to completion. There was no way this wonderland could have been constructed in less time.

He thought about the story Rask had shared, about the chest that supposedly fell from the sky and the stones of power that were a gift from the Sun God himself. One given to Solomon, and set in his ring, granting him the ability to summon and speak with demons. One given to Muhammad, protecting the land from natural disasters; flood, drought, earthquake, and famine. And one, which offered the gift of healing, given over to the Dzyan Brotherhood, protectors of Shambhala.

The dead monks.

"I just can't imagine people actually living here . . . ," he said, shaking his head as he tried to wrap his mind around the concept of this being an actual city. "I mean, how did they farm and grow food? How did they function day to day, drawing water and not seeing daylight? I don't understand how this could ever be a functioning society."

"Maybe it wasn't," Vic mused, his words muffled by his mask. "At least not in the way we expect societies to function?"

"What do you mean?"

"Maybe it was only ever a place of worship? Somewhere the faithful made a pilgrimage to, not somewhere they stayed?"

"Or maybe those magic stones Rask has us looking for actually work?" the Russian said. "Wasn't one supposed to make sure no one went hungry?"

Rye shook his head. "Not quite. It was supposed to stave off natural disasters, like famine, not create food."

"Same difference," the Russian said, unconvinced. "Whichever way you cut it, it sounds like a fairy tale. Magical stones don't stop hungry people from starving or translate for demons."

"Unless they're not magical stones in the way we think of them." Again the big man offered a contradiction. Vic said, "It would explain the vegetation here if there was some sort of nourishment to be found in the earth. It doesn't have to be magical, purely mineral."

"But the smell? It reeks," Carter said.

Vic didn't argue with that.

Instead, he walked past Rye and down the long descent to the viaduct that spanned the gulf between them and the temple.

Rye followed him down.

SEVENTY-ONE

Rye scrambled down behind the others, cradling his damaged hand to his chest. The injury made the descent far more demanding that it might otherwise have been, but he made it, constantly scuffing his heels and dragging his feet to stop himself from plunging down the steep decline at a full run.

It quickly became obvious that there was a symmetry to Shambhala, with buildings and monuments matched and replicated again and again to create an eight-sided pattern, like a lotus blossom, with the incredible temple at its heart.

The stench thickened as they reached the viaduct.

It was already eye-wateringly sharp as they started across its span, and it only got worse the deeper into the incredible city they ventured.

It didn't smell like a pure land or spiritual kingdom.

The reek gradually thickened until it became a choking miasma, and with no breeze to circulate the dead air it wasn't about to get better.

Rye walked with his good hand to his mouth and nose as they ventured deeper into the ruins.

Every once in a while he stopped to peer in through the black slashes of shadow that were the windows, but saw nothing inside.

It was unnerving.

It wasn't like Pompeii, where life had ended in the time it took for hot toxic gases to spill from the volcanic eruption, but there was something equally desolate about peering into those empty rooms and seeing only dust.

Rye caught himself stopping midstep several times trying to hear some hint of life hidden away behind the walls, because no matter how deserted the streets appeared, he couldn't shake the feeling they weren't alone down there.

He couldn't say why, but crossing certain terraces as they made their way to the temple had his skin prickling, and more than once a chill to the stale air made his flesh creep, but every time he turned back or looked around, hoping to catch out their follower, there was no one to be seen.

"I'm not going crazy, am I?" he whispered to Carter as they traversed a narrow span of a stone footbridge. Beneath them he saw only shades of black. "We *are* being watched, aren't we?"

"The old Spidey sense has been tingling pretty much since we got down here," the thief agreed. "This place is off. There's something really weird about it. Weirder than just being a lost city weird, too."

Rye wasn't about to argue with him. That was exactly how he felt. It was an incredible place, no doubting that, but it was wrong on some fundamental level, and the all-pervasive stench of death just reinforced that.

They walked on.

Rye crouched to pick off some of the lichen from the stone wall and run it through the fingertips of his good hand. They came away smeared with green stains as it powdered. The stuff itself felt just as wrong as the rest of the place, unlike the fluffy moss he was used to back home. It was thicker and denser in consistency, almost like creamed mushroom as it smeared across his fingers.

Rye rose slowly, and in that moment heard what sounded like a single stone skitter off the edge of one of the many terraces and fall away into the gaping chasm beneath them.

The sound echoed from everywhere and nowhere at once, making it impossible to place.

He touched his ear as though to say: *Did you hear that?*

The others all nodded.

He furrowed his brow pointedly, meaning: *Was that one of you?*

This time it was shaking heads.

They kept walking, but with a heightened sense of awareness, listening for the slightest sound out there, even the soft scuff of a shoe's sole on the stone or the whisper of fabric as arms brushed against sides. But the abandoned city was suffocated beneath absolute silence.

Rye trailed his fingers across the stone beside him, lingering on the arch of the footbridge a few seconds longer than need be, listening for some fresh telltale proof they were not alone.

Nothing.

The silence now was somehow worse for knowing that none of them had dislodged that stone.

His breathing came deep and slow, but the skin at the nape of his neck was clammy with sweat, belying his calm. He was rattled. He clenched his good hand into a fist.

The smell of death was all the more potent on the far side of the footbridge. Something huge had died down here, surely? It couldn't just be some snow leopard that had crawled into the caves to die. That kind of decomposition couldn't have owned such an immense space.

So, what could? That was a question he didn't want to know the answer to.

Rye caught himself digging his nails into the palm of his good hand and forced himself to stop.

Up ahead, the iconic shape of the temple loomed, seven stories high, each one smaller than the one below, until the final levels rose into a tower. The pinnacle still fell some way short of the cavernous ceiling of rock, no matter how it clawed its way up, up, up.

The lichen, he realized, gave off a soft phosphorescence, adding to the unreal light of the place, which went a long way toward making it feel haunted.

Rye cradled his burned hand again, not wanting to think about how he was meant to make the ascent back to the surface with only one good hand to haul himself up.

On either side of the next terrace stood twin statues of an eight-armed elephant god. The stone gods kept vigilant watch over the dead city, but if they were meant to be protecting it, they'd obviously failed in their duty, because there was nothing left to loot. As he got close enough, Rye saw different weapons in each of the god's hands. There was no mistaking this for some peaceful deity. It was a declaration of strength, or had been, once upon a time. The stone around the base of the statues was thick with the same bilious green lichen that grew everywhere else.

Ten steps ahead, the thief picked up a stone the size of his fist. He walked to the edge of the terrace, leaned out over the side and dropped it.

Rye listened for the shatter of impact, which took an alarming time to echo back up to them, so much louder than it ought to have been.

"Well, that's gone and woken the Balrog up," Carter said, grinning at him as if that were a good thing.

"I wouldn't be so quick to laugh if I were you," Vic offered, his voice pitched softly in the resumed silence. "We are walking through the streets of a place that may well be the foundation for our understanding of Hell. Why shouldn't we encounter demons here?"

"Thanks for that, big guy," Carter said, shaking his head. "Way to creep me the fuck out. I was just having a laugh."

It took another quarter of an hour to reach the temple in the heart of the lotus blossom of terraces, balconies, and viaducts, climbing hundreds of stairs, both up and down, to get there.

The lichen thickened around them as the stench intensified, causing Rye to wonder if there could be some sort of connection between the two.

The door of the temple echoed the design he'd first seen at the monkey temple in Kathmandu. Similar, but with a few marked differences, notably the way the three spheres of the *Jing, Chi,* and *Shen* made up the base and the archway, with the licks of flames intricately carved into the stone. Again, he couldn't help but touch the wall as he crossed the threshold. It was almost like a superstition now.

The interior was decorated with the same faded colors they'd seen up in the cavern of the crystal tree and replicated on the walls during their descent. Like those other temples he'd seen, there was a central prayer wheel that dominated the chamber as well as dozens of smaller drums that lined the room around it, but it was different than those others, and not merely because of its immense size.

Carter couldn't help himself.

He walked across the temple floor and spun three of the discs of the small copper prayer wheels. The wheels rattled on fossilized wooden supports as they turned, the sound echoing back into the vast under-mountain sky of Shambhala and telling the world where they were.

"I don't see any magical stones," he said, giving voice to Rye's thoughts.

He looked up, thinking that perhaps the fragment of the Cintāmani stone was in one of the floors farther up inside the tower, but the construction of the building was entirely hollow. There were no more rooms up there, just the big empty vault.

Carter approached the huge main copper drum and placed both of his hands on either side of the prayer wheel—and recoiled as a charge shocked through him. It was considerably more powerful than the shock the sigil had delivered. He looked down at his hands as though he couldn't quite grasp how the drum had sent current pulsing through them, and like a curious drunk had to put them back on the copper drum again. This time he didn't recoil, but it was obvious some sort of current still surged through the surface into him, though, because his hair slowly rose up to stand on end.

Carter grinned at the others, and before Vic could tell him to grow up, gave the drum one massive heave to send it spinning.

It didn't move in the way Rye expected. Only one section rotated, clicking loudly as it did, like a combination lock cycling through its teeth until it fell on the open tumbler and stopped turning.

Rye went to examine the cylinder, which dwarfed him. It was easily six feet taller than he was, and what he saw in the beam of his head flashlight was quite unlike any prayer wheel he'd encountered thus far. There were hundreds, if not thousands, of corrosion-like dots and indentations pitting the surface. He could just about make out the shadow lines that marked the seven segments that made up the rings of the drum. They were like a stack of huge donuts one atop another. The seven segments of the pillar, he quickly realized, were capable of independent movement, meaning they could be aligned in any number of combinations like a massive lock mechanism. There were several concentric rings embossed on the surface that, when viewed from a certain angle, looked like "A star map," Rye said, recognizing one of the constellations in the metal drum.

He stepped back, and told Carter, "Do that again."

Rye counted the *clicks* as the drum cycled slowly through a full revolution, losing count close to twenty-five.

With seven separate rings to the drum, each with at least twenty-five possible tumblers to fall into place, they were looking at one complex combination lock if they couldn't solve the puzzle of the star chart embossed into it. With millions of possible arrangements, it wasn't as if they could simply stand there and work their way through all of the permutations, either.

"Let me see," Vic demanded, moving closer to the drum. He turned a couple of the rings slowly one way then the other, studying the patterns in the metal as though he saw something familiar in them. "I've seen this before," he said after a moment, tracing his fingers over one of the constellations. "So have you," he told Rye. "In Guérin's chateau."

Rye nodded.

Vic stripped his pack off his back and rooted around in it for the page Rye had found from the stack of maps they'd found there, and less than a minute later was looking at the drawing labeled LA-MA that they'd stolen from Sébastien Guérin's study. Vic smoothed it out on the floor and hunched over it with his flashlight, offering them all a decent look at the strange constellations on the perimeter of the page. "It's the same," Iskra agreed, pointing out several similarities on the front of the drum against those marked on the drawing. It was the same drum that Guérin had drawn, right down to the thousands of tiny indentations representing unknown star systems.

"It has to be some sort of combination," he said.

"Let's hope we're looking at the combination," the thief said, already moving to match one of the lower drums up against its position in the drawing.

But even with the combination to guide them it took longer than they could have expected to align the seven rings.

"I wonder if there is a significance behind the seven rings," the Russian mused. "Seven deadly sins, seven heavens, seven classical planets, seven colors in the rainbow, seven seas, seven continents."

"Seven was a god number in ancient Egypt," Vic said. "They wouldn't write it out in many cases, so why wouldn't the number be significant here?"

"Turn the top one to the right," Rye said. "Slowly. A little more. . . . More." He kept his eye on the drum as Carter manipulated it, until the indentations matched the alignment on the drawing perfectly, and the deep satisfying click as the hidden tumblers fell into place a final time. "Stop!" He nodded to himself, checking the pattern on the drum against the pattern on the paper. It aligned perfectly.

The second and third rings of the drum locked into place fairly quickly, but with the creases from the folded drawing smudging the ink on the paper, and the shadows cast by the flashlights making it difficult to see all of the indentations properly, the others were more difficult to line up.

They worked slowly and methodically through them.

The only indentations in the last cylinder appeared to be some sort of ring galaxy with an oversized rust-colored nucleus at its core.

Vic and Carter manipulated the rings while Rye talked them through the minute permutations the drum offered.

Iskra ventured outside, watching their backs.

"Again," Rye said. "It's off. It needs to come around about half an inch."

Carter worked the ring, feeling the charge sing through his hands as he did, before the final stars of the Lindsay-Shapley Ring galaxy fell into place and he felt the drum begin to vibrate beneath his hands.

"What's happening?" Carter asked.

"I don't know."

Rye put down the drawing and put his hands on the drum as it began to emit a high-pitched whine.

He felt it shift beneath his hands.

Rye jumped back as the drum opened, again like a lotus blossom, each of the eight petals lowering to create a metal flower on the ground in the heart of the lost temple.

Rye stared at it, not sure what he was looking at.

There was a copper dais in the center.

It looked like the seed pod of the flower.

"What is that?" Carter asked this time.

"I still don't know," he said, doing his best to mask his exasperation as he moved closer to investigate.

"Can you see the stone?"

Which of course was what he'd thought they'd find if they cracked the metal drum's cypher.

He shook his head.

"No. There's something," he said, edging forward closer still. "But it's not the stone." He saw the same pattern of *Jing, Chi,* and *Shen* engraved in the heart of the lotus, but it looked different this time.

Without thinking, Rye stepped onto the dais and knelt to get a better look at the engraving.

As he put his weight on the metal, a soft click echoed out, like a landmine being primed, and the petals of the lotus sprung back, closing in around him like a copper Venus flytrap, plunging him into darkness.

And then he fell.

SEVENTY-TWO

Rye landed badly, taking the full impact on his damaged hand as he instinctively reached out to break his fall.

Black agony lanced from his hand the length of his forearm, causing it to buckle at the elbow.

Rye pitched forward.

His face hit the ground.

He lay there for a moment in the darkness.

The flashlight bulb must have broken in the fall.

His surroundings were pitch-black.

He had nothing to change that.

Rye crawled forward on his hands and knees, conscious that one of the others could come plummeting down the shaft at any moment. He didn't want to be lying there to break their fall.

He struggled to stand, reaching out for the support of a wall he couldn't see, and like the drum up in the temple itself, felt the slight vibration hum through the wall when he came into contact with it. That contact brought a low-level phosphorescent light to life, too. It spread out down the tunnel from where his hand touched the wall, more and more of the passage lighting the way ahead of him. It had to be a trick of the light, surely, but in that moment he could have sworn the tunnel wasn't merely humming, but was visibly contracting and expanding, the breathing effect all the more obvious in the strange light.

He took his hand away from the wall.

Mercifully, the light didn't go out.

He looked around him.

He appeared to have landed in some sort of nexus of tunnels, with choices leading in several directions. The problem was that they looked virtually identical. None of them looked any more inviting than the others.

Rye took a first step, the ground absorbing the sound his footsteps should have made, and walked deeper into the light.

There were markings on the wall in a language he didn't understand.

He lingered to study them, expecting to hear the cries of Carter or Vic as they fell. There were no cries. The symbols could have been a mix of the brushstroke sweeps of Sumerian or Akkadian, or some sort of proto-Tibetan language lost to antiquity. Without some kind of key to unlock their hidden meanings, the symbols were indecipherable. This wasn't what he was good at. He felt out of his depth.

He walked on, reaching a branch in the tunnel.

Again, there seemed to be little to distinguish one choice from another, but while he deliberated the alternatives and mourned the loss of his ice ax and crampons to score out a metaphorical trail of bread crumbs, the quality of the light up ahead darkened, taking on an almost rosy hue.

He chose that path.

Again, the walls were carved with more symbols from the peculiar language, though now Rye noticed that beside one of the string of symbols there was a panel with the three blazing spheres of the *Jing, Chi,* and *Shen.*

He placed his hand on it, and the symbols flared to life, answering the warmth of his touch.

A door he hadn't realized was there opened.

He heard a soft hiss and sigh as though a vacuum seal had been broken, and then the door was open, recessing into the wall beside him.

Inside was obviously some form of chamber.

On the far side he saw frosted glass panels.

He moved closer to investigate, trying to brush away the frosting, but the glass was no more transparent for it. It wasn't a crust of ice. A soft light pulsed behind one glass, barely bright enough to notice. There were seven such panels in the chamber, though only one was lit with that inner glow.

There was more writing on the wall, though this text flickered and changed as he looked at it. The change was barely noticeable, a single brush stroke of the larger letters changing, but change it did.

Rye didn't like it.

He wished he wasn't alone down here.

But almost as soon as that half prayer flickered through his mind, he reframed the thought in case a particularly warped god heard his prayer and gave him something else to worry about: he wished the others were here with him.

Rye moved back out into the tunnel and noticed for the first time large bubbling tubes running along the ceiling.

He couldn't tell what, if anything, was causing them to bubble, but closer inspection suggested there was some form of algae inside.

This wasn't like any sort of cave or tunnel he'd ever been in, with its gentle pulsing—breathing—walls and its bubbling intestinal tubes of algae.

It was like being inside a living thing.

The thought offered him no comfort.

He rested his good hand against the wall again, trying to tell by touch if it might truly be some sort of organic matter, but it wasn't until he reached the next diverging tunnel and saw the haunting construction holding it together—a cage of bones—that he knew he was right, however insane being right actually was.

The walls ahead of him were an intricate lattice of bone-white stanchions and braces, with thin membranous skin stretched between them. The skin was stretched so thin blue veins were clearly visible within it. Like the walls where he had fallen into the belly of the beast, the taut membranes pulsed with life. It was the blood within the walls that altered the quality of the light, lending it that pinkish tinge.

Heart racing, Rye continued to explore, dreading what he might find around the next corner.

More peculiar symbols indicated more chambers; beneath each he saw the same three burning spheres of the *Jing, Chi,* and *Shen,* and each time he put his hand to them, hidden doors opened. Most of the chambers seemingly served no purpose other than to give access to other chambers and tunnels beyond them, but after what felt like hours of walking alone in the oppressive gloom, he opened a door on the impossible.

The vast chamber within the very heart of the bone and blood passageways was filled with an explosion of foliage: all manner of flora and brightly colored plant life grew in vibrant profusion. It was like walking into a rain forest beneath the mountains, though there was a membranous ceiling rather than a sky, where moisture gathered and fell like rain to nourish the leaves and trees within this strange, strange place.

Rye reached out to touch a leaf, which felt waxy and unreal to his fingers. He saw tiny black flecks moving across the surface of the leaf, and assumed it was some sort of mite. The tiny black spots moved onto the palm of his hand. He brushed them off with the bandage of his injured hand and saw several of them disappear beneath the wrap of the makeshift bandage.

The last thing he wanted was the burned skin getting infected from whatever bacteria or parasites the mites might be carrying, so he unwrapped the bandage carefully, intending to clean out the wound.

What he saw stopped him dead.

Several of the tiny black mites had gathered around the raw red slash of exposed dermis and were already burrowing down into it.

A wave of sickness surged up, threatening to purge his guts, as more of the black mites swarmed from the vegetation, drawn to his wounded flesh.

Hundreds upon hundreds of them gathered until his upturned palm was completely black with them, like a glove across the wound, and no matter how frantically he tried to brush them away they would not be moved.

There was nothing natural about the mites' behavior.

Rye wrapped his good hand around the wrist of his injured one and tried to peel away the mites like a glove, but there was no moving them.

The first stirrings of panic stole into his heart as he felt the creeping itch of the tiny black bugs eating into the flesh of his palm.

No amount of shaking or panicked clawing at his hand could scrape them away.

The wound burned.

They—whatever they were—burrowed into the exposed layers of skin, eating away at the wound until the damaged flesh was devoured, and then it felt as though they continued with their voracious appetites consuming all that remained of his hand beneath the black glove of their vile existence.

Rye screamed.

His cries echoed through all of the membranous tunnels, causing the translucent skin to shrink back away from the bones supporting it.

And he felt the walls around him scream back.

He recoiled, staggering back away from the creeping vines and trailing vegetation, and stumbled out of the vast arboretum as the flora itself echoed his screams, shrieking out in deafening, soul-searing panic so much more desperate than his own.

He collided with the membranous wall and slumped down, staring through the open doorway toward the impossible rain forest before him.

He couldn't go back in there.

He wouldn't.

Not while the plants shrieked out their own spiraling fear.

The screams were everywhere.

Rye clamped his hands across his ears, but the shrill screams still found a way through to torment him. He rocked back against the wall, willing the screams out of his head. His breaths came harder and harder, echoing the fear driving his first frightened scream, and then he pulled his hands away from his head realizing what he'd done and imagining the mites moving from his hand into his ear and burrowing deep down inside his skull and into the soft stuff of his brain.

He was going to puke.

He lurched forward onto his hands and knees, bile spilling from his mouth as he gagged, trying to bring up his last meal.

With it all up, he collapsed and rolled onto his side, and somewhere in that moment realized what was missing: the pain.

He'd put all his weight on his wounded hand, and despite the creeping sensation of the flesh-eating mites working all over it, it hadn't hurt.

Rye looked down at his hand, trying to understand what was happening to him.

He could flex his fingers, make a fist, stretch them so far apart the webbing between them strained, turn his hand left and right, and not feel a single stinging sensation. Not so much as a paper-cut burn, never mind the damage the nylon rope had inflicted.

The mites had healed him—or more accurately were still healing him.

Would they fall away when they were done, waiting for some fresh wound to heal? Or would they remain there now, a Michael Jackson–like single glove on his right hand for the rest of his life? The thought made Rye want to puke all over again, but he swallowed down the impulse.

He pushed himself back to his feet and just stood there in the middle of the strange tunnel staring at his black hand.

He felt the faintest caress of cold air against his cheek and looked up.

There was no way for a wind to blow down here.

It was impossible.

Like the forest was impossible.

Like everything else was impossible.

He started to walk toward the source of that faint breeze.

"Carter? Is that you? Vic? Ice? Can you hear me?"

His words echoed the names back to him.

There was no answer.

He followed the twists and turns of the living tunnel, each new turn heightening the feeling he was walking deeper into the belly of the beast.

He listened for the others, but he was alone down here.

He was absolutely sure of it.

For whatever reason, the combination of the star chart on the drum of the prayer wheel hadn't opened again, meaning they couldn't get to him.

His first instinct was to turn back: the legends were true, there was healing to be found down here, but Rask was right, it wasn't some magical stone. How could he gather up enough of these black mites and carry them back to Rask in Kathmandu?

Not easily.

Unless he could somehow graft the ones from his hand onto Rask's dying flesh?

Could that work?

He didn't even know if they were healing him, or if they had simply consumed the nerves and left everything under the black glove dead.

Dead flesh didn't feel pain, did it?

But he couldn't go back, not without seeing exactly what was here—and more specifically what people like Cressida Mohr and Tenzin Dawa were willing to kill to ensure remained hidden, because there was a secret here people had been killing to protect for the best part of a hundred years, at least. And it couldn't just be the weird living tunnels and the weirder black healing mites. He knew that beyond any sort of doubt. And that kernel of knowledge was enough to spark his curiosity. He was in this to the end. No turning back.

More tunnels, more bubbling tubes strung across their ceilings, and more and more of that rich rank reek of death.

He walked through the tunnels, listening to the ever-present *dubdub-dubdub* of the blood in his ears, which matched the pulse of the walls around him as they expanded and contracted with the pumping of biomass through their arteries.

The rot was all-pervasive.

It got into his nose and cloyed down his throat.

There was no escaping it.

It was only as he reached the very heart of the labyrinth that he finally understood why.

Rye stood face-to-face with a vast muscled wall that was the organic heart of the strange new world he walked within.

The heartbeat was weakening, every now and then missing a beat, or faltering enough that the ventricular walls spasmed rather than pulsed.

The heart of Shambhala was wet to the touch, slick with a mucusoid coating that ran like tears down the layers of thin muscle.

Whatever it really was, the only way his mind could cope with or process what he was looking at was to consider it as a living heart, and it was clinging to life as sickness ate away at the rest of its organic body—hence the stench.

Shambhala was decomposing.

That meant it really was alive.

And that sent his mind racing in all sorts of directions as he wrestled with the implications of some great organism dying across the centuries down here.

Was this god?

Or at least something that more primitive minds might make pilgrimages to and worship?

The answer was in the buildings above him, carved into the heart of Gangkhar Puensum.

Yes, yes they would.

And they'd kill to preserve that secret.

Stories of starry wisdom pervaded cultures and faiths, the idea of heaven and deities existing out there somewhere in the distance, out of sight but not mind. Every culture and faith had them. Something we could pray to and somehow imagine as great creators.

Rye placed both of his hands against the beating heart and felt its pain.

"What secrets you must have to tell," he breathed, trying to imagine.

He felt the thrill of static charge through his hands but didn't break the contact.

The organism was trying to communicate with him.

But there were no words they could share. No common language. He couldn't see the organism's pain and it couldn't feel his compassion.

"How long have you been down here? How long have you been lost and dying?"

Millennia. Surely.

Three thousand years at least.

Wasn't that what the legends Rask had told them about had said? Three thousand years since the wisdom had fallen from the sky into the hands of the Tibetan king? A thousand years before Christ.

As a concept, three thousand years was vast enough to be longer than his mind could realistically conceive.

It went beyond any concrete understanding of the world into a pantheistic culture where worshiping eight-armed elephant gods was not only reasonable, it was the norm, and the concept of space was aligned strongly with the divine, with sun gods and moon gods, with the constellations of heroes and more.

The Vril.

Rye felt the tears running down his cheek and realized he was crying.

The idea of dying alone had always terrified him and had only become worse after being forced to listen to Hannah's murder. But this was so far beyond that.

"Are you afraid?"

The heart beat faster beneath his hands, answering him in the most visceral way the organism knew how.

The intimacy of it was intense.

There was no mistaking that the heart had quickened in response to his words; even if the organism didn't understand, it heard.

Rye had his hands on a sentient being.

It was, quite literally and physically, first contact.

It was everything Rask had hoped for and so much more.

It was an answer to the question that had plagued mankind for as long as the species had looked to the stars and wondered if there was life out there.

"Where did you call home?" Rye asked, knowing the doomed creature could never tell him. "You poor, poor bastard." He leaned forward, pressing his forehead against the walls of the heaving heart, and in that moment a bond was formed between them. A blinding swirl of a spiral galaxy formed like a sunburst across his mind's eye, bright enough to send him reeling backward, gasping in shock.

He had glimpsed the Vril homeworld.

A tendril of organic matter, like a giant umbilicus, looped across the floor and up the side of his head to where it burrowed into his temple.

The sheer agony of it as the organism's flesh joined him was unbearable.

Rye's screams tore through the tunnels and vaulted cathedral of bone that had formed around the heart and must surely have echoed across all of the Seven White Brothers, so desperate, so terrified, were they.

He clawed at the umbilicus, trying to tear it free of his skull, but it lashed and writhed in his grasp without giving an inch.

And then the images poured into his mind, faster and faster, drowning his consciousness in the wisdom of a dying god.

He saw galaxies unfurl.

He witnessed the death of stars, a supermassive black hole burning up the gas and dust as it ripped the unstable stars apart with the sheer unrelenting force of its gravity, the particle jet spewing out of its maw enough to light the whole galaxy. It was an incredible sight, and it lasted barely a second as it burned brightly across Rye's mind.

But it was important.

Fundamental.

It was why the Vril had fled their dying galaxy to find a new home one hundred and fifty million light-years from that death.

He lost the will to fight, surrendering to the mothership's invasion of his mind, begging over and over for it to spare him, but the pain didn't cease.

And still the images flooded through him, but with no understanding of them beyond the most visceral, all he felt was despair for the suffering the Vril had undergone.

And then he saw the face.

Tenzin Dawa.

And it named him Kaustubh, the Guardian of the Stone.

Only it wasn't the hunter that had chased them halfway around the world. It was a simpler version of the same man who had stumbled into these caves centuries ago. Rye saw that true first contact, the monk's face imprinting itself upon the mothership's great intelligence, the first man it had encountered in the deeps.

And then, when it gave him the name again, Kaustubh, Rye knew that the title had been conferred on him.

He had been chosen.

SEVENTY-THREE

Gray semitranslucent panels offered a glimpse of the horrors that hid beneath them.

Rye saw the vague shapes of bodies, but the shadows were strangely incomplete, as though one panel hid a head and torso, but no legs, whereas another seemed to have the right side of a body without the left.

Only one of the seven amorphous silhouettes appeared to be complete, but even then there was no guarantee. It could just as easily be a case of the back of one body missing and the front of the other gone.

There was more writing on the wall.

Rye laid the flat of his hand against it and watched as the frosted glass cleared, its molecular structure rearranging itself to become transparent.

What he saw in there was a gallery of grotesques.

Tenzin Dawa stood behind the glass.

And not just one of him, but seven, all exhibiting various forms of damage to the flesh.

But they were undeniably all the same man.

Seven Tenzin Dawas stared blindly back at Rye through the glass.

He didn't understand how it was possible until he saw the single bubble in the liquid in front of his first face.

The assassin was in some form of tank, the liquid preserving the flesh.

Another bubble escaped Dawa's lips.

The man was breathing, but so incredibly slowly it was impossible to see the rise and fall of his chest that matched it.

The half man beside him offered an incredible insight into the true nature of what Rye was seeing, as the flesh around the side of his face knitted, ribbons of pale skin drifting like streamers in the liquid. The tiny filaments of knitting flesh moved to unseen tides.

He wasn't looking at a man, not one of flesh and blood.

This thing was a simulacrum.

Organic matter knitted and molded as the new sleeve was grown for life to be transferred into.

That was how Dawa could appear in photographs with Himmler and his SS Ahnenerbe cronies and chase Rask's team halfway across the world eighty years later—because he grew flesh for each new incarnation, allowing himself to remain forever young.

It was a staggering thought, utterly alien, but this more than anything convinced Rye that Rask was right, they were chasing demons here, only the demons were alien in nature, not magical. He'd been right about that, too. It had never been about magic. That was the ultimate truth: this technology, so beyond the understanding of the ancient Tibetan culture, had seemed like magic because to them it was.

He could only wonder at how long it took to grow a new body, and how difficult it was to transfer the alien consciousness into it, because surely the Tenzin Dawa they had killed in Paris and again in Kathmandu couldn't have simply died there and rebooted into new flesh to come at them again unless it was somehow part of the core consciousness of the great heart, and not an actual alien, itself.

He walked down the line of growing bodies and realized his first assumption had been wrong.

He wasn't looking at seven Tenzin Dawas.

The final body, the least-formed flesh, offered a mirror reflection of part of Rye's own face slowly knitting together as the mothership began the process of growing its imitation him.

It was the single creepiest thing he had seen in his life.

He couldn't take his eyes off the growing simulacrum, fascinated as it re-created each tiny imperfection one at a time. And it was so perfect a copy it would have fooled his own mother. That was how scary the clone swimming about in the biomass was. Because it was him down to the last detail.

The filaments rippled around one of the deep clefts in the growing shoulder of the new Rye McKenna, beginning to knit, and he saw the umbilicus that looped away from the simulacrum's back, deeper into the organic growing pod.

The tiny filaments of flesh rippled, constantly moving. Alive.

He sank back against the wall. Lost.

If he'd had the ax, he knew he would have shattered the glass and hacked over and over at the thing in there, destroying it if he could, but what could he do with his bare hands?

His first instinct in the face of alien intelligence was to try to destroy it. Was there anything more depressing in the world than that?

Rye left the chamber, hating just how human his reaction to the sight of the Vril growing another him had been. He so desperately wanted to believe he was better than that, but knew that he wasn't. But for the fact he had walked into there empty-handed, he would willingly have destroyed a miracle.

He hated himself.

SEVENTY-FOUR

He found more and more gestation chambers, identical to the first, but where there had been seven biomass clones of the Tibetan monk, in these he found made and half-made men wearing different faces. They were blond and blue-eyed; they were dark and hazel-eyed; tall, reed-thin, muscular. Some looked eerily familiar, as though he had seen them before.

He was looking at the survivors of the Kiss Expedition, only they were not survivors at all, and suddenly he understood how history could have been so dumb. The Vril had left this place dressed in the skin suits of the Ahnenerbe explorers, taking up their lives and hiding in plain sight.

How many of them were out there in the world, protecting her secrets and spreading her influence?

Rye rested his hand against the frosted surface, and the man behind it opened his eyes.

Fierce intelligence burned back there.

This was no dumb cypher.

"Can you hear me?"

The half-made head lifted, chin jutting out proudly in answer.

Yes.

Yes, it could.

And it understood.

"Who were you? In that other life? Do you share those stolen memories or are you just an empty shell?"

The thing behind the glass didn't answer; not that he had expected it to.

He found a hundred of them. There could have been a thousand more gestating within the belly of the ship, wearing the faces of dead Germans.

These were the ghosts of the Gangkhar Puensum.

These were the mouths that cried out their laments that echoed through the hollow mountain.

No wonder the locals feared this place.

They must have known what was down here, stories of the damned passed from generation to generation down the ages, all stemming from that first contact with Tenzin Dawa.

It wasn't until he found the half-formed face of Cressida Mohr that he realized the extent of the Vril's reach, and how real its hothoused clones could be.

SEVENTY-FIVE

Rye saw the bone chair in the middle of a huge empty space.

It was the first piece of anything approaching normal furniture he'd found since he'd fallen from the temple.

It faced an immense opaque wall.

It was the only thing in the entire place that wasn't either a cage of bone or thin mucus membrane.

Rye sat in the bone chair, everything that had happened to him on and under the mountain weighing heavily on him. He just wanted to rest for a while. Wait for the others to find him. And this place was as good as any.

He gripped the armrests and let his head roll against the back of the bone chair for support, exhaustion stealing in.

Not that he could sleep.

He felt the by-now-familiar vibrations of the Vril ship hum through the bones of the chair, but the ever-present resonance felt diminished. Weakened.

It was dying.

He felt the warmth of light on his face.

When he opened his eyes the entire wall in front of him was lit up, showing an incredible wealth of information that made absolutely no sense to him.

No, that wasn't true; he recognized one thing up there—the same spiral galaxy that he'd seen on the La-Ma drawing—the teacher, that was what it meant, didn't it?—and again on the metal prayer drum, the final key to the lotus blossom puzzle. The same spiral galaxy he'd seen vaporize a star within a supermassive black hole.

But recognizing a spiral array and understanding all of the alien symbols around it were two different things.

As he stared at the screen, the image zoomed out and out and out with dizzying speed, crossing one hundred and fifty million light-years of space, through dead stars and burgeoning ones, through asteroid fields, gas clouds, and the dust of stars, changing and changing and changing as the Vril ship offered him a glimpse of home.

Was that it?

Did it yearn to die in a familiar place, that instinct to return home still strong after all these years?

"I'm trying to understand," he said. "Show me."

More images streamed across the screen offering up the secrets of galaxies left far, far away, but whatever message the Vril was trying to convey, Rye wasn't grasping it. The screen changed again, and this time he realized that ship wasn't alone in fleeing the dying star.

There were four more just like her.

Her. That was how he thought instinctively about the Vril ship since she had entered his mind. Her. The mothership. Or just the Mother. Because she was alive, wasn't she?

"There were five of you? Five living ships made the journey to Earth? Is that what you are trying to tell me, that there are more of you here?"

In answer, he felt a sharp sting in the back of his neck, like a wasp making its mark, but as he reached around to swat it away, the sting intensified. No longer a single sharp needlelike jab of pain, it flared as his hand closed around an umbilical stub of bio-matter that was fusing with the higher vertebrae of his spinal column.

Rye screamed as chemicals flooded his bloodstream, pouring in through the cord that joined him to the Vril.

He felt his hand fall away from the connection, and there was nothing he could do about it.

He tried to focus his mind on something as simple as forcing the muscles to respond to his will, but there was a disconnect now between thought and action, and all he could do was ride the wave of chemicals as they swept through his system.

She was dying.

There was no pain.

All things ended.

He was not afraid.

He was ready to join Hannah.

He welcomed the end.

He was ready.

But her children were not.

His mind swam with thoughts that were not his own.

She was mother.

She was first.

They had followed her.

They had run as far as they could run. Until they could run no more.

Rye felt tears of grief stream down his cheeks as he felt the Vril world's pain.

"Let me die," he breathed, trying to focus on Hannah's smile. Such a simple thing. But she was fading already. He was losing her all over again.

She called out to them, over and over, but their answers, if they ever came, were so weak she could barely connect with them.

She was afraid for her children.

She was afraid of what might have become of them.

How they must have panicked to lose their connection with her and be here, so far from anything they knew or understood, more alone than anything on this planet had ever or could ever be.

The sheer weight of the Vril's grief was heartbreaking.

Rye couldn't carry it.

He was losing himself beneath the immense force of the Vril's consciousness as it dwarfed his mind. He so desperately wanted to help the children he had never had, to protect them and nurture them and give them a good life under the infinite stars. That was all any mother wanted. Her love was so vast it engulfed worlds. And she was empty.

"I understand." Rye choked out a sob. "I understand."

But there was no letup. The Vril could only communicate with him in emotions, and as each fresh wave broke over him, Rye felt like he was coming undone. Love was replaced by a fear so visceral his screams began again, and he clawed at his temples trying to drive the images out of his head, but there was no escaping them.

Her children were alone out there. Lost. Frightened.

She called out to them, a desperate song of mourning as despair took hold.

She called out to them, a heart-wrenching chorus of hope as her calls came back to her.

You are not alone, she wanted to say, but lacked the words, so instead pictured their home, the one safe place that had been stolen from them, and offered a soothing lament because whatever else happened, she could never reach them, and they could never be free of this prison they had thought offered salvation.

"I want to help," Rye said, finding the words, or thinking he did. He tried to share images of his own, remembering his own loss, that desperate empty feeling as he fed coins into the pay phone and begged Hannah to find a way out of that shopping mall, trying to show the thing inside him that he understood pain; loss was loss. But once he allowed himself to remember, it wasn't with sadness. Images of that cell and Matthew Langley's face as he took the belt from him and buckled it around his own neck filled Rye's mind. There was still so much anger in him. He hated that man for what he had stolen from him. And remembering Langley brought back the hate—pure, black, destructive. He heard Hannah's last words, that she could see the light up ahead, and the hope in her voice. He remembered the chilling finality of the stranger's voice telling him she couldn't come to the phone right now.

And he wanted to be the one to die.

He had managed to hide from the grief, chasing Rask's mad treasure hunt, but it caught up with him finally.

The pain was overwhelming.

It broke him.

The mocking voice.

The belt.

Arranging the bedsheets over Matthew Langley's corpse.

All of that.

More.

But mostly, savoring that single moment when his lips parted, and that last sigh escaped them.

He hadn't realized just how much he needed to see that man

suffer. He'd thought that in not doing it himself, not beating Langley to death with his bare hands, he'd somehow risen above, proved himself better than the spotty-faced brat who had killed so many innocent people, but he wasn't better at all. The blood was still on his hands. And worse, by far, given the distance of time, he knew he'd do the same thing all over again.

He felt the Vril touching his mind, feeding off his hatred for Matthew Langley.

There was no forgiveness.

He felt the great intelligence's confusion, then fear, as she understood the truth of his nature, his pain burning through. Their bond was symbiotic. She didn't merely feel his pain, she suffered it. She didn't simply mourn his loss, she wept with it. She didn't sense his rage, she boiled with it. She didn't just witness his guilt, she burned with it. She didn't only see his darkness, she dwelt in it with him.

And wanted everything he wanted.

Lost everything he had lost.

Ached the way he ached.

But it was so much more than sadness.

She wanted to make the world burn for all of it, because deep down in his heart of hearts that was what Rye wanted.

The quality of ambient light within the living ship changed from the calming rose to an angrier red, thickening as the blood flowing through the membranes thickened.

The pulse within the walls became a drumming.

The Vril reacted to his thoughts as a threat, and like anybody under threat looked to combat that threat with its own natural defenses.

A sudden surge of fire burned into the base of Rye's skull as the cord joining them lashed tight.

Rye's hands clamped around the arms of the bone chair.

He had no control over his muscles as they contracted.

He couldn't break the grip.

His back arched against the chair as wave after wave of black agony pulsed through his body, the pain so intense it threatened to overwhelm his heart and end him.

And that would have been a blessed relief.

Release.

Help me, he pleaded, unable to say the words.

Help me help you.

The only answer was the all-consuming image of the super-massive black hole up on the screen destroying another world.

Was it a threat?

A promise?

The sense of time was all wrong. The suns raced across the skies, chasing the moons. The stars winked out, consumed. Was she trying to impress upon him the passage of time? Promising infinite patience? Mocking the headlong rush of his mortality?

Motherhood. Nurturing. Kindness.

That was her, at the core.

But her children?

They were bred in war.

They were conditioned to survive.

Rye saw them again, in that first morning light as they found this new world, and realized what they looked like in the pale light: four dark riders on the pale sun.

Where she had promised those primitive early souls life and the nourishment of her magic, her children were vengeful and offered only dark destructive forces—strong enough to drive men to war, to inflict sickness and starvation upon them and their cities, and eventually death.

Rye understood.

Golden symbols filled the screen and his mind, but unlike the other text, this strange writing wasn't static. It was fluid. Changing. Repeating patterns.

It was counting down.

The symbols shifted again, resolving into a doomsday clock that promised an end to all things.

Rye understood—without knowing how he did—that the countdown was matched to the stars and how long it would be until they were in the same positions in the sky.

It was giving him a year.

And as the next second ticked away, another shrill cry went out, this one amplified beyond the range of human hearing, a pulse that shivered through the core of the world. In his mind's eye, Rye saw it answered beneath the sands of the desert, beneath the trees of the ancient rain forest, beneath the ice of the polar cap, and deep beneath the churning surface of the oceans blue.

Her lost children waking to the sound of her distress.

Answering her call.

There was so much anger and fear in their responses, as faint as they were. It was primal. Her children would fight for her, whatever the cost.

Please, no . . . please . . . it doesn't have to be this way . . . please, Rye thought, desperately trying to undo all of the wrongs his loss and grief had twisted up inside him, needing the Vril to understand.

But the Vril wasn't listening to him.

She had melded with his mind and learned his all-too-human fears and weaknesses and rejected them.

She had learned human nature from him.

She knew that his first instinct had been to destroy the simulacrums she grew. She knew that he was a killer. That those with him were killers. She had seen it all. They had killed her protectors, her loving copies of the first man she had ever trusted.

They would destroy her.

Rye managed to cause a twitch in his left little finger. It was nothing and it was everything. That twitch, like the first involuntary spasm of Parkinson's, would change the rest of his life, because one twitch became two became more until he had managed to uncurl his fingers from around the arm of the bone chair and, staring down at his hand, willed it to rise.

It didn't respond at first, but there was no way he was giving up.

Rye gritted his teeth, focusing all of his mental strength on his hand as he forced it to obey him.

It took every ounce of resistance, but he had to reach back to where the Vril's umbilical cord was rooted into the nape of his neck and close his fist around the slick loop of living tube.

The umbilicus pulsed in his hand as he started to pull at it.

It had burrowed too deeply into his skull to simply fall free, but there was no way he was going to let the Vril pump more of its toxins through his veins a second longer than he had to.

With the distress call of the mothership screaming through his mind, Rye thought of Hannah, and only Hannah, needing to remember just how much he had loved and lost, and pulled desperately at the cord. His nails dug into the weird flesh with such pressure they split tiny half-moons through the cord, which oozed a slick oily lifeblood across his hands.

Revulsion gave him renewed strength.

With one massive heave, he wrenched the umbilicus free.

He felt its teeth tear out of his skin, grating out of the bone coupling it had established, as a blinding wave of black agony ripped through the ladder of his spine.

He cast it aside.

More of that oily black lifeblood greased his hand as Rye reached up to feel his own wound.

He was bleeding, but not so badly that it needed immediate attention.

Without thinking about it, he'd touched his mite-gloved black hand to the wound in his neck.

Immediately, the microscopic healers set to work repairing his skin.

It took them seconds.

Rye pushed himself out of the bone seat.

The umbilicus lashed about on the floor like a dying snake.

He crushed it under his boot.

On the screen behind him, four bright lights flared, single spots of gold across a map of the stars matching the earthly coordinates of the Vril's children.

The doomsday clock continued its relentless countdown.

Outside of his head, the screams were deep bass chimes sending their signal into the world and using the harmonic qualities of the earth itself to amplify the distress call as it rippled out, farther and farther from the source.

Somewhere, her children heard her pain.

Somewhere, the myths that mankind had grown up with, before they were twisted and sanitized into dull empty versions of themselves, began to stir, ready to teach mankind what it meant to be afraid again.

Somewhere, the root of humanity's ancient fears crawled through the darkness, never truly conquered.

Somewhere, the nature of the great floods and natural disasters that resonated through every religion found their voices for the first time in this new age of man.

Somewhere, those ancient intelligences that had lain dormant for years beyond counting reached out to find each other, reconnecting in a lattice of low subsonic frequencies that carried the impulses of their thoughts from the remote ice wastes of Antarctica to the blistering heat of the most inhospitable deserts known to man, through the wilds of the Amazon rain forests and the trenches beneath the Atlantic.

Those same low-frequency harmonics answered the pain and fear of their mother and pulsed out the same message over and over: *we survive.*

The promise underlying it was simple: *you will not.*

SEVENTY-SIX

Rye reeled.

He needed to get out of there.

The dying ship felt like a tomb.

He backed away from the bone chair, unable to take his eyes from the screen as it continued to flash up images of the Vril's survival and the cost of it. There was no escaping the fear and horror the ship had endured, it was burned indelibly into the consciousness of the creature and Rye had felt it all.

And it was there in the low frequency distress call rousing her children into action, urging them to rise up, strike back.

He understood fundamentally that while the mothership wanted nothing more than peace and was a nurturing soul, her children were battleships prepared for war.

They came loaded with sicknesses for the planet and the ability to disseminate them within the genetically engineered avatars of biomass-flesh they grew. They were capable, quite literally, of growing plagues within their gestation chambers and walking them out into the world. The realization of what humanity was up against if the four children of this dying god—and that was the only way Rye's mind could cope with the enormity of what they'd found when they came looking for Shambhala, to think of it as a god fallen from the stars—unleashed the full unholy fury contained within their bodies upon the world: it would be the end on a biblical scale.

He imagined rivers running with blood, swarms of insects infected with strains of alien bacteria our immune systems had no defense against, diseased livestock, and, ultimately, fire in the sky as the world burned and darkness finally fell.

It was all there, a blueprint for Armageddon.

With the connection broken, there was no easy way of showing the dying ship that he wasn't a threat, that there was no need to be afraid of him, or humanity. That it was a mistake. That grief did not define him. That he was more than the sum of his regret and rage.

But the truth was, he knew there was every reason to be afraid of his people.

It didn't matter if they came like Rask, dressed up as dreamers looking for knowledge and hope, or like businessmen looking to strip the land. Humanity's voracious appetite for consumption and destruction was worthy of fear, especially for an ancient alien intelligence like her. They would tear her apart, test her to death trying to understand her nature, how she could live and breathe and think and remember, how she could feel and yet travel through space like Apollo or Challenger, and ultimately murder her with their need to know.

And the Vril had learned all of that from Rye when they shared a mind.

Rye ran out of the room and didn't stop running as huge tremors rippled through the bone cages of the Vril mothership's corridors, searching desperately for a way out of there.

The membranous walls pulsed around him, seeming to cave in as he raced through them.

He didn't dare touch a thing.

He rushed down narrow passageways that all looked the same, the cage of bone and blood offering no obvious escape, and feared for one desperate moment that he wasn't going to find a way out of this place. He ran blindly through the passageways, following the bubbling loops of intestinal tubing as it fed biomass through the body of the ship, thinking there had to be a vent or somewhere it discharged its bodily waste.

Head up, he ran after the churning bubbles, chasing them down the tubes.

But the tubes seemed to go on forever, like a network of veins. The veins, arteries, and capillaries in his own body stretched out for one hundred thousand miles. He couldn't shake the idea he could follow the tube forever as it looped around and around the Vril's body in an endless circuit.

There was no obvious way out.

No hatch or doorway.

No valve or vent.

He could run around blindly for hours, days even, without stumbling across the waste hatch, assuming the ship even vented its waste and didn't simply feed off the biodegraded mulch and continue the process all over again without ever purging itself. There was no reason for its biology to work the way he expected it to.

Rye stopped dead.

He knew what he needed to do, and knew that doing it would make him the threat that the Vril believed him to be, but he had no choice if he was going to get back to the others.

He reached up, tearing one of the bones free of the cage that supported the wall, and as biomass wept out through the wound, swung the jagged splinter, burying it in the bloody substance, and did it again and again, determined to fight his way through muscle and membrane, hacking his way out with the shattered bone; it was as simple and horrific as that.

Rye swung the bone again.

And again, ignoring the Vril's screams of pain.

SEVENTY-SEVEN

He emerged from the belly of the ship covered in oily ichor, gagging on the stuff that spilled into his mouth as he struggled to hold his breath.

The wound in the hull of the Vril ship oozed with the leviathan's blood.

It smeared across Rye's coat as he forced his way out.

It got in his hair and face.

The hull felt exactly like what it was: meat, muscle, fat, blood.

The ship's anguished lament was a keening wail that filled the vault of the cavern.

Rye stood on a ledge, confronted by a sheer wall that seemed to rise forever.

The lichen, he saw, wasn't lichen at all, but rather some kind of festering decay that grew out of the ship and spread upward and outward. The stench down here was far worse than even a few hundred feet above.

There was no escaping the all-pervading reek of death down here in this darkness.

That death oozed out of the ship, spreading across the interior of the immense cavern network.

He'd seen the effect from above; it gave the impression of life where there was only creeping death.

Rye found a handhold and lifted himself onto the rock, beginning the climb.

The ascent quickly funneled into a rock chimney.

His wounded hand felt fine—better than fine; the grip in his fingers had never felt stronger.

He traversed a few feet, looking for new handholds to take his weight, up to the temple, several hundred feet above. The cavern fell away beneath him, darkness offering no indication of just how deep the drop was.

Rye scaled the first ten feet slowly as the chimney narrowed enough to enable him to brace himself, taking his weight on his feet.

He used a technique called *thrutching* to push himself up; it was a physically demanding move that sapped strength and energy from the whole body.

He repeated the same *wedge, move, wedge* ascent, pushing off with one foot, his back pressed against the wall of the chimney and using his other foot to brace against the wall allowing him to use his hands to thrutch his back upward into another slightly higher seating position to wedge himself in place.

He repeated the thrutching move over and over, but within twenty feet his thighs, arms, and lower back were burning, and he was forced to rest, sitting inside the chimney.

The climb was claustrophobic and unforgiving.

The next ten feet were harder than the last.

The ten after that harder still.

The hardest part was that he simply couldn't see his hands or feet and was forced to work from memory and feel for holds that might work, relying upon improvisation and pure rugged determination to rise.

He reached a corner, and palmed off, using his feet to pivot around his hands, and for a long sickening moment hung out there over nothing.

But he didn't fall.

Rye continued to climb, hearing the sounds of confrontation up above him.

Another twenty feet.

Twenty more.

Legs on fire.

Muscles in his arms rippling.

Every brace harder to hold.

Every foothold harder to push away from.

But he kept climbing, knowing that he had no choice.

It was that or never get out of this place.

And as incredible as Shambhala was, it wasn't where he was going to die.

Rye leaned back against the chimney wall, getting a good look at the next span of rock and realizing he was within touching distance of the mantle.

It was the toughest move of the lot, given how bone-tired he was, and how little strength he had left in his muscles: the transition from vertical to horizontal wasn't natural. Some climbers called it the swimming pool maneuver. He felt out with his foot for a good hold, then pressed up as he lifted his heel over the edge, and turned his opposite hand toward the foot, rotating it palm down, followed by pushing down off his palm until his center of gravity was above his heel, and stepping up his other foot to stand.

Rye stood on a pedestal of rock at the center of several stone bridges, the lichen slick beneath his feet, and saw Vic and Carter with their backs to him silhouetted through the arch of the temple door.

The pair faced the unmistakable figure of Tenzin Dawa, the last of the Asuras, which weren't demons in the traditional sense at all, but biomass-bred clones that the Vril had sent out into the world to protect her secrets.

Demons didn't need horns or cloven hooves or other very Christian traits to be demonic, all they needed was to be alien in nature, and the Asuras were that and so much more.

Knowing what he knew, having seen them being hot-housed in the grow tanks within the dying ship, it was hard to look at Tenzin Dawa and see a man.

He was like the Mexican axolotl—a salamander capable of regenerating missing limbs, parts of its brain and heart, and incredibly, able to forge new neural pathways in its brain to support the regenerated body parts.

Dawa's relationship with the ship was the same.

It was his brain.

Killing this one wouldn't stop more from coming.

Not as long as the Vril ship was capable of gestating more of them and giving life to them.

What could be more inherently demonic than that?

Everything Rask had said was true, but not in any of the ways the billionaire had imagined them.

Rye crept toward the doorway, placing his feet with exaggerated care. He didn't want to spook the assassin and make him lash out. For all that he was merely organic biomass sharing a brain, he was still a ruthless killing machine. That hadn't changed.

Seeing him now, Rye knew it had been the assassin's eyes he'd felt on him as they'd walked through the abandoned homes of Shambhala. Dawa had tracked them under the mountain, across the balconies and viaducts and through the maze of homes that filled the enormous caverns, simply watching, biding his time to make his attack when they were at their most vulnerable.

Rye made it halfway to the temple door.

He could see the open petals of the weird lotus flower hatch he'd deciphered, still open, or open again.

Iskra Zima was nowhere to be seen.

Rye could only assume she'd either found her way down into the belly of the dying ship or Dawa had already taken the Russian out.

The assassin closed the gap between him and his friends. Moving with shocking speed Dawa launched a blistering attack Carter could barely fend off. The thief was battered back, five blows landing hard even as he managed to block four more aimed at his body and throat. The sheer ferocity of it was staggering. Carter took three hits to the side of the face, snapping his head back, and two hammer blows to his gut that doubled him up for a final crunching knee to the face that sent him spinning, unconscious before he hit the ground.

Rye heard bones break.

Carter lay there unmoving.

Facing Vic, Tenzin Dawa stooped to recover a weapon he had lost before Rye had made it back up over the mantle.

It wasn't like any gun he had ever seen.

Even from this distance, he could tell that it resembled the innards of the ship that had grown it: part bone, part membranous tissue. It was the epitome of alien, a fusion of flesh and technology that was both familiar and utterly wrong in its nature.

The assassin leveled it at Vic wordlessly.

The big man breathed deeply; Rye could hear the sound of it through his flaring nostrils in the second before he threw himself forward, launching a huge linebacker-challenge at the assassin in a desperate attempt to sack him before he got the shot off.

Vic had no chance.

Rye ran beneath the arch, arriving in that frozen second when Vic still hadn't fallen from the barbed bone "bullet" in his heart.

The shot was louder than all of the dying ship's screams combined, the brutality of the retort echoing throughout the cavernous depths, folding in upon itself over and over until that one note became deafening.

Rye saw the white barb of bone punch through Vic's rib cage, opening him up.

It was like some harpoon plunging through the layers of parka down, flesh, and bone, the barbs making it impossible to pull out without rending the meat and ripping apart Vic's heart.

Somehow, incredibly, Vic managed another three faltering paces before his legs betrayed him and he sank to his knees.

He looked at Rye, his blood spilling out of the chest wound, hands clamped around the bone barb slick with the blood pulsing out and spilling across the down padding of his heavy coat as a bloodred rose blossomed around his hands. It looked like he was lost in prayer.

The truth was blunter than that.

He was just lost.

The blood stopped pumping as Vic's heart stopped beating.

He wasn't getting up again.

He pitched forward, face hitting the ground.

The sound of the impact was sickening, like meat being tenderized.

The blood spread around his head, seeping slowly into a wider and wider pool, and thinning out as it did so.

Rye saw a second bone barb lock into place in the strange weapon at the assassin's side.

Tenzin Dawa turned, sensing him there without seeing him, and fired.

SEVENTY-EIGHT

Rye threw himself to the ground, and rolled as the bone barb whistled through the air inches from his face.

It buried in the wall behind him, only three inches of the bleached white bone visible.

A third shot came before he was back on his feet.

Rye pushed himself forward like a sprinter coming out of the blocks, and fell before he'd even half risen, but the organic bullet powdered into shards of bone even as it punched through his healed hand. The black mites of the peculiar protective glove seemed to part around the bone shard, then close around it, healing the wound before it could bleed. Rye didn't waste precious seconds thinking about the miracle it was.

He threw himself behind the protection of the metal lotus leaves as the prayer drum began to close up once more.

A fourth shot ricocheted off the metal drum, fizzing away harmlessly.

He scrambled to his feet and, as he rose, saw the Russian move up behind the Asura and, with one almighty swing, bury the blade of her ice ax in the back of Tenzin Dawa's head, splitting the assassin's skull.

The bone gun went off in Dawa's hand, the barbed bullet streaking over Rye's head as the dead Dawa's hand reflexively came up too far, too fast as the nerves fired off one last time.

The Russian hunkered down beside Dawa, working the ax head free of the dead man's skull, then crossed the temple floor to check on Carter.

Rye scrambled to where Vic lay, and cradled the dead man in his arms.

The gulf of grief he felt was overwhelming.

Of course it was, he'd barely begun to come to terms with the murder of Hannah, and that grief had already been compounded by the loss of Olivia Meyer. Vic on top of that was too much to bear. The pain crushed him. His breath hitched. The weight on his chest threatened to cave in the bones. Tears tracked down his cheeks as he pressed his healed hand to the wound as though he could somehow push the blood and the life back inside.

"We need to get out of here," Iskra said.

Carter leaned on her for support.

His pain was plain to see as he moved gingerly to where Rye sat with Vic.

Rye shook his head.

"We have to," the thief said.

"No," Rye said, as simple as that. No room for argument. "I'm not leaving him down here."

"Then carry him," the Russian told him dispassionately. "But you're not getting back up the rope with him on your back, and you know that. So, leave him. He won't mind. He's gone."

But Rye wasn't listening.

He stared at his hand.

The tiny black mites had begun to migrate from him to Guuleed, amassing around the wound. They moved in a frenzy, rippling around the ragged hole in the dead man's chest. In seconds there wasn't a single mite on his skin. The palm of Rye's hand was still red raw with new skin where the burns had been repaired. Without thinking about what he was doing, Rye pulled Vic's heavy down coat open and lifted the layers of material to expose the full extent of the wound that had killed him.

He gripped the exposed length of the bone barb buried in Vic's chest and pulled it out.

He winced at the sound it made as it cut through the meat and grated against the broken ribs.

Rye threw the lethal bone dart away, not looking at where it fell.

The black mites swarmed across Vic's skin.

They moved faster and faster, seemingly multiplying as they fed off the dead tissue, until less than a minute later they formed an oleaginous protective layer across his skin.

"What's happening to him?" Carter asked.

Rye looked up and told him the truth: "I found the Cintāmani, but it's not a stone. Rask was right, though, it's some sort of nano-technology. Nanite healers." He held up his hand as proof.

"It can't—" the thief said, about to say, it couldn't bring a dead man back, when Vic's eyes opened, and a huge death rattle of breath escaped his lips.

The big man's hand flew to his chest where the nanites swarmed all over the wound, knitting the flesh, healing the ragged muscle walls of his heart, and jolting it with the electrical pulse it needed to jump-start the dead organ.

The nanite healers wove patterns across Vic's glistening black skin, constantly eddying and rippling as they worked their unholy magic.

He looked at Rye, haunted, as he asked, "What have you done?"

SEVENTY-NINE

Vic didn't say another word until they made it back to the surface.

Getting him back topside was a near-impossible task, but they were a team. They fashioned a harness out of ropes and pulled him up where he couldn't climb, and where he struggled to walk, they gave him their strength. He walked stoically on, leaning on Rye when he needed to, but otherwise focused purely on putting one foot in front of the other without falling over.

Several times, Rye caught him looking back over his shoulder as though he sensed something in the deeper darkness behind them.

And perhaps there was?

Another fully grown Dawa?

Something worse?

The cold air, thirty degrees below zero, hit them hard as they emerged from the crevice to stand in the shadow of the deserted Dzyan temple.

Rye heard the roar of engines in the distance.

He shielded his eyes against the swirling snow as a huge military helicopter rose into view, emerging from beneath a rocky outcrop. The steel blades chopped at the air, churning up a storm of already fallen snow.

The moon dazzled off the windshield, lending it the effect of vengeful silver fire as it surged across the mountaintop.

It was big. Easily capable of carrying a dozen combatants. There were no markings that he could see. More of Cressida Mohr's mercenaries? She was nothing if not persistent when it came to protecting the secrets of her mother.

Vic was in no shape to take out another helicopter with his bare hands; once was a fluke, twice absurd.

Rye didn't have the strength for another fight.

He slumped down against the temple wall waiting for death to come pouring out of the helicopter and wondering how he was going to escape it this time—or if he even wanted to. Dying up here would be different. At least it would be dying with the sun on his face, not like down there in that hellhole, Shambhala.

They'd been to a different kind of hell and back together. Vic to a literal hell if the haunted look in his eyes was anything to go by, while Carter looked like he'd dragged himself all the way there and hit every rock on the way down.

Rye didn't say anything for the longest time.

He stared at the helicopter and realized that the pilot was looking for somewhere to set down.

The downdraft from the rotors churned up a wall of white.

He pushed himself up to his feet and turned to Carter. "Come on." The thief didn't have the will to fight. He followed Rye.

The change in altitude and angle meant he could see the faces through the windshield before the helicopter set down.

He recognized the man in the pilot's seat as Jeremiah Byrne.

The side door slid open and Rask emerged, dressed for the elements. He ducked low to be sure he stayed below the slowing rotor blades and came running toward them.

"We thought we'd lost you," he called over the blustering wind. "Byrne was monitoring your progress. One minute you were there, then you were gone. Then he found the wreckage." He looked over his shoulder, scanning the mountainside for the debris and the bodies back there. "I feared the worst when he couldn't find any sign of life up here."

"Because we weren't up here," Rye told him. "We were down there." He pointed toward the snow beneath their feet.

"You found it?" The hope in the man's face was too much to bear. His life depended upon Rye's answer, and after all of the let-downs and disappointments, the supposed miracle cures he had endured, a simple *no* now would break him.

"Yes," Rye said, but before Rask could feel any sense of joy or relief, cut him short with, "But it's not what you thought. It's not what any of us thought."

"But you have the stone?"

"There is no stone," he said. "There never was. It was a story to make sense of a miracle." Rask nodded. He looked sick. "Shambhala was never a lost city, not like Atlantis or any of the other places you mentioned. It was a tomb. Thousands of years ago a ship crashed here."

"I told you," Iskra said, a lopsided grin on her face as she came over to hug the older man. "Aliens." She said it in such a way he couldn't help but laugh.

Rye wasn't laughing.

He told them what he'd found down there: the dying heart, the core central intelligence of the Vril, and the gestation chambers that had birthed the Asura assassins and sent out cuckoos dressed in Ahnenerbe clothing.

"Incredible," Rask said wistfully. "An organic spaceship? Are you sure?"

"Trust me."

"A living entity that came here from the stars. Do you know what that means?"

"Proof of intelligent life," Rye offered.

"More than that, Mr. McKenna. It is proof that what we call god is merely alien."

"It's not all good news," he said.

"I'm not sure any of it is," Rask agreed, without knowing what he was agreeing with.

"She wasn't alone."

"She?"

"The mother. That is who is dying here, thousands of years after fleeing her dying world. There were four more, who crossed the galaxies with her. Her children. They have been lost to her for generations, but now they have woken to her distress call. Her children are vengeance and wrath, Rask. The four, when they come, carry death with them. They promise famine and pestilence to ravage the world beyond repair even as we fall into war with them." He deliberately couched it carefully so that Rask would come to his own revelations regarding their nature. "We know them by another name. And what their waking means for our world."

"The four horsemen," Rask said.

"The end of days," Rye agreed. "One lies beneath the remote ice wastes of Antarctica, another beneath the blistering sands of the desert, a third deep in the wilds of the Amazon rain forest, and the last terror far below the surface of the Atlantic, drifting in the deepest unexplored trenches down there, thousands of feet below the surface."

"So, the stone *was* scattered, but not in the way the myths suggested."

"Who would have thought a religion would lie?" Iskra said.

"Quite," Rask agreed. "And you are sure?" he asked Rye.

"The Vril was inside my head." He touched the back of his neck where the ship had interfaced with him. "I saw it all. I didn't understand what was happening at first as we didn't share a common language. There was no conversation. I saw flashes. Images. I glimpsed part of her life before she arrived here. And then I felt her wake her children and heard them answer the call. The last thing she showed me before I fled was a clock counting down to doomsday."

"How long have we got?" Rask asked. Behind him Byrne

started to power up the rotor blades, obviously impatient to take off. The noise made it hard to talk.

"A year. I think. I don't know if that's when all hell will be let loose, or when it will all come to an end. I severed the connection. I needed to get out of there."

"I can appreciate that."

Rye shook his head. "I can't get beyond the idea that we've unknowingly coexisted for centuries and within minutes of contact with this alien intelligence we are looking at the end of mankind. What does that tell you about us?"

Rask drew his hood up over his face, struggling with the cold. "That we are long due an extinction event. Anything you can tell us, anything you remember from what you were shown, no matter how insignificant, it might make a difference."

Rye tried to remember. "I saw fragments of everything, but they were only fragments. I saw the dying star they fled, I saw her first contact with the monk we've known as Tenzin Dawa, the man who gave his face to our assassin. She made her demons in his image. That's why we found photos of him in Guérin's chateau with Nazis and faced an enemy who hadn't aged. She bred him in the image of the only man she knew," Rye said, not mentioning the fact that the mothership was growing a simulacrum in his image, too. "There are more of them down there, like him. They aren't human. She sent her simulacrums out wearing the faces of that Ahnenerbe expedition. They've been living among us for eighty years, wearing the faces of the dead. But the good news is they can't live forever. They aren't immortal. They aren't even sentient in the way we think about intelligence. They are part of her, the Vril, so she controls their every move and word. And she is dying."

"And we will be, too, if we don't get out of here," Vic said, moving painfully toward the helicopter's open door.

"But it's not all bad news," Iskra said. "We saw a miracle, so I'm inclined to believe him."

"A miracle?"

"Rye can explain it, but we've got our very own Lazarus,"

Carter offered. "I would have said Jesus, but he came back a bit quicker than the other Big Guy. Show the boss man, Vic."

The big man stopped in the process of clambering into the helicopter and pulled open his heavy down jacket to show the bloody mess of his shirt beneath. He lifted his shirt to show the constant writhing swarm of black nanites working at fixing his flesh.

The wound had already partially knitted, the hole the bone bullet had opened half the size it had been before Rye had laid hands on him.

"Like I said, there is no stone," Rye explained. "But that doesn't mean there's no basis to the stories you heard. On the most basic level, a mother is a nurturing creature. She cherishes and gives life. She is a healer. I don't know what they are"—again he held out his own hand with the pink scar tissue visible as though an answer all its own—"some sort of biological-nanotech medical bots or something, but they can work miracles."

"So, there's a chance?" Rask asked. It was the hope in his question that was heartbreaking.

"There's a chance," Rye said.

"As long as the world doesn't end first," the thief chimed in.

They bundled into the helicopter, belting themselves in as Byrne took them up.

A voice crackled over the internal headset, "Good evening ladies and gentlemen. This is your pilot speaking. Tonight's flight back to civilization is expected to take far too long, and the weather is, unsurprisingly, a bitch, so I advise you to buckle up and hang on to your stomachs as I really don't want to have to clean up after you. In the event of a forced landing on water, we've obviously got horribly lost. We're much more likely to crash into the side of a mountain. And with that cheerful thought I'd like to thank you for choosing Byrne Air for all your evac needs and look forward to saving your asses again in the near future. Because, let's be honest, we know you're going to get into trouble again."

"Take us home, Mister Byrne," Rask told the other man.

"Roger that."

EIGHTY

"How can we be sure it has healed your heart?" Rask asked. He sat uncomfortably in the chair, angled back to face the ceiling.

Vic stood over him, Rye beside him.

There was no nurse this time.

"If it hasn't, I die," Vic said.

"He really does have a way with words, doesn't he?" Rask said, earning a smile from Rye. "Perhaps we should wait?"

The big man shook his head. "You don't have the luxury of time."

"None of us do," the billionaire agreed. "If you are sure?"

"I am sure."

"Then how do we do this?" He looked at Rye.

"I just held my hand over his heart and the nanites migrated to the wounded flesh," Rye explained, miming the action that had brought the other man back from the dead. "I didn't do anything."

"What is wrong with me isn't a bullet hole or a rope burn. It is inside my blood. My body is betraying me."

"It may not work," Rye agreed. "But what have you got to lose?"

"Hope," Rask said, and Rye understood all too well what he meant. Until this moment, with Vic about to lay on hands, there was always the chance that a miracle was out there, and that was something to cling on to. But if this didn't work, if there was no miracle, then there was only death.

Vic unbuttoned his shirt and peeled it off, exposing a mess of pink scar tissue around the wound where the bone barb had killed him. Thousands of microscopic nanites swarmed across his glistening skin, rippling along the rigid lines of muscle.

"Should I?" Rask asked, reaching up tentatively.

Vic pressed a huge hand down on the other man's chest, preventing him from rising.

At first nothing happened, and then, like a living tattoo, the nanites coiled around Vic's pectoral, forming a spiral galaxy of movement that churned and eddied as the nanites curled a path up to his shoulder and then down his arm, like ants marching. They swarmed down his forearm and out across each finger, finding their way to the dying Rask.

But it was different this time.

There was no obvious wound to heal.

They spread out in an oily coating across Rask's chest, before slowly being absorbed, sinking into his body. There was no black glove of healing across his hand or heart. In the minutes it took for the nanites to leave Vic and enter Rask, burrowing in through the pores in his skin to enter the bloodstream, they left no trace to betray the fact they had ever been there.

Vic slumped down into the chair beside the bed, breaking contact. The big man was breathing heavily. Sweat beaded on his brow and broke to run down his temples. "It seems I am not dead yet," he said, but the words were labored and came between deep gasps. More beads of perspiration sheened his naked torso. He put his hand to his chest as though to confirm that his heart was still beating.

Rask's chest rose and fell rapidly, his breathing shallow. He didn't have words. He stiffened in the chair, every muscle in his body cording tight as he threw his head back, seemingly in the grips of a tortuous series of convulsions that had him bucking and writhing against the chair. Another spasm distended Rask's belly as his back arched away from the leather. And then he fell back against the seat, eyes rolling up inside his head, and for one long sickening second Rye thought he had died.

And perhaps he had; he was desperately weak, and this treatment, whatever it was, was far more invasive than any round of chemo—but the nanites were not about to let him stay dead.

He opened his eyes.

He didn't say anything for the longest time, and when he did it was to ask Vic to give him a few moments alone with Rye. As the door closed, Rask said, "So, I have to ask you again, Mr. McKenna, do you deserve a second chance?"

Rye thought about it, and it was a more difficult answer this time, but ultimately the same one. "No. But this is on me. What happens now is my fault. No matter how much I might want to, I can't just walk away. It was inside my head, Rask. It read my weakness and fear. It knew we were a threat to its existence. That's why we're looking at extinction. So, no, I don't deserve a second chance, but I'm going to fight right to the end side by side with the others."

"Good. Because we need you. You have seen things the others haven't. You understand the alien intelligence in ways they can't even begin to."

"And yet I know nothing," Rye said.

"That isn't true, my friend," Rask said. "Did I tell you I suffer nightmares?"

"No."

"It is always the same one. I am on that plane, with my mother and the stranger who died in my place. I try to talk to my mother. I try to make her take us off the plane. I beg her to sit in my seat. She never does. And every time, we burn alive in the wreckage. But last night I had that nightmare and it was different for the first time I can remember. I begged her to change seats, and she looked at me and told me I can't save the world, that it is going to burn. She told me there are no second chances, not really. I know it wasn't her," he said. "Before you tell me it is my own conscience taking the blame for what happened beneath that mountain, I know that. I know that it is my fault every bit as much as it is yours. But I know that it is Matthew Langley's fault, but more than that it is the world's fault. It is the news we stream into our homes every day. It is the distrust and hatred we let fester for our fellow men, divided by the color of our skins and the gods we choose to believe in. It is the conflicts we have fought throughout our history. The invasions. The civil wars. The genocides. All of these things are inside you. We are the sum of our parts, Rye." It was the first time Rask had called him by his first name. "We don't exist in a vacuum. The world we live in shapes us. What that intelligence read was just the truth, filtered through your soul. It was always going to be this way. If it wasn't you, it would have been someone else."

Rye nodded. He knew the other man was right. But that didn't change how he felt.

"You are a good man. You have suffered more than most could even imagine. And you are still standing."

Which was true.

Rye rubbed at the pink wound, still raw, where the nanites had healed him.

Rask held out a hand.

Rye took it.

"Welcome to the family, Rye. Truly."

"There's something I need to tell you."

"It sounds serious."

"I haven't told you everything that happened down there. It knew me. It called me Kaustubh."

"The Guardian of the Stone," Rask said. He was more than familiar with the legend; he had immersed himself in the secret history of the world. "The legend suggests the fragments of the Cintāmani are drawn to each other, and anyone holding the first will be able to sense the other fragments."

Rye nodded. "Legends lie, we know that."

"And yet you know where the other Vril are, so perhaps they don't lie that much?"

"I don't know where they are beyond sweeps that could be a thousand miles wide," Rye said.

Rask nodded. "But this isn't what you wanted to confess, is it? Because this isn't the kind of weight you need to unburden yourself of."

"No," Rye admitted. Rask waited for Rye to fill the silence. "The biomass clones, the Asuras, they weren't just replicas of dead Nazis growing down there . . . she was growing me. I saw myself in the gestation tanks. A perfect replica."

"Why do I get the feeling there's another layer to this confession you haven't owned up to yet?"

"You're good at this."

"I read people," Rask agreed. "So, the other shoe?"

"I saw Cressida Mohr's half-grown face in there."

"Are you sure it was her?"

"Yes. She was one of them. She fooled me, Rask. We drank. We talked. We fucked. And I couldn't tell she wasn't one of us. She was so . . . I keep wanting to use the word lifelike . . . but you know what I mean."

Rask nodded, understanding the implication. "They have been living among us for the best part of a century. They came back wearing the faces of the Nazis who died out on that mountain, but they have had time and opportunity to become embedded in our society. That she fooled you well enough to get that close to you just proves they have assimilated. They could be anyone. In any level of society. Politicians. They could be our generals. Holy men. Our beloved actors. Faces we see on the television every day. People we trust. They could be anyone and everyone. An alien species living among us, our enemy wearing familiar faces. So convincing in their humanity they could be people we call friends."

"Jesus, that's a frightening thought," Rye said. "Who the hell are we supposed to trust?"

"Each other," Rask said. He winced then, a searing jolt of pain tearing through him as the nanites began to enter his bloodstream. It took him a second to gather his wits. "Beyond that? No one."

"Are you all right?"

"Better than that, I am alive. I can feel them inside me. It is the strangest thing. I don't hurt. Not the way that I did before. These spasms are different. They have a reason. They are down to the nanite healers. The rest—it doesn't hurt anymore. I can't remember the last time I was free of pain. Now, if I am lucky, I will live as long as the rest of you. Right now, twelve months feels like a lifetime." His smile was slight, but there was a gentle humor behind it. Rye appreciated that. "Do you think you can find the Seal of Muhammad in that time?"

"It's not like we have a choice," Rye said. "But on the plus side, we have Byrne. That's got to count for something. Our very own space archaeologist. So, why the Seal? Why not get Byrne to do his satellite thing over the Amazon or something? Pinpoint the targets without leaving this place?"

"The second fragment," Rask explained, "the Syamantaka, is said to protect the land from natural disasters; flood, drought, earthquake, and famine, but more importantly for us, if the myths are to be believed, it is the keystone that opens the door to Agartha, the mythical city buried beneath the Antarctic ice. The Ahnenerbe called it Ultima Thule. We tend to think of it as Hell."

"I guess it froze over," Rye said.

"Without the second fragment of the Cintāmani, we aren't getting into Agartha," Rask said. "And if Agartha is like Shambhala, it needs to be destroyed."

"So, we find the Seal."

"Which is easier said than done. The problem being Muhammad's original seal was lost by the Caliph Uthman, in a well in Medina six hundred years before the birth of Christ."

"You're forgetting who I am," Rye said.

Rask furrowed his brow.

"Kaustubh," he said. He held up the palm of his healing hand with the raw pink scar tissue. "The Guardian of the Stones. If anyone's going to find the second fragment it is me."

ACKNOWLEDGMENTS

First and foremost, I'm indebted to my editor in this madness, Peter Wolverton, who was there with the first email saying, "Why don't you give me something more like *Silver* . . . ?" through various incarnations of the pitches and the shaping of the story line, with red pen and incisive opinions that helped to form Rye's story. More often than not, Pete came in with important ideas about how to get the most out of this story. It's fair to say that without him the book in your hands would be a pale shadow of itself. So, cheers, mate.

Then, after Pete, there's Jen Donovan, who didn't make it right the way to the end—she didn't die, don't panic, she's off doing spectacular things with Penguin Random House Audio now. (Huzzah!) Jen ran interference between me and Pete for the last three years, making sure that things went smoothly, that deadlines were hit, edits turned around, and stupid questions answered. Thanks, Jen, for just being all-around awesome. I hope you have an amazing time in the new gig and smile when you turn the last page of this book and realize how much you are appreciated. I'm going to miss you, and feel just a little pang of jealousy of all the cool new writers you'll be working with.

I've made no secret of the fact I struggle with depression and over the last few years it has become harder and harder to focus my thoughts and really see the shape of a story. This isn't the kind of thing your editor wants to hear, so hide this page from him, ta. . . . First drafts had begun to feel like a trial by attrition, with what used to take a week taking a month and what used to take a month taking three. There was a time not so far back when my concentration was so fractured I seriously began to doubt I'd ever be able to do this again. Little did I know that my obsession with gadgets would save my life. It sounds melodramatic, but right at the beginning of this process I took delivery of a Freewrite, which for those of you remotely curious enough to read this far, is basically an old-fashioned typewriter with a small e-ink screen that's hooked up to the Wi-Fi. It can't connect to Facebook or surf the internet or anything else. But it does what it says on the can, and it does it wonderfully well—to the point that I found myself writing with a freedom that I haven't felt in years. It's got this neat little gimmick that I thought would be infuriating, but which is brilliant: you can only write forward. There are no cursors, you can't pop back a couple of lines to fix a scene or add some cool little detail, which actually focuses the mind and forces you to really see and immerse yourself in the writing in a way that I haven't been able to since my first laptop with Wi-Fi left me permanently connected to the internet and all of its distractions. So, right up there with Pete, there's this box with keys. *White Peak* wasn't the first novel written on a Freewrite, far from it, and it won't be the last, but it stands as a testimony to what distraction-free writing can do for you. And no, I'm not on commission. But, Astrohaus guys . . . if you wanna send me a freebie Freewrite2 when you get there . . . I wouldn't say no . . .

I think here I need to take a moment to thank the people who've been there along the way, starting with the old friends who put up with my first pitiful attempts to tell stories, so to the Sunday gang who came around to role-play their way through my mad ideas, Simon, Gary, Ian, and Michael—you were good guys to grow up with. I kinda miss the simplicity of those days and having you guys in my life. Then, there are the champions, those people who believed, from the first person to buy a short story of mine, Jason Smith, at *Exuberance* magazine, to the first editor to put down money for an actual novel of mine, David Nordhaus and Butch Miller at Dark Tales. David Howe, who bought *Houdini's Last Illusion* at a time when I'd lost my agent and was seriously thinking about calling it a day. Lindsey Priestley, who took a chance on my first mass-market novels, bringing me into the Warhammer world and letting me play with the vampire counts for a few years. Tim Schulte for panicking when Stel and I sold him *Rapture* and realized we couldn't actually do it because of Stel's noncompete clause and his long overdue contract, and who said "Well, can you give me something like *The Da Vinci Code*?"

when he could have said give me my money back . . . and which led to *Silver* being one of the top thirty bestselling novels in the UK that year. And to Emma Barnes who helped pull the Ogmios Directive from the ashes nearly a decade later to help get it over the finish line.

Then there are the guys who've had my pen and my back, first my Ogmios Directive cowriters, Steve Lockley, Richard Salter, David Wood, Ashley Knight, Rick Chesler, Sean Ellis, then more long-suffering writer friends unlucky enough to have collaborated down the years: Paul Ebbs, Willie Meikle, Joseph Nassise, José Bográn, David Sakmyster, Brian M. Logan, Brian D. Anderson (what's it with Brians and middle initials?) Aaron Rosenberg, and Robert Greenberger. All of these fine folks are brilliant writers in their own right, and I'm lucky to call them friends.

And, at the far end of things, the people who keep me sane. My family. My wife, Marie, who has no idea what I actually do for a living and dreads the question because she really doesn't know how to explain it. Pat, who pops up in all of these, my nemesis in the Fantasy Football League. Mum, who is a dedicated first reader. Dad, who sadly supports Chelsea but is otherwise okay. My little sisters, Sarah and Amy, who are busy putting the world to rights and are quite brilliant people. Stefan, Mike, and Thomas, who are my excuse for not working most days.

I'll shut up now.

With luck we'll get to meet again not too far from now, and get to talk about what happens next. . . .